PRAISE FOR KE

"Readers coming in cold to this thriller won't have   it missing the series' previous books: It reads just fine as a standalone plot, its wintry twists and turns paced adroitly and warmed up with a touch of romance."

—*The Oregonian* on *A Merciful Secret*

"Elliot delivers a fast-paced, tense thriller that plays up the small-town atmosphere and survivalist mentality, contrasting it against an increasingly connected world. The romantic angle is subtle, with the established relationship between Mercy and Truman slowly and satisfyingly maturing as they solve the mystery."

—*Publishers Weekly* on *A Merciful Secret*

"Each Mercy Kilpatrick mystery improves on the last . . . In this third installment, the whodunit, a tale that blends a hint of the paranormal with some all-too-human ghastliness, is engaging, but the real power comes from watching Mercy evolve as an individual."

—*RT Book Reviews* on *A Merciful Secret*

"In the debut of her new Mercy Kilpatrick series, Elliot crafts an eerily fascinating small town. An air of menace is palpable throughout the story, and the characters hide a wealth of secrets and twisted loyalties."

—*Romantic Times Book Reviews* on *A Merciful Death*

"In Elliot's latest gripping novel the mystery and suspense are top-notch, and the romance embedded within will quench love story junkies' thirst, too. The author's eye for detail makes this one play out more like a movie rather than a book. It can easily be read as a standalone but is obviously much better if the prior three are digested first."

—*Romantic Times Book Reviews* on *Targeted*

"Elliot's latest addition to her thrilling, edge-of-your-seat series Bone Secrets will scare the crap out of you, yet allow you to swoon over the building romantic setting, which provides quite the picturesque backdrop. Her novel contains thrills, chills, snow, and . . . hey, you never know! The surprises and cliffhangers are satisfying, yet edgy enough to keep you feverishly flipping the pages."

—*Romantic Times Book Reviews* on *Known*

"Elliot's best work to date. The author's talent is evident in the characters' wit and smart dialogue . . . One wouldn't necessarily think a psychological thriller and romance would mesh together well, but Elliot knows what she's doing when she turns readers' minds inside out and then softens the blow with an unforgettable love story."

—*Romantic Times Book Reviews* on *Vanished* (Top Pick)

"Kendra Elliot does it again! Filled with twists, turns, and spine-tingling details, *Alone* is an impressive addition to the Bone Secrets series."

—Laura Griffin, *New York Times* bestselling author

"Elliot once again proves to be a genius in the genre with her third heart-pounding novel in the Bone Secrets collection. The author knows romance and suspense, reeling readers in instantaneously and wowing them with an extremely surprising finish . . . Elliot's best by a mile!"

—*Romantic Times Book Reviews* on *Buried* (Top Pick)

"Make room on your keeper shelf! *Hidden* has it all: intricate plotting, engaging characters, a truly twisted villain. I can't wait to see what Kendra Elliot dishes up next!"

—Karen Rose, *New York Times* bestselling author

A
MERCIFUL
SILENCE

ALSO BY KENDRA ELLIOT

MERCY KILPATRICK NOVELS

A Merciful Death
A Merciful Truth
A Merciful Secret

BONE SECRETS NOVELS

Hidden
Chilled
Buried
Alone
Known

BONE SECRETS NOVELLAS

Veiled

CALLAHAN & MCLANE NOVELS
PART OF THE BONE SECRETS WORLD

Vanished
Bridged
Spiraled
Targeted

ROGUE RIVER NOVELLAS

On Her Father's Grave (Rogue River)
Her Grave Secrets (Rogue River)
Dead in Her Tracks (Rogue Winter)
Death and Her Devotion (Rogue Vows)
Truth Be Told (Rogue Justice)

A
MERCIFUL
SILENCE

KENDRA
ELLIOT

Published by Montlake Romance, Seattle

www.apub.com

Amazon, the Amazon logo, and Montlake Romance are trademarks of Amazon.com, Inc., or its affiliates.

ISBN-13: 9781503901315
ISBN-10: 1503901319

Cover design by Eileen Carey

Printed in the United States of America

For my girls
My biggest fans

ONE

There it is.

Eagle's Nest police officer Ben Cooley hit his brakes, thankful he'd been driving a cautious thirty miles an hour. He squinted, trying to see through the smears created by his windshield wipers. Ahead of his car, one-third of the road was gone, washed down the steep side of the hill. It looked as if a monster had bitten a ten-foot-wide chunk out of the asphalt. The last three days had dropped several inches of rain in Central Oregon, and he could swear the cities were about to float away. This sort of continuous downpour happened all the time in the Willamette Valley on the other side of the Cascade mountain range, but not in his beloved—and usually dry—high desert.

To the left of the road was a gut-turning drop-off that vanished into a forest of pines. On his right the rocky hillside sloped upward, and several impromptu waterfalls cascaded down, flowing across the road. The water was supposed to feed into the ditch and funnel beneath the road to flow safely out the other side, but the quantity of water had overpowered the culvert.

"Don't know how the other side of the state puts up with months of this rain." No one was around to hear Ben mutter to himself. He made a conscious effort not to do it within listening distance of the other guys in his department. The last thing the police chief needed to hear was that his seventy-something officer was losing his mind.

Ben hit his flashers, called in his location, and popped his trunk.

The highway department tried to keep up with the weather, installing nets and culverts and natural drains to keep the streets safe, but every year *something* happened to this poor road. And since its vehicle traffic was quite low, it ranked near the bottom of the state's priority list.

Ben set out cones and flares, wondering if anyone would even use the road before the flares burned out. He went back to his car and got Lucas on the radio.

"We need the highway department out here to assess the safety," Ben told the Eagle's Nest dispatcher and office manager.

"That bad?" asked Lucas.

"Definitely. The guardrail along the south edge is gone. A car is going to come by, not see the hole in time, and end up forty feet down the hill, stuck in the pines. They need to close the road."

"I'll call it in."

"Send Royce or Samuel out here with some roadblocks right away because the highway department will take hours to get here. I've blocked the road in one direction with my car, but we need something else."

"Will do."

Ben carefully walked to the edge of the wide gap, always curious about the engineering of roads. He saw the dirt-and-rock support under the asphalt had simply washed away, defeated by the continuous power of the water. The thick border of the black asphalt looked like a broken Oreo cookie wafer.

He moved as close as he dared, aware he didn't know what supported the asphalt under his feet . . . if anything.

Peering into the giant washed-out section, he spotted the edge of a huge concrete culvert six feet below the road. A slow rivulet flowed out of it while a hundred times the amount of water surged outside the culvert.

The culvert is probably jammed with rocks and dirt.

He bent over, resting his hands on his thighs, and craned his head to get a look inside the culvert.

His gaze locked on one round, pale rock.

With eye sockets. And teeth.

TWO

Twenty-four hours later, FBI Special Agent Mercy Kilpatrick watched as bones were removed from the culvert. The Eagle's Nest Police Department had reached out to the state police for help with the removal and investigation of the remains. The team from the state police had gotten a good look inside the large pipe and immediately requested a medical examiner, who had asked for a forensic anthropologist, who had then suggested the FBI be brought in.

A long chain of requests for assistance had landed Mercy on the site.

Beside her, Eagle's Nest police chief Truman Daly stood with his arms folded across his chest, his sharp gaze watching every move of the forensic anthropologist's team. What had started as his case had ended up being Mercy's. The chance of that happening had been small, and she was slightly amused, considering they'd been dating for about six months. Mercy had heard about the situation the moment Ben Cooley reported the skull to Truman and had been aware of every step of the investigation after that. A perk of sleeping with the police chief.

"That's the fifth skull," she whispered to Truman, knowing he could count just fine.

He nodded, his stance stiff.

It looks a lot smaller than the others. A shudder rippled through her.

The entire group of observing professionals was quiet and respectful. Two state police troopers were there to handle any traffic—which meant they stood around a lot. A forensics team from the state carefully removed the remains under the watchful eye of a tall, elegant black-haired woman Mercy knew was the forensic anthropologist, Dr. Victoria Peres.

The anthropologist ran the scene, giving orders and being in three places at once. Mercy watched her gently accept the fifth skull and study it for ten seconds longer than she had the others. Dr. Peres's jaw tightened, and she passed it off to one of her assistants.

The rain had stopped overnight, and the water rushing under the road had slowed to a trickle. Mercy knew their respite wouldn't last long. More rainstorms were expected, blowing in from the Pacific and down from Canada. A double whammy of weather.

At least it was better than ice.

Or feet and feet of snow.

Her thigh twinged, a reminder that she'd been standing in the same position for an hour and that less than two months ago, she'd been shot in that leg as she pursued a killer. She still couldn't move as comfortably as she'd like and had learned the hard way not to ignore her body's warning signs. "I need to sit down," she whispered to Truman, hating her weakness.

Truman jerked as if she'd shocked him. "Your leg?" Concern filled his brown eyes.

She grimaced and nodded, looking around for a perch. The bumper of the medical examiner's vehicle was the closest, and she took a seat. She lost her good view, but she wanted to be able to walk tomorrow. She'd be no help to anyone if she couldn't move.

Was that last skull a child's?

"Well look at that, the FBI sitting down on the job again."

Mercy closed her eyes. She didn't need to see Chuck Winslow to recognize his voice. The internet reporter had become a thorn in her side over the last two months. Truman claimed Winslow had developed an obsession with writing about Mercy. The reporter had published how she'd been shot in the leg and had strongly implied that it'd been her own fault for being friends with the shooter's brother. He wove the facts to suit the story he wanted, even dropping hints in his story that Mercy had refused to arrest the killer for his first two murders because she knew him. Her integrity had been stung by that story, and Mercy knew she'd screwed up when she'd cursed at the reporter over the phone when he asked personal questions about Kaylie, her seventeen-year-old niece. Winslow had gloated about it for weeks.

He reminded her of a grade school boy who would punch a girl because he wanted her attention.

She hadn't read anything about her and Truman's relationship in his articles. Anyone could find out that Truman spent a few nights a week at her apartment. Maybe Chuck was a bit lazy. It was a good thing she'd talked Truman out of confronting the reporter about his coverage of her, but Mercy knew that if Chuck included her relationship with the police chief in his stories—or personal details about Kaylie—she wouldn't be able to stop Truman from losing his temper.

She didn't look in Winslow's direction, keeping her gaze toward the recovery scene. Truman started to turn toward Chuck, but Mercy tugged on his sleeve. "Don't give him the satisfaction," she ordered. She knew the reporter was at least twenty feet away, behind the yellow tape, his view of the crime scene strategically blocked by tarps and tents.

"Asshole," Truman muttered. "One of these days . . ."

"Careful!" the forensic anthropologist snapped at one of her assistants. The assistant didn't flinch, but everyone nearby did. The two women had climbed up from the culvert to the blacktop, their hands full with buckets of dirt and bones. The state's structural engineers had shored up one side of the washed-out hole and deemed the site safe enough for the bone removal, but one engineer had stayed at the scene, noting the dwindling runoff and keeping a sharp eye on the movement of the mud.

Dr. Peres watched her assistant add the skull to the growing collection of bones and debris. The evidence would be taken to the medical examiner's office, where the bones would be studied and hopefully reveal a lead for the investigators. Mercy had already pulled up a list of missing people from the immediate area. Since she didn't yet know the sex or age of the remains, it might turn out to have been a waste of time, but Mercy had felt the need to do *something* to get the case moving.

"Dr. Peres." Mercy pushed to her feet after her fifteen-second relaxation period. "I'm Special Agent Kilpatrick." She held out her hand to the tall woman. An intelligent but impatient brown gaze met hers, and even though the doctor had been digging in mud for hours, there wasn't a hair out of place from the large bun at the back of her neck.

"No, I don't know who these people are yet," the doctor immediately stated. Extreme patience filled her tone as she shook Mercy's hand, but Mercy saw her annoyance flash. Dr. Peres seemed to be the type of person who just wanted to do her job and not be bugged by the police until she was ready.

Mercy raised a brow. "You're not a miracle worker?"

"Not today. Try me next Tuesday."

Mercy leaned closer. "Was that last skull from a child?" she asked in the softest possible tone.

Dr. Peres gave an imperceptible nod.

"How many more are in there?"

The doctor glanced from side to side, checking for listening ears. Truman had stepped away a polite distance. "I believe we've found them all, but I won't guarantee that until the culvert is completely empty."

"Just this end was blocked, right?"

"Correct. It appears that three-quarters of it was empty. We'll need to check the surrounding area too." She sighed. "There's no telling how much of the remains have washed away."

How can the doctor put together this puzzle when several pieces might be missing?

"Do you have an age and sex on the last skull?"

The doctor's large brown eyes narrowed, her lips thinning.

Mercy pushed on. "I'm not asking for perfect answers, but I *know* you have a rough idea. I'm simply looking for a place to focus my efforts while I'm waiting for your report. I'm trying to save some time."

Dr. Peres's face softened, and she looked over at the vehicle holding the bins of recovered bones. "That last skull belonged to a child between the ages of five and eight. I'm leaning toward female, but I'm not positive yet." She met Mercy's gaze. "Sexing a skull is hard at a young age. Clothes and hair help, but we've found neither. One of the other skulls belongs to a young person too. I estimated in their teens."

"Five skulls."

"So far." Dr. Peres gestured toward the downward slope of tall pines. "Who knows what we'll find down there?"

The scope of the search suddenly hit Mercy. Acres and acres of dense sloped woods and rushing water. "It could take days," she gasped, overwhelmed by the task.

The anthropologist simply nodded. Her eyes looked tired, but Mercy believed she wouldn't give up until she was completely satisfied. She'd heard rumors about the state's Bone Lady. *Tough. Brass balls. Ice princess. Damn good at her job.*

Mercy wouldn't mind the descriptions for herself.

"Are you taking the remains back to Portland?" Mercy asked, wondering how many trips to Dr. Peres's office at the medical examiner's building were in her future.

"I'm going to use a facility here at the county morgue," Dr. Peres told her. "I prefer to be close to a scene like this. Especially when it could take quite a while to get all the missing pieces."

"That will make it easier on me too." Mercy paused but couldn't stop herself from asking the question. "Have you seen anything to help us yet, Dr. Peres?"

"Call me Victoria. Did you get a look at any of the skulls?"

"Only from a distance." Bones didn't make Mercy squeamish. In fact, she found them fascinating and wished she knew how to read them the way this doctor did.

"It appears they all had powerful blows to the head in the temple area. The teeth have been forcibly broken. Someone took a hammer or club and bashed them in the mouth several times."

Mercy's teeth and jaw ached. "Postmortem?"

"I suspect so, but I'm not positive yet."

"Were they trying to hide the identity?"

"They didn't do a very good job if that was their goal. There's plenty of teeth left, and people can even be identified by the roots of the teeth if we have previous dental X-rays. I've called for a forensic odontologist to come take a look."

"Which skulls?" The idea of the child being hit in the mouth made her queasy.

"All of them."

"Wait—what? All of them had the same injury?" A memory started to poke and prod in the back of her brain.

Victoria nodded. "All." Her eyes narrowed as she studied Mercy's face. "Why?"

Mercy simply stared back at her, her mind scrambling to uncover the memory emerging in her mind. *Broken teeth. Smashed in the mouth.*

It rushed to the surface.

It'd happened before. A family who'd been murdered in their home. Mercy had been in grade school, but she'd overheard her parents discussing the brutal destruction to their mouths. The imagery had horrified her and stuck in her young imagination.

Then it'd happened again two months later. Two families murdered.

She'd never heard of that type of mass injury again until this moment.

THREE

"Grady Baldwin was arrested more than two decades ago for the murders of the Verbeek and Deverell families," Mercy informed the other agents in the meeting room at the Bend FBI office. "I checked, and he's still in the Oregon State Pen in Salem."

"What was his motivation?" asked Special Agent Eddie Peterson. He leaned forward, his elbows on the table and his fascinated gaze locked on Mercy's face, clearly wishing he'd caught her case.

"Baldwin claims he had no motivation because he didn't do it," Mercy said. "The state argued that he was attracted to Maria Verbeek, hit on her, and she'd turned him down. He was a handyman of sorts and had worked on both the Verbeek and Deverell homes during the six months before they were murdered. I'm trying to set up an interview with him."

"All those children," data analyst Darby Cowan said quietly as she made notes on her laptop.

"Exactly," said Mercy. Between the two families, four children had been murdered with their parents. Mercy pulled up the photos of the families on the big wall screen. The Deverell family photo showed everyone in red pajamas in front of a Christmas tree. Happiness and mischief radiated from the family. The father held mistletoe over his wife's head and kissed her cheek as she laughed at the camera. Ten-year-old Michelle and twelve-year-old Glenn had their arms around a black Lab wearing a Santa hat, and Mercy idly wondered if someone had adopted the dog.

It'd been over twenty years. Odds were the dog was also dead.

The Verbeek family picture was more sedate, shot outdoors in front of a river. Dennis and Maria Verbeek stood formally behind their three blonde daughters. Only the children smiled, and Mercy couldn't look away from one of the daughters, Britta, a fifth grader who had been a year ahead of Mercy in grade school. Mercy remembered the shock and astonishment from the other students and teachers when the family was killed. The other girls, twins Astrid and Helena, had been in first grade at the same school.

"Which girl survived the attack?" asked Eddie.

"Britta. The oldest," answered Mercy. "She was hit in the temple with the weapon but survived the blow. He knocked out several of her front teeth, but she must have been unconscious during the blow and didn't react. He probably assumed she was dead."

"Blessed Jesus Christ," Darby murmured. "The world we're in . . ."

"Where does she live?" asked Jeff.

Mercy took a breath. "I looked her up. She moved to the outskirts of Eagle's Nest last summer. Before that she lived in Nevada, Colorado, Arizona, and New Mexico."

Everyone at the table exchanged glances. "She lives here now," repeated Darby. "After how many years of living away?"

"As best as I can tell, this is the first time she's been back. An aunt in Nevada took her in after the murders years ago."

The room was silent. Mercy's stomach had done a small spin when she learned Britta Verbeek had returned after decades of living else-where. She suspected the other agents were feeling the same thing.

"Weird," Eddie finally commented.

"That's putting it mildly," said Darby.

"I'm trying to reach her," said Mercy.

"And we still don't have a lead on the identities of our current case?" asked Darby. "Those remains were all bone, so they've been dead for a while. Who doesn't report an entire missing family?"

"Don't assume it's another family," Jeff pointed out. "It could be a mix of individuals."

Mercy nodded. Individuals had been her initial thought, and she'd considered that the site might have been a serial killer's dumping ground. It wasn't until she remembered the past family murders that she'd wondered if this was another family. "I pulled a list that includes missing children between five and twelve in our county. Dr. Peres—the forensic anthropologist—gave me a narrower age frame, but I widened it a bit, and I went back thirty years. I wanted to include the time frame of the other murders."

Eddie sighed. "How many names on the list?"

"Five for Deschutes County."

"Only five children unaccounted for in thirty years?" Jeff asked. "That's not horrible."

"Unless you're one of their parents," added Darby.

"Touché," admitted Jeff. "You've been in contact with the National Center for Missing and Exploited Children?"

"Yes," Mercy stated. "I'm waiting on a callback."

"Do you know how difficult it will be to follow a trail thirty years old?" Eddie's eyes were hopeful, but he slowly shook his head in sympathy.

"I do." It was a challenge. One she wanted to tackle.

"I'll help you look into Grady Baldwin's family and friends," said Darby. "And get an in-depth history on Britta Verbeek."

"Thank you," said Mercy. "I know he has a brother still in the area. Don Baldwin."

"When will the road be open?" asked Jeff.

"They can't get started on repairs until the medical examiner releases the scene," Mercy stated. "And that won't happen until we're positive we have every shred of evidence collected." The rugged slope of the hill flashed in her mind. "It will be a difficult scene to process. How far down do we look for evidence? The water could have washed it miles away."

"We'll have to work with what we have," said Jeff. "I think the skulls found so far will be very helpful. When will the forensic anthropologist have an initial report?"

"Tomorrow," said Mercy. "But I'm going to stop by there tonight to meet the odontologist, and I'll try to get more information from Dr. Peres."

Jeff glanced at the time and tucked his pen in his pocket, signaling the meeting was over. Eddie and Darby immediately headed out the door, Darby typing one-handed while she walked, balancing her laptop on the other hand.

"Any work getting done on your cabin?" Jeff asked Mercy conversationally as he shoved in his chair.

Mercy swallowed hard. Her boss hadn't known she owned a cabin in the Cascade foothills until it recently burned to the ground, destroyed by her friend's brother during his hunt for a woman he believed had ruined his life. The woman had survived; Mercy's cabin had not. A decade of Mercy's prepping and hard work had gone up in flames as her cabin burned. It'd been the source of her sanity, a place she could run to if the world started to crumble.

A safe house. Prepared with years of food and fuel and a solid defense.

Mercy had grown up looking over her shoulder for the end of the world. Her parents had ingrained in her to take nothing for granted and taught her the skills to feed and protect herself in a crisis.

Jeff thought she had a mountain getaway. A place to escape for a weekend of skiing. He didn't realize she had created a fortress with enough stores to last at least five years. She didn't correct Jeff's thinking; she didn't correct anyone's assumptions.

Her secret was hers. If the United States' food sources or power grid collapsed, she couldn't save everyone. For the sake of her own survival, only Truman and her family knew her secret.

"All the burned rubbish has been hauled away," she told him. "The area has been cleared and prepped to start building again. But they can't get started for another month or two."

Against her instincts, she'd hired a builder. She'd wanted to tackle the project herself, keeping her secret hidden from the world, but Truman had put his foot down, logically pointing out that it could take her a year to simply build the frame. She relented and hired a builder to do the basic structure; she would do the customizations herself.

Along with Truman.

Luckily her barn of supplies hadn't been touched, but she still felt naked and exposed without her cabin. She'd rapidly outfitted the barn with a sleeping area, but it was rough. No running water or heat. But it settled her anxiety.

A bit.

She wouldn't relax again until she had her hideaway.

Who am I fooling? I never relaxed to begin with.

There was always something to improve or prepare. Together she and Truman had gone over the cabin plans. It would be bigger than her previous A-frame . . . but not too much. A bigger house took more fuel to heat. The home would have a true second story, not just a loft. Truman had suggested a safe room, believing it would appeal to Mercy's protective nature. She'd violently disagreed, imagining being trapped in a box as her home burned around her, unable to fight and defend herself. They'd compromised on a hidden closet big enough to hide in if immediately needed. The same type that had protected her niece in the barn when the killer had come hunting.

"The builder promises to have it done by the end of summer," she added. "Then I'll finish the interior myself."

"Perfect. Just in time for skiing. Will your leg be ready to hit the slopes?" Jeff asked with concern.

The same man who had burned her cabin had shot her in the right thigh. The residual pain from the injury still woke her up at night, along with nightmares of how defenseless she'd been as he'd aimed his gun at her head. In her dreams she died, but in reality he'd been shot a split second before by his brother.

Mercy had no intention of skiing. "I don't know. It hasn't healed as quickly as the doctor expected."

"It hasn't even been two months. You had a huge hole in your leg. Give it time."

"I'm trying to be patient." Mercy smiled, feeling like a liar. She couldn't run, she couldn't walk very far, and she could barely do the stairs to her home. The first week she'd overworked her leg and received a stern lecture from her doctor and Truman along with more nights of agonizing pain. It'd been a tough lesson to learn, so now she tried to listen to her body instead of pretending a bullet couldn't slow her down.

"You'll have to throw a housewarming when your cabin is done."

"We'll see. It will be pretty bare bones. Just the basics, you know," she hedged. The idea of people congregating in her hideaway created an itch deep inside her skull.

Rule one of a secret hideaway: keep the location a secret.

"But I'll figure out something," she added noncommittally.

"Great. Let me know what you find out from the odontologist about the skulls."

"Will do." She exhaled a sigh of relief as her boss left the room.

I hate lying to people I trust.

FOUR

The El Camino flew by Police Chief Truman Daly, leaving the rumble of a powerful engine in its wake.

Truman immediately had two thoughts.

I haven't seen an El Camino in decades.

What kind of license plate was that?

He dropped his scone into his Tahoe's cup holder and hit his lights and siren as he pulled onto the two-lane highway. The speeder had to be driving at least twenty miles an hour over the speed limit. Truman hadn't recorded his speed, but his gut told him the license plate would be all he needed to pull over the El Camino.

He pressed the accelerator and picked up his radio to let Lucas know what was going on.

"Try to wrap it up quickly," his office manager told him. "My mom dropped off pulled pork here at the station. It's not going to last."

"Did she use the Dr Pepper sauce?"

"Yep. Royce and Samuel are already digging in."

"Save me some," Truman ordered. "Because I have a hunch this might take a while."

"You need county?" Lucas's voice sharpened. The twenty-year-old man would make a good cop, but he was happiest maintaining the organization of the tiny Eagle's Nest Police Department and telling everyone what to do.

"That's a good idea. Or state. Whichever is closest. The license plate looked homemade."

"Gotcha," Lucas replied in a knowing tone. "I'll make the calls."

Truman pushed the Tahoe up to eighty-five and gained on the white El Camino. The driver was enjoying the gentle curves of the highway, cutting from one lane to another to straighten his course. This particular highway wove between flat ranch lands dotted with sagebrush and lava rocks. No other traffic was present. Normal for this stretch of remote road.

Everything around the tiny city of Eagle's Nest was remote. The Central Oregon town was thirty minutes from Bend and several hours from Portland, the biggest city in the state. Distance wasn't the only thing that separated Eagle's Nest from population-dense Portland. They were separated by the Cascade Range, whose peaks averaged around ten thousand feet. The big city sat at the north end of the fertile Willamette Valley, while Truman's small town perched on the high desert. Politics in the valley were generally blue; in Eagle's Nest they were firmly red. And Portland's median household income was double that of Eagle's Nest. They were two different worlds.

Truman wouldn't trade his city for anything. It was God's country. Sun, rivers, mountains, lakes. Forests to the west and fields to the east. And he laughed at the rush-hour traffic that made the locals moan. He'd lived in San Jose—he didn't mind Eagle's Nest's two-minute wait at 5:00 p.m. to turn onto the highway.

The El Camino started to slow. Truman held his breath as he drew closer, squinting at the license plate.

No state DMV authorized that plate.

It was white with blue lettering and had a flag on one side. The vehicle pulled over, and Truman stopped behind it. There was no point entering the small numbers along the bottom of the plate into his computer. The license plate read US CONSTITUTIONAL LICENSE PLATE in big letters above the numbers.

He sighed. Over the radio Lucas announced that a Deschutes County deputy was minutes away.

Might as well get this over with.

Truman put on his cowboy hat, stepped out of his truck, and sniffed the air, noting a damp odor; the rain was coming back. He slowly approached the El Camino. It wasn't in bad shape for a vehicle that had to be at least thirty years old. The paint was shinier than Truman's dusty SUV's, and he saw only one dent on the driver's side. There appeared to be a single person inside, and the bed of the vehicle was loaded with plastic tubs and fresh-cut lumber. The driver made eye contact in the rearview mirror, and Truman saw he was young, maybe in his twenties or thirties.

Truman stopped a few feet behind the driver's door, getting a good view of the front seat through the rear window. No apparent weapons. Yet.

A traffic stop in Arkansas nearly a decade earlier flashed in Truman's brain. It hadn't been his stop, but not a single cop in the United States would ever forget it.

It'd been in the news for months.

The homemade license plate had brought the memory front and center.

Maybe I should wait for county.

His hand hovered over the butt of his gun.

"Did I do something criminal, sir?" The voice from the car was calm and polite.

Truman tensed at the man's emphasis on the word *criminal*. "License and registration, please." He took a step closer. Now he could see the man's lap and both hands. No weapon.

"Did I do something criminal, sir?" he repeated. "You cannot stop me unless you suspect me of a criminal act."

Moving closer, Truman decided the driver was in his midtwenties. "What's your name?" he asked the driver.

"I don't have to identify myself," he stated, piercing blue eyes meeting Truman's. "That's my right. I know my rights."

"You have an illegal license plate on your car, and you were exceeding the speed limit."

"I don't care what your highway traffic act says. I have no contracts under that act. I've canceled them all so you can't enforce them on me."

I don't have the energy for this today. "Let me guess. You're a free man and have a God-given right to travel freely."

"That is correct, sir."

The man's confirmation told Truman he was of the same beliefs as the two men who'd leaped out of their vehicle and murdered the cops in Arkansas.

A sovereign citizen. Someone who believes they are above all laws.

Truman kept a sharp eye on the man's hands. "Well, you've endangered other innocent people by speeding, and your plate tells me that you haven't paid the taxes to drive on these beautiful roads of ours."

"I know my rights. You're enforcing corporate policy, sir, and unless you suspect me of a criminal act, you have no right to detain me."

A Deschutes County cruiser stopped behind Truman's vehicle. "How about you simply tell me your name?" Truman asked politely. "That way we can have a civil discussion."

"I'm not operating in that capacity."

The capacity of being sane?

"I am the human being that owns the entity. You know a legal person is a nonhuman entity, right?"

"How about you share your entity's name?" Truman didn't bother to try to understand the man's logic. There was no logic when it came to dealing with sovereign citizens. They firmly believed every word they said, indoctrinated by the internet and other like-minded people. Most were polite to a point but had an arsenal of word magic and pseudo-legal phrases to make anyone's head spin.

The man considered Truman's question and then handed him a plastic card from his wallet. "Are you the Deschutes County sheriff?" the driver asked, twisting his neck to see Truman's uniform.

Right now, I wish I were. Sovereign citizens recognized only a sheriff as law enforcement because sheriffs were elected by the public.

Truman took the card without answering and stared at it. "What is this?" he blurted, confused by the identification the man had handed him.

"That's my diplomatic identification card."

Truman was pretty certain the young man in the dirty jeans and yellowing white T-shirt wasn't a diplomat. But according to the card, which showed the name Joshua Forbes, his photo, the word *ambassador* across the top, and the seal of the State Department, he was exactly that.

Completely bogus.

Truman had heard of the cards but had never seen one before. He'd now met his first card-carrying sovereign citizen.

"I don't suppose you have an Oregon driver's license?" Truman asked.

"Don't need one. This card shows the state has recognized my claim as a sovereign citizen. I am not a citizen of the United States. I have diplomatic immunity, and I am the representative of Joshua Forbes. This card replaces all other forms of identification."

Why not just state your name is Joshua Forbes?

The man stuck his head out the window and got a look at Truman's Eagle's Nest uniform. "Sorry, Mr. Daly, but you have no claim over me. I only stopped to be mannerly."

Joshua's tone was still polite, but Truman suspected that wouldn't last long.

"How much did you pay for this card, Joshua?"

Joshua frowned. "What does that matter?"

"Because this is a money-sucking scam. This card has no authority whatsoever. Who sold it to you?"

"I don't expect you to understand it," Joshua said, his blue eyes narrowing. "It's above your law."

"No, it's not. It's no one's law. Someone took advantage of you. What'd it cost? Three thousand dollars?"

The young man was silent.

"All you did was pad someone's pockets. He's selling hopes and dreams, not legal IDs. This card doesn't declare that you're exempt from US taxes and laws. It declares that someone is running a scam."

"I had to get an apostille—"

"An apostille simply confirms the notarization was legitimate. Not the document. I don't suppose he sold you lifetime car insurance too?"

"It's good for—"

"It's good for shit." Truman felt a microscopic twinge of sympathy for the young man. Money was dear out here. This man had probably spent years of savings on the printed garbage. "Here's a life lesson for you: if it sounds too good to be true, it probably is. You know your license plate is illegal too, right?" Truman was relieved to see a second county patrol unit stop behind the first. He and Joshua were currently outside Eagle's Nest city limits, but when he'd first spotted the speeder, they'd been in Truman's territory. He'd be more than happy to let county take over Joshua Forbes.

"I have an unimpeded, God-given right t-to t-travel as I wish," Joshua stuttered. "You're violating my rights."

Two county deputies approached as rain started to sprinkle. "I like that license plate, Truman," said the tallest one. His casual tone belied the sharp, understanding look in his eyes. The deputy had taken in the entire situation with one glance. Both men had their hands near their weapons, their alert stances stating they knew how violent SCs could turn when facing law enforcement.

"I don't think Josh here knew he was breaking the law." Truman handed the diplomatic card to the tall deputy, whose eyes lit up and face filled with a grin as he showed it to the second deputy. The second one looked fresh out of high school to Truman.

"Our supervisor would love to see this card," the tall deputy said. "He's fascinated with these guys."

"I know my rights." Joshua's voice rose an octave. "You're violating my rights."

"Why don't you step out of the car?" suggested the tall deputy.

"I do not consent!" Joshua tightened his grip on the steering wheel, anxiety filling his face.

"All we're going to do is have a discussion about where you got your plate and your . . . diplomatic card," Truman said in a calm voice as his heart rate accelerated. Joshua was pushing his luck. "It's illegal to create and sell those."

"I do not consent!"

"You can get out of the car on your own free will or I'm going to assist you," said the tall deputy.

"You do not have authority over me!"

The younger deputy whipped open the car door, and the other repeated the command to get out of the car. Joshua lunged for his car door's handle, attempting to yank it closed. "I do not consent! You are violating my rights! I will sue you for violating the rights of a free man!"

The tall deputy impressed Truman with a quick maneuver with the driver's arm that had Joshua out of his seat and his chest on the damp gravel in the blink of an eye. Together the three of them cuffed the struggling man as he continued to shriek about consent and violated rights.

Truman stepped back and brushed the dirt off his knees, shaking his head. The stop hadn't gone the way he'd hoped, but at least no one had been hurt. *Why didn't he just step out of the car?*

"These people make no sense to me," admitted Truman, meeting the gazes of the two deputies. "You got him?"

"Yep. We can take it from here. Unless you want to handle it," the older one said with a wink.

Hell no.

The sky opened up and the rain turned into a downpour. Truman squatted next to Joshua, who was facedown in the gravel, and he spoke in a quiet voice, the rain dripping off the brim of his hat. "You seem like a decent guy. I'm going to assume you got sucked into something that sounded pretty terrific. Take a little time and educate yourself, okay? A real education. Not extremists on the internet."

"Fuck off!" Joshua sent a furious look that seared into Truman's brain. "You are going to regret violating my rights."

Ouch.

Truman sighed and stood. He shook hands with the deputies and went on his way, thankful Deschutes County was willing to book the sovereign citizen.

Time to see if there's any pulled pork left.

FIVE

It was nearly 8:00 p.m. by the time Mercy reached the small building where the local medical examiner kept an office. Typically bodies went to the medical examiner's primary building east of Portland for autopsy, but Dr. Natasha Lockhart had a small facility in Bend for herself and an assistant. Two vehicles were in the lot, and Mercy hoped one belonged to Dr. Peres. The other she assumed was the odontologist's or Dr. Lockhart's.

Inside, Mercy followed the sounds of conversation and found Dr. Peres in a large room with three stainless steel tables. Bins from the recovery were stacked along one wall, and Dr. Peres had set out four dirty skulls on one table. She and a petite blonde woman were deep in discussion, studying a fifth skull in the small woman's hands, and didn't hear Mercy enter.

"Dr. Peres?" Mercy asked quietly, not wanting to startle them and have a skull drop.

Both women turned. Victoria Peres had a scowl on her face, while the blonde woman gave Mercy a wide smile. Mercy couldn't help but smile back. She was tiny, with wavy hair and warm brown eyes. Mercy immediately felt like a giant. No doubt the tall Dr. Peres felt the same way around the woman.

"You must be Agent Kilpatrick." The blonde woman held out her hand, balancing the skull in the other. "I'm Lacey Ca—Harper."

Mercy took her hand. "Caharper?"

"Harper," Lacey said firmly. "I married recently. Victoria was one of my attendants," she added with a quick glance at the forensic anthropologist.

Dr. Peres gave the first smile Mercy had seen from the woman. "Dr. Harper is the forensic odontologist I told you about."

"I'm still not used to hearing 'Dr. Harper,'" admitted Lacey. "My husband, Jack, loves the sound of it, but I've been called Dr. Campbell for too many years. My father was Dr. Campbell too."

"As in the former state medical examiner?" Mercy asked. She'd met the man a few times in Portland before he retired.

"That's him."

"You didn't want to follow his path?"

"Teeth are *sufficient* for me, thank you," she said with a small eye roll.

Mercy gestured at the skull in Lacey's hand. "What do the teeth on that tell you?"

Lacey's eyes lit up. "All sorts of things. But I'll let Victoria start. She's been looking them over." Lacey set the skull in the line with the others. Three of the skulls had mandibles set next to them. Victoria hadn't exaggerated about the damage. Broken and missing teeth made the group look as if they'd been stolen from a Halloween store. Again Mercy's attention was caught by the smallest skull. Many of its tiny teeth were brutally shattered. Each skull also had a spiderweb of fracture lines near a temple. Some had a hole or two in the same area.

Are those impacts the cause of death?

"I haven't had time for a proper examination of each skull," Victoria said, distinctly reluctant to share any findings. "I still need to clean them up better."

"But you have first impressions," Mercy coaxed. "I'll take them all with a grain of salt, understanding they aren't concrete and could change."

"This isn't how I work." Victoria frowned.

"Completely understandable. It's a risk I need to take because we must move as fast as we can."

Victoria took a deep breath and exchanged a look with Lacey, who lifted one shoulder. "We *are* positive about some things," Lacey pointed out.

"True." Victoria gestured at the five skulls. "You ever play that game of 'one of these things is not like the other'?" Her voice took on a lecturing tone.

"Like from *Sesame Street*?" Mercy was amused. Clearly one of the skulls was much smaller.

"Yes. And I'm not referring to the size of the child's skull. I'm talking about ancestry."

"Oh." Mercy looked again. To her all the skulls were similar. Dirty ivory in color, with eye sockets, an opening where the nose had been, and seams across the smooth parts. She couldn't see them as people. Except for the tiny one. Every time she looked at it, for no reason she pictured a young girl with blonde curls. "I don't know what I'm looking for."

"Exactly. But before I get into ancestry, first of all, there is one adult female, one teenage female, and two adult male skulls in addition to the child's skull." She ran a finger above the eye sockets of the first large skull. "See how the bone juts out over the orbits of the eyes? And how the forehead slopes back? This one is male. Now compare it to the one next to it. The brow ridges are smoother; the forehead more vertical. Not to mention the skull is smaller and the bones more delicate. It's also much lighter than the other one."

Mercy looked at the next two skulls in line. "The third is a male and the fourth is female," she said slowly.

"Correct." The forensic anthropologist was pleased with her new student.

"And the child?"

Dr. Peres gently lifted the small skull and looked directly into the deep spaces where its eyes should have been, a thoughtful expression on her face. "Lacey and I have agreed the child is between five and eight. I feel the structure has more feminine characteristics, but like I said at the scene, it's difficult to tell at this age."

"She was hit in the mouth and the side of the head," said Mercy as she blinked rapidly, staring at the damage to the temple. The killer had abused the child the same way as the adults.

"The blow to the side of the head was perimortem—right before she died or else immediately after. I can tell by the edge of the broken bone."

"Bastards," breathed Mercy.

"Quite," agreed Lacey.

The three women were silent for a long moment as Victoria gently set the small skull back down.

"What did you want to tell me about ancestry?" Mercy asked, needing to fill the lull.

"Three of the adults are Caucasian. One is Asian."

"Interesting. Let me try to figure it out." Mercy studied each skull and finally had to admit defeat. "Again . . . I have no idea what I'm looking for. They all look alike to me."

"Start with the shape of the eye orbits," suggested Lacey.

Mercy pointed at the first. "This one's orbits are very round. The other four are sort of angled." Now it was very obvious to her.

Lacey picked up the first male skull and turned it upside down to show Mercy the top teeth. "The maxillary incisors are a good indicator too . . . even though three have been broken off, the fourth shows a shovel shape with defined ridges when viewed from the lingual."

"Tongue?" Mercy asked in confusion.

"Viewed from the tongue side of the teeth," Lacey clarified. She showed Mercy the smooth shape of the back of a front tooth on another skull for comparison.

"When they're side by side, I can see the differences. If I had a single skull, I'd be lost," admitted Mercy.

"That's why they pay me the big bucks," said Victoria, and Lacey gave a snort of laughter. "Well, sort of big bucks."

"The Asian skull is darker," Mercy observed. "Does that mean anything?"

Both Victoria and Lacey frowned. "We were just talking about that," said Victoria. "It could be from a few things. Possibly it was buried longer than the others, or the dirt right around it was a different composition, staining it darker."

"Buried longer?" Mercy's ears pricked up. "We're considering that this might be a family. But if one has been buried longer and is Asian, maybe he doesn't belong." She couldn't help but smile a little as she referenced Victoria's earlier words about the *Sesame Street* game.

"Maybe he married into the family," suggested Lacey. "Your theory is still viable."

"It is," agreed Mercy. "None of the others have the slightest Asian characteristics?"

"Not really," said Victoria. "I have to take dozens of measurements to see where the skulls fall in the ancestry guidelines, but the two prominent features—the orbits and the incisors—aren't apparent in the others."

"Do you mind if I take some photos?" Mercy asked.

"Go right ahead," answered Victoria.

As Mercy snapped pictures with her work phone, Lacey asked, "I heard this might be similar to some past murder cases?"

Mercy didn't take her gaze away from her work. "Yes. A little over twenty years ago. The main similarities are the blows to the teeth and the possibility that this is a family. But they caught the killer back then. He's in prison."

"Uh-huh. Sometimes that doesn't matter," stated Lacey.

Mercy looked up from her shooting. "What does that mean?"

The woman shrugged and lightly traced the faint line across her neck, not meeting Mercy's gaze. "Sometimes someone else takes up the cloak and continues the deadly work."

An odd prickling started on Mercy's scalp. *What happened to her?*

"Lacey." Victoria touched the woman's arm, concern in her eyes. "Are you okay?"

Lacey looked up and forced a smile. "Yes. It's been years now." She finally met Mercy's gaze. "I'll tell you about it over a beer sometime."

Mercy nodded. *After I Google you.*

SIX

It was nearly ten o'clock when Mercy returned to her office. After seeing the skulls, she wanted more information about the old family murders. Her brain was spinning in a dozen directions with a million questions. She couldn't fall asleep if she tried. Truman had called as she left the medical examiner's office, and she'd told him she was headed back to the office. He wasn't surprised and offered to meet up and bring food.

She'd suddenly realized she hadn't eaten since breakfast, and every starving nerve in her stomach roared with hunger. Pleased with his thoughtfulness, she told him to bring whatever sounded good to him. Quickly.

Thirty minutes later she was eating pork massaman curry straight out of the container, occasionally trading off with Truman and his carton of pad thai as they looked over the old murders together. Boxes and boxes of records had arrived from the Deschutes County Sheriff's Office. She'd briefly scanned some summary reports before her meeting with Jeff, Eddie, and Darby earlier, but now that she had the physical evidence and written records, she wanted to take her time.

"Shouldn't you be focused on finding the identities of the current victims instead of wading through solved cases?" Truman asked.

"I'm doing both." His question didn't bother her; it was pertinent. "I've gone through missing persons records, and we prepared a short statement for the local news. It should be on the eleven o'clock edition tonight."

"You'll be mobbed with leads."

"We'll sort through them. We didn't mention the possibility of a missing family, but we did include the fact that there was a young child. Until I get a report from Dr. Peres, the only information I have on the adult skulls is their sex and that one of the females is probably in her teens. I can only do so much with that and the missing persons records. And who knows? We might find more remains down the slope."

"They're still looking?"

"We'll have a team out there for at least a few more days. Depends on the weather, safety, and what they find. Until I have more evidence on the current case, this is a good place to start."

Truman glanced pointedly at the storage boxes. "This could take a week to wade through."

Mercy moved a few boxes aside, lifted a lid, and chose a three-ring binder. "I want to start with the Verbeek family. I plan to go visit Britta Verbeek tomorrow."

"The girl who survived."

"Barely survived. She was in the hospital for weeks. They thought she'd have permanent brain damage from the blow to her head, but from what I found about her online, she appears to have recovered well."

"What did you find?"

"She works for a business that builds websites . . . her portfolio features a lot of restaurants and small businesses. She changed her last name to Vale a long time ago, but I couldn't find any marriage records, so I suspect it was a personal choice."

"Can't say I blame her," said Truman. "No doubt weird people have contacted her to ask rude questions about her story. Probably some reporters too."

Mercy opened the binder and set aside her pork, searching for interviews with Britta Verbeek.

"How was the Verbeek family discovered?" Truman asked.

"A neighbor stopped by in the morning. And Britta was lucky he did. It was a summer weekend, so the kids weren't expected at school and the father wasn't expected at work. No one might have noticed for days that something had happened, because the Verbeeks lived on a dozen acres out in the middle of nowhere. According to the neighbor, the front door was open. When no one answered, he went in."

Truman poked at his pad thai with his fork. "I can't imagine."

Mercy scanned the neighbor's interview. "The father was found in the living room, the mother in the hallway, and the three kids in their beds."

"Weapon?"

"A hammer."

Truman looked up, his fork motionless in his noodles. "Seriously? That's it?"

"A big hammer." Mercy imagined a madman swinging the hammer. "The father had broken bones in his hands and abrasions on his arms. The mother did too. She was found in the hall outside the girls' bedroom."

He set down his fork. "Trying to protect her girls."

"It appears the girls didn't wake. They all had single blows to their heads." Mercy closed the lid on her pork, her appetite gone. "Britta was on a top bunk. He probably didn't have the right angle to get a killing blow."

"The neighbor was cleared?"

"He was. The medical examiner estimated the deaths occurred between eight and midnight. The neighbor's work shift covered the hours, and he had several witnesses to back up his presence at work."

"Why did he stop by?"

"He was going to borrow a rototiller for the weekend. Phone records show a short call between the two homes the day before, which the neighbor said was about the rototiller. And the machine was sitting out and dusted off beside the Verbeek home, looking ready to go."

Truman leaned closer to see the neighbor's interview. "Steve Harris. I know him . . . if it's the same one. Now he lives in a house just off the main drag in Eagle's Nest. Older man. Rather crabby. A get-off-my-lawn type of guy. I dealt with him after he accrued a dozen parking tickets and refused to pay. He couldn't accept that the curb right in front of the hydrant on his street wasn't a legitimate place to park. Still doesn't."

"He sounds charming. Let him park there. He'll get a surprise when the fire department bashes in his windows to get to the hydrant."

"That's what I told him. He responded that he'd sue the fire department."

Mercy could only shake her head. "I'm sure I'll interview him at some point." She flipped through several pages. "All the detective notes say Britta had no memory of what happened. She remembers going to bed and then waking up in the hospital days later."

"I've read that kids are dead to the world when they're sleeping. Sometimes smoke alarms won't even wake them."

"Poor child woke up without a family." Mercy's heart contracted in pain for the girl.

"Was anything taken from the home?"

"No one was sure. Nothing obvious was missing. Guns and some money were left behind." Mercy ran a finger down several pages. "It looks like Britta never went back into the home. I'd think she'd be the only one who could tell if anything was missing . . . although a child that young might not know. It looks like the detectives came to the same conclusion."

"Any other . . . assault of the female victims?" Truman asked delicately.

"No." Relief had filled Mercy when she verified that fact. But it didn't help with the motive for the attack.

"But they think a sexual motive was behind the murders? He was interested in the mother, right?"

"I read that in the summaries. It said one of Maria Verbeek's friends believed Grady Baldwin made a pass at Maria." Mercy checked the summary of the contents on the binder. "That interview isn't in this binder."

"I'd like to see that one too."

Mercy went back to the boxes and opened another binder, reviewed the contents, and then grabbed a third. "Here it is. Janet Norris." She sat back down and found the detective's notes on the interview, then slid the binder over so Truman could read too.

"Janet didn't say Grady Baldwin by name," Truman asserted. "Janet states the pass was made by a workman at the house."

Mercy tapped her fingers on the table. Truman was right. "I wonder if they had an inaccurate accounting of the workmen. Everyone who knew which persons had worked in the home were killed. Except for Britta."

"A good point. But Grady Baldwin was convicted."

"They had physical evidence. A hammer with his fingerprints. His prints in the home. No alibi."

Truman sat back and rubbed his eyes. "I have to imagine Grady had a decent lawyer who poked all the right holes in the prosecutor's case."

"I hope so."

"What did the other crime scene look like?"

Mercy wasn't going to open the other case boxes when she had binders from the first still on the table. "Two months earlier the Deverell family had been killed," she recited from her research earlier in the day. "They hadn't arrested Grady Baldwin yet, but he'd been interviewed because he'd worked on the Deverells' home too. It was another late-night home invasion type. That time all the family members were in their beds."

"Any sexual assaults?"

"No."

"Anything stolen?"

"Again, they were unsure."

Mercy reread Janet Norris's interview summary. The woman had stated that Maria Verbeek rarely went into town, and that they'd worked in the same hotel for a short time. Mercy found the family photo of the Verbeek family that she'd shown at the FBI case briefing. Maria looked like a timid woman. She stood a half foot behind her husband, at his side, her hands clasped in front of her, her shoulders rounded.

She looked as if she didn't have an assertive bone in her body.

But she'd fought to the death to save her girls.

I hope they put away the right person.

SEVEN

The next morning Mercy was filling her coffee mug as her niece Kaylie sleepily stumbled into the kitchen.

"You're going to be late for school," Mercy said as she watched the teen cram a bagel in the toaster.

"I'm skipping first period. The teacher's still sick and the sub is just babysitting us. There's no point for me to sit there and read a book."

Mercy fought back a lecture on the teen's attendance record. Kaylie got great grades; Mercy had nothing to complain about.

This isn't how raising a teenager is supposed to be.

Kaylie was easy. Which immediately made Mercy suspicious. Where was the teen angst and drama? The two of them had experienced some hiccups, but for the most part the six months they'd been together had been smooth sailing.

"Cade around?" Mercy asked about Kaylie's on-again, off-again boyfriend. Mercy approved of the hardworking young man, but Kaylie's world was rapidly growing beyond Cade's. Her amazing baked goods were displayed every day at the coffee shop she'd inherited after the death of her father, and she had talked about starting a new bakery south of Portland, where there were more people and shoppers. Then the next day she'd discuss marketing a line of brownies to grocery stores. Then she'd express an interest about a job in law enforcement. Her niece knew her options were open and limitless, and Mercy loved listening to her explore the possibilities. Even if she didn't seem very focused.

That will come.

"He's gone for the next three weeks. New project." Disappointment rang in her tone.

"He has solid, stable work," Mercy pointed out. "And most of the time he enjoys it."

"I know. He's happy at this new job." Kaylie smeared cream cheese on her bagel. "I heard they found a bunch of bodies under the road up on March Mountain."

"What else did you hear?" Mercy asked, startled at the abrupt change of topic and curious as to what rumors had started to circulate.

Kaylie gave her a side eye. "I saw a picture online of you at the scene in an article. You looked tired."

"Sheesh. Let me guess. I was sitting on the bumper of a vehicle. How bad was the caption?"

"Not bad."

"Kaylie," she said in a warning voice.

The girl sighed. "Okay. It said you were sitting around waiting for others to do the investigation. I know that's not how it was," she quickly added.

"One of these days I'm going to kill Chuck Winslow." Mercy sipped her coffee too fast and burned her tongue. She swore out loud.

Today is not off to a great start.

"The reporter only does it to annoy you. Ignore him," advised Kaylie.

"*Reporter* is a kind word for him. He's a bottom-feeder."

"Who are the victims they found?"

"We don't know yet. Have you heard of anyone missing around town? Is anyone speculating on who it could be?"

The teen took a big bite of bagel. "Not that I've heard," she said around the mouthful.

"Keep your ears open. There's often a bit of truth buried in rumors."

"I'm around high school students all day."

"They listen to their parents talk."

"Is it true a family was murdered?"

Mercy set down her coffee mug, exasperated. "There. See? How did you hear that? No one was supposed to talk about that."

Kaylie tucked her hair behind her ear. "I heard something at the Coffee Café last night." She took another bite and blinked innocently.

"We don't know who they are or if they were a family. That's pure speculation, and I'm looking into it today." She waved a finger at the teen. "Don't be part of the gossip problem."

"Never."

Mercy raised a skeptical brow at the girl.

Five minutes later, Mercy climbed in her Tahoe. She had a local address for Britta Vale but no phone number. Tax records indicated the woman was self-employed. She was the owner of the website business, so Mercy crossed her fingers she'd find her at home.

Mercy's additional research had explained the forensic odontologist's odd comment about prison not stopping a killer. A few years earlier, Lacey Harper had been the target of a serial killer. Someone had decided to finish the job another serial killer had started decades before. Lacey had survived both men's attempts to kill her.

Mercy doubted she would smile as much as the blonde woman did if she'd been through that much trauma. Being shot two months ago had made Mercy noticeably cranky. At least in her opinion. Some rolled eyes and glares from Kaylie since that time had confirmed Mercy's suspicions.

Time for me to get over it. I've got nothing to whine about.

I can still walk.

Her GPS took her on a wet, winding trip thirty miles out of Bend. Mercy revered privacy, and it appeared Britta Vale did the same. The terrain was flat, with clumps of huge trees and fields of scattered volcanic rock. She took the final turn off the two-lane road and was pleasantly surprised to find a well-maintained gravel driveway. A wood fence lined one side of the drive, and Mercy idly wondered if Britta kept cows or sheep in the field. A wide creek rapidly flowed through the pasture, full of the recent rains. A few minutes later she stopped in front of an old white farmhouse. Fields flanked the house on two sides, and a small ancient grove of fruit trees was to the east.

The paint flaked from the two-story building, and large pieces of railing were missing from the wraparound deck. Lace curtains appeared at most of the windows, and a newer Ford pickup was parked next to the home. As Mercy stepped out of her Tahoe, faint barking greeted her, and she spotted a black Lab inside, watching through a tall window next to the front door, alerting the residents that company had arrived. Its wagging tail defied the belligerent barks.

Overall, Mercy liked the home. It felt shy but friendly. Sequestered but welcoming.

The size of the large window next to the door caught her attention. *Easy to break and enter.*

She shut down that part of her mind as she approached the house. She wasn't here to assess the home as a fortress. Recently she'd sunk a lot of brainpower into considering every possible angle of security as she designed her new cabin. The weaknesses of her old cabin had been exposed during its destruction, and Mercy was determined to anticipate all vulnerabilities. She'd been mentally entrenched in the process for so long, it was difficult to turn off.

The door opened, and a woman appeared. In one hand she gripped the Lab's collar. With the other she balanced a rifle against her shoulder.

Not threatening but making her stance clear.

Mercy approved. And stopped moving forward.

Mercy stood with her right shoulder and hip slightly farther back and casually held her hands out in front of her stomach, the palms up. A nonaggressive pose, but she was ready to move to the gun in her shoulder holster if needed. "Britta Vale?"

"Who wants to know?" The woman's tone was polite but direct. Her long hair was black. The flat-black, obviously dyed tone that half of Kaylie's friends wore and that Mercy prayed her niece would never attempt on her lovely hair. Blunt-cut bangs just above Britta's eyebrows gave her a no-nonsense look.

"I'm Special Agent Mercy Kilpatrick from the Bend FBI office. You're welcome to call them to verify me."

"Take three steps closer."

Mercy took three measured steps, her hands still exposed. She felt the weight of her weapon at her side and watched Britta for any warning movements. The woman stood perfectly still, the dog's wagging tail a contrast. At this distance Mercy could meet Britta's gaze. The woman had light-blue eyes and skin that looked as if it'd never seen the sun. She also had a huge tattoo that wrapped around the front of her neck. Mercy couldn't read it but wondered how painful the process had been. She swallowed, imagining tiny sharp needles jabbing at the tender skin on her throat.

The woman released the dog, who instantly sat, its dark eyes still locked on Mercy.

"Are you here about Grady Baldwin?"

"Yes," Mercy answered.

"Is he out? I'm supposed to be notified if he gets out. No one has said anything to me." Britta's voice shot up an octave as the words spilled out of her mouth, terror and anger flashing in her eyes. Her fingers tightened on the butt of the rifle, and Mercy tensed.

"He's not out and he's not getting out."

The woman lowered her chin a notch, and her shoulders moved as she exhaled. "I have nightmares about police vehicles abruptly showing up at my home, trying to get me to safety. They're always too late." She nodded at Mercy's Tahoe. "You're clearly armed, and you have government plates, so you understand my reaction."

"I do. You *are* Britta, right?" The woman acted like a survivor, but Mercy wanted to be certain.

"I am. Why are you here?"

"Yesterday we uncovered five bodies. Possibly a family—we aren't certain about that. But each one of them had been struck in the mouth. Their teeth and jaws shattered."

The pale woman went a shade whiter as she slapped a hand across her mouth, and the dog whined, leaning hard against her thigh.

"I'm sorry I don't have coffee. I gave up caffeine years ago."

"The herbal tea is fine." Mercy took a sip. It tasted of grass and flowers. The two women sat at a small table in Britta's large kitchen. Zara, the Lab, had sniffed Mercy thoroughly, accepted some scratches behind her ears, and then planted herself next to Britta's chair. The woman had stroked Zara's fur nonstop since she found out the reason for Mercy's visit, and Mercy wondered if Zara served as a sort of service animal for anxiety. The dog's calm manner and serene dark eyes created a soothing presence.

"Your last name seems familiar," Britta stated, studying Mercy from head to toe.

"I was a year behind you in grade school."

"I don't remember you. Did you have an older brother?"

"Two of them. And an older sister."

"That's probably it. I went to live with my aunt immediately after . . ." She looked away, and her jaw muscles flexed.

"I remember," Mercy said gently. "The whole school was rattled. Students and teachers."

Britta stared into her teacup. "Are you sure he's locked up?"

She had asked the question four times now.

"I'm positive. I called last night and requested a visual check."

The woman nodded absently and rubbed Zara's head more vigorously.

"He always swore he didn't do it," Britta stated, staring off into the distance.

"Evidence placed him at the scene. His fingerprints were on a hammer and in the home," Mercy countered.

"*I know.* No one knows the evidence better than I do," Britta snapped as her pale gaze returned to Mercy and flashed in anger, but she immediately calmed. "Please excuse me. I'm a little rattled."

"You have every reason to be," Mercy asserted. "But I'm curious why you mentioned his claim to be innocent while you know the evidence."

The woman's gaze fixed on Mercy. "How long ago were they killed?"

Britta hadn't answered her question.

"We don't know yet. But the remains were fully skeletal."

"Where were they found?"

Mercy shared an abbreviated description of the scene as Britta shed her sweater. Underneath she wore a short-sleeved T-shirt, and her toned arms were covered in an assortment of tattoos. There was little room left for more. She emitted the aura of a woman who could take care of herself, and Mercy figured the fear and uncertainty she'd just witnessed were rare for Britta.

She looked like a survivor who was determined to never again be a victim.

Britta was not her mother's daughter. At least not the mother Mercy had seen in the pictures.

"I read that you moved here last summer," Mercy said. "What prompted you to come back?"

"I've lived in a lot of places," said Britta. "I'm lucky that I can work anywhere there is internet. My job doesn't limit me." She scowled and took a long drink from her cup. "I'm not sure why I came back.

For a long time I've felt as if I'm searching for something, but I can't name what it is. All my other homes have felt stale after a time. I find that moving to a completely new place invigorates me in a way I can't describe. I love the space available to me here, and I feel like I can stretch out my arms." Her face fell. "I'm sure I'll feel suffocated at some point and move on again, but the last nine months here have been fine."

"You rented the home?"

"Yes."

The house had very little furniture. Even the table only had two chairs, but Britta had hung large framed black-and-white photos on the wall. Stark trees and muddy, deep ditches, icy rivers and broken fences, a lone gravestone with a somber flag. They were powerful images, colorless and stripped down to their essence. Sort of like the woman in front of her. Three long foreign-looking swords were mounted next to the photos. Deadly and silent. Mercy had no doubt they were real. Britta's kitchen counters were completely empty, but there was a cozy chair with a lamp and small bookshelf in the sitting room that looked like a good place to curl up on a rainy day. No TV.

Britta noticed her scan of the first floor. "I travel light. I don't like clutter."

Mercy's gaze went to the crowded tattooing of her arms. Britta stored her possessions on her skin.

"Yesterday I read the reports from your family's death," Mercy said. "But I'd like to hear your words."

"I was interviewed dozens of times. Surely you read those." Britta's spine was rigid, her chin up, her lips pressed in a line.

"I did." Mercy had been up half the night reading. "But you were ten years old. Looking back as an adult, what goes through your head?"

Britta looked away. "I'm not doing this today. I'm sorry, Agent Kilpatrick, but you can't show up on my doorstep and expect me to unload. I spent a decade in therapy learning how to survive with my memories. They're all neatly packed up in manageable boxes. You're asking me to rip them open and scatter my emotions across the floor. I can't do that."

She slid her chair back and stood, her face carefully composed in a blank shield.

I pushed too hard.

Mercy fingered the handle on her mug of tea. "That was rather presumptuous of me, wasn't it?"

"Yes."

"I apologize." Mercy stood and set her card on the table. She held Britta's gaze. "I can't pretend to know what you've been through—"

"No, you can't." Britta leaned closer, holding Mercy's gaze. The lamplight gave her eyes an eerie glow. "There are few people in this world that know what it's like to wake up and find out your family has been murdered and that you are now alone. It never leaves you. The survivor's guilt eats away at your brain until you're convinced you've pissed off death and it will return one day for painful revenge. Every noise in the night. Every person who knocks on my door. I wonder if my borrowed time is up."

Mercy held her breath, unable to break eye contact. Anger and pain fueled Britta's words.

"I can state out loud that I won't be punished for surviving. Therapy taught me to say and believe those words, but my heart doesn't trust that belief. My heart trusts nothing. And do you know what? It's my heart that gets me out of bed every day. It drives me forward. I'm too damn stubborn to let fear overtake every aspect of my life. When the fear does strike at night or when a federal agent shows up on my doorstep, I power through. It may take a few minutes, but every time I come out on the other side."

Mercy couldn't speak.

"You'll leave here today and go back to your office to see your FBI buddies and go on with your normal life. Maybe you'll hit a Starbucks drive-through. Get coffee orders for everyone. Be the office hero for the afternoon. You know what I'll do? I'll take Zara on a run. We'll run and run until I can't breathe or think about the demons you stirred up with your visit today. I don't care if it's raining. All I want is to be damned exhausted when I crawl in bed." She straightened, briefly looking uncertain, as if she'd just realized how close she'd leaned to Mercy. "That will be my evening."

Mercy waited a long moment. "Are you done?"

Britta nodded.

"My evening will be spent digging through the dozens of case boxes from the Deverell family and yours—just like I did last night until two a.m.—searching for a needle in a haystack that might point me in a direction to solve the current murders. That's after I stop at the morgue to see skeletal remains again. No Starbucks. No office hero. I'm just doing my job." She kept her tone light and matter-of-fact. Britta didn't look away.

"You're not the only victim here, Britta. I respect everything you've gone through. But you're upright and walking. My priority is the people who can no longer do that. I'd appreciate any help you can give us. Someone else has committed murder, and I doubt they are finished. A small fact might be tucked away in your memory to help us figure out who it is."

"I'm not opening my brain up for your perusal." Britta's hand crept up and touched the side of her head where Mercy knew the killer had hit her with a hammer.

"Think about it."

"I just did."

Her resolute expression stated she was done with the topic.

But there was a streak of honor in Britta that hovered underneath the tough exterior. One that Mercy hoped would step forward to prevent another human from experiencing her horror. Mercy prayed she hadn't overstepped her bounds and scared Britta further away.

One step at a time.

EIGHT

Lucas handed Truman an envelope as he walked into the Eagle's Nest station for work that morning. "This was taped to the front door."

Truman noted his name on the outside and opened the envelope as he strode down the hall to his office.

He studied the single piece of paper and halted. *What the fuck?*

He laughed and then read it again. *Is this for real?*

Joshua Forbes claimed that Truman had trampled on his God-given rights and he wanted $3 million in compensation. Truman had heard of judges and police officers receiving this type of letter. It was a jumbled mess of legalese and fantasy.

The signature at the bottom captured his attention.

joshua; forbes SLS

What the hell do I do with this?

He walked back out to the waiting area, where Lucas was working at his computer. "Check this out."

The young man's eyebrows rose as he read. "Holy shit. Does he really believe he can get that kind of money out of you? I'd like to see a case where an SC was successful with a demand like this."

"I'm sure one doesn't exist."

"Did you assault him?" Lucas asked with a gleam in his eye.

"Hell no. All I did was stop his vehicle and ask some questions. County took him to the ground and I helped cuff him, but it was an easy arrest. At the most he got his clothes a little muddy."

"So he should be suing you for the cost of his laundry."

"His clothes weren't that clean to begin with," Truman pointed out.

"What's with the weird signature?"

"That's an SC oddity. The best I've been able to figure out is that it shows the letter was really signed by Joshua the human being, not the legal entity Joshua Forbes, created by the United States. I think the SLS stands for *sovereign living soul*."

"In English, please."

"There's no easy way to explain it. You need to watch one of those three-hour lectures on YouTube, but the way I understand it is they believe the United States has done some illegal machinations that created a straw man for every physical person. Your taxes are billed to your straw man, and laws apply to the straw man, so he as a person isn't liable for the taxes or held accountable to our laws. The actual human is only accountable to God. By signing the letter this way, he's showing that it's really him, not the US's straw man."

Lucas stared at him. "Everyone is two people," he recited slowly. "One is a fake entity that is accountable to US laws, and the other is the real human being that can do whatever the fuck he pleases."

"Bingo."

"It's notarized, and is that his fingerprint at the bottom?"

"They like to notarize everything—I'm surprised it wasn't delivered by registered mail, and I suspect you're right about the fingerprint."

"Isn't he in jail?" asked Lucas. "How'd he get it notarized and delivered?"

"Probably had a friend do that part for him. His arraignment is tomorrow. I'll try to be there."

"This is so cool," announced Lucas. "Can I post a photo of it on Twitter?"

Truman grabbed the paper out of his hand. "No. And don't talk about it to anyone else."

Lucas's face fell. "I'll black out your name."

"No." Truman headed back to his office, done with the conversation. He sat in the chair at his desk and leaned back, reading the letter again, wondering if he should show it to an attorney. Joshua Forbes had no real laws behind his claim, although Truman knew Joshua firmly believed he did.

"What's he going to do? Take me to court?" Truman mumbled. A judge would laugh himself off his chair. Truman filed the letter in a drawer. Mercy would be the person to show it to. While assigned to the Portland FBI office, she had worked in Domestic Terrorism, and sovereign citizens had been involved in some of her cases. She'd said that the majority of them were harmless and kept to themselves, but some of them associated with militias and took their beliefs seriously enough to create disruption in the current government. Usually they fought with paper, overloading the courts by filing nonsense complaints and liens.

He knew Mercy would review the letter even though she was focused on her new case. There had been an obsession in her eyes when she talked about the small skull found in the culvert.

Violence against kids got under her skin. His too.

The old crime reports he and Mercy had reviewed last night had stuck in his head. More horrible attacks against children.

Why murder the entire family?

Someone isn't right in the head.

Not that those who murdered a single person were right in the head, but to take out an entire family spoke to a new level of illness.

Truman wanted the new case solved as much as Mercy did.

But what can I do?

Steve Harris. The man's face popped into Truman's mind. The neighbor who'd discovered the Verbeek family.

Truman had interacted with him several times. Not usually on the best of terms, but he felt Steve respected him even if he didn't respect the fire hydrant in front of his home. Truman knew Steve's small house. It was three blocks away from the police department.

None of my business.

He logged on to his computer and discovered that Steve still owed the city for three parking tickets. They were about to be sent to collections.

Maybe I should be neighborly and give him a warning.

Truman put on his hat and walked out into the rain.

"We've got a lead."

"I'm listening," Mercy told Jeff as she drove away from Britta Vale's home, where she'd silenced her phone for her interview. There'd been three missed calls and two texts from Jeff.

"I'm sending you the address. There's a family missing. It's possible they've been missing for months."

"Sounds like a good lead."

"Deschutes County Sheriff's Department is already at the home. It's not far from where you're at."

"On my way." Mercy pulled over and plugged the address from his text into her GPS. She could be there in twenty minutes. She frowned at the map, surprised that someone lived in the desolate location. She would have expected it to be only rock and shrubs and wildlife.

Twenty minutes later she put her Tahoe into four-wheel drive to get through the mud. No one had done maintenance on the private road in ages. She rocked and bounced her way down into a valley, crossing her fingers that she wouldn't get stuck. Fresh tracks assured her that the county vehicles had made it. Moments later she found the home.

If Britta Vale's home was welcoming, this home advised people to stay away. The house looked abused and exhausted.

Three broken-down trucks sat in front of the home. Two still had wheels; none had windshields. The front of the home hid behind overgrown bushes. It had a sagging roof, and Mercy spotted several squatty outbuildings with pens to the left of the house. One she assumed was a chicken coop, and the others looked as if they would hold small farm animals. She parked next to a Deschutes County vehicle and slid out. A familiar figure stepped out of the home and Mercy recognized Deschutes County Detective Evan Bolton.

Mercy pulled up her hood in the misting rain and went to greet Bolton. The detective always looked as if he'd just wrapped up a difficult interview. He had a seen-it-all gaze in his brown eyes, even though he was a bit younger than Mercy.

She shook his hand. "What did you find?" she asked him.

"Something happened here, but who knows how long ago. There's a lot of old dried blood in the bedrooms, and all their stuff is still here, but the place is deserted. I assume this family didn't move away to a new city."

Not with dried blood left behind.

"What's the name?"

"Last name is Hartlage. Richard and Corrine Hartlage own the home."

"Kids?"

"Judging by the pictures inside, they have one young girl and a teenage girl."

The small skull flashed in Mercy's brain.

"Relatives? Neighbors?"

"We're searching for relatives. I sent a deputy to the closest homes, which are a good mile or two away, to get some information about this family."

"Vehicle registrations?"

"There's a missing Chevy Suburban. Fifteen years old. I put out a BOLO on it." Bolton pointed at the three old trucks. "None of these are registered."

"Not surprised." The silence of the property was overwhelming. "Are there animals?"

"The doors to the pens and the buildings were open when we got there," said Bolton. "I can tell there had been chickens in one pen and other animals in the other buildings . . . There are bales of hay and some feed bins."

"Someone let the animals out. I guess that's good." Mercy turned in a circle as she eyed the remote location. "I assume they're totally off the grid out here? No utilities to pay or fall behind on?"

"Nothing. Self-sufficient."

"Does it appear the home has been empty a long time?"

"Come take a look."

Mercy followed Bolton up the steps. "I think more than four people lived here," Bolton said. "You'll see what I mean."

A smell of mildew and old dust pervaded. "Was that window open like it is now?" Mercy gestured at a large one in the living room. Water had stained the wall and wood floor below the window. The boards had started to curl.

"Yes," said Bolton. "There are a few windows open. The wood floor is saturated over there."

"Not surprising after the storms we've had."

She took a quick pass through the kitchen, noting the layer of dust on the counter and the few dishes in the sink. "Did you look in the fridge?"

"It's pretty nasty."

"I'll take your word for it." Her stomach was already tight at the sight of the empty home. The weather must have been better when the family was last here. It hadn't been warm enough to leave windows open since September. A crime scene tech with a camera in hand moved into the living room from the hallway. He nodded at Mercy and started taking photos in the kitchen.

She followed Bolton down the hall and glanced in the small bathroom. A holder with five toothbrushes sat on the counter. The next doorway was to a tiny bedroom. Pink walls. Old white furniture. My Little Pony sheets on one twin bed, plain blue on the other. Clothes and Barbies on the floor.

Rust-colored stains on the pillows.

Mercy took three steps to the My Little Pony bed. The covers were pushed back, and a reddish-brown trail was smeared from the pillow to the floor. Then it stopped. It was the same for the blue bed.

"He put them in something."

"It's the same in all the rooms. The blood trails abruptly stop."

The next bedroom appeared to belong to the mother and father. Men's and women's clothing hung in the closet. The queen-size bed had dried blood on both pillows. Both sides of the bed had bloody stains down the sides of the mattress and box springs to the floor, where it had pooled in the carpet. No blood trail to the door, but blood spatter went up the walls and across the ceiling, showing how the killer had raised and swung the weapon.

Mercy stared at the blood patterns.

They were bludgeoned.

"The other bedroom is similar," said Bolton. He led her to the last room.

This room was slightly smaller, and the bed was the same size as the last one. It also had a bloodstain on the pillow. Mercy checked the small closet. Adult male clothing. "Another man lived here?" she asked, thinking of the second male skull. "Did you find a wallet?"

"We haven't found IDs anywhere in the home. No wallets with credit cards or anything. I suspect he took them."

"He may have wanted to use the credit cards. Jeez. He could have been charging up a storm for months and no one would know."

"No doubt the cards were frozen once no payments showed up."

"Good point. But he still had a wide window of opportunity." Mercy made a mental note to check the Hartlages' credit reports.

"Think this is related to yesterday's discovery up on March Mountain?" Bolton asked.

"It's a good possibility. Same number of victims. Obviously they've been gone from this home for a long time."

"The remains you found were skeletal. How long does that take?"

"Depends on the environment they were left in." Mercy took a deep breath. "So far there doesn't appear to be any clothing or even shoes with the bodies we found. Either they were stripped before they were buried in the culvert, or possibly the bones were recently put in there."

Bolton scowled. "They were dumped somewhere else first and then moved to the culvert?"

"I'm speculating out loud. I know they can test the bones to analyze the soil they were buried in, and then they can analyze the soil and debris in the culvert. I'm curious to find out if they're the same."

Bolton stared at her for a long moment. "You don't think they were in that culvert for very long."

"We have to consider that as an option. Why hadn't they already washed away? We had rain last fall and this spring."

"But I heard the water was flowing around the culvert. Maybe it's been doing that for months."

"True. This is just a theory bouncing around in my brain." She studied the blood on the pillow. "You said there were some family pictures?"

"This way."

On a small table in the living room were six framed photos. A young girl with dark hair clutching a white-and-tan cat smiled in one. Another frame held a school photo of a teenage girl. The others showed the girls with their parents.

"What's her name?" Mercy picked up the picture of the young girl. She was missing two top teeth, but her wide smile proved she didn't care.

"I found some coloring book pages in the pink bedroom with the name Alison signed on them. I haven't figured out the teenager's name yet."

The tiny skull suddenly had a potential name. No longer would Mercy think of it as "the child." Now it was Alison.

Maybe.

"Dammit." She set down the picture and looked away. It'd been easier to think about the bones when they were nameless.

"I think we found the murder weapon outside."

"Saving the most important evidence for last?" Mercy asked.

"I like to make an impact." Bolton's smile didn't reach his eyes.

They went out the front door and around the side of the home. In the tall grass next to the home lay a large hammer. It'd been washed by the rain and probably frozen by the snow over the last few months. *Will there be any fingerprints?*

"Awfully cocky to leave it behind," Mercy murmured.

"I took it as a big fuck you," said Bolton.

"What kind of hammer is it? I've never seen a head like that before." Two-thirds of the head was a solid cylinder shape before it narrowed to a point at one end.

"I don't know either. I've got an evidence team on the way," Bolton said. "I'm not touching it until then."

"I want the photos from this scene as soon as possible."

"Not a problem."

"Ask your team to look for dental or medical bills. We need the name of their dentist to get copies of their dental X-rays. If they don't find any paperwork, check with the local dentists and see if any of them had the Hartlage family as patients."

Bolton nodded as he tapped a notation into his phone.

"Meeeeooooow."

A white cat with tan patches wound itself around Mercy's ankles. "Oh my God." The cat's blue gaze met hers as it rubbed the side of its face against Mercy's shin. *It's the cat from the photo.* It was skinny but not deathly thin. "How on earth . . ." Shock and pity shot through her.

"The cat must have been living in one of the outbuildings. Catching mice."

"You poor thing." Mercy scooped up the cat and it immediately started to purr, pressing its head against Mercy's hand.

"Looks like you acquired a cat." Bolton leaned to one side and studied it. "A female cat."

Mercy stared at Bolton. "Hell no, I didn't."

"Why not? I bet your niece would love it."

True. "My place is too small."

"Does it allow pets?"

"Yes."

"Then I'm sure you can work it out." Bolton finally gave a real grin. "Or we can drop her off at a shelter."

No! "Maybe." The cat vibrated contentedly under Mercy's stroking hand.

"I'd noticed two small pet bowls on the floor in the kitchen. And there was a cat bed in the pink bedroom. I bet she misses her people." Bolton ran a hand over the cat's back.

Damn him.

"We'll see," Mercy admitted. "Maybe there are some Hartlage relatives who would take her in."

But deep down she suspected she'd just acquired a cat.

NINE

Truman knocked on the front door of Steve Harris's home.

The house didn't have a garage, and Steve's truck was parked on the street, directly in front of the fire hydrant. Looking around, Truman realized that the man really didn't have anywhere else to park unless he went down the street quite a way. His neighbors' vehicles filled both sides of the street. Yes, it was a safety issue, but Truman figured it'd only take the firemen an extra thirty seconds to bash in the windows of the truck to access the fire hydrant. Bringing up the issue on this visit wouldn't get him any insight into the Verbeek family murder.

Steve answered the door. In his midfifties, Steve was a tall, angular man with an oddly wide face that didn't suit the rest of his body. He was bald except for a little hair above his ears. His eyes immediately narrowed at the sight of Truman on his front porch.

Truman held up a hand before Steve could speak. "I'm not here about the violation I just walked past at your curb."

Steve relaxed a fraction, but his gaze was still suspicious. "Then what do you want?"

"I'm doing a little research about some cases from twenty-odd years ago."

"The Verbeek murders," he stated in a flat tone. The suspicion vanished from Steve's eyes, replaced by a distant emptiness.

"Do you mind answering a few questions?"

"Why? Why do you care about something that happened so long ago?"

Truman paused, weighing how much to reveal. "Something came up recently that has us reviewing the murders of those families."

"Why? Grady Baldwin was tried and found guilty. The cases were closed, right?"

"They were." Truman didn't want to say that it was possible something similar had happened recently. *How can I phrase this?* "Sometimes we have to look at the past to find answers for the present."

"What does that bullshit mean?" Steve shoved his hands in his pockets, his stance stiff, blocking the door.

Truman gave up on tact. "It means something violent has happened and we're looking at the old cases for help." He looked directly at Steve, all his cards on the table.

Steve considered him for a long moment. He took a step back and gestured for Truman to come in.

The inside of the home was surprisingly nice. From the outside, the old bungalow-style home looked as if it hadn't been touched since the 1960s. But inside, it had been updated with nice wood floors, baseboards, a modern fireplace, and contemporary furniture. The home smelled of coffee and bacon.

Truman took a seat in an upholstered chair that was uncomfortable and stiff. Steve sat in a matching chair. "What happened?" Steve asked.

Truman mulled it over.

"You can't tell me," Steve stated before Truman could speak.

"Not yet."

Steve slowly nodded. "It's serious?"

"Yes."

"What do you want to know?"

"Tell me about the morning you found the Verbeek family."

Steve looked away, rubbing his jaw. "It's been a long time. I try not to think about it. Never seen anything like that before. And I haven't since, thank God."

"What made you go in the house?"

"The door was open a bit and no one answered my knock, so I pushed it." He wouldn't meet Truman's gaze. "I knew something was wrong . . . It didn't smell right either. I called out and stepped inside. Dennis Verbeek was on the floor in the living room." He looked down at his hands. "Blood had soaked his head and the floor. It wasn't quite dry, but he was cold. I found Maria in the hallway. She was the same."

He cleared his throat and his knuckles went white as his hands tightened.

"Maria was outside the girls' room. I checked the twins first. They were bloody and cold like their parents, but when I touched Britta's arm, she was still warm."

His gaze met Truman's. "Those girls were beaten in the head. I don't understand the kind of person who does that to adults, let alone helpless small girls."

"You called 911 from the Verbeek home?"

"Yes. I was too scared to move Britta from the top bunk bed . . . I was afraid I'd injure her worse. She was unconscious, with a head and mouth injury. There was nothing else I could do, so I waited for the ambulance and prayed she continued to breathe."

"Did you know Grady Baldwin?"

Anger filled Steve's face. "I knew who he was. I'd never talked to him. I knew Dennis Verbeek had hired Grady to help him reroof his home a few months before."

"He made a pass at Maria Verbeek and got turned down?"

"So they said."

"You don't believe it?"

Steve shrugged. "I have no doubt that Grady Baldwin killed that family. They had evidence against him, but I doubt that was why he did it."

"Why do you say that?"

The man looked away. "I don't care to speak ill of the dead," he said with discomfort in his tone.

"What if it helps someone else?"

He looked back at Truman, his eyes serious. "This is just my opinion, but Maria wasn't the type to attract other men."

"You can never tell what attracts another man."

Steve grimaced. "True. But Maria would never look anyone in the eye. She always seemed terrified of speaking to anyone and practically hid behind her husband. Why would Grady hit on her?"

"Maybe he likes the victim type."

"Maybe." Steve didn't sound convinced. "I celebrated the day they put Grady Baldwin away," he stated. "I testified at his trial, and he sat there in the courtroom, staring straight ahead, no emotion at all." He took a deep breath. "I had to describe the condition I found those little girls. Those twins . . . Astrid and Helena . . . they were tiny girls, and their little heads had been caved in. I'll never get that sight out of my mind. It rushes in sometimes . . . Those memories can completely knock me down for a day." His voice cracked. "It's gotten better over the years, but it's not gone."

"I appreciate you telling me," Truman told him, feeling guilty both for making the man revisit his hell and for talking to someone on Mercy's review list.

It's not like he's a witness in the new murder. The case he was involved in is closed.

"I don't know what happened to Britta. I know she went to live with an aunt or something. I tried to find her online a few years ago with no luck. I frequently wonder if she's okay . . . if she's a well-adjusted adult, or living on the street somewhere. I may have seen that horror, but Britta lost her family. I can't imagine how that could affect a child."

The man sitting across from him wasn't the jerk who had argued with Truman about fire hydrants. Caught up in his memories, Steve looked broken.

"I know the FBI has been in touch with Britta," Truman said kindly. "She's doing okay and doesn't live on the streets. I can't tell you much else." He'd had a brief phone call from Mercy after she'd talked with Britta.

Steve raised his head and met Truman's gaze. "Truly?"

"Yes."

"Thank you for telling me." Steve seemed lost in thought for a few moments. "I've wondered about her for years. I hope this helps me sleep better at night."

"Since the Deverell family had been murdered two months earlier, what went through your mind that day?"

"After I found the Verbeeks, I figured right away that it was the same guy. Once the cops discovered that Grady Baldwin had worked in both homes, they knew they had a strong suspect."

"You said earlier that you didn't think the motivation for the Verbeek murder was Maria Verbeek. Why do you think he did it?"

"He was insane," Steve said in a low voice.

Truman knew the answer wasn't ever that simple.

Several hours after he left Steve Harris's home, Truman pulled open the door to the Brick Tavern, wishing he had backup. Samuel was at least ten minutes out.

Who gets in a bar fight in the middle of the afternoon?

Surprisingly, the bar was brightly lit inside, and he had a clear view of two men wrestling on the floor. A few bystanders idly watched.

"Hey, Chief." The owner, Doug "the Brick" Breneman, appeared at his side, looking unconcerned about the brawling men. The Brick had been his wrestling name in Portland in the 1980s, when *Portland Wrestling* was on TV every week. He had been a local celebrity back then, and he was still built like a brick. Rectangular bald head, thick neck, and barrel torso. People had never stopped calling him Brick.

"What happened?" Truman asked.

"Dunno," said Brick. "It's the Moody brothers, Clint and Ryan." He pointed at the men. "The one in the red shirt is Clint. They're both pissed as hell at each other, which isn't anything new. I tried to separate them, but I'm not as young as I used to be. Got back issues, so I turned up the lights. Usually that will stop a fight, but it didn't work this time."

Truman scanned the room, checking for anyone who looked as if they would cause a problem if he separated the two men. His gaze stopped on Owen Kilpatrick, Mercy's brother. His surprise at seeing Owen was compounded with relief at the knowledge that the man would have Truman's back if trouble arose. Brick would too.

Truman strode to the fighting men. Clint had a grip on Ryan's ear, attempting to slam his head into the floor. Ryan was kicking and punching but landing few blows. "Police! Break it up!"

The men continued as if they hadn't heard. The brothers were muscular and fit, but Truman had an advantage because both were severely inebriated.

"I said break it up!" Truman grabbed Clint's shoulder and yanked him backward. He landed on his back, his head bouncing off the floor. *Shit.*

Ryan lunged for Clint, but Truman knocked his legs out from under him, making the man land on his chest. "I said that's enough!" He planted a foot on the center of the man's back and pointed at Clint. "Stay right there!" He noted Owen and Brick had both moved within an arm's distance of Clint, ready to keep him from diving at Ryan under Truman's foot. He lowered himself to a knee on Ryan's back, and told him to spread his arms out on the floor and then bring the right one behind his back. Truman cuffed one wrist and asked for the other arm, which he promptly secured.

"I didn't do anything!" Ryan protested.

"Bullshit," said Brick. "Now shut up."

Truman left the man on the floor on his stomach and turned to Clint. "On your stomach, arms out."

"But Chief—"

"*Now.* This is for my own safety."

Clint shot him a dirty look and laid his sweaty face down on the floor. Truman tried not to think about the filth of the tavern's floor. Clint followed Truman's orders and was quickly cuffed. Truman exhaled, letting go of some tension. Police work was full of what-ifs. His training had taught him to be prepared for any issue, how to study behavior and movements to anticipate a suspect's next move, and that even a simple face-to-face discussion could turn deadly. People were insulted when the cuffs went on, but that was how it worked.

Truman went back to Ryan. The man turned his head, struggling to make eye contact from his prone position on the floor, clearly drunk.

"What happened here, Ryan?" Truman asked.

"Nothin'," Ryan spit out. "My brother is an asshole!"

"You swung at me first!" Clint yelled back.

"That's bullshit!"

"You're the bigger asshole!"

"Shut the fuck up!"

"Both of you shut up," Truman ordered. He hauled Ryan to a sitting position, noting how the man swayed, and then did the same with Clint. Truman couldn't decide which man was more drunk. He turned to Brick. "You filing charges?"

"Nothing's broke."

Truman had figured that would be Brick's answer.

After a quick pat down, Truman said, "I need to see IDs from both of you." After some awkward maneuvering due to the men sitting on their wallets and having their hands cuffed, Truman finally opened the first wallet. He found a diplomatic card identical to the one he'd been shown by Joshua Forbes but with Clint Moody's name and photo. He looked at Clint and showed him the ID. "This all you got?"

The man squinted blearily at the card. "Nah, that's just a joke. My regular license is in there."

Truman found a legitimate Oregon driver's license. Clint was twenty-eight.

"Told you not to carry that crap," Ryan told his brother. "It's illegal."

"Shut up!" Clint shot back. He looked nervously at Truman. "Like I said, it's just for fun."

Truman checked Ryan's wallet next. No diplomatic card. Just a normal license. He was thirty.

"These are expensive." Truman held up the fake ID. "I'd like to know where you got it."

"A friend gave it to me. He didn't charge me anything."

"What's that friend's name?"

Clint looked away.

Truman bit his cheek at Clint's stubborn silence. *Does he not realize he's sitting on the floor in cuffs and about to go to jail?* He sighed. There was no point in arguing when the men were clearly inebriated.

Eagle's Nest officer Samuel Robb pulled open the bar door and entered at that moment.

"Damn. I missed the fun," the buzz-cut, brawny officer said as he took in the two men on the floor. "What do you have?"

Truman briefed him on the fight and fake license. "I want them locked up until they're coherent."

Samuel nodded. "Will do. I got this one." He grabbed Clint's arm and easily hauled him to his feet. "This way, princess." The two men disappeared out the door.

Ryan sat silently, his head down, still swaying. Truman hoped he wouldn't puke in the back seat when he drove him in.

"Nice job." Owen approached and shook Truman's hand.

"Thanks." The simple fact that Owen approved of Truman's police work was a big sign of the change in Mercy's brother. He'd been suspicious of police and government all his life. Enough to make him rub shoulders with a growing militia several months ago. He'd learned from his mistake and had grudgingly also accepted his sister as a federal officer.

"I heard Joshua Forbes will be arraigned tomorrow," Owen commented, his words casual but his eyes alert as he studied Truman.

"I heard that too," said Brick.

"Word travels fast."

"He's not the sharpest tool in the shed," added Owen.

"I noticed that," said Truman. "You know him well?"

Owen shrugged. "Everyone knows the Forbeses."

"Not me."

"They try to stay under the radar," said Owen. "His dad had a few run-ins with the courts and police back in the day. He's in a wheelchair now, and that's reined him in. But Joshua seems to be following in his footsteps."

Brick nodded. "Right here in this bar, I've overheard him try to convince people about the straw man theory. He's pretty fervent in his beliefs."

"People fall for it?" asked Truman.

"Hard to say," answered Brick. "It's easy to get people's attention when you tell them they're not legally obligated to pay taxes and that the government actually owes them money. Making the life change is a difficult commitment, but sometimes people are just hungry and desperate for answers. No taxes sounds like heaven."

"Have you seen these?" Truman showed Owen and Brick the fake diplomatic license. "I'd like to find the supplier."

Owen grinned. "You arrested the supplier the other day."

"Joshua Forbes made it?" Truman was surprised.

"Yep. Sells them too," said Brick. "Makes a pretty penny, I believe."

Truman nudged Ryan with his boot. "Is that who your brother got this from? Joshua Forbes?"

Ryan wobbled and nearly tipped over. "I don't know where he got it. He doesn't tell me shit, and he's an idiot for carrying it around."

Truman scowled, wondering if he could get forgery added to the charges against Joshua Forbes. "Glad to hear you weren't sucked into this scam, Owen."

Mercy's brother looked grim. "I stay away from big talkers now. Besides, everyone knows those aren't legal. Well, everyone but the sovereign citizens who want to believe."

"Good."

Ryan suddenly fell to one side and moaned. Truman jumped backward as the man vomited where Truman's boots had been a split second earlier.

Truman's stomach heaved at the odor, and Brick cursed like the professional wrestler he'd been.

Better here than in my vehicle.

TEN

Two miles away from the scene at the Hartlage house, Mercy parked at the closest neighbor's home. Kenneth Forbes's house strongly resembled the Hartlages', but there was a long ramp to the front door. An ancient sedan without license plates sat beside the home, weeds growing around its tires.

Does he live alone?

Earlier a deputy had briefly visited Kenneth Forbes, returned to the Hartlage crime scene, and reported that Forbes believed Corrine Hartlage's brother had lived in the home with the family, but didn't know his name.

"What else did he tell you?" Mercy had asked the deputy. "When did Mr. Forbes see them last? Has he been by the farm recently?"

The deputy had looked at his feet and shuffled them. "He wasn't very cooperative, ma'am. And he's disabled. I didn't want to pressure him."

Mercy had exchanged a look with Detective Bolton. The deputy was very young. "I'll go talk to Mr. Forbes," Mercy stated.

Still in her vehicle, Mercy looked at the cat, who'd curled up on the passenger seat and gone immediately to sleep. *I thought cats hated cars.*

Should I stop at a pet shelter?

If a Hartlage relative wanted the cat, leaving it at a shelter could lead to a hot mess. Mercy decided she'd keep it until they heard if anyone was interested in it.

I'll tell Kaylie up front that it might leave.

As Mercy got out of her vehicle, the front door opened, and a man in a wheelchair appeared.

"Mr. Forbes?" Mercy stopped ten feet from the ramp.

"Who wants to know?"

"I'm Special Agent Mercy Kilpatrick. I'm investigating your missing neighbors and could really use your help."

The man gave a short laugh. "Help? Do I look like I can help anyone? You're just here to ask more questions. I already told that other policeman all I know."

Kenneth Forbes appeared to be in his midfifties. His short hair was salt and pepper, and his face was well weathered and lined. Even at this distance, Mercy could see his eyes were a piercing blue. Anger radiated from him.

"Did you know the girls, Alison and Amy? There's a lot of blood in their room, and it appears they've been missing for months." Mercy lobbed the loaded question at the man. If missing children didn't affect him, he wasn't human.

He was silent for five seconds. "Blood?"

"Yes. In all the bedrooms. The house hasn't been lived in for a long time, but their belongings are still there."

His cheeks tightened as he flexed his jaw, and he spun his wheelchair around. "Come in then," he said over his shoulder.

It wasn't the welcome she'd hoped for, but she'd take it.

The home was extremely plain inside, with wide paths for his wheelchair. He motioned for her to sit in an old easy chair by the front door. He maneuvered his wheelchair so he could face her, crossed his hands in his lap, and looked at her expectantly, his eyes still hard. "What do you need to know?"

No coffee. No tea. No small talk.

"When did you see any of them last?"

He grimaced. "I'm not sure. Last summer, I guess. And that was just passing them on the road."

"But they're your closest neighbor."

"No, I'm *their* closest neighbor. My son lives a quarter mile away from me." He frowned. "Just because I live near someone doesn't make us friends. I didn't need anything from them, so I rarely interacted with them. Are they dead?"

Mercy blinked at his bluntness. "We don't know."

"You said there was blood."

"I did. But we didn't find any bodies there."

"Why does the FBI care about a missing family? Shouldn't this be handled by the sheriff?"

"Missing children are always our business," Mercy stated firmly. "Did you know the children?"

"I've seen them."

Mercy waited.

"I've never talked to either one." He shrugged. "Wouldn't even know their names if you hadn't said them. I've only spoken with Richard. He told me his wife's brother was living with them, and I got the impression he wasn't very happy about the intrusion."

"But you don't know his name either?"

"No, but I've seen him once or twice."

"Was the brother Asian?"

Kenneth gave her a confused look. "No. Why on earth would he be Asian?"

"Just following up on a possible lead."

Who is the Asian skull?

"Do you know who can tell me more about this family?" she asked.

He looked beyond her, scratching his chin. "Maybe my son. If he's met them, I'm unaware of it, but he is the next-closest neighbor."

"Do you live alone?" Mercy asked curiously.

Defensiveness filled his face. "I do. My son brings my groceries and helps me out."

"I noticed the car out front."

"Haven't taken it out since my accident ten years ago. Thrown from a horse."

"I'm very sorry," Mercy said awkwardly. His anger had returned during the statement.

"Me too. Fucking hate this chair." The bitterness in the room was suffocating.

Mercy pulled out her business card and set it on the accent table. "Can you give me your son's address?"

"Don't need that. Just turn left after you leave my drive and then take the next left off the main road. But he's gone for a few days."

"Do you know when he'll be back?"

"No." The anger rose again.

"Can I get his phone number?" She wrote down the number he rattled off. "Please call me if you think of anything that might help us figure out what happened to this family."

"Don't know nothing. I rarely saw them. I hardly see anyone."

Mercy escaped the hostile-feeling house. She darted between the puddles in the yard and climbed into her Tahoe, shaking the drizzle from her hair. The sour atmosphere still clung to her. The cat raised its head, gave a jaw-stretching yawn, and went back to sleep. Mercy stroked her back, wondering how long the cat had been alone at the Hartlage home.

Does the cat miss her owners?

Mercy pictured the skeletal remains she suspected might be the Hartlages.

There'd been two male skulls in the culvert. One Asian, one Caucasian.

Kenneth Forbes claimed the brother-in-law wasn't Asian.

If the Hartlage family was in the culvert, is the father or brother-in-law still alive?

◆ ◆ ◆

"I might have gotten a cat," Mercy told Rose over a late lunch.

"Might?" Rose asked in surprise, nearly dropping her glass of soda.

"I might have to give it back if someone claims it." Mercy shared that morning's cat-acquiring incident with her sister at the diner in Eagle's Nest.

"Where is the cat now?"

"I stopped and bought cat litter, cat food, a cat bed, and a covered litter box and dropped her off at my place before coming here."

"Does Kaylie know?" Rose grinned.

Mercy grimaced as she took a bite of her BLT. "I texted her so she wouldn't be surprised when she walked in the door. She was ecstatic, of course."

"Of course she was. She's a teenage girl."

"I don't need a cat."

"No one *needs* a cat . . . until you get one and wonder why you never had one before."

"Just like a baby?"

Rose laughed and touched her rounded stomach. "Honestly, I don't remember what it was like to not be expecting this little one. I think that's a pregnancy hormone thing. It's made my brain forget how life was before."

"I've heard you forget the pain of birth too. Makes you willing to go through it again," said Mercy. She suspected that was a lot of bull.

People didn't forget pain. She remembered every bit of the agony from when she was shot in the leg.

Rose looked thoughtful. "I've heard that. I can't say I'm not worried about the pain. But my biggest fear is getting to the hospital in time."

"Call me and I'll drop whatever I'm doing."

"Nick has promised the same thing."

"How is it going with Nick?" Mercy asked. She tried to meet Rose once a week for lunch and catch up, but this was their first visit in three weeks. Nick Walker had been very clear about his attraction to Rose. At least to Mercy. Rose had been slower to believe his interest was real. Rose's baby had been conceived during a rape by a serial killer, and Rose struggled to believe that any man could consider becoming involved in her situation. The baby hadn't bothered Nick, and neither did her lack of sight. The adoration that Nick consistently showed for Rose took Mercy's breath away. And the two of them were officially dating now.

A faint blush appeared on Rose's cheeks. "Good. We went out to dinner in Bend last night." Her brows came together as she frowned slightly.

"What is it?"

Frustration crossed Rose's face. "He's a bit overprotective. Always asking if I need help or trying to do things for me."

"Ah." Mercy believed that. Many men assumed Rose was a helpless flower, but she could do almost anything. Except drive a car. Rose was tough as nails under her rose-petal exterior. "He needs to spend more time with you. I'm sure he'll figure it out."

"I hope so."

"Stand up for yourself now. The two of you need to learn if you can work together. Don't back off because you're afraid of offending him."

"You make it sound like we're coworkers."

Mercy shrugged. "Dating and marriage is a balance. He has a lot to learn about you and vice versa."

"He always wants to know how I feel and how each prenatal visit went. I finally said I'll let him know if there is something unusual to share. It's a small thing to be annoyed about . . . I should be happy he's interested."

"He did lose his wife to breast cancer," Mercy pointed out. "I can see him having anxiety about your health, but is your relationship at the point where you're sharing everything about the baby with him?"

"It's pretty serious," Rose whispered with a small smile. "He told me he's in love with me last week."

"Oh, Rose. That's wonderful!" Mercy's heart warmed at the happiness on her sister's face.

"We've talked a lot about the baby"—she sucked in a big breath—"and how it was conceived. He's such a good man, Mercy. He swears it makes no difference to him."

"Have you accepted that yet?"

Her sister was quiet for a second. "I'm getting there. We haven't been together that long."

Rose hadn't said that she'd told Nick she loved him too. "You need to feel absolutely certain of his commitment to the baby before you tell him you love him, right?" Mercy asked softly. She'd seen the dedication on Nick's face, but Rose had to make her own decision.

"Is that horrible of me?" Rose tipped her head to the side a little, reminding Mercy of Kaylie.

"I don't think so. Your baby is your priority now, right? Your actions and decisions are based on what's best for your baby . . . even if it might break your heart."

Rose held perfectly still. "That's exactly how I feel," she whispered. "I can't go any further with Nick until *I know*."

"You'll know soon," Mercy said, remembering when she'd realized she loved Truman. "One day you'll simply realize that he's the right one."

"I hope so."

"How long do you have left?" Mercy asked.

"Three months." A dreamy smile filled her sister's face.

Mercy was glad to see her sister's happiness about the baby. The thought of the challenge of her being blind and raising a baby gave Mercy anxiety but not Rose.

"I hope . . ." Rose trailed off, a thoughtful look on her face.

"You hope what?"

"I hope as an adult, my child will look back and be grateful to have a mom who was different. I'll learn as much from her as she does from me."

"Her?" Mercy jumped on the pronoun.

Her sister laughed. "No, I'm not hiding the sex. I'll be as surprised as everyone else. But in my mind, I think of it as her."

Mercy did too. "She'll be lucky to have you as a mom. What will you do about your preschool when the baby comes?"

"I'm going to close up for the summer. I usually do anyway, but I don't know what I'll do in the fall. Mom has offered to watch the baby while I teach, but if possible I would like to bring the baby with me. I'll know better what I'm capable of once she's born." Rose leaned toward Mercy. "Just promise you'll be in town the week I'm due. Seriously . . . I don't want to have this baby at the farm. Even if Mom is a skilled midwife."

"I promise. You've also got Mom and Dad as backup drivers. Nick too. You could even call Kaylie or Truman or an ambulance, if it comes to that. There are a lot of options."

Rose sat back, her face clearing as she nodded. "True. I've had dreams that I can't get there and it's just me and the baby alone at the farm. Something is wrong, and I can't take care of her."

Mercy reached across the table and took Rose's hand. "That won't happen. No apocalypse is scheduled before the baby is to be born."

Her sister laughed, and Mercy sighed in relief, but part of her brain immediately started to make plans in case a national crisis happened before Rose's baby was born.

I'll bring Rose to my cabin. Shit! The cabin won't be done by then.

Her heart sped up and her lungs tightened.

I'm unprepared. Rose's baby could suffer because of it. I need to check my medical supplies—

Stop it.

Mercy took deep breaths and searched for a different topic. "Are you familiar with the Hartlage family?"

Rose finished her grilled cheese sandwich as she considered the question. "First names?"

"Corrine and Richard."

Her sister shook her head. "I don't recognize them. Do they have something to do with you getting a cat?"

"They own the home I was at this morning. That's where I found the cat."

"They're the missing family?"

"Yes. Do you know Kenneth Forbes?"

Understanding flashed. "I do. He's in a wheelchair, right? Got thrown from a horse and can no longer walk."

"That's him."

"He's an SC. Whole family is."

Sovereign citizen.

"No wonder he didn't want to talk to me this morning." Mercy sighed. "I don't care what he believes. I just want to find out what happened to this family."

"Is this missing family related to the bones found at the road on March Mountain?"

"We don't know yet. It's possible. Hopefully we'll find out soon." Mercy checked the time. "Do you need a ride home?"

"No, Dad is at the feed store. He said he'd drive me when I was ready."

Mercy pictured her father exchanging gossip and shooting the breeze with the other men who tended to congregate at the feed store.

The constantly brewing free coffee probably had a lot to do with the frequent gatherings. *How many times did I wait for him to finish his conversations when I was little?* As a kid she had explored every inch of the feed store to fight her boredom. Sometimes there had been baby chickens to hold. Mercy could still feel the yellow fluff under her fingertips. Those had been the best days.

Mercy hugged and kissed her sister goodbye and headed toward her vehicle. She was tempted to wait and see her father, but it wasn't the right time yet. *He'll let me know when he's ready to accept me back into the fold.* It'd already been six months. It'd been fifteen years and six months since they'd parted ways because she'd refused to live under her father's iron fist. Hopefully it wouldn't take much longer.

Truman called as she drove back to her office. "How's your day?" she asked.

"Good. Only one bar fight so far."

"Already?"

"It's five o'clock somewhere. Say, I wanted to ask you if you've ever received a letter from a sovereign citizen claiming you owe them money for trampling on their rights."

Mercy grinned. "Not me personally, but I saw a few when I worked in the Portland office. We had a few judges get them."

"I got one from the guy I pulled over with the fake ID and plates yesterday."

"Awesome! How much money does he want?"

"Three million."

"You just made my day," she stated. The letters had been a big source of amusement at her old office. "Did he use a funky signature?"

"Yep."

"The lure of never paying taxes is very strong. People will subscribe to any scheme, no matter how convoluted it is."

"Do I need to do anything about this?"

"No, but email me a copy. I'll file a report and check the FBI's records to see if your guy has done anything else. SCs love to create stacks of paperwork and bog down the legal systems, but they rarely take physical action."

"According to your brother Owen, this guy is also creating and selling diplomatic licenses."

"Isn't that like Owen, to keep that little piece of illegal activity to himself?" Mercy wasn't surprised. Her older brother wouldn't report someone unless physical harm had happened. "Sounds like I need to open an investigation. Get that letter to me, and I'll go from there."

"He's being arraigned tomorrow. I plan to be there."

"Let me know if anything else crops up about him."

"Will do." He sounded relieved. "I love you. I'll miss you tonight," he said in a husky tone.

His voice sent good shivers up her spine, and she ended the call. She blew out a breath and leaned back in her seat.

What was my life like before Truman Daly?

She barely remembered. She recalled faint memories of quiet evenings in front of the TV and weekends full of work on her cabin. Now he was an element of her life as routine as breathing and eating. She'd been comfortably independent and alone for a long time until Truman showed up and disrupted her normal. She'd fought her growing need for commitment for months, worried that loving him would mean losing herself.

How wrong she had been.

Thank God he was persistent.

ELEVEN

"You found the Hartlage girls' dental X-rays but not the parents'?"

That evening Mercy questioned Dr. Harper, the forensic odontologist, in the room where the remains were being studied. The dentist had two skulls sitting near the computer screen where she was talking to Mercy. One was the tiny skull. Mercy tried not to look at the destroyed teeth; she'd seen them enough. The skulls had haunted her dreams.

"We got lucky when we called a pediatric dentist," said Dr. Harper. "Hopefully we'll find out that the parents were patients at one of the dental offices where I left a message. The adult skulls had dental work done, so somewhere there are records. I was happy to have found the kids' dentist on the eighth phone call."

"What about patient privacy laws?"

"The dentist hesitated because of those. I had your boss give him a call. He convinced him."

Jeff could talk anyone into anything.

Mercy looked at the computer screen in front of Dr. Harper. To her eye, it showed a jumbled mess of small gray films that had no rhyme or reason. "How did you take those precise X-rays of the teeth? You don't have that kind of dental equipment at this location, do you?"

"I called in a favor," said Dr. Harper with a sparkle in her brown eyes. "A local dentist I graduated with from dental school let me use her machine. Saved me from driving back to Portland just to take films."

"Smart."

"Always." Dr. Harper turned back to the screen. "Now," she said in a teaching tone of voice. "Across the top of my screen are Alison Hartlage's films I received from her dentist's office."

"Tiny little films," remarked Mercy. The images showed white-and-gray shapes that she knew were teeth. *How does Dr. Harper know which teeth they are?*

"Normal for a child of this age. Below those are the films that I took on the smallest skull."

"You took a lot more films."

"It's typical for pediatric offices to only take two or four films of the molars at Alison's age. I shot a lot of views of the skull's teeth for our records."

Even Mercy's unpracticed eye could see the broken and jagged teeth on Dr. Harper's recent films. Anger tightened her throat. "Fucking asshole," she whispered.

"Breaks my heart," said Dr. Harper. She cleared her throat and touched the screen. "If you look here at the film I took, there is a whiter mark on this tooth. It's a composite filling—a white filling—on her six-year molar." Her cursor dragged the film next to one of Alison Hartlage's films. "This film from Alison's dentist has the exact same-shaped filling."

Mercy held her breath. "Is that the only thing that matches?"

"No. There are two other composite fillings that match." The dentist touched the screen again, pointing out the similarities. "And even if there weren't any fillings, the shape of her first molars is distinctive. It's clear to me that this is positively Alison Hartlage."

"Even though he broke her front teeth?"

"Oh yes. In a child this age, the front teeth change the fastest anyway . . . the kids are constantly losing baby teeth, and the adult teeth are growing in. She wouldn't have lost her deciduous molars for a few more years. Right here, you can see the adult premolars below the baby teeth. They wouldn't have grown in until she was much older."

"Can you tell how old she was?"

"Kids lose and grow teeth at different rates. Looking at the films, I can make an educated guess of her age." Lacey smiled. "But her dentist gave me her date of birth. She's six and a half."

A sense of finality washed over Mercy. This was Alison. No question.

"What about her sister?" Mercy asked.

"Amy." Dr. Harper brought up more films on her screen. "I'm also positive one of the other female skulls is Amy. She was fifteen."

"Two people identified." The accomplishment tasted sour in Mercy's mouth.

"No doubt two of the others will turn out to be her parents," said Dr. Harper.

"I'm not assuming anything," said Mercy. "A neighbor said the brother-in-law who was living with them wasn't Asian. So—"

"So either the brother-in-law or the father could still be alive." Dr. Harper's eyes opened wide.

"Maybe his skull washed down the bank."

"I know they searched the area for a long time. They've brought in some more bones," said Dr. Harper, "but I don't know if they're done. You know there was a creek way down the slope, right?"

"I heard that. I wonder if some bones made it that far. Is Dr. Peres around?"

"Not at the moment."

"Did she find evidence that there were more than five skeletons?"

"Like more than ten femurs?"

"Exactly."

"My understanding is that she's annoyed so many bones are missing. She hasn't mentioned finding too many."

"A lot of bones could have been completely washed away." Mercy sighed. "That would include skulls."

"Very true."

"It's also possible none of those skulls are the parents of Alison and Amy."

Dr. Harper nodded with sympathy. "Until I have dental X-rays to compare them to, we won't know."

"Hopefully one of your calls to a dentist will yield some results. It's late, so I assume you won't hear anything more until tomorrow. Are you sure you called all of them?"

"I called every one within thirty miles of Bend. It's possible they traveled farther than that for dental care, but it's not typical. Especially since their kids went to one in town." She frowned. "I will say that the Asian skull has had some horrible dental work. He had two amalgam fillings done, and they have huge overhangs and decay underneath them."

"What does that mean?"

"Someone didn't know what they were doing . . . or they didn't care if they did a decent job. He also has several teeth that should have been repaired. I imagine they were giving him serious pain."

"Then it's possible he avoided the dentist for several years. I'll have to concentrate on another way to identify his remains."

"Do you really think these are related to those cases from twenty years ago?"

Mercy made herself look at the destruction on the skulls. "We have to consider it. I've never seen abuse like this outside of those other two cases, and all of them happened in the same county."

"But the bodies were left in their homes twenty years ago. These were moved."

It was a primary difference between the old cases and new.

"Maybe the parents weren't killed." Dr. Harper's sad gaze met Mercy's, and she knew exactly what the odontologist was thinking. It was a possibility she couldn't ignore.

Who would do that to their children?

TWELVE

The next morning Mercy yawned at her desk for the tenth time.

She'd slept poorly, unable to get the small skull and broken teeth out of her mind. She'd woken up too early and paced in her home. The cat had curled up with Kaylie in the teen's bed, and Mercy hadn't held back her smile as she watched them both sleep. The cat was affectionate and had immediately attached herself to Kaylie. The thought of the sweet animal shivering alone during the winter made Mercy want to cry.

I hope no one claims her.

She checked the time. Her phone call with Grady Baldwin was in one minute. She cleared some papers off her office desk and mentally ran through the questions she wanted to ask the convicted mass murderer.

Her desk phone rang. She answered, identified herself, and was soon connected with Baldwin.

"What does the FBI want with me?" Baldwin bluntly asked without exchanging pleasantries. He sounded as if he'd smoked cigarettes for the last twenty years in prison.

Mercy eyed the old mug shot of Baldwin on her screen and wondered what he looked like now. In the mug shot, the tendons stood out on his thick neck, and his glower made her shudder. He looked as if he had spent a decade lifting weights. *Or was the muscular build from his physical work?* Grady was now in his fifties, and she pictured him with softening jowls and graying hair.

"I have questions about the Verbeek and Deverell murders."

"Doesn't everybody? I'll tell you the same thing I tell everyone else. I got nothin' to say because *I wasn't there.*"

Mercy had expected the statement. "You've had a lot of time to think about it. Who do you think did it?"

"Do you have a suspect?" A faint glimmer of hope was in his tone.

"No."

"Then why the fuck are you talking to me?"

She and Jeff had discussed whether or not to tell Baldwin about the new victims. The discovery of the skeletal remains had already made the news, but the empty Hartlage house and the identification of the Hartlage children had not. They'd agreed to only tell Baldwin the information that was already public.

"Is this about those remains found on March Mountain?" he asked.

How did he instantly connect that case to my phone call?

"You heard about that?"

"I'm popular recently. A reporter tried to schedule a visit with me yesterday. I turned him down, but I looked up what he'd published recently."

"Who was the reporter?" asked Mercy through her teeth.

"Something Winslow."

Chuck Winslow. How did he connect the dots to Grady Baldwin?

Probably the same way she had. Her memory had recalled a common factor between the cases. No doubt Chuck had talked to a local who also remembered.

"The remains have raised some questions," Mercy admitted. "There's a few similarities between the new case and the two old ones. Enough to make us take a second look at the old murders."

"Probably because whoever murdered the Verbeeks and Deverells is still walking around. Drinking beer. Going fishing. All the shit I used to do."

The bitterness in his tone struck Mercy deep inside. So many freedoms were taken for granted. Until they were taken away.

"Take a look at the Verbeek girl," Baldwin suggested. "I think she's hiding something."

"Britta? She was unconscious."

"So she says," he snapped.

"She was a child."

"She had eyes, didn't she? She's still scared of something."

Mercy gripped her phone, Britta's description of the anxiety she lived with echoing in her head. She was scarred for life. "What do you mean, she's still scared? How would you know?"

Baldwin was silent.

Suspicion filled Mercy. "Mr. Baldwin, do you know where Britta is now?"

"I know she's moved back."

"*How* do you know that?"

"I have a little bird on the outside."

Mercy briefly closed her eyes. "Why would you bother keeping tabs on Britta Verbeek?"

"She goes by the last name of Vale now. I've got nothing better to do with my time. I've always thought that girl knew something. Her behavior tells me she's nervous."

"You have someone following her?"

"Nah, nothing like that. My brother Don keeps tabs on her movements through the internet." His tone turned coy. "She's moved around a lot, hasn't she?"

Mercy was stunned into silence. *Does Britta know he's watching her? Maybe she has a reason to feel paranoid.*

She moved Don Baldwin's interview up her to-do list.

"Mr. Baldwin," she finally said, "are you saying you've been watching her for over twenty years? Don't you think that's a bit . . . abnormal?"

"If there was one thing that might lead to your release from prison, wouldn't you keep tabs on it?" he said angrily.

"But twenty years—"

"It feels like seventy to me. I don't belong in here, and I have the right to keep my eyes and ears open. We're not doing anything illegal."

"Have you contacted her?"

Silence.

If Grady Baldwin had been sitting in front of her, Mercy would be tempted to kick him. "Jesus Christ," she exclaimed. "Why would you do that? The girl is a victim."

"She knows something."

"Why do you keep saying that?"

"Because she's the most likely person."

"But what if no one knows *anything*?"

"I haven't contacted her since she was a girl."

"What did you do back then?"

"I sent some letters begging her to tell the police what she knew. It was easy enough to get her aunt's address."

Mercy wondered if Britta ever saw the letters. If Mercy had been her aunt, she would have taken them to the police and never told the girl.

"Did she reply?"

"No. My lawyer told me to stop."

"So the letters were reported to the police."

"Yeah." Disgust filled his scratchy voice. "They investigate a letter, but they never follow up on any tips that I've sent them."

"What tips are those?"

"Other crimes that are similar to the Verbeeks and Deverells. The cops don't care because they already put me away for the murders. They don't want to look like idiots and have to admit they made a mistake by arresting me."

Mercy fumed. "I've never met a detective with that attitude."

"Well, I've met plenty."

"If they thought your tips held any weight, they would have investigated them. Or maybe they did, and it turned out to be nothing."

"Nothing? You call murdered families *nothing*?"

"What families?" Mercy grabbed her pen.

"Phoenix, Arizona. The Smythes. Denver, Colorado. The Ortegas."

Mercy wrote down the names and cities. "These aren't close to us at all."

"No, but they were close to someone else."

"Who?"

"Britta Verbeek. Like I said, she moves around a lot. Death seems to follow her."

THIRTEEN

My father was a cruel man.

I didn't realize this until I was older. I thought it was normal to rule a family with an iron fist.

Mother said it was because of the war. Father had seen horrible things during the war and returned as a different person. She told me his friend had died right beside him, his blood and brains splattered on my father's gear. My father saw dismembered bodies and people suffering from mortal wounds with no immediate help available. Countless times he had feared for his own life as he served our country. When he was finally home, he heard bombs and guns in his sleep.

When he was able to sleep.

My punishments for bad behavior were swift and memorable. No time allowed for explanation or excuse.

"Discipline should be immediate," he said. "You put other people at risk if you don't learn what you did wrong."

I found this to be unfair, especially when I was punished for the actions of someone else. My father went with his own view of family squabbles. My pleas of innocence didn't matter.

A broken dish would warrant a spanking.

A bike left in the driveway would result in the bike being given away.

I never understood how these small things could put other people at risk.

One time I dropped a bowl of spaghetti. I had finished my meal and was taking the dirty dish to the dishwasher. It slipped out of my hands. To my relief the dish didn't break, but the leftover sauce in the bottom of the bowl splashed all over the floor and up the cupboard doors.

A hand was immediately at the back of my neck, pushing me to the floor. "Clean it up!" A dishrag thrown on the floor in front of me. *Of course I would clean it up.*

I started to clean, fuming because he hadn't given me a chance to start on my own. From the corner of my eye, I saw his boots planted in a stiff stance as he watched every move I made. I rinsed the rag frequently, the red sauce difficult to get out of the grooves of the linoleum. I wiped down the cabinets and put the bowl in the dishwasher. To my eye everything looked perfect.

I helped clear the rest of the table and believed the incident was over.

At one in the morning, he hauled me out of bed. Bleary eyed, I stumbled down the stairs not comprehending his furious words. In the kitchen he pushed me to the floor again, and I landed hard on my hands and knees. "You missed spots!"

I frantically looked and saw nothing. "Where?"

He slapped the back of my head and I flinched. "Open your eyes!"

I looked closer, running my hands across the floor, not seeing what he saw. "Where is it? I don't see anything." Terror shook in my bones. I knew his tone. It meant he needed to administer pain.

His foot landed on my back, crushing me down to the floor, and my nose made a sickening *crack*. Blood dripped. The new spots on the floor resembled the spaghetti sauce.

"Dammit!" he swore. "Another fucking mess."

Still on the floor, I slapped my hand to my nose, and pain shot to my brain at the touch.

"Look right there!" He knelt and pointed.

From my view on the floor I could see under the cabinet. The sauce had splashed up under the cabinet and I'd missed it. I blinked back tears, pain still rocketing from my nose. "I see it," I mumbled, tasting blood in my mouth. My stomach heaved at the metallic flavor.

Don't puke, don't puke.

A wet dishrag dropped beside me. I shakily picked it up, keeping my other hand over my nose, feeling warm blood flow between my fingers. I scrubbed at the dried sauce until I saw no more, double- and triple-checking the area. Then I cleaned up my blood.

He stood behind me and silently watched every move.

I stood, rinsed out the dishrag, and then laid a clean one beside the sink from the kitchen drawer. I clenched the wet one in my hand to take to the laundry and grabbed a napkin to hold below my nose. Facing him, I stood silently, my gaze on the floor, waiting to be dismissed.

He made me wait a full ten seconds.

"Did you learn something?" he finally asked.

"Yes, sir."

"Look me in the eye when speaking to me!"

I immediately looked up, my stomach knotting in fear. His gaze was furious, and I hated him. Despised him with every angry cell of my body.

"Don't let it happen again."

"No, sir."

"Go to bed."

I ran. I put the dishrag in the laundry, grabbed a dark-colored bath towel, and then crawled in my bed, covering my pillow with the towel, terrified to get blood on the sheets. My legs shook for an hour. My nose throbbed, but I didn't dare wake my mother to ask for help.

I lay in bed and imagined the death of my father.

FOURTEEN

Truman realized too late that it had been a mistake to invite Royce along to Joshua Forbes's arraignment.

The young cop wouldn't stop talking or asking questions. Sitting by Truman in the courthouse, Royce delivered a running commentary under his breath as the judge arraigned other defendants. Twice Truman had told him to be quiet, but the cop's lips kept moving.

Truman was ready for the judge to ask Royce to leave.

Joshua sat at the front in the county jail's bright-orange inmate clothing. His chin was up and his shoulders held stiffly back. He stood out from the other inmates, who slouched and stared at their feet. Truman hadn't seen the sovereign citizen turn around, and he wondered if Joshua knew he was there.

The judge called Joshua Forbes.

"Finally," Royce muttered.

Truman liked Judge Parks. The older man was direct and took no bullshit from lawyers or defendants. He'd already made one defendant cry that morning.

Joshua rose and stepped in front of the bench, his hands cuffed behind his back.

Judge Parks looked at him over his reading glasses. "You've got quite a list of charges here, Mr. Forbes. No license, no registration, speeding, resisting arrest. How do you plead?"

"I am not Joshua Forbes."

Even from his seat in the back, Truman could see the gleam in the judge's eye at Joshua's statement. Joshua didn't know what he was up against.

"Well, who are you?"

"I am the representative of Joshua Forbes. I'm here to challenge the jurisdiction of this court," Joshua announced. "It has no authority over me."

"What the hell?" Royce whispered.

Truman shushed him.

"Why is that, Mr. Forbes?" The judge's tone was polite.

"This is a maritime admiralty court—"

"No, it's not," shot back the judge.

"Maritime?" Royce asked. "Does he mean like in the ocean?"

"I have no idea," whispered Truman.

"Is this a common-law court?" Joshua asked.

"No."

"I am not accountable to your laws."

"The laws apply to everybody," answered the judge.

"I am not a US citizen. I am sovereign under God."

Royce started coughing uncontrollably, and Truman slapped him on the back, glancing at the judge. The judge was focused on Joshua.

The judge removed his reading glasses. "Is that a not-guilty plea on the charges?"

"I will not plead. I am only here to challenge jurisdiction."

"When there is no plea, I enter a plea of not guilty for you," said the judge. "Do you have an attorney to represent you at trial?"

"No. I will represent myself."

"This court strongly recommends you have an attorney."

"There is no need. I know my rights."

The judge sighed. "Of course you do." He proceeded to schedule a trial for Joshua and dismissed him.

Truman didn't miss the stunned look on Joshua's face.

"Did he really think the judge would dismiss the charges?" Royce whispered behind his hand to Truman.

"Of course he did. Just like he believed his diplomatic license gave him the right to drive however he wanted," Truman answered. He stood. "We're done here."

◆ ◆ ◆

"Mercy, you've got a visitor," the FBI office manager, Melissa, stated as she stepped through Mercy's open door.

"Who is it?" Mercy glanced up from her computer screen, where she'd been searching for information on the out-of-state murders that Grady Baldwin had told her about. They existed, but public details were scarce. She'd have to contact sources in both cities for more information.

"She wouldn't give her name. But she's got black hair and a Lab with her."

Britta.

Mercy pushed back her chair and followed Melissa out front. Britta Vale sat in the small waiting area, Zara at her side. Again Mercy noted Britta's constant stroking of the dog and wondered if the dog always accompanied her. Zara didn't wear one of the service animal vests that Mercy always viewed with skepticism. Anyone could order a vest off the internet.

The tall woman was dressed for the rain in boots and a hooded jacket, her neck tattoo barely visible. Raindrops glittered on Zara's fur, and she had wagged her tail as Mercy entered the room. Mercy greeted Britta and patted Zara's head.

"Can I talk to you outside?" Britta asked as she glanced at Melissa, who'd returned to her desk behind a glass window.

"It's raining," said Mercy, curious as to what the woman wanted. "Why don't you come to my office?"

"I'd rather not. Right outside the door is a covered area."

Mercy agreed and buttoned up her thick cardigan as she followed Britta. Outdoors, the woman had a hard time looking Mercy in the eye. "What is it?" Mercy finally asked.

Britta took a breath and met Mercy's gaze. "Someone was outside my home last night. Do you know who it was?"

Mercy stiffened. "No. What happened? Did they threaten you or do some damage?"

"Nothing happened. I think they left when Zara barked." The woman's throat moved as she swallowed. "I'd hoped you'd know if it was some sort of police investigation."

"They would have come to your front door like I did. Why do you suspect the police?"

"I don't. I just hoped . . . I don't like to think of the alternative." She bent over to rub Zara's head.

"Tell me what happened," Mercy ordered.

Grady Baldwin said his brother kept tabs on Britta through the internet. Has he changed to doing it in person?

"It was about two in the morning. Zara went crazy barking and jumping at the front door. I'd installed a lot of outside lights, so I have a good view right around the house. I looked out, expecting to see a coyote or cougar, but I didn't see anything." She swallowed again. "But I couldn't see beyond the lighted area. It was pitch-dark last night."

Mercy waited. *She wouldn't come to me with a possible coyote sighting.*

"This morning, when I let Zara out, she immediately headed to the orchard on the east side of the house. I had her on a leash because I didn't want her taking off after a cougar trail."

"What did you find?"

"Boot prints under a tree. I don't think they got any closer to the house than that."

"That was plenty close. Could you see more tracks?"

"I followed them for a little bit, going in the direction of the main road, but then the prints disappeared because the rain washed them away except for right under the trees."

"Did Zara try to follow the prints?"

"She led me all the way to the road, where she stopped. I think they parked on the road and walked in."

"Someone knew exactly where they were going," Mercy added.

It's the right decision to contact Grady's brother soon.

She was pleased Britta had come to her with her concern. Even if Britta didn't admit it, on some level the woman trusted her. "How is the security at your home?"

"The best. It's the one thing I sank money into before moving in. I don't rent a place unless the owner agrees that I can add new locks, outside lights, and a security system. I need it for peace of mind."

Mercy understood the turmoil on Britta's face. She had her own needs for peace of mind. Knowing that her cabin wasn't rebuilt yet was giving her a low level of constant stress. *The supplies are still up there. And makeshift sleeping quarters.*

But it wasn't the same as the solid four walls of her cabin.

"What are you going to do?" Mercy asked.

Frustration crossed Britta's face. "I don't want to move again already. I'm prepared to protect myself if needed."

Mercy frowned. "Britta . . . do you have a suspicion of who it was?"

"No."

Her answer was too quick for Mercy. And most people wouldn't consider moving just because they'd found the footprints of a prowler. She decided to take a risk. "Britta, have you ever been contacted by Grady Baldwin?"

Her gaze flew to Mercy's, and Mercy knew she was about to lie. But Britta pressed her lips together for several seconds. "A long time ago he sent letters to my aunt. I was still a kid. My aunt didn't tell me about them, but I found them. I think she reported them to the police, because they stopped."

"You didn't tell your aunt you found them?"

"No."

"What did Grady write?"

Britta looked away. "He wanted me to tell the truth about what I'd seen that night. He believed I knew things that would set him free."

"Do you?"

She met Mercy's gaze again. "No. I remember nothing." She zipped up her jacket a few inches to her chin and rearranged her grip on Zara's leash.

"I think we should talk inside," suggested Mercy.

"No. It was stifling in there. The rooms are too small."

Mercy agreed. Both the waiting area and her office were definitely not roomy. "How many times have you moved since the murders?" She knew the answer, but she wanted to open the subject with Britta.

Britta's brows came together. "Why?"

"I'm trying to understand what your life has been like." Grady Baldwin's claims of similar murders in those other cities went through Mercy's head. She wasn't about to mention them to Britta before she finished investigating.

Britta raised one shoulder in a dismissive gesture. "I haven't kept count."

"You told me before that you move when you feel uneasy in a location. Were your other homes approached like last night?"

The woman paused, holding Mercy's gaze. "I don't know. Maybe."

"Why would someone do that?"

"I'm a single woman living alone, although I've lived with other people at times in the past."

"Roommates? Boyfriends?"

"Both."

"Did they think there had been prowlers?"

"No one ever saw anything, but everyone always agreed it was possible because we lived in suburban areas. This is the first time I've lived out in the country."

"Are you armed?"

"Besides my rifle, I own a handgun and keep it beside my bed. I practice once a month."

Mercy wasn't surprised.

"Did you figure out the identities of the remains you found?" Britta asked. "The ones with the . . . damaged skulls?"

"Not yet." Mercy watched her closely. The identification of the children hadn't been released to the press yet.

"I can't get the thought of them out of my head," Britta said angrily. "Why did you tell me about them the other day?" Accusation shot from her tone and gaze.

"I can't stop thinking about them either," Mercy admitted. "You know I told you in hopes that you could help us out. The way they were murdered was too similar . . ." *To your family.*

"I know nothing. I knew nothing as a ten-year-old, and I know nothing today." Desperation permeated her tone.

The emphasis of Britta's words struck Mercy's bullshit meter. Britta was trying too hard to make her point.

Grady Baldwin was right. What is she scared of?

FIFTEEN

That afternoon, Mercy stared at the red spray paint that now coated the edge of the concrete culvert. The vandal had also sprayed the wet dirt, but the paint hadn't stuck very well. Broken beer bottles covered the area, the crime scene tape had been ripped down, and the wood stakes marking the search area had been ripped out and tossed aside.

Mercy was at the crime scene to meet Dr. Peres because a second group of bones had been found farther down the hill. She sighed at the disrespectful damage.

Dr. Peres was grim. "Pissed me off when I found it."

"I can't say it pleases me," said Mercy, wiping from her nose the rain that had sneaked past her hood. "But no one had the manpower to keep a watch here twenty-four seven. At least all the initial evidence had been removed."

"I usually want to examine the scene again," Dr. Peres stated. "I'm thorough, but I always double-check to see if I missed anything." The anthropologist put her hands on her hips. "I'd like to know who made this mess."

"That makes two of us. Drunk teenagers? Drunk adults?" Mercy asked. "Who knows?"

"Or someone who isn't happy we found his burial site," Dr. Peres asserted, a knowing look in her dark eyes.

It'd crossed Mercy's mind too.

"What's done is done," said Dr. Peres. "And I'm pleased the searchers found another cache of bones. There's no evidence that our vandals knew about it."

Mercy stared down the steep hill. Her thigh throbbed at the sight, and she hadn't even started the descent. She rubbed the complaining muscles, feeling the lumpiness of the scar where the bullet had entered her leg. *I have to do this.*

She carefully followed the tall woman down the slope. Someone had tied ropes between the trees, creating a much-needed safety line. The two women wore vests with straps and carabiners that they hooked to the ropes as they slowly stepped downhill. The ground was damp under the trees, mostly protected from the heavy rain, but Mercy could see where the water from around the culvert had created a wide, washed-out channel that wound between the trees. The dirt around some tree roots had washed away, and the trees had fallen, leaving huge spidery roots exposed to the air. It was against the trunk of one of these fallen trees far down the hill that the cache of bones had been found.

The dirt under Mercy's left foot gave way, and she grabbed for the rope. Her hands flailed in the empty air, and she landed on her back, then began sliding down the slope. Her breath was knocked out of her lungs as the strap of the carabiner jerked her to a halt, stopping her from a dangerous journey down the hill. She lay in the dirt, panting, digging her hands into the bank, petrified the carabiner would give way. Her right thigh screamed in pain, and she fought to catch her breath.

"You okay?" Dr. Peres asked from above, gripping the safety rope, concern on her face.

"Yep." The word was casual, not revealing that her heart was trying to beat its way out of her chest.

"Need a hand?"

"I've got it. Give me a moment." Her right leg felt as if it'd run a marathon, the muscles useless. She took a deep breath and hauled herself to her feet with pure arm strength and willpower. She crept back up to the safety rope, forcing her right leg to move. She kept a tight grip on the line as she followed Dr. Peres, paying better attention to the placement of her steps. Her leg shook from the strain. No wonder the search for more bones had taken so long. Dr. Peres looked over her shoulder and took in Mercy's dirty pants and coat.

"That was why we put in the safety line. Sorry about your clothes."

"I've got another outfit in my vehicle." *As always.* She never went anywhere without a duffel or backpack stuffed with clothes, food, medical supplies, water purification tablets, and ammunition.

Preparation.

The women worked their way down the hill with no more accidents. At one of the fallen trees, Mercy exhaled as the ground flattened out near the trunk and gingerly placed all her weight on both feet at the same time.

"I'll get my team out here tomorrow to officially excavate the area," said Dr. Peres. "I thought you'd like a first look."

Mercy nodded and crouched beside the downed tree. The pine was easily four feet in diameter and had landed perpendicular to the downhill slope, held in place by the thick trunks of still-standing pines. Beneath one section of the fallen tree, water had washed away the dirt and still trickled downhill unimpeded.

Are there more bones farther down the hill?

She knew a lot of the slope had been explored, but the searchers weren't done yet.

To the right of the wash under the tree, branches had trapped mud and debris when the flow of the water was heavier. It took Mercy a moment to spot the bones that had caught the eyes of the searchers. Several small white nubs stuck out of the mud. Around one, a searcher had dug a little deeper to reveal that the nub was a bone.

"A femur," stated Dr. Peres as she pointed to the exposed bone. She pulled out her camera and took several photos of the area before she gently brushed away loose debris. Two more nubs were exposed further. "Bingo," the anthropologist said under her breath.

Mercy fought back the urge to start randomly digging. It was best left to the experts and their careful processes. She stood back and watched over Dr. Peres's shoulder as she carefully moved small tree branches and rocks, photographing every step.

"Aha!"

Mercy's heart sped up. She'd spotted the smooth section of bone at the same time as Dr. Peres. The anthropologist gently removed the packed soil around the bone. A minute later she had a skull in her hand. No mandible. Its front teeth had been shattered, and Dr. Peres clucked her tongue in sympathy as she brushed mud from the bone.

"Male. Adult," Dr. Peres stated. "Caucasian."

"Possibly the Hartlage father or brother-in-law," said Mercy. "Whichever we don't already have."

"Possibly," the doctor repeated.

"We still need the dental records for the adults." Frustration filled Mercy. *I have to assume one or more of the Hartlage adults could be alive.* "DNA testing will take a long time."

Dr. Peres did some more superficial digging, unwilling to disturb most of the site. No more skulls.

In her gut Mercy believed this was the Hartlage family, but she didn't have proof outside of the children's dental records.

How does the Asian skull fit in the picture?

Possibly this was a dumping site for multiple murders. The Hartlage family might be only a few of many deaths.

Mercy had run a search for a missing adult Asian male within the state of Oregon. From the last thirty years, two relevant cases were still unsolved. The men had been in their sixties and seventies when they vanished. Dr. Harper had examined the dental records in the missing men's files; they didn't match the Asian skull's dentition.

"I'll take this skull with me and clean it up tonight," said Dr. Peres. She surveyed the ground near the fallen tree. "I wonder if they'll find more skulls tomorrow?"

That was Mercy's question too.

Mercy limped up the stairs to her apartment.

Driving home had almost been too much for her leg. Continuously pressing the gas pedal had taken an amazing amount of concentration. Now she just wanted Advil, a hot shower, and her bed.

Thank goodness there is a bench in the shower.

She pushed open the apartment door and was greeted by a screech from Kaylie. "Don't let her out!"

A low white flash shot from the kitchen and Mercy slammed the door behind her. The cat slid to a halt, meowed, and wound herself between Mercy's legs, her tail wrapping around Mercy's calf. The cat didn't appear to resent that her escape route had been cut off. Mercy bent over to pet her and was rewarded with a throaty purr.

"I swear she's smiling," said Kaylie, who had appeared from the kitchen. "I think she likes you more than me."

"I was the first person she'd seen in a long time."

"She needs a name."

"We don't know that we can keep her." To Mercy, giving the cat a name would mean her stay was permanent.

"I took her to the vet today," said Kaylie, scooping up the cat and pressing her cheek against the cat's fur. "She's not chipped, but she has been spayed. Her blood work looked good, but she's underweight."

"An easy fix."

"Especially with the way she's been eating," agreed Kaylie. "She's a pig."

"I can't blame her."

"We could call her Piggy." Her niece blinked innocently.

"Hell no. That's a horrible name."

"I was thinking about names that tied to your job. Glock, Beretta, Ruger."

Mercy patted the cat. Her fur was as soft as a bunny's. "She's a girl. Those names aren't girly at all. Not to mention they sound violent. And more accurate names about my work would be Paperwork, Phone Calls, or Headaches." She stroked one of the tan patches on the cat's side. "How about bakery- or coffee-related names? Cupcake, Latte, Mocha, Cookie."

"Biscotti," murmured Kaylie. "Or Snickerdoodle, Streusel, Dulce de Leche, Café au Lait."

"I like Dulce de Leche. It fits with her tan patches, and we could call her Dulce for short, which means 'sweet.'"

"Perfect." Kaylie planted a kiss on the cat's forehead and set her down. "She's definitely sweet."

We weren't supposed to name her yet.

Mercy acknowledged that she'd failed on that objective.

Dulce hopped onto a dining table chair and settled down as if she'd always lived there, her blue gaze locked on Mercy. Dulce had lived through a tough winter on her own, and Mercy suspected she would have gone on to survive another just fine without people. The cat was very self-reliant. Just as Mercy strove to be.

You're a survivor too, aren't you?

Will a relative take you home?

They were still trying to contact the Hartlages' closest relatives. So far Darby had located the father's uncle in Arizona. He didn't care about the deaths and only wanted to know if he'd get some money. Darby continued to search.

The suspicion that Dulce had a permanent home with her and Kaylie grew stronger.

"Have you read or heard the news today?" Kaylie asked as she started to wipe down the kitchen counter, not looking at Mercy.

Kaylie's tone was too casual, and Mercy's radar went off. "I haven't. What did you hear?"

Her niece focused on scrubbing at an invisible spot. "You haven't read anything new about your find up on March Mountain?"

Crap. "What did he write now?"

Kaylie indicated her laptop on the table. The article was still open. Mercy spotted Chuck Winslow's name and quickly scanned the article, her fury growing as she scrolled.

He didn't.

He did.

Chuck Winslow had written a recap of the murders two decades earlier and then stated that Britta Verbeek had recently moved back to the area and was currently using the name Britta Vale. He'd listed her work website.

Every nut and reporter in the country is going to hound her.

He went on to quote Grady Baldwin's declaration that he hadn't committed the murders and, without stating it outright, implied Baldwin's belief that Britta was holding back something that would exonerate him.

Baldwin told me he didn't talk to Winslow.

Rereading the article, she realized that wasn't true.

"Dammit." She fumed, wondering if her conversation with Baldwin had encouraged him to reach out to Winslow, seeing a way to get his side of the story out in public again.

The only positive she saw was that Winslow hadn't mentioned Mercy's name or the missing Hartlage family. He stated that the bones found on March Mountain had a few similarities to those in the old cases. *Shit.* The sentence read almost exactly how she'd stated her reason to Grady Baldwin for the interview.

Baldwin must have contacted Winslow after I left.

Winslow didn't mention the murders that had supposedly followed Britta from city to city. No doubt Baldwin had shared that theory, but Mercy hadn't found the claim credible after more research, and Winslow must have come to the same conclusion. One family had been killed by a relative, another family had all died in a car wreck, and another had died in a house fire. All of the deaths had been explained. Baldwin was grasping at straws by pushing the theory that mysterious deaths had followed Britta.

Poor Britta. Sympathy for the woman filled her. Britta needed her privacy, and Mercy wondered what this exposure would do to her psyche.

Asshole. Chuck Winslow had no idea of the emotional trauma his article could cause the woman.

Or did he?

"What is it?" Kaylie asked. "You look like you want to strangle someone."

"I do. Chuck Winslow would do just fine."

"He doesn't mention you," Kaylie said helpfully.

"No, but he's mentioned a woman who's been through enough."

"Britta Vale? It sounds like the police need to investigate her."

"That's my point. There's nothing concrete to back up what he's implying about Britta. It's all speculation from a man who desperately wants out of prison. I've talked to her twice."

"Well, that's horrible. What's she like?"

Mercy turned to her niece, wondering how to best describe the unusual woman. "She's different. The trauma from her past has stripped away all the bullshit that people hide behind . . . the fake layers . . . the socially correct facades. Her essence is what's left, and it's very strong.

She's scared at times but determined. Blunt. Self-sufficient. I like her," Mercy admitted with some surprise.

"What are you going to do about her now?" asked Kaylie.

"I'll check in with her. Wait . . . I don't even have a cell phone number for her. Both times I've talked to her in person. I'll have to drive out there." She grimaced, not knowing when she'd find the time.

Kaylie frowned. "Don't put it off. It sounds like she's alone and needs people like you who understand her."

Admiration for her sensitive niece touched Mercy, and she hugged the girl, kissing her on the forehead.

"Damn, you're a good kid."

"I know."

SIXTEEN

"I'm starting to despise this case." Mercy's heart was a thick lump in her throat.

"Me too," agreed Truman. Until now, he'd been silent beside her during the drive.

Mercy had received a 2:00 a.m. phone call—never a good thing—with a report that a family had been murdered in their home. A neighbor had found the family when she went to investigate why their dogs were howling.

Truman had been in bed next to her when the call came in and had insisted on accompanying her to the scene.

Her headlights lit up the one-lane gravel road, and the falling rain looked like liquid silver. Up ahead she spotted several county vehicles and a home with all its lights on. She parked behind a county unit, got out of her SUV, and pulled up her hood against the rain. Frantic barking sounded from behind the home. Mercy didn't see a fence around the house and assumed the dogs were tied up or kenneled. She and Truman checked in with the deputy manning the scene log, bootied up, and then looked for Detective Bolton, who'd made the call to Mercy. A pair of deputies stood in the kitchen making small talk. They nodded at Mercy and Truman as the two of them entered, and one went to get the detective.

The home was nice, Mercy noticed. Someone had updated the flooring with wide plank boards, and stainless-steel appliances shone in the kitchen. Not high-end appliances, but definitely newer models. The cabinets had been painted white, and the countertops were granite and uncluttered. Time and money had been spent to remodel the home.

A family lived here. Books for children and adults filled a bookcase. A football, *Star Wars* figures, and two lightsabers were scattered on the rug next to the large sectional. A professional photo showed four smiling faces as the family posed in the middle of a golden wheat field.

The family name was Jorgensen. Father, mother, two sons.

Mercy studied the photo. Everyone looked happy. Her breath caught at the way the mother wrapped her arm around one of the boys, pulling him close, joy on their faces. Family. Love. Togetherness.

Gone.

Evan Bolton appeared from the back of the house. *He's become the Angel of Death.* Mercy only saw him when someone had died.

He must think the same of me.

Bolton greeted the two of them, and she noticed he didn't mention Truman's presence at a scene outside the Eagle's Nest jurisdiction. She took it as a sign that he'd grown to trust the two of them.

"My evidence team isn't here yet," Bolton told them. "But we've confirmed the front door was open. My men have cleared the house and immediate area around the home. No sign of anyone or a weapon."

"The neighbor came over in the middle of the night because the dogs were barking?" The late-night visit felt odd to Mercy.

"The neighbor was very worried. She said the Jorgensen dogs are usually no problem, but tonight they wouldn't stop howling. She called the Jorgensens and they didn't answer. The backs of the two homes are about five hundred feet apart, but the neighbor's driveway goes out to a different road. It takes a few minutes to drive from one house to the other. When she got here, she saw the door was ajar and the dogs were going wild in their kennel. She stuck her head in the door and called for the family." He shook his head, looking glum. "No one answered, so she went in and found them."

"Where is the neighbor?" asked Mercy.

"I talked to her, and then she went back home with one of my officers to get some warmer clothing. She was wearing a nightgown. They should be back any minute. She was pretty shaken."

"Does the home have a camera security system?" Truman asked.

"No. The neighbor does, but the cameras cover the front of her home. Nothing catches the road or the back of her house."

"Still worth a look," Truman said. "The killer might have cut through her property."

"Agreed," answered Bolton.

"What do you know about the family?" Mercy asked.

"Ray and Sharla Jorgensen. Their boys are Luke and Galen. According to the neighbor they were eight and ten."

More murdered young children. "Let's take a look," she said, steeling herself.

The first bedroom belonged to the boys. Twin-size beds stood against opposite walls and between them was a wide low table on a Seattle Seahawks rug. A giant Lego city with skyscrapers and a sports stadium covered the table—an impressive project. Mercy forced herself to look at the children. Someone had pulled back the covers of both boys, and they lay on their sides as if they were still sleeping. One's head was so soaked with blood, Mercy couldn't tell the color of his hair. The other was blond. Both boys had suffered blows to the head and mouth.

She blinked rapidly, comparing the children to the photo in the living room.

Truman's gaze was expressionless, his emotions tucked away, but she spotted a brief flash of sorrow and sympathy as he glanced at her.

The lump in her throat grew larger, and she couldn't speak. Instead she gestured for Bolton to take them to another room.

As they walked the narrow hall, behind her she heard Truman curse under his breath.

The parents' large bed had a cream-colored velvet headboard. Ray Jorgensen's side of the bed had multiple blood trails going up the headboard. He'd been hit several times. Sharla was on the floor. Her pillow had spatter from her husband, and her blood had soaked into the carpet and splattered on the side of the nightstand.

"It looks like she woke up while her husband was being killed and tried to get away. The killer caught up with her," said Bolton.

"The MO looks the same as the Hartlage family," Mercy said. "The injuries are the same, and their attacks happened in their beds."

"But the bodies weren't left behind," Bolton pointed out.

"Maybe the dogs or the neighbor scared him off before he could finish," suggested Truman. "Or he's abandoned that part of his plan. Moving bodies is a lot of work."

Mercy crouched next to Sharla. The woman's eyes were open and starting to cloud. Shock and terror were frozen on her face.

Did she know what was happening?

Her mouth was bloody, several of her front teeth broken or missing.

Why does he do that?

"I heard you're looking at some old cases in conjunction with the remains found on March Mountain," said Bolton, his gaze locked on Mercy.

She exchanged a glance with Truman.

"Those cases were solved. The guy is in prison," Mercy stated as she stood up.

"Then why are you going through them?" Bolton asked. His expression stated he knew Mercy was holding back.

Mercy gestured at Sharla's mouth. "Because the two families that were killed two decades ago had the same injuries. And he killed complete families in their beds by bludgeoning them."

Bolton pressed his lips together as he slowly nodded. "Copycat?"

"I don't know. Grady Baldwin, who was put away for them, claims he didn't do the murders."

"Of course he'd say that. Did he leave the families in their beds?"

"He did."

"But you found a family's bones in a culvert? That's very different."

"And we haven't confirmed it's the Hartlage family. The daughters have been identified, but not the adult remains."

Bolton stared at her. "The parents could have left town after killing and dumping their kids?"

"Possibly. But there was blood found in all the beds in the home."

"If I was trying to make people think I was dead, I'd leave behind some blood," Bolton stated.

"The blood splatter at the Hartlage home was consistent with a victim in each bed."

Bolton relaxed a fraction. "That's hard to fake. I guess if they were really organized, they could have put an animal in each bed and beat it."

Mercy had attended a blood spatter seminar that demonstrated exactly that. The instructor liked to use pigs.

"We don't have lab results on the blood yet, but no animal fur was found in the beds. We have toothbrushes and hair from the bathrooms of the home, so we'll be doing DNA analysis at some point. I still hope to find the parents' dental records. It's much quicker to confirm identity."

"Good." Bolton turned his attention back to the victims in the bed. "At least we know who the victims are here."

Mercy glanced at Sharla again. Even under all the blood, Mercy could tell she was one of the adults in the family picture out front. The man was too. Scanning the room, Mercy noticed an open dresser drawer. The room was extremely neat, and the open drawer felt out of place. Glancing inside, she saw an open jewelry box that appeared to have been rifled through. She doubted Sharla left her jewelry so scattered. "I suspect he was looking for some valuables. Does anything else appear to have been gone through? What about wallets?"

Bolton checked the adjoining bathroom as Truman opened the master closet with a gloved hand. "His wallet is still in the pocket of the jeans on a hook," said Truman. Bolton joined him, slipped the wallet out, and opened it. "A couple of twenties," commented Truman. "If he was looking for fast cash, he didn't look very hard."

Mercy went out to the living room, where she'd noticed a purse and a bowl of keys on a small table by the door. *Why didn't he grab the purse?* Looking inside, she saw cash in Sharla's wallet too. *Easy money.*

Truman and Bolton joined her. "Money isn't his motivation," she said. "Maybe Sharla did leave her jewelry a mess."

"Most crimes come down to money or sex." Truman pointed out a fact Mercy knew all too well.

Sharla was fully clothed in pajamas.

"Not money or sex," Mercy murmured. "What does that leave?"

"Revenge . . . anger . . . or just fucked up in the head," said Truman.

"There's always a reason," agreed Bolton.

"What did Ray and Sharla do for work?" asked Mercy.

"I don't know yet," admitted Bolton.

"And why didn't the dogs wake everyone up?" Truman asked. "They threw a fit when we got here. I can't see someone getting in the house without them sounding the alarm, even if they are kenneled outside. I would've expected Ray Jorgensen would get out of bed to investigate."

"Good point," said Bolton.

"I hope the neighbor can help us out." Mercy glanced at the time. It was past three in the morning.

There'd be no more rest for her tonight.

Truman stood on the front porch of the Jorgensen home, listening to the rain fall on the porch roof and breathing the clean air. He'd needed to step away from the scene.

Those boys.

All too easily he could picture the pair as they played in the yard and fought with their lightsabers. He'd done the same with his sister.

Headlights appeared down the long drive, and he assumed the deputy was returning with the neighbor. The vehicle drew closer, and he spotted the light bar on the roof. After it parked, a woman in a hooded thick coat and boots got out along with the deputy.

Truman turned around and spoke through the open front door. "The deputy is back with the neighbor."

Mercy and Bolton immediately stepped out. "Let's talk to her out here," suggested Mercy, pointing at the bench and chairs on the wide covered porch.

Truman agreed.

The woman followed the deputy up the steps, pushing back her hood as she stepped into the dry area. Truman estimated her to be in her fifties. Her face was lightly lined, and she was tall like Mercy. She moved with athleticism and energy, but sorrow shone in her eyes. She'd been crying.

Mercy introduced herself and Truman.

"I'm Janet Norris."

A flicker of confusion flashed on Mercy's face, and Truman knew she was trying to place the name. Even though Mercy had been away for fifteen years, she frequently encountered people from her past. Truman didn't recognize Janet or her name. The deputy who had driven her conferred quietly with Bolton for a few seconds, then stepped inside and grabbed another deputy. The two of them jogged down the stairs and got in their vehicles to leave.

"I don't need every one of them here to maintain the scene and wait for the evidence team," Bolton explained. He turned to Janet. "Let's have a seat out here."

Relief crossed her face, and she sat on the bench. Mercy sat beside her as Bolton took one of the chairs, and Truman stood, leaning against the porch railing.

"I know you've already talked to Detective Bolton about what happened," started Mercy. "Can you tell me from the beginning?" she asked with an encouraging smile.

Janet's hands twisted the hem of her coat as she focused on Mercy. "The dogs woke me. They were braying and howling like crazy. I've never heard them do that. I waited awhile, expecting them to stop, but they didn't, and I couldn't get back to sleep."

More coat twisting.

"I finally called Sharla's cell phone," Janet continued. "She didn't answer. I tried Ray's too, with no luck, and then called the landline. I didn't call it first because I didn't want to wake the boys," she hurriedly explained to Mercy, including Bolton and Truman with quick glances. "I finally decided they'd gone out of town. I was surprised because usually we ask each other to keep an eye on each other's place. I debated for a while, but the dogs didn't let up, so I decided to do a quick check on the dogs."

"That was kind of you," Mercy said.

Janet shrugged. "I feed the dogs when the Jorgensens go out of town, so they're used to me. Tonight I wondered if some animal had gotten into their kennel. They're good dogs but getting up there in years. Both are moving slower than they used to."

"What did you notice when you arrived?" asked Mercy.

"Well, the outside lights were on. That's normal. When I got out of the car, the dogs renewed their braying. I assumed no one was home, so I went to the kennel first. Both dogs looked fine and were happy to see me. No coyote or cougar in there with them."

"Were there any lights on in the house?" asked Truman.

"I could tell there was a light on in their kitchen, but I knew that didn't mean someone was up. After I saw the dogs were okay, I decided to knock on the door. That's when I saw it was partially open. I opened the door and called out for Sharla." Janet moved her gaze to her hands and popped open the bottom snap of her jacket. Then snapped it closed. And repeated.

"What did you do next?" Mercy gently asked. She leaned toward the woman. "I know this is difficult," she said in a lower voice.

Janet blew out a breath and kept fiddling with the snap. "I stepped in the house and called for Sharla and Ray." She wiped a tear from her cheek and dug a tissue out of her coat pocket. "I could smell it. I know what fresh death smells like. I was raised on a ranch, and we butchered animals." She looked up. "It's an odor you never forget.

"I told Detective Bolton that I turned on some lights, and then I looked in the bedrooms. I studied each of them to make certain they were dead, but I didn't touch them. That's when I called 911." Tears flowed from both eyes. "Those little boys. I'll never forget the sight."

The sight was burned into Truman's retinas. *I'll never forget either.*

Mercy took one of Janet's hands and squeezed it. "Thank you. I know that was really hard."

"You have no idea." Janet's voice cracked as she wiped her nose and eyes.

Mercy knows exactly what it is like.

"What did Ray do for work?" Mercy asked.

Janet's shoulders slumped a little as she relaxed, appreciating the change of topic. "Ray worked for an investment firm in Bend. I don't know his exact position, but he was high up the chain."

"Which one?" Bolton asked.

Janet named a firm Truman had never heard of.

"Isn't that the one that was caught up in a scandal last year?" Bolton asked. "Something about falsifying their clients' reports, inflating how much the investments had returned? I thought they went under."

"They almost did," agreed Janet. "A lot of people were fired, and the company paid the fines. Ray was under a tremendous amount of stress, but the company survived."

"I wouldn't put my money with them," Bolton stated. "Did Sharla work?"

"Sharla was a stay-at-home mom, but she was always doing those work-from-home product sales. You know . . . the kitchen gadgets, skin care, and jewelry that you sell to friends. I've probably attended a half dozen parties at her house, trying to be supportive of her work. She was a great salesperson. Very outgoing and kind." Tears appeared again.

"What do you do?" asked Bolton.

"I work at the front desk of the DoubleTree in Bend." Janet wiped her eyes. "I can't believe this is happening again."

Truman caught his breath at her words. Mercy and Bolton both straightened in their seats.

Again?

SEVENTEEN

Mercy struggled to find her voice.

Is she talking about the Hartlage family? How did she find out?

"What do you mean, it's happening again?" she managed to ask Janet.

The woman turned a tearful face toward Mercy. "My friend's family was murdered a long time ago. He left them in their beds just like this."

Mercy connected the dots.

Janet Norris. She was the friend of Maria Verbeek, Britta's mother. That's why her name is familiar.

"You're talking about the Verbeeks," Mercy stated evenly, trying to hide the shock that reeled through her.

Janet's eyes widened. "Yes, how did you know?"

"I've read the case reports. You said that Maria told you she'd fended off an advance from Grady Baldwin." *What are the odds that Janet is connected to the Verbeeks and the Jorgensens?*

It is a small community.

The woman blinked several times as her mouth opened the slightest bit. "You have a very good memory," she said slowly. "But I never named Grady Baldwin. I only said it'd been a workman. Maria didn't tell me who it was."

"You're right," Mercy admitted. "I remember reading that now."

Janet frowned, confusion clouding her eyes. "When did you look at Maria's case? Why would you? They caught the guy."

Mercy couldn't share the investigators' questions about the Hartlage family. They didn't have all the pieces yet. "I read it very recently." She paused, searching for the right words. "All I can say is that we had good reason to review the case."

The older woman held her gaze for a moment, plainly expecting a better answer.

"I'm sorry, I can't say more at this point." Mercy gave her an apologetic look.

"Grady Baldwin didn't kill those families?" Janet asked in a hushed tone.

"That's not what I'm saying. Let's focus on the Jorgensens right now. Have you seen anyone suspicious in the area recently?" Mercy was determined to bring Janet back to the current case.

Janet ran a shaky hand through her hair. "Umm . . . not that I can think of. I can't see this house from mine, and I can't see out to the road either. I haven't had any visitors recently."

"When did you last talk to one of the Jorgensens?"

"Oh, jeez. It's probably been at least two weeks. The boys were climbing in my apple tree and I asked them to get down. It's old and I don't trust the branches. I sent them home with some cookies because I didn't want them to think I'm that crabby old neighbor."

"When did you last speak to Sharla Jorgensen?" Bolton asked.

"I couldn't tell you. Long time. Around Christmas, maybe?" Janet tipped her head as she concentrated. "They were nice people . . ."

Mercy saw something flash in Janet's eyes. "But?"

Guilt crossed the woman's face. "I don't want to spread rumors."

The three investigators exchanged glances. *There are always rumors.* "Spread away," said Mercy. "We understand that's what you're sharing with us."

"Well, Sharla wasn't happy. She'd asked me questions about getting a divorce. I don't know why she asked me—I don't know anything about it. I've never even been married."

"Did she say why she wasn't happy?" Mercy asked. *Cheating? Money issues?*

"She believed Ray was having an affair. I asked her if she'd confronted him, but she hadn't—at least she hadn't back in December. Maybe she finally did." Her lips turned down, a nauseated look on her face.

Mercy remembered the blood spatter and injuries of both adults. It wasn't possible that one of them had killed themselves after killing the rest of the family. "Neither of them hurt the other," stated Mercy. "That wasn't indicated in the crime scene." She glanced at Truman and Bolton, who both nodded in agreement.

"I'm happy to hear that . . . Well, there's nothing to be happy about here," admitted Janet.

Mercy was writing a mental list of leads to follow. *Ray's work situation. Possible affair.* "Did you live next door here when you were friends with Maria Verbeek?" she asked.

"No. I moved about ten years ago. Back then I lived closer to Eagle's Nest."

"Do you remember the exact conversation you had with Maria about the workman who made a pass at her?"

Janet gave a sad smile. "Yes. Maria was a housekeeper at the DoubleTree for a little while. That's how we met. She told me about it at work and was confused that he'd tried to kiss her. No one had ever done anything like that to her. She was very reserved. I told her to take it as a compliment but to threaten to tell her husband if he did it again."

Mercy remembered how Maria had appeared as if she wanted to fade into the background in the file's family photo. "She never told her husband?"

"I don't know, but I'd guess not. I always thought he was an ass. Very controlling. Maria couldn't go anywhere without getting his approval first." Janet pressed her temples with her fingertips. "This is surreal. I've already gone through this once. How is it happening again?" She looked at each of them. "Did they arrest the wrong man back then?" she whispered.

Mercy wondered the same thing.

"What the fuck did you do?"

Mercy blinked. She'd grabbed her cell phone off the nightstand and answered without opening her eyes. Now she checked her clock. It was nearly 9:00 a.m. She'd come home at 5:00 a.m. from the Jorgensen scene and crashed.

"Who is this?" Her voice was full of sleep.

"Dammit, Mercy, it's Britta Vale."

Mercy sat up, surprise shooting through her veins. "What happened?" Now she was wide awake.

"I'm getting emails through my website. Nasty emails accusing me of hiding the facts about my family's murder." Britta's voice cracked. "How did they find me?"

"Oh God." Mercy put a hand to her forehead. "I was afraid something like this would happen. You were mentioned in an article online last night—with your new last name and your old."

"Why did you tell them about me?" Hot anger spiked her words.

"It wasn't me!" Guilt swamped Mercy even though it wasn't her fault. "Grady Baldwin gave a media interview. He knew you returned to the area and changed your name."

"How do you know that?" she shot back.

Mercy cringed. "I talked with Baldwin the other day. He already suspected we were looking at your family's case. His brother informs him about anything to do with the cases that sent him to prison. He even knew what cities you've lived in."

"*What?* Did you know that when we spoke the other day?"

She couldn't speak. It stung to know she'd inadvertently hurt the woman. "I didn't see the point in telling you right then. You were spooked enough. I had no idea Baldwin would expose his theory to the public. Chuck Winslow has no ethics. He shouldn't have printed it."

"He's an asshole."

"So you *have* met him."

"No."

The firmness of her answer made Mercy smile. "You said you were renting the house, right?"

"Yes, but people who are determined to find someone know how to find shit out. Utility companies . . . I pick up my mail at the post office . . . I could be followed home. Dammit! I'm going to have to leave town." Anger and frustration came through the line. "I've had a weird feeling for the past week. I've constantly felt as if I'm being watched."

"You feel that way because of what happened at your place the other night. Keep your guard up."

"Always."

"I'm so sorry, Britta, but I suspect the emails will die down before you can move. There can't be that many people interested in Grady Baldwin."

"You'd be surprised at the number of social justice warriors online. They hear a whisper that someone in prison might be innocent, and they blow it up in social media. Then I'll have a thousand people emailing me." Britta sighed. "I might have to turn off the contact form on my website. Shit!"

"You don't know that will happen. Let me call Chuck Winslow. Maybe I can get him to take down the article." As soon as the words left her mouth, Mercy winced. Winslow would never do her a favor. He'd print that the FBI had asked him to take it down and use that as proof of Baldwin's claim of innocence.

"Really?" Hope infused Britta's voice.

"I'm sorry, but now that I think about it, Winslow is the type of jerk who'd shout long and loud that the FBI asked him to take down an article."

"You're right. I wonder if he'd listen to me." Britta didn't sound optimistic.

"Probably not. The best course is to not give the article any more attention, and it will fade away."

"It's online. It's permanent. Anyone who searches my name—new or old—will find it."

Mercy was silent. *She's right.*

"I'll change my business's name, get a new website domain, and let my current clients know. Crap, that's going to be a lot of busywork."

"It's a good plan."

"It's a pain-in-the-butt plan. I know people feel very powerful when they make threats online, but actually following through is another story. They're usually all talk. But still . . . I don't need this in my life. I still might have to move. Again."

Mercy abruptly remembered where she'd spent most of the night. "Britta," she slowly started. "A family was murdered last night."

Silence.

"And the circumstances are a lot like your family's deaths."

A sharp intake of air sounded over the line.

"I wanted you to be prepared before it hits the news."

"What is going on?" Britta whispered.

The Hartlages have been missing since about the same time Britta came to town.

And now another family had been murdered in their beds.

I'm making assumptions. Mercy had seen Britta's fear and shock when she first told her about the remains in the culvert. It'd felt real.

But she'd been fooled before.

"I'm really sorry to dump it on you this way. Especially after the mess Chuck has started. I hope you don't have to leave town." It was true. She admired the way Britta hadn't let her past destroy her.

"We'll see." Britta hung up without a goodbye.

Mercy stared at her screen. *Now I have your phone number.* She was surprised Britta didn't hide it on outgoing calls.

Fury at Chuck Winslow raged through her again. He was an independent reporter. There was no boss she could complain to.

One of these days I'll have it out with him.

She immediately rejected the thought as she pictured Winslow's next headline: "FBI Agent Threatened Me."

Mercy crawled out of bed.

She had murders to focus on, not a reporter.

EIGHTEEN

My father was a drinker.

He was a falling-down, shit-faced, hateful, angry drunk, and my mother always made excuses for him. She feared him too. I heard it in her quivering voice and saw it in her wide eyes. He was quick to slap her when angered, then blamed her for causing him to lose his temper. She spent her whole life tiptoeing on eggshells around him, scared to awaken the beast.

When he was drunk, he talked, ranted, and raved.

He didn't care if no one was in the room; he talked to the walls, the TV, or a lamp.

No one was ever with him, but I'd hear him beg over and over, "Stop talking to me." But most of the time, he talked about the war. I would listen from behind a door, fascinated and horrified by his descriptions of death and destruction. He spoke of the thrill when he had control of someone's life—the decision of whether they lived or died. I heard the yearning in his tone as he described the hours-long high after killing the enemy, and I knew he craved that power again.

Looking back, I understand that beating on us kids and our mother was his way of achieving that power.

Eventually I learned to turn everything off. No one could hurt me if I didn't feel anything.

Take away my toys? It didn't matter because I didn't care about them.

Scream and yell at me? It didn't matter because words couldn't touch me.

I remember feeling removed from my punishments, as if I were standing to one side, observing the veins pop on my father's temples and the cords in his neck grow taut. I was simply an observer.

I grew thick walls around my emotions. I learned not to want things—toys, time with friends, biking through the woods. If they didn't happen, I wouldn't be disappointed. I expected nothing from anyone.

My world grew flat and empty. But I was in control of it. I wouldn't be one of those stupid people who let emotions dictate their behaviors. I wouldn't be the stupid child on the playground who cried because no one would share the swings.

Losers. All of them.

Even my father, who drunkenly ranted and raved at chairs and lamps. No control.

But my anger started to build inside me. I could keep my other emotions under control, but I needed an outlet for the anger. I tested my mother even though I knew she was a victim of my father like me. One day I yelled at her that she was stupid for making a bologna sandwich for my lunch when I'd told her countless times I prefer peanut butter and jelly. Satisfaction ran through me at the shock on her face.

Is this what my father feels?

The rush of power fed an empty hole in my chest, and I shamed her again.

She told me to make my own lunch and left the room.

Pleased, I made my sandwich. It'd never tasted better.

Dinner with my family went as normal. Us kids knew to be silent. Mother and Father discussed plans for the following day.

I was in bed when my father came in. Without a word he hauled me out of bed, down the stairs, and out the back door. I didn't care. I checked out of my body and watched as I stumbled behind him, his grip tight on my upper arm. At the barn he threw me against the fence, ripped down my pajama bottoms, and whipped me with a thick branch. His words punctuated the strokes. "Don't you ever speak to your mother like that again."

I couldn't control the pain and I screamed, embarrassed by the tears that ran down my face.

He kept whipping, and I knew he enjoyed it. "You're just like me," he panted between strokes. "I see myself in your eyes every day. Need to whip it out of you."

I glanced back at the house and saw my mother's silhouette in her bedroom window. She was watching.

I hated her for letting him beat me. I hated everyone.

After that I behaved at home because I feared word would get back to my father.

My deeply hidden anger still grew; it festered. I kicked our dog in the ribs one time, furious at her continuous barking. The sad look of betrayal she gave me was enough to make me never do it again. Animals weren't the answer.

I wanted to conquer the anger the same way I'd tackled my other emotions. My father was controlled by anger; I wouldn't be.

I was determined to never be like him. No matter what he said.

I eventually learned to tuck it away deep inside. Hide it from everyone. I spent as much time as possible outdoors, seeking physical outlets for my excess energy. It helped. I bought a journal and hid it in my room, transcribing my deepest fears, desires, and needs.

After a month I burned it. Terrified it would fall into my father's hands.

The words I wrote would have earned me another beating. Maybe worse.

I continued to hide any actions I thought would trigger my father. When the Deverell family was killed and no one knew who had murdered them, my curiosity got the better of me.

Weeks after the murders I snuck away and rode my bike to the Deverell home. The police were done with their investigation of the house, but still no killer had been named. Boards had been nailed over the windows. I'd heard someone had broken the glass and wondered who had covered them up. *Neighbors? Police?*

I crept around to the back of the home, trying the doors, and then spotted a small high bathroom window that hadn't been broken or boarded up. I stacked firewood until I could reach the window, planning to smash it with a rock. To my delight it was unlocked, and I shimmied in, knocking down the shower curtain rod and landing awkwardly in the bathtub.

I tiptoed around, expecting a cop to appear at every turn. The house smelled musty and metallic. Black fingerprint dust covered every surface. I touched the black powder and then studied the smear I made on the wall. Panic swept through me and I grabbed a towel from the bathroom to wipe the place I'd touched.

In the first bedroom was a large bed, and I knew it must be the parents'. The bedding had been removed, and a hole had been cut in the carpet. But there were dark stains on the mattress. *Blood?*

I stepped closer, staring at the oddly shaped stains. I leaned over and sniffed. *Yes, blood.*

I'd heard the entire family had been killed in their beds. Blows to the heads. I crept from room to room. Each one was the same. No bedding. Stains on the mattresses.

How much do people bleed?

The kitchen and living room looked normal. Like the family was simply away for a day. Books, cups, and papers were scattered about the tables and counters. More black dust.

It became difficult to breathe. My breaths grew frequent and shallow, and I wondered if the boarded-up windows had blocked fresh oxygen. I sprinted to the bathroom, shakily replaced the curtain rod I'd knocked down, and crawled out the window. Outside I leaned against the house, taking deep gulps of the fresh air. I wiped my forehead and discovered it was covered in sweat.

I rode my bike home, thinking about what I'd seen and wondering if any of the Deverells had known they were about to die.

I've never forgotten that house.

NINETEEN

Finally some progress.

Delighted, Mercy hung up the phone in her office. Until this moment it had felt as if the Hartlage case had completely stalled, but that phone call had breathed new life into the case.

"Lunch?" Truman appeared at her door with a large paper sack.

Three good things in a row: new evidence, lunch delivery, and Truman.

"Absolutely." Mercy cleared an area on her desk.

"Why are you beaming?" he asked as he handed her a spinach salad. He looked as tired as she felt after their long night at the Jorgensens'.

"Because I just heard from Dr. Harper. She found a dentist who had Corrine and Richard Hartlage as patients."

"Nice!" Truman pulled up a chair and opened his steak sandwich. "Are they emailing the films?"

"That's the one bad thing. They don't have digital films, but the office is making copies and overnighting them." She took a bite of strawberries and spinach. "I'm getting spoiled. I expect instant delivery these days."

"I thought most offices had gone to digital films," he commented.

"They have. But this office is in Burns."

"Oh," Truman said with understanding. Burns was a tiny remote city in eastern Oregon. Everything moved slower in that rural half of the state. "You told me she'd called every dentist around here. What made her look for a dentist in Burns?"

"Because two years ago, the Hartlages moved here from Portland. Do you know how many dentist offices there are in Portland? Poor Dr. Harper didn't even know where to start calling. I dug a little deeper. Ten years ago they lived in Burns. I figured she'd have better luck pinpointing a dentist in a town of less than three thousand."

"But the films will be ten years old—or older. Will they be helpful?"

"I asked the same question. Dr. Harper said she can definitely use them to determine if these skulls are the Hartlages."

"Impressive," admitted Truman as he popped the last part of one half of his sandwich in his mouth. Mercy looked down at her giant salad. She'd eaten two bites.

"Was the brother-in-law a patient too?" asked Truman.

"No," Mercy said, stabbing her fork into a strawberry. "I don't know if I'll ever find his dental records—we haven't even found his name—and we need to know who the Asian skull belongs to. With the skull we found yesterday we've got the right number of Caucasian skulls to match the Hartlage adults, so the Asian one is a big mystery."

"And they're still searching the area, right? Hopefully they don't find more victims."

"Amen." They ate in companionable silence for a few moments. "Did you get any sleep?" she asked him.

Truman crumpled up the paper from his finished sandwich. "A few hours."

"Same."

"I got a call from your contractor. He said you didn't call him back."

"Oh, crap. I forgot." Mercy's brain scrambled to recall the message her contractor had left on her voice mail regarding the construction of her new cabin.

"He said the parts for the photovoltaic system will be here in four weeks." Truman leaned forward, catching her gaze. "You didn't tell me you were going with that power system again."

"I made a decision." Warning bells went off in her head at his quiet tone. She shoved a huge bite of spinach leaves in her mouth.

He pressed his lips together. "You know best what you need done up there, but that's the fourth big decision that you have left me out of. I felt completely out of the loop when he talked to me about the system as if I knew everything about it."

His words were gentle, but she knew she'd hurt him. She set down her fork. "I'm sorry. Sometimes I forget that you're in this with me."

"You forget?" He looked stunned.

Open mouth, insert foot. "What I mean is that the cabin has been my baby for years. I'm not accustomed to discussing it with anyone. It's a habit. I'm on automatic pilot when it comes to dealing with it."

He nodded but didn't look convinced.

She reached across the desk and took his hand. "I love you. This is *our* project. I'll try harder to include you."

"I haven't paid for any of the construction yet." His eyes narrowed. "How much have you paid out?"

"It doesn't matter—"

"Yes, it does. You just said this is our project. That means I contribute."

Pride and independence rose within her. Plus she made more money than the small-town police chief. "I'm using the insurance payout."

"But you had to meet the deductible."

"I used the money I was saving for a down payment on a new house."

"Mercy . . ." Disappointment filled his face.

He has pride too.

"When the insurance money runs out, we'll divide everything, okay?" His obvious hurt stung deep in her heart. She'd made two big blunders and not even noticed. *This relationship stuff is hard. I need to share the pain-in-the-butt and expensive stuff too . . . not just the happy stuff.*

She'd been on her own for a long time. The routines and decisions that felt perfectly normal to her felt exclusionary to Truman.

"Okay," he said, standing up and collecting the garbage from their lunch. "I need to get back to work."

I didn't convince him.

She'd have to show him she meant it.

"I do too." She came around the desk and kissed him goodbye.

I will try harder.

◆ ◆ ◆

It was nearly midnight when Truman's officer Samuel Robb woke him up with a call to come to a scene. It took Truman a full ten seconds to connect faces to the names Samuel stated.

The Moody brothers.

Ryan Moody had returned to the home he shared with his brother, Clint, and found a lot of blood in Clint's bedroom. Clint Moody was missing. Samuel had already checked with the local hospital and clinics to see if Clint had come in as a patient. No luck.

On the drive over, Truman wondered if one of the brothers had finally been pushed over the edge, lost his temper, and done away with the other.

The Moodys lived in an older Eagle's Nest neighborhood. The homes sat on large lots with the garages behind the houses. The road was gravel, and Truman's headlights shone on dented and crooked mailboxes along the street. He pictured teens cruising along the street with a baseball bat, trying to knock the boxes from their posts. As a teen Truman had hung with friends who'd played mailbox baseball, but he'd never taken the bat. He'd laughed along with them but passed on destruction of property, knowing his uncle would hang him if he was caught. Looking back now, he knew the cops would have arrested him for simply being in the car, not caring that he claimed he'd never touched the bat.

Truman parked next to Samuel's patrol vehicle and spotted his distinctive silhouette in the front door of the Moody home—the cop's slightly spread legs, his crossed arms, and his buzz-cut head. He was reliable, sharp, and physically fit. The only one of his officers who checked all three boxes. Truman felt secure when Samuel backed him up.

Truman met Samuel on the small concrete porch. "What do we have?"

"Ryan is a mess," said Samuel, "and Clint's truck is gone."

"Ryan doesn't believe he drove somewhere?"

"With the amount of blood in the home, the only place I would drive is to the hospital."

"Maybe he drove off the road if he's severely injured."

"I put out a BOLO on his truck. It's a ten-year-old Ford Ranger. Black."

Truman stepped closer and lowered his voice. "I broke up a bar fight between these guys the other day. Could Ryan have hurt his brother?"

Samuel pressed his lips into a line as he considered. "Ryan's a big guy. Physically he could do it. But if he's acting about being upset, he's got me fooled. I got in fights with my brothers all the time. Doesn't mean I'd really hurt them."

He knew Samuel had good instincts, but all of them had been conned before. Truman would make up his own mind. "Show me the way."

Inside the small house, Ryan sat on the couch with his head in his hands, staring at his feet. He didn't look up at Truman, and Samuel gave a jerk of his head for Truman to follow him. He'd talk to Ryan in a few minutes. Obviously the man wasn't interested in speaking at the moment.

They stopped at the first bedroom. The king-size bed nearly filled the entire room. A flat-screen TV hung on the wall, and several game consoles sat on a small table beneath it. A sheet hung over the window, and a curtain and two pairs of dirty jeans lay on the floor.

Blood had soaked into the pillow and splattered on the wall. The heavier spots still glistened with moisture.

"Jesus." Someone had been brutally beaten. Recently. "Did you see any blood on Ryan or his clothes?"

"No. And I checked the sinks and showers. All dry. No wet towels in the laundry. If he did this, he cleaned up somewhere else."

The covers were shoved back, and more blood smeared the sheets. "I don't see any heavy bloodstains or trails on the carpet," Truman said. "A little spatter here and there."

"I noticed that too. I'm sure county will spray it and check for blood."

Truman squatted and studied the carpet. "It's not wet. No one cleaned up the rug. Is there blood elsewhere in the house?"

"I've done a quick search and didn't see anything." Samuel gestured at the bed. "With an injury like that, I'd expect blood trails. There's nothing."

Truman pulled the flashlight off his belt and shone it under the bed. Dust bunnies, dirty Kleenex, and a paper plate holding several old pizza crusts. A small white object caught his eye. "Samuel, get a photo of this."

Samuel took a picture of the mess under the bed with his department cell phone, and then Truman used a pen to move the white object closer.

It was small and pointy, with blood covering two-thirds of an end. A tooth.

"One of his teeth was knocked out," said Samuel. "No question this guy was seriously injured."

Truman imagined the tooth arcing through the air to land on the floor and then accidentally being kicked under the bed by the attacker. "Have you found a weapon?"

"No. But I haven't searched outside yet. County is sending an evidence team."

"Good call." Truman stood and stared at the pillow, a suspicion simmering in his thoughts, thinking of Mercy's current cases. "This blood pattern reminds me of a case Mercy is working on." A stomach-lurching notion struck him. "Any kids live here? Does either man have kids?"

"Ryan said just the two of them live here. I guess their kids could live somewhere else."

"I'd like to talk to Ryan now."

This time Ryan looked up when Truman stepped into the living room, recognition flashing in his eyes. After Ryan and Clint had sobered up in the Eagle's Nest holding cells, Truman had let them go after a stern lecture that he didn't want to see them again for beating up on each other.

And here they were . . . well, one of them.

Ryan's eyes were red, and he wiped his nose. He wore jeans, work boots, and a John Deere cap. He stood as Truman approached. Truman noted his fingernails were dark around all the edges, but it was the deep stain that comes from years of grimy physical work. His hands and knuckles had scabbed abrasions that Truman recalled being fresh on the night of the bar fight. He also had a colorful bruise on his cheekbone and a healing split lip from that night.

Truman didn't see any new injuries.

"Before we start, do you or your brother have kids?"

Ryan stared, a confused look on his face. "No. Why?"

"Just checking." Truman gestured for him to sit back down, and took a seat in a chair facing him. Samuel stood in his usual pose with his arms crossed. "What happened when you got home?"

Ryan cleared his throat. "Nothing happened. I pulled up around nine and was a little surprised that Clint's truck wasn't here because I know he has to get up early, but I didn't think much of it. I'd been home for a good two hours before I noticed the blood in his room. I'd left the light on in the bathroom across the hall and caught the stain on his sheets out of the corner of my eye." He took a shuddering breath.

"Did you touch anything in the room?"

"Only the light switch."

"What did you do next?"

"I checked all the other rooms and then called you guys. While I was waiting I called the hospital. No one under his name had been admitted."

"No John Does in the hospital either, and I checked all the emergency clinics," added Samuel.

"Is anything missing?" asked Truman.

Ryan wiped under his nose with the back of his hand. "The only things worth stealing are the TVs and game systems. Everything is still here."

"No guns? Cash?"

"Guns are in a safe. I noticed it was locked, but I didn't look inside."

"Let's check."

He and Samuel trailed Ryan to the other bedroom, where a large gun safe took up most of the closet. Samuel gave him a pair of gloves to do the combination lock. Ryan spun the dial and seconds later opened the heavy door. Truman spotted three rifles and six lockboxes that he assumed held handguns. Ryan checked each box as Truman watched over his shoulder. Every weapon was present.

Back in the living room, the men took up their previous places. "What's your brother do? Has he had any angry encounters recently?"

"He works at the lumberyard."

"Walker's Lumberyard?"

"Yeah, he's been there about five years. He hasn't mentioned any arguments recently."

"Where do you work at?"

"I'm a plumber for Dawson's Plumbing. I usually work an eleven-to-eight shift."

"Do you know of anyone who had it in for your brother? What about bar fights?"

"Clint didn't have any enemies. He was easygoing. If there were bar fights—well, except for the one you broke up—I haven't heard of anything recent."

In his time as a cop, Truman had always heard that the victim had no enemies. Everybody always loved the missing person.

Later the truth would come out.

"I'm going to take a look outside around the house," Truman stated. Ryan simply nodded, his gaze back on his feet.

Truman signaled for Samuel to stay inside and keep an eye on Ryan. Outdoors he stood on the porch for a long moment. The gravel road had streetlights, but the closest one was in front of the house to the left. Trees and bushes blocked any views of the Moody home from the right and left neighbors. But the home across the street stared directly at the Moody house. Lights were on inside and out, and the curtains moved as he watched. Truman hoped the brothers had a nosy neighbor.

He did a quick circuit around the home and the garage behind it, sweeping the ground with his flashlight. He peered through the side door window into the small garage and learned why the brothers parked out front. The garage was packed with junk. Still wearing his gloves, Truman tried the handle and discovered it was unlocked. He stepped inside, smelling mildew and motor oil but nothing worse. There were mattresses, old dressers, tons of stacked boxes, dusty ten-speed bikes, and a motorcycle. He checked every place he thought a body could be hidden. The evidence team would be more thorough. He backed out and shut the door, resuming his lap around the house.

Out front he shone his flashlight in the old Ford Explorer, which he assumed belonged to Ryan.

Did the attacker take Clint's truck? If not, where is the attacker's vehicle?

Either the attacker had arrived on foot, or he wasn't alone.

Could Clint have driven away?

Truman seriously doubted it, judging from the blood in the room.

The Deschutes County evidence team arrived, and Truman gave some brief instructions before turning them over to Samuel. He knew giving the case to a Deschutes County detective was an option. *Not yet.* At the moment it was simply a missing persons case.

He strode across the gravel street to see who was still up.

◆ ◆ ◆

"I don't sleep much anymore," Sally Kantor told Truman.

She'd insisted on serving him a cup of instant coffee and set out a plate of chocolate chip cookies. Truman took one cookie to be polite. After the first bite, he knew he'd have to exercise self-control not to eat the rest of the cookies. They sat in her living room, which had a large window that faced the Moody house. Her old TV was on a table next to the window, and Sally sat in a recliner that faced the TV and window. Next to her was an end table loaded with novels, crossword puzzle books, and knitting supplies. A bed pillow and comforter were squeezed in the recliner with her. It was *her* spot.

She was a petite woman with a small hump at the top of her spine, and she wore a pink quilted satin robe that zipped up the front. Her pink embroidered slippers reminded him of ones his grandmother had worn. She'd proudly told him she was eighty-four years young, and she moved with an energy that surprised him. Her curly gray hair was short and neat, and her smile compassionate. She'd opened the door before he knocked, stating that she'd watched him walk across the street. Curiosity and excitement had danced in her dark-blue eyes as she welcomed him into her home.

"I usually knit late in the evenings. It doesn't take much thought, and the rhythm helps my brain slow down. When I'm tired I turn off the light, pull up my blanket, and sleep right here." She clapped her hands twice and the light went out. She immediately clapped again to bring it back on. She wore a wide grin when Truman was able to see her again. "I know my Clapper is corny, but it's one of my favorite things," she admitted.

As a child he'd been fascinated with the product.

"But you're not here to have coffee and cookies with an old woman. What happened across the street? I've been watching since the first police vehicle pulled up with its lights flashing."

"Do you know the Moody brothers?" Truman asked before taking another bite of heaven.

"Of course. Clint and Ryan. I can always count on them when I need a bit of muscle to move something around here. Polite boys."

"Did you see either one of them today?"

"I saw Ryan get home from work a few hours ago. Clint's pickup was there earlier today. He gets off work at the lumberyard around three, I believe. I didn't actually see him, just his vehicle."

"Did you see any other vehicles over there?"

She frowned at him. "What happened? Did someone break in? I've always been a little nervous living here by myself, but I've got Betty Lou in case someone tries something." She spread open her bag of yarn and knitting needles, tipping it toward Truman to expose a revolver nestled among the skeins of yarn. "I know my way around a gun."

Of course she does.

"There was an unfamiliar pickup at the home earlier today," she continued, setting the bag aside. "I saw two men get out and head toward the house, but I didn't think anything of it."

"What time was this?"

She tapped her lips with one finger as she thought. "Well, I'd already watched the local news, which finished at five thirty . . . I'd say they showed up around six."

"Did you see them leave?"

"No. I made my dinner and cleaned up the kitchen. When I came out the driveway was empty. No vehicles at all."

"How long do you think you were in the kitchen?"

"Maybe a half hour."

"Did you get a good look at the two men?"

She cocked her head. "Not really. It was raining and getting dark. But my impression was that they fit in with Ryan and Clint. You know, solid, hardworking men. Jeans, boots, caps. I saw them as two friends coming to visit."

Like every other man in Eagle's Nest.

Truman made a notation about the clothing on his pad. "What color was the truck?"

Sally grimaced. "A dark color. I don't know if it was dark green, blue, or black. I know it wasn't white or any pale color. And don't bother to ask me the make. I don't pay attention to stuff like that."

Truman tried a different approach. "Would you say it was identical to the truck Clint drives?"

She thought hard. "No. It was different somehow. I only saw it from the back. They'd already parked next to Clint's truck when I looked up, but the back of the truck wasn't the same as Clint's."

Congratulations. I eliminated one specific year and make of truck.

"Were either of the men heavyset?"

Sally shook her head.

"Would you say they moved like young men? No slow steps of an older man?"

"Not old. Are you going to tell me what happened over there or not?" Impatience colored her tone.

Truman put away his notebook. "We don't know. Clint is missing and there's quite a bit of blood in the home."

"Oh, my!" Sally touched her hand to her chest. "That poor boy. Such a nice man."

"The brothers get along as far as you know?"

"For the most part. Whenever they were in my home, they were gentlemen. But I've heard a few shouting arguments. And my hearing isn't the best, so they must have been loud for me to hear them all the way across the street. But who doesn't have those?"

"You never saw them or heard about them hitting each other?"

"Oh, Lord no. Do you think Ryan did something to Clint?" She asked. Her thin eyebrows shot up. "That's ridiculous. They're brothers."

So were Cain and Abel.

Apparently Sally hadn't heard about the recent bar fight between the brothers. Truman handed her a business card. "You've been very helpful. Call me if you see the truck again or remember anything unusual from across the street."

"Are you going to find Clint?"

"That's the plan."

"They're good boys," she repeated, but uncertainty shone for the first time in her eyes. "I hope nothing horrible has happened."

"You and me both."

TWENTY

The next morning Truman stared at the lists of priors for Clint and Ryan Moody.

"You're kidding me," he mumbled. The day of the bar fight, Samuel had checked to see if either man had outstanding warrants. Both were clear. He'd mentioned to Truman that the men had several priors, but he hadn't gone into detail.

Now Truman saw that the brothers had a history of arrests for assault and drug use, and a long list of traffic violations. All of which had occurred outside of Eagle's Nest.

They're good boys.

He shook his head as he remembered Sally Kantor's words. Maybe the Moodys behaved themselves around the senior citizen, but they didn't appear to care what other people thought. He took a closer look at the assaults. Mostly bar brawls. *And Ryan claimed his brother was easygoing.*

By the looks of the arrest records, it was a regular thing. Truman wasn't surprised that Ryan had stretched the truth about the bar fights.

Clint's disappearance can't be related to the cases Mercy is working on.

Other than the similar bloodstains left in Clint's bed and the lack of a blood trail, it didn't feel the same.

Truman had slept at his home alone the night before, and hadn't told Mercy about his late-night call-out yet. They'd exchanged their normal brief morning texts but no work talk. *I'll call her after I have more information.*

He tapped his fingers on his desk as he thought. Ryan's record was as bad as Clint's. There hadn't been any local police calls to the men's home, so maybe they did get along with each other. But each had a history.

Ryan Moody had agreed to stop by the station later that morning. Looking at the time, Truman decided he could fit in a quick stop to Walker's Lumberyard and talk to Clint's employer, Nick. He liked Nick and figured he'd be a reliable source of information on Clint.

Ten minutes later, he strode in the door at the lumberyard and brushed the rain off his coat. He'd called ahead to make certain Nick was in, so the man was waiting for him, his German shepherd, Belle, at his side. The men exchanged greetings, and Truman rubbed Belle's soft ears. He gave Nick an abbreviated version of what he'd discovered at the Moody home the night before.

"Holy crap. That's awful." The tall man looked stunned. "I left a message on his cell phone when he didn't show up for work. I figured he had a hangover or was sick . . . although I was surprised he didn't answer his phone."

Truman remembered seeing a cell phone on Clint's nightstand and assumed the evidence team had taken it.

"A hangover? Does that happen often?"

A thoughtful look crossed Nick's face. "Not really. My guys know I don't put up with that shit. They need to be on their toes when handling the lumber—it's heavy. And if anyone had an accident while driving the forklift because they were hungover, they'd be out of a job. They know this."

"Did Clint get along with his coworkers?"

Nick considered the question. "He did. He was the type to lose his temper pretty quick, but then he'd be laughing the next minute. No one held it against him. I'd say everyone likes him."

"Can you think of anyone who'd want to hurt him? Did he mention any arguments outside of work?"

"I can't think of anything he mentioned like that."

"How'd he get along with his brother, Ryan?"

Nick's brows slowly rose on his narrow face. "You don't really think . . ."

"I have to consider everything."

The man gave it careful thought before speaking. "Clint's worked here less than a year. I think I've seen his brother stop in once. I knew they lived together, and he's occasionally bitched about Ryan. But it was what I would expect of two brothers sharing a house." He gave a wry grin. "One time Ryan ran into Clint's truck in their driveway, and I know there was an issue about who would pay for the damage. Clint was in a foul mood for a few days about that."

"When was that?"

"During the snow and ice earlier this year. Ryan slid. Claimed he couldn't have prevented the accident."

"Anything else you can think of that might help? Did Clint ever talk about leaving town?"

Nick shook his head.

Truman held out his hand. "Thanks for your time. Let me know if you think of anything else."

"Anytime."

Truman was about to leave when he stopped and looked back. "How's it going with Rose?" Belle's ears perked up at Rose's name.

An easy smile crossed Nick's face. "Good."

"Take it slow." Truman had a soft spot in his heart for Rose. He'd witnessed the hell she'd been put through last fall. A weaker person would have been emotionally and mentally destroyed. Thankfully Rose was made of tough material. Like Mercy.

"I will."

Truman pushed open the door, thinking about the blind woman and the quiet lumberyard owner. He made a silent wish that they'd have a good future together.

As he left the lumberyard, he realized he'd forgotten to feed Simon that morning in his exhaustion after two nights with little sleep. Truman still had a good half hour before Ryan Moody was to show up at the police department for an interview, so he headed toward home, surprised his cat hadn't made her needs known before he left for work.

Maybe she did and I was too tired to notice.

He'd started his coffee maker without any water that morning.

He pulled into the driveway of his house and sat in his seat for a few seconds.

Damn, I need a nap.

He'd have time to stop and get some caffeinated fuel after feeding Simon. The thought of espresso and Kaylie's apple coffee cake from her coffee shop perked him up. He got out of his SUV and headed toward the front door.

He knew someone was behind him a split second before the blow hit him in the right kidney. Lightning shot from his lower back to the core of his brain, and he forgot how to breathe. He stumbled forward and fell to one knee as his right hand grabbed the railing to the porch stairs, stopping him from landing on his face.

Protect my gun.

He started to push to his feet and turn to face his attacker as his left hand tried to reach his weapon at his right hip. His balance relied on his right hand's still gripping the railing, preventing him from using his gun hand. His body burned as if a mine had exploded in his back.

The second strike hit his left kidney, and Truman fell to both knees. Both his hands shot forward to stop his skull from crashing into the concrete steps. Fire radiated from two places in his back. Bright lights flashed behind his eyes, momentarily blinding him.

A baseball bat?

"Fucking cop!"

"Asshole!"

Two attackers.

He tried to turn again. A blow hit his temple, and the flashes of light went black.

Simon will be hungry.

His head bounced off the concrete, and then he knew no more.

TWENTY-ONE

"This has to be boring for you," Dr. Harper said to Mercy as they looked at dental films in the medical examiner's office for the second time that week.

"Heck no. I find it fascinating," corrected Mercy. It was true.

The Hartlage films from the Burns office had been delivered to Dr. Harper, who'd called Mercy within an hour to tell her the first Caucasian skulls they'd found were definitely Corrine and Richard Hartlage. Mercy asked Dr. Harper to demonstrate how she'd come to the conclusion.

Again the small grayscale rectangles on the screen looked like a jumbled mess to Mercy.

"How long did it take for you to learn to read these?" she asked the dentist.

Dr. Harper tilted her head as she thought. "It feels like I've always known, but we learned to identify the teeth in films very early in dental school. Years of working with them after I graduated also taught me hundreds of things I never encountered during school. I've easily examined fifty thousand films. Everyone has unique qualities to their teeth, the roots, and the bone around them."

Mercy looked again. She could recognize fillings and crowns and root canals, but that was about it.

"What did you find?" she asked.

"Let's start with Richard Hartlage." Dr. Harper's lips twisted. "The copies his old office made aren't the greatest. They're dark. I would have told the assistant to redo them, but I can work with them. I put the films I shot at the top of the screen."

Mercy nodded, noting the films on the bottom were much darker.

"On my film, he's missing two molars on the lower right side." She indicated a wide empty space on her film. "On the dark film, he has those teeth, but do you see how the crest of the bone steeply angles down toward the roots of both of those teeth? This was caused by gum disease. Over time it destroys the bone that anchors teeth. A healthy bone level would have been higher on the root, just below the bulbous part of the tooth, like on this one." Dr. Harper pointed at another tooth on the film. The crest of bone was flat.

"You're not surprised that those teeth are missing on the films you took."

"Not at all. When comparing old films and new, teeth and their roots can always be missing on the newest films, but you can't add a tooth and root that weren't there before. Unless you count implants, but those are completely different. They look like screws in the jaw."

"That still doesn't prove this is Richard. It could be someone else."

"It doesn't. But then I look at the amalgam filling on tooth number thirteen on this old film, and it's still the exact same shape on the new. Same with these three other amalgam fillings. They are identical on both sets of films. But on number five, the old film shows an amalgam filling that involves two surfaces of the tooth. Now that tooth has a filling that involves three surfaces."

"There's an inconsistency?"

"No. The filling was replaced with a bigger one. Fillings will never be replaced by smaller ones or disappear, but they *can* be replaced with larger ones. If tooth five had no filling, I'd know this isn't Richard."

"You're convinced it's him?"

"Without a doubt." Confidence rang in her voice.

"And Corrine?"

Dr. Harper pulled up new films. "Corrine had better dental health. Her old films show no fillings, but she's received two amalgam fillings which show up in the films I took on the skull."

"Then how can you be sure it's her?"

Mercy swore the dentist's eyes twinkled.

"There are other markers besides fillings. Look at the roots on this tooth. See how the ends suddenly point toward the back of the mouth instead of going straight down?"

Mercy noted that all the other teeth had perfectly straight roots.

"I'd hate to extract this tooth with those difficult root tips—I'd send her to a specialist if she'd needed it removed. But my point is that the roots are identical on both sets of films. The same tooth on the opposite side of her mouth does the same thing, and they match."

"It's not a common root formation?"

"It's not uncommon. But these are identical." She moved one of her films over the old one and Mercy saw that everything lined up perfectly. The crooked roots, the straight roots, and the shapes of the other teeth. "I had to retake the new film a few times to match the angle of the old one, but I caught it."

"It's Corrine," Mercy stated.

"Yes."

"That poor family." The photos from the home flashed in her memory. *Alison, Amy . . . gone.*

"We didn't find any remains of shoes, or belts, or wallets," Mercy mused out loud. "Does that mean they were put in the culvert naked? Or were they already skeletal remains when they were hidden there?"

"Did you see the soil report that was just finished?"

"Not yet." She made a mental note to check her email.

"I read it. The soil tests indicate that the bones have been there the whole time."

"Interesting." Mercy tried to imagine the work involved in dumping an entire unclothed family in the culvert. "I wonder if he put them in the other end first. Maybe the bodies are what caused part of the backing up of the culvert to start with."

"And the bones were eventually washed out the other end?" suggested Dr. Harper.

"Yes. They were really embedded in the debris backing up the culvert, weren't they?"

"They were." One side of Dr. Harper's lips curved up. "Could be ironic that the way he disposed of the bodies is what caused them to be eventually found."

"And it's reasonable that the remains could have skeletonized since last summer?"

"Absolutely."

"How will we figure out if the last skull is the brother-in-law?" Mercy asked. The brother-in-law could be the murder suspect she was searching for. *But did he kill the Jorgensens too?* "I still don't know his name. I can't find any records of Corrine's family, and Richard's uncle was no help."

"There's always DNA testing, but it will take time. We can compare the unknown skull's DNA to Corrine's. If they're siblings, they should have about fifty percent matching DNA."

"I plan to get that test rolling as soon as possible," Dr. Victoria Peres said as she entered the room. "Nice to see you, Agent Kilpatrick. I'm glad we had some good news for you." She frowned. "I guess it's not *good* news, but helpful news."

"Definitely helpful," agreed Mercy, noticing Dr. Peres carried a skull. "Now we're down to two mystery skulls instead of four."

"Actually we're down to one mystery skull." The usually calm and collected woman spoke in a voice that was higher than normal.

Mercy's skin tingled. "What did you find?"

Dr. Peres held up the skull, and Mercy recognized the different shape of the eye sockets. "That's the Asian skull," said Mercy.

"Yes." The forensic anthropologist flipped it over and indicated the opening on the bottom. "Can you see in here?" She shone a penlight inside the skull.

Mercy leaned closer, wondering what the doctor expected her to see. She couldn't read every bump and fossa the way Dr. Peres could.

"It's always bothered me that the color of the skull was slightly different from the other five," Dr. Peres said. "And it felt more brittle to me. I was about to run dating tests on it when I spotted something inside. I blame myself for not getting it fully cleaned out right away. Stubborn dirt and the awkward location kept me from seeing it."

Mercy searched the inside of the skull. Her gaze stopped on some small scratches. "Is that a year?" Mercy took the penlight from the doctor and moved closer to the opening. "It says *1969*. But what do the letters spell?" She squinted. Someone had awkwardly carved the numbers and letters inside the skull.

"I think they're someone's initials."

"Someone put the identity inside?" Her mind raced. *It must be a birth year and the victim's initials.*

"No. I think this is a war trophy from Vietnam."

Mercy drew back, horrified at the thought. "Seriously?"

"It's my theory. I've heard of soldiers smuggling back skulls or bones or clothing from wars. All the wars."

"That's sick."

"There's a market for it."

"That's even sicker."

"Let me see it," requested Dr. Harper. She opened a case and took out a pair of glasses with loupes attached to the lenses. Mercy's dentist wore the same type. "The initials are HRR. I assume they belong to whoever originally brought home the skull?"

"Who knows?" asked Dr. Peres. "It could have had multiple owners over the last fifty years."

"But why place it in the culvert? And was it put there at the same time as the Hartlages?" questioned Mercy, thinking out loud.

"I suspect you won't know the answer to that until you make an arrest," Dr. Peres said solemnly.

It wasn't the answer Mercy wanted to hear, but she knew the forensic anthropologist was correct.

TWENTY-TWO

My father had a love of all things military.

I didn't understand his fascination with these items because of his hatred of his time in the war. He condemned our government, which sent men to war, but would make special trips to see war memorabilia for sale. Mother looked upset every time he came home with a new purchase, but she never said anything about the money he spent. I suspect she knew better. Even I knew Father was in charge of the money. Mother had to ask several times when she needed to buy us clothes for school.

He had quite a war collection by the time I was ten. The items were kept in a big wooden armoire with a lock. When he was drunk he'd set a chair in front of the armoire and lovingly handle each item. If he was in a good mood, he'd let us touch some items in his precious collection. He'd tell us which war the item was from and speculate on the type of man who'd used it. Sometimes he'd recite stories about his collectibles . . . the men who carried the guns, wore the clothes, earned the medals. I knew the stories weren't true; some of these wars had happened before he was born. How could he know who'd used those things?

He'd let us try on the hats. There was a black metal helmet worn by Germans from a very old war, and a weathered tan hat with a brim and a dirty-looking metal pin with an eagle and a shield. He claimed this one was used by Americans. It smelled old . . . like dust and gasoline and oil. Both were too big on my head.

My favorite hat was the red beret. It was slightly crushed but would mold to my head better than the others. Its patch had a star and a gold wreath, but Father said it wasn't American. It was from Vietnam. The manufacturer's label was in a foreign language, so I suspected he told the truth. Another neat thing from Vietnam was the camouflage-covered helmet. Someone had written *Born to Kill* on it with a fat black marker and drawn peace signs.

He wouldn't let us touch the weapons. He had about a dozen knives with battered scabbards, and the prize of this collection was a long bayonet. I don't remember what war it was from. He had several handguns, but I thought they looked like the weapons used on cop shows on TV and they didn't hold my interest. The one gun I did like was a French submachine gun. It was long, black, and deadly. It looked like someone had added parts to a regular gun. My father claimed it had been stolen in another war and then used by Vietnamese guerrillas. Most of his memorabilia was from the Vietnam War . . . including some collectibles that shocked me.

He rarely talked about his war. The keepsakes from his war were pushed to the back of the armoire, and he rarely brought them out. When I'd find the armoire unlocked, I'd look through them, wondering which belonged to him and which he'd bought. He called the camouflage from his war "chocolate chip." I never knew if that was a joke or real. He had a medal in a box. I don't believe he earned it, because it was on a red-white-and-green ribbon and imprinted with a foreign language, but I could read the year. 1991. I suspected the Operation Desert Storm patch was his.

All these items were his obsessions. I believe he cared more about them than about his kids. Or wife. Sometimes he would lock himself in the bedroom for days and drink. Mother would sleep on the couch and tell us to leave him alone. I could hear him rooting through the armoire, muttering or swearing to himself.

After one long binge, Mother pried open the bedroom door. She'd been listening and pacing outside the door for an hour, concern on her face. When it opened, I saw him motionless on the bed, wearing the chocolate chip camouflage. I stayed by the door and watched her creep close to bend her head to listen by his mouth. I saw his chest rise and she silently dashed back out of the room.

I swear I saw disappointment on her face.

TWENTY-THREE

"Where's the boss?" Officer Ben Cooley asked Lucas.

"Last I heard, Truman was going to the lumberyard to talk to Nick Walker." Lucas frowned at the clock on the wall. "That's been hours ago, and I left a message when he missed an appointment this morning, but I haven't heard from him. I'll try his cell." He immediately punched numbers on a phone.

Ben sighed. He hated to bug Truman, but his wife was hounding him to get next Saturday off. Samuel had offered to switch shifts with him, but all changes had to be okayed by Truman. Ben's wife wanted to buy tickets for some play in Bend, and she needed to know *today* if Ben could get the evening off.

He wouldn't mind missing the play. He always fell asleep.

"No answer," said Lucas. "I'll try the radio."

"It's not a big deal," Ben hedged, hating to put Lucas out.

"He should have told me where he was going next," Lucas pointed out, a slightly miffed tone in his voice. "He's not picking up his radio either."

"I'll head over to the lumberyard," said Ben. "Maybe Nick knows where he went next. Back in a bit." Ben grabbed his cowboy hat and headed outside, thankful the rain had stopped.

Ten minutes later he parked at the lumberyard and strode to the front door. Truman's Tahoe wasn't in the lot.

"Hey, Ben," Nick said from behind the counter, his face lighting up with a smile as Ben entered. The tall man leaned on his forearms, writing up something in a ledger.

Ben wiped his boots on the mat, and Belle peeked around the side of the counter, her black ears pointed in Ben's direction. "I'm looking for Truman."

Nick's face cleared. "He left hours ago. He was only here for about ten minutes."

"What did he talk to you about?"

The man's shoulders slumped. "He told me Clint Moody is missing and blood was left behind."

"Yeah, that happened last night. We're keeping an eye out for his truck."

"Truman asked me if he got along with his brother." A questioning gaze met Ben's.

"Well . . . now . . ." Ben understood what Nick was asking. The possibility that one brother had caused the disappearance of the other didn't sit well with Ben, and he could see Nick felt the same. "He's missing. Coulda took off for an impromptu trip. Maybe he got in an argument with his brother so he didn't tell him he was leaving."

"Maybe." Nick didn't look convinced. "I had the impression Truman was headed back to the station when he left, but he turned the wrong way out of the parking lot."

"Oh yeah? I'll hunt him down."

"Don't you have GPS tracking on your department vehicles?"

"We've looked into it. Too spendy."

"*Hmph*. Maybe it's time to consider it again so you're not wasting time looking for one another."

"I'll bring it up. See you around." Ben headed back to his vehicle. As he pulled into the street, he turned in the direction Nick had mentioned. If Truman had been going back to the department or back to the Moody home he would have gone the other way. In this direction the most logical location was Truman's home.

I bet he's home sound asleep.

Ben knew the last two nights had been long ones for the police chief. He relaxed as he headed toward Truman's, confident he'd find the boss sacked out on his couch.

Truman's vehicle wasn't in the driveway. Ben knew he occasionally parked in the garage, so he parked at the curb and headed up the driveway to take a look in the garage door windows before ringing the doorbell.

"Meeeooooow!"

Simon glared at him from the window next to the front door. Ben grinned and waved at the indignant cat before he peeked in the skinny horizontal windows in the garage doors.

No Tahoe.

Ben frowned. The cat expressed her displeasure again, and Ben decided to ring the doorbell.

He waited.

Simon continued to complain through the glass to him, and Ben rang the doorbell again. *Of course he's not here. There's no vehicle.* He slowly walked away, half expecting Truman to sleepily open the door as he left.

No luck.

Where to next? Ryan Moody's house?

Ben stopped, his boot in the air, his gaze locked on blotches on the driveway.

Blood.

The biggest spot was still wet in the center. Ben studied the entire driveway. The blood was on the side closest to the house. *Where Truman's driver's door would have opened.*

Maybe he hit a dog in his driveway and drove it to the vet.

His heart pounding, Ben went to his car, popped the trunk, and found his blood-testing kit. His hands shook as he slipped on gloves and opened the small box. He studied the directions. He hadn't used this type of kit in years, but he knew it would tell him if the blood was human.

Squatting next to the biggest stain, he dipped the kit's long Q-tip into the blood. He broke the seal on a small container of liquid and stuck the wet end of the Q-tip in and stirred, letting the blood mix with the liquid. He put the lid back on and shook the tiny container. He set it down and ripped open a small envelope from the box, then shook out a white plastic stick with two windows on the flattest side.

He removed the lid of the container of the blood mixture and dripped three drops into the smaller round window on the stick.

He held his breath as he watched it soak up the stick toward the other opening. If one line showed in the second window, it meant the test was working. If two lines showed, it meant the blood was human.

Two lines appeared, and Ben nearly dropped the test.

Shit.

I need to call Lucas.

◆ ◆ ◆

"That's great about confirming the Hartlage parents," Jeff told Mercy late that afternoon as they met in his office. "What else do you have?"

He always wants more.

Eddie sat beside her in front of Jeff's desk, listening to her recap of the latest developments. She missed working with Eddie, but he was up to his neck in another case.

Mercy shared Dr. Peres's theory about the Asian skull.

Jeff's brows shot up. "I've heard people buy stuff like that. I consider it to be in the same class with serial killer memorabilia."

"What is wrong with people?" asked Eddie.

"Everyone has their little secrets and obsessions," said Jeff. Mercy caught him looking at her and immediately studied her notes.

Does he know the true reason I have my cabin?

"Chuck Winslow published an article that outed Britta Vale," Mercy added. "Now she's being harassed online."

"I repeat," said Eddie. "What is wrong with people?" He shifted in his seat, a black glare in his eyes.

"Is she safe?" Jeff asked.

"I think so. She said someone would have to dig deep to figure out where she lives. I can't imagine anyone would go to that effort. It's much easier to sit at a keyboard and vent, but she did have a prowler the other night. She found footprints outside her home, and her dog went ballistic."

"Before or after the article?" Eddie asked.

"Before."

"Probably not related, then," Jeff said. "But she does need to take precautions living in the remote place that she does."

"She's very cautious," asserted Mercy, remembering the rifle during their first visit.

"What are your next steps?" asked Jeff.

"I need to interview Don Baldwin, Grady Baldwin's brother—who, by the way, has been keeping tabs on Britta for Grady for the last twenty years."

"Could he be her prowler?" Eddie suggested.

"I wouldn't rule it out." She looked at the list in her hand. "I'd like to talk with Britta again. I feel like she's holding something back, but I don't know what. She's reached out to me twice now, so I think she's starting to trust me."

"That's the old cases—the solved cases," Jeff reminded her. "What are you doing on the new?"

"I'm waiting for some evidence on the Jorgensen case. And I want to talk with Janet Norris again. I told you she was Maria Verbeek's friend, right?"

Jeff nodded. "That's a coincidence I don't like."

"Me neither." Mercy went back to her list. "The investment firm Ray Jorgensen worked for had some legal issues not too long ago. I want to look into those and the neighbor's statement that Shaila Jorgensen asked questions about getting a divorce. Back to the Hartlage family, I keep stumbling over one aspect of their case—I can't figure out the brother-in-law's name. I know Corrine's maiden name was Palmer, but for the life of me I can't find his name or someone who knows him."

"No other relatives?" asked Eddie.

"I found Richard's uncle, who didn't know anything about Corrine's family. Darby has been digging, and she's stumped too."

"Maybe he wasn't a brother-in-law," suggested Jeff.

Mercy blinked.

I was so hung up on one aspect, I didn't consider any others.

"I didn't think of that!" Mercy wanted to bang her head on Jeff's desk. *Case tunnel vision.*

"Who originally told you the other man was Corrine's brother?"

"Kenneth Forbes. The neighbor said that was what Richard told him. I've been operating on hearsay." She closed her eyes and tipped back her head. "Stupid. Stupid. But I still haven't come across anything that indicates who he is."

"What about his mail in the house?" Eddie asked.

"None. And there's no mailbox at the home, so they must get their mail at the post office. I suppose if mail is no longer picked up, they return to the sender? I'll check."

"Good—"

The office door opened. "Mercy?" Melissa, the office manager, interrupted, worried lines creasing her forehead. "You've got a call. He seems very insistent."

"Who?" Mercy glanced at Jeff, embarrassed that their meeting had been disturbed.

"One of Truman's men. Ben Cooley."

Mercy checked her silenced phone, and alarm shot through her. She had four missed calls from the Eagle's Nest Police Department. "Something's up, Jeff. Can I take a minute?"

"Is there anything else we need to cover?"

"Not really."

"Then we're done. Tell Ben hello from me."

Mercy darted to her office and picked up the call, not bothering to sit down. "Ben?"

"Sorry to bug you at work, Mercy. Have you talked to Truman today?"

"No. He texted me early this morning, but I've been on the go all day." She tightened her grip on the phone. "What happened?"

"Well, we don't rightly know," Ben said slowly, reluctance in his voice.

"What *do* you know?" she asked firmly. *Get to it, Ben!*

"No one's heard or seen him since around nine this morning. He even missed an interview he'd scheduled for this morning. That's not like him. I've followed his steps best I could, but I hit a dead end."

"It's nearly four o'clock." Mercy forced her lungs to work properly. "How can you just be calling me now? I would think I'd be one of your first calls."

Ben was silent on his end.

"Ben? *What happened?*"

"We wanted to check all possibilities first because we didn't want you worried."

"Well, *now* I'm definitely worried. What possibilities?" She wanted to reach through the line and shake the older man to get him to talk faster.

"I found human blood in his driveway on the driver's side next to where he usually parks. It was fresh."

Mercy leaned on one hand on the desk, dizziness threatening. Her tongue stopped functioning and her mouth went bone-dry.

"His phone is going straight to voice mail," Ben continued. "His wireless carrier says his last location was his home. We checked the hospitals and clinics before calling you. We've put out a BOLO on his vehicle, and all the guys have clocked in to do patrols, looking for his Tahoe. We'll find him," he said in a caring tone.

Blood?

"His SUV is missing?" she whispered.

"Yes. He couldn't have been too hurt if he managed to drive away."

If he was the one driving.

"I'll be there in forty minutes." She ended the call. Sweat had bloomed under her arms and dampened her lower back. This wasn't like Truman. Panic exploded in her head and chest, making her legs shake. She shut it down. *Panic doesn't help anyone.*

"I have to go," she said out loud to her empty office.

Her brain shifted into get-shit-done mode.

I'll tell Jeff I'm leaving for the day and then follow up on Truman's recent calls.

Hold tight, Truman.

She refused to consider that it might be too late.

TWENTY-FOUR

The stress and concern in the Eagle's Nest Police Department were palpable.

When Mercy had stepped through the door, the four men inside had turned toward her as one.

Royce Gibson had immediately hugged her, and the young cop had whispered in her ear, "Don't worry. We'll find him," as his voice cracked.

Ben Cooley patted her on the back, a grandfatherly look on his face that made her want to curl up in his lap and hide.

Samuel was his usual resolute self, standing strong, his arms crossed on his chest, determination filling his gaze. No hugs; that wasn't his style. Lucas was working the phone and held up a hand to her as he spoke into his headset.

This is Truman's family.

She'd locked her emotions behind a tiny door deep in her mind during the drive to Eagle's Nest, but being among these concerned men who loved their boss nearly broke that door down. Her eyes burned, and she struggled to stay in control.

"We've got county and state on board. County offered a detective, and he should be here soon," Samuel stated. His tone told her the experienced cop had taken the lead among the men. "All their patrols are keeping an eye out for Truman's vehicle. I suspect he went off the road." The other men looked to him and nodded hopefully. "We've all been driving the roads for a few hours, and we'll get back out there, but we wanted to be here when you arrived."

Samuel's face blurred in her vision.

"Thank you," she choked out. "You guys are too kind."

Lucas got up from his desk. The young man slipped an arm around her shoulders and squeezed. It was like being hugged by a huge body-builder. Lucas planted a kiss on her temple. "The two of you matter to us," he said hoarsely. "He'll turn up."

She wouldn't lose hope.

And she refused to think about her last discussion with Truman. When she learned she'd disappointed him by forgetting to include him in the cabin decisions.

I'm so sorry, Truman.

"I want to see the scene." Mercy felt as if she could verify Truman's blood by looking at it. *He's a physical part of me.*

Stupid thought.

"How about photos?" Ben suggested.

"To start with," she said reluctantly, wondering if the men were protecting her from seeing something. "Did you go in his house?"

"I did," said Ben. "Everything looks perfectly normal—no blood inside. No evidence that he hurt himself in the house or cleaned up a cut in the sinks or shower. His cat was acting weird, though . . . it was like she knew something was up. I fed her."

She followed Ben to a computer screen. The photos were already up. She studied each one. Ben was right. The blood was on the driver's side of where Truman usually parked. She zoomed in on the largest pool of blood, taking heart because it wasn't big enough to indicate someone had bled out. In fact, if the spots had fully dried, no one would have noticed them unless they specifically looked.

She focused on the big spot, her mind probing for Truman as if she could mentally speak with him.

Truman?

No one answered.

I'd know deep inside if something horrible had happened, right?

"What's he worked on in the last twenty-four hours?" she asked, keeping her thoughts from spinning off into drain-circling pessimism. *Focus.*

"Last night he and I responded to a missing persons case," Samuel told her. "Clint Moody, age twenty-eight. His brother found blood in his bed and couldn't locate Clint or his vehicle. He's still missing."

Mercy stared at him, her heart sinking. "Like Truman? Blood left behind and a missing vehicle?"

Samuel scowled. "There are similarities. Truman had told me he'd originally wondered if Clint's case was related to yours. He said the patterning of the blood left behind in the bedroom resembled your cases. But this wasn't a family, no body was left behind . . . and the vehicle was missing."

"Truman didn't tell me about that case." *He didn't have a chance to.*

"Ryan Moody, Clint's brother, came in this morning. Said Truman had set up the time to talk to him about his brother," added Lucas. "He waited around awhile and I finally told him I'd have Truman call to reschedule."

"How was Ryan?" Samuel asked. "He was a mess last night."

"He said he didn't sleep at all last night. His eyes looked like it."

"Did you contact Truman to tell him Ryan was waiting?" Mercy asked.

"I shot him a text and then forgot about it," said Lucas. "I checked it later and it didn't indicate it'd been read."

Same with my texts to Truman. "What time did you text him?"

"Nine-oh-seven."

"His phone was probably off by then."

"We checked with our wireless provider. Truman hasn't used his phone at all today."

That's not good.

Mercy sucked in a deep breath. "Let's start a timeline." Ben nodded and headed to the back of the building. He returned a minute later with a large whiteboard and marker.

"What else has he handled? What did he do today?" Mercy asked, looking from man to man.

"He was here by seven," Lucas told her. "He was in his office most of the morning and then said he was going to talk to Nick Walker at the lumberyard. He left around eight thirty."

"I talked to Nick," said Ben. "He said Truman wasn't there more than ten minutes." Ben made notes on the board.

"What time was he supposed to talk with Ryan Moody?" she asked Lucas.

"Nine."

"Was Ryan on time?"

"Yes."

"Where did Truman go earlier in the day yesterday?"

Lucas sat back down at his computer and tapped the keys. "Domestic dispute call. The Dalrymples." The other three officers sighed and nodded. "A monthly occurrence. Usually whoever responds just talks to them for a while and they cool down. He also issued two speeding tickets—Neil Herrera and Gordon Pittman."

"Can you follow up on the tickets, Royce?" Mercy asked. The young cop nodded. "And Ben on the Dalrymples?"

"I already went to the Dalrymples'," said Samuel. "They said Truman did the usual. Put them in different rooms and talked with them. Said he was there about a half hour. I gathered they're both pretty fond of Truman. Said he's always patient."

Mercy looked at Lucas to indicate he should continue. "Minnie Neal reported her lawn mower had been stolen," he said.

"It's been raining for weeks," Mercy pointed out. "She wanted to mow?"

"Beats me," said Lucas. "In Truman's report it says she noticed her shed door was ajar and that appeared to be the only thing missing. She acknowledged it could have happened months ago."

"Ben?" Mercy asked.

"I'll talk to Minnie," he agreed.

"That's it for yesterday," said Lucas. "Pretty normal day except for the Moody case."

"Two missing vehicles. Two missing men," stated Mercy. "Let's focus there," she said.

The door opened, and Deschutes County Detective Evan Bolton stepped inside, brushing the rain off his sleeves.

Goose bumps rose on Mercy's arms as she remembered her previous thought about Bolton being the Angel of Death.

No.

Ben and Royce left to check on their assigned people and resume searching for Truman's Tahoe. Mercy and Samuel brought Bolton up to speed.

This additional set of sympathetic male eyes was about to push her over the edge. She steeled her core and concentrated on covering every angle.

No case tunnel vision allowed.

"What about that letter he received from the sovereign citizen?" Mercy asked. "He sent me a copy, but I haven't looked at it yet. He told me that supposedly that guy is selling the diplomatic licenses. Has anything else come of that?"

Lucas scratched his head as he exchanged a glance with Samuel. Both shook their heads. "Not that we've heard of."

"What is this?" Bolton asked.

Mercy told him about the letter demanding $3 million and then described the fake diplomatic licenses and license plates.

"You know," Samuel said, "Truman broke up a bar fight between the Moody brothers a few days ago. One of them had one of those stupid licenses—I don't remember which brother."

"I'll check," said Lucas.

Mercy's spine tingled as she felt a few pieces of the case fall into place. "That can't be a coincidence. One of those brothers and Truman both missing."

"Clint Moody was the brother with the fake ID, according to Truman's report," said Lucas. "Truman mentions in his report that someone in the bar told him Joshua Forbes was making them. The sovereign citizen who sent Truman the letter."

Mercy and Bolton looked at each other, agreement flowing between them. "Did Truman get too close to something?" Bolton asked. "Where's Joshua Forbes right now?"

"In the county jail," reported Lucas. "Truman and Royce went to his arraignment two days ago."

"I'll call and get us in to see him tonight," said Bolton, pulling out his phone and stepping away from the group.

"Where do you want me?" asked Samuel.

"Scouring the roads for Truman's Tahoe and Clint Moody's vehicle."

Samuel gave her a casual salute and disappeared out the door.

He's a good officer. Respectful and dependable. She hadn't missed the concern for Truman in his eyes, despite his stiff stance. It was the most emotion she'd ever seen in the tough cop.

"Joshua Forbes got out on bail today," stated Bolton as he returned.

"What time?"

"Noonish."

"Too late to have anything to do with Truman's disappearance—assuming something happened to him before he was scheduled to meet with Ryan Moody at nine."

"Never assume," Bolton recited.

"I try not to."

"I have Joshua Forbes's address."

"What are we waiting for?"

TWENTY-FIVE

Mercy parked behind Detective Bolton's vehicle, a strong sense of déjà vu affecting her.

I was just near this area.

The Hartlage home with the missing family was two miles away. Bolton had been there with her.

Memories of the sad, empty home and the small skull filled her thoughts. *Alison and Amy.* Mercy was no closer to finding their killer.

She got out of her car, pulled up her hood against the rain, and joined Bolton. The mobile home in front of them was dark.

"We were both just out here," she said to Bolton.

"I had the same thought," he said. "But I don't know what this could have to do with that case."

"Coincidence?" Mercy suggested, as her brain refused to accept the answer.

"Usually I don't believe in coincidences." He turned to the house. "Looks like no one is home. Let's check."

She followed him toward the house and then hung back, watching the home and windows as he knocked.

Silence.

He knocked again. "Joshua Forbes?" he said in a loud voice. "I'm Detective Bolton with Deschutes County. I'd like to ask you a few questions."

Mercy felt a clock ticking down on their window of time to find Truman. *Tick tick tick.*

She moved to the side of the home, shining a flashlight toward the back of the house. "No fence."

"Let's take a quick look around."

The two of them cautiously circled the house. Nothing was behind the home except for a wet garbage pile. "There's no car," Mercy stated. "I can't tell if he's been home today or not." Frustration filled her at the minor roadblock. It was too early in the case for this.

"I think most guys who get out of jail immediately hit the bars or a steak house."

"True. But I don't want to search every bar for him. Either we look for some relatives or—shit."

"What?"

"Joshua's last name is Forbes. I interviewed a Kenneth Forbes about the Hartlages because he was the closest neighbor. He's in a wheelchair and mentioned his son lived nearby and helped him out. That son has to be Joshua Forbes. I didn't make the connection until now." She dug in the pockets of her coat for her little notebook. "Kenneth Forbes gave me his son's cell number so I could ask him if he knew the Hartlage family. I called and left a message, but he never called me back." She quickly dialed the number and got voice mail. *Dammit.* "Truman didn't mention the name of the guy with the fake license to me . . . not that I would have remembered. It was a few days ago."

"Sounds like we need to visit the father for our next stop."

"He's not a pleasant person." Mercy remembered the older man in the wheelchair. "Very bitter. I didn't find out until later that he's an SC, so don't expect any help from him. Especially considering that his son was recently arrested."

"Great," replied Bolton dourly. "I'll follow you."

Mercy drove to Kenneth Forbes's home and was pleased to see lights on. No other car was present except for the old abandoned sedan she'd noticed on her first visit. She lowered her expectations about finding Joshua Forbes tonight. She already had no expectation of help from his father.

Dammit. Are we chasing the wrong lead?

As on Mercy's previous visit, Kenneth Forbes rolled out onto the porch before she and Bolton could reach his home. This time he had a rifle across his lap.

"What do you want?" he hollered at them.

"Mr. Forbes, I met you the other day," said Mercy, holding up a hand to block his bright outdoor lights from her eyes. "I'm Special Agent Kilpatrick. I talked to you about the Hartlage family."

"I remember. I'm not senile yet," he snapped. "Who's with you?"

"I'm Deschutes County detective Evan Bolton."

"You're the ones who locked up my boy."

"So I heard," replied Bolton.

"Damn fool. Thinks he's untouchable."

Mercy and Bolton exchanged a glance. *And the father doesn't believe his son should be untouchable?* Mercy felt a little hope that Kenneth Forbes might cooperate.

"Is Joshua around?" Mercy asked. "We stopped by his home, but no one is there."

Kenneth didn't invite them in out of the rain. "I haven't seen hide nor hair of him for days. Even before he was arrested."

"Did you know he was released today?"

The man gave a short laugh. "Shit, yes. I posted his damn bail. I sent a friend to withdraw the money from my account and pay it." He looked grim as he shook his head. "You'd think I'd hear from Joshua after that. No thanks or nothin'."

Mercy realized he was slightly drunk and suspected that was advantageous for their questioning.

"Where do you think he went?" she asked.

"Hell if I know. Did you check the bars?"

"Not yet," she admitted. "Where does he work at?" she asked, wondering if they could find him there in the morning.

"Not working. He's between jobs. Usually works construction, but it's been slow with the rain. And don't bother asking me the last company he worked with, because that boy don't tell me anything. He's probably worked for a half dozen different companies in the last two years. Bounces around like a beach ball."

Mercy suspected Joshua liked to get paid under the table.

"How about his friends?" Bolton asked a question for the first time.

Kenneth glared at him, and even through the rain, Mercy could see the annoyance in his sharp blue eyes. "You two act like I run my son's life. I don't know who he hangs around with."

"Do the names Clint or Ryan Moody ring a bell?" Mercy wasn't ready to give up.

He scratched his short beard. "Moody might be familiar. Don't know the first names," he said absently. Kenneth seemed to refocus, and suspicion narrowed his brows. "Why do you want him, anyway? You need to haul him back to jail? I just paid to get him out."

"Nothing like that," Mercy quickly assured him. "We want to ask him about a missing persons case."

"That why you asked about the Moody name?"

"Yes."

"Good luck getting him to answer any calls. I've left two voice mails and he's ignored them."

"Do you need some errands done?" Mercy wondered if he was low on groceries if his son hadn't been around.

"Nah. I'm well stocked. Say . . ." He looked uncomfortable, as if he wanted to say more.

Mercy waited.

"Did you figure out what happened to those girls?" he asked gruffly.

Alison and Amy Hartlage. "They were murdered in the home," she said in a quiet voice. *Is that sympathy in his tone?*

His eyes widened. "How do you know?"

"We found the remains. We're working on the case."

He shifted in his chair, looking down at his hands. "Just askin'."

"Thank you for your help, Mr. Forbes. If I leave my card, will you have Joshua contact us when you see him?"

He shrugged. "I can't make him do anything."

Mercy went up the ramp to the porch to hand him her card. Now she smelled the alcohol. He took the card without looking at it.

She and Bolton walked back to their vehicles, and she wondered if they'd just wasted another twenty minutes.

"I'm going to check in with Lucas," she said, dialing her phone.

"I'll try the cell number for Joshua again," replied Bolton.

Lucas had no news for her. No Tahoe. No Truman.

Bolton immediately reached Joshua's voice mail.

"I'll request a location and list of recent calls from Joshua's wireless provider," said Bolton. "But we probably won't have a result until tomorrow. What do you want to do next? Checking bars seems fruitless."

"I think we should shift gears and go to the Moody home."

"Agreed."

Tick tick tick.

TWENTY-SIX

Mercy was nearly to the Moody house when her phone rang. She recognized the Eagle's Nest Police Department's phone number on her dashboard, and her heart climbed into her throat. She couldn't hit her answer button quick enough.

"They've found Clint Moody's truck," Lucas told her. "But not Clint."

Not Truman.

Disappointment made her want to pull over and cry.

She swallowed the lump in her throat. "Send me the address. I'll tell Detective Bolton."

"I'm sorry it wasn't the news you wanted, Mercy." Lucas sounded as crushed as she felt.

"Soon," she told him. "If they can find Clint's truck, they'll find Truman's."

Am I reassuring Lucas or myself?

Her hands were shaking too hard to pull Bolton's phone number up on her dashboard, so she steered her Tahoe to the side of the road and parked. Bolton did the same and was out of his vehicle and at her door as she opened it.

"What happened?" Tension made the tendons in his neck stand out.

"Moody's truck has been discovered." Her voice sounded wrong, flat. "Without Clint."

He went perfectly still, as if he was waiting for more news. "I'm sorry, Mercy," he finally said.

She forced a weak smile. "It's a step in the right direction. Lucas sent me the address. I'll forward it to you in case we get separated."

"I'll be right behind you." He put a hand on her shoulder, his eyes sad. "Truman will turn up."

Bolton had headed back to his vehicle before Mercy registered the kind gesture. She'd always known Evan Bolton was a good investigator, but he always felt . . . detached when she encountered him. As if he was just riding along with life, waiting for it to finish up. She'd never gotten a peek behind his shields before just now.

She closed her Tahoe door, punched the address from Lucas into her GPS, and pulled a U-turn. Bolton's headlights followed her, the rain blurring the outline of his truck.

A lot of good people had her back. And Truman's. For the first time since she'd heard the news of Truman's disappearance, she felt a small measure of calm.

The ticking clock in her head quieted by a few decibels.

◆ ◆ ◆

"I don't understand how the truck got through a locked gate," Mercy said to the county deputy who'd located Clint's truck.

The truck was partially submerged in a pond at the bottom of the abandoned rock quarry. Only the cab's windows and part of the hood were visible. She watched as a county evidence team rigged big lights to shine on the truck and started taking pictures. She was stunned at their fast response. Bolton told her the team had been waiting for the signal to roll the moment they heard the Eagle's Nest police chief was missing.

But this isn't for Truman.

"The padlock on the gate looked new to me," said the deputy. "The key I had didn't work, so I cut off the lock. I suspect whoever dumped the truck here did the same thing and then replaced the lock."

"The truck might not have been found for months," Mercy murmured.

"We're lucky a few teenagers got tired of being stuck inside due to the rain. They got their dirt bikes around the gate and tore around in the quarry. I see a lot of it during the summer months."

"They rode in the rain?" Mercy was skeptical.

The deputy shrugged. "Why not? They're boys. Anyway, they called in the truck. I suspect they found it a few hours ago but didn't think anything of it once they'd looked to see if anyone was inside. They got their riding time in and then reported it."

Mercy eyed the deputy's waders. "And you checked it out more thoroughly when you got here. Do you always have waders in your vehicle?"

"Yes," he answered simply. "The windows were down on the truck. I grabbed a pole and felt around in the dirty water inside the cab. The boys were right. There's nothing in there."

"I bet someone left the windows down to ruin evidence," said Bolton, glowering at the submerged truck.

A tow truck worked its way down the winding road to the bottom of the quarry.

"We need to drag the pond."

Neither man replied to Mercy's statement; they had both been thinking the same thing.

She walked away from the two men, following the edge of the pond away from the bustle around Clint's truck, her gaze glued to the black water.

Is Truman in there?

Fighting back the urge to plunge into the pond and search, she shoved her hands in her pockets. Tears threatened, but she couldn't look away from the water. Its surface constantly rippled under the falling rain. Her gaze bounced from one movement on the water to the next, as she hoped to spot something that everyone else had missed.

What's done is done. If he's in there, there's nothing I can do.

Hot tears tracked both her cheeks, and she furiously brushed them away. "Fucking hell. Damn you, Truman! *Where are you?*"

You can't do this to me.

With a start she realized she had to contact his family. His parents were in California, his married sister in the Seattle area. Mercy had never spoken with or met any of them. The thought of telling his family he was missing made her tears run faster, and her stomach churned at the thought of making those horrible calls.

I'll ask Ben to do it.

Guilt shamed her for being too weak to face his family, but right now she was struggling to even stand upright. She took a few steps toward the water, again searching for something . . . anything.

"What the hell?" A hand grabbed her upper arm and yanked her backward.

She blinked at Bolton as she caught her balance. "Wh-what?"

"Don't go in the water."

"I wasn't going to."

He pointed at her boots, and she looked down. They were wet to halfway up her calves.

She was speechless, blinking at her wet boots. "I didn't notice," she murmured.

"Hey." Bolton took hold of her other arm to turn her toward him. "We'll find him."

But there was doubt in his brown eyes. Uncertainty and fear broke loose and roared through her, making her thoughts turn darker.

"You don't know that," she whispered. "I don't know that. *No one knows.*" Her vision tunneled on his face.

He gave her a small shake, and she broke his grip with a rapid swing of her forearms. "*Do not* shake me," she snapped as anger replaced her fear.

Bolton took a step back, his eyes cautious. "I'm sorry. You suddenly went white. I thought you were about to pass out."

"I'm fine." She straightened her shoulders, seizing inner strength from her rush of anger. "Back to the truck."

She marched away.

I can do this.

The scent of coffee woke Mercy.

She stared at the ceiling in her bedroom for two seconds and then snatched her silent phone off the dresser.

Truman?

She scanned for missed calls, missed texts, and relevant emails. Nothing. The silence about Truman was crushing. No news that progress had been made overnight while she slept. She sent Truman her usual morning text and watched the screen, waiting, hoping.

Nothing.

Finally she set down her phone and lay stiffly, searching for motivation to crawl out of bed, since it was nearly seven. Cupboards banged in the kitchen, and she realized she had an important task.

I need to tell Kaylie.

Last night her niece had been asleep when Mercy got home. Mercy had collapsed into bed after several hours at the rock quarry and then proceeded to lie awake forever, her mind spinning as she made a to-do list for the next day. Several times her thoughts had been overtaken by Truman, wondering if he was safe, or warm, or dry, resulting in a desperate need to hit something. She'd considered going to her cabin site and doing something physical, but cell service was spotty up there, and she didn't want to miss a call.

She swung her legs out of bed and made herself go face Kaylie.

The teenager sat at the table, dressed in plaid flannel pajama pants and a baggy T-shirt, eating a bowl of oatmeal. Dulce sat on the chair next to her. Kaylie glanced up as Mercy walked in and did a double take, concern on her face.

"Rough night? I didn't hear you come in."

Mercy pulled out a chair across the table from her niece. "You don't look ready for school."

Kaylie grinned. "It's Saturday. Cade's coming to town and we're going shopping."

My days are blending together.

"You haven't seen him in a long time." *I'm stalling.*

The girl gave a one-shouldered shrug. "It's his job. Now we just hang out when he has a few days off. I think we're better off as good friends."

Mercy agreed.

Kaylie froze, holding a spoonful of oatmeal halfway to her mouth. "What is it? What happened?" She dropped the spoon in her bowl, staring at Mercy. "You look ill."

"Truman is missing," Mercy blurted. "He's been missing for almost twenty-four hours."

The relief at getting the words out turned to pity as her niece's face crumpled. Mercy moved to the chair next to Kaylie, scooping up the cat and placing her in the girl's lap, where Kaylie clung to the animal. "Where is he? Is he . . ."

"We don't know anything." Mercy wrapped both arms around the teen, resting her forehead against the girl's temple. "Every cop in the state is looking for him."

"But how can he just *disappear*?" Tears flowed.

"I wish I knew." Kaylie had lost her father less than a year ago, and Truman had filled in when a father figure was needed. He and Kaylie had a tight connection. Another loss would devastate her.

I can't think like that yet.

"We'll find him," Mercy promised. "It's a good possibility that he drove off the road somewhere and doesn't have phone service." *And is too hurt to get out.* She refused to tell Kaylie about the blood.

Kaylie lifted the cat and buried her nose in her fur as she cried. Dulce licked at the tears on her cheek.

"I'm so sorry." Mercy didn't know what else to say.

"Your stupid jobs," the teen spit out. "Both you and Truman. Someday you might not come home either." Fresh tears.

Mercy said nothing and held the girl tighter.

Her phone rang. Mercy let go and grabbed the phone from the kitchen counter, answering without looking at the number. "Agent Kilpatrick."

They were to start dragging the pond this morning.

"Mercy, it's Lucas. We've found Truman's truck—not Truman, but his truck." His words rang with repressed excitement.

"Send me the address. I'll be there as soon as I can."

TWENTY-SEVEN

An hour later, Mercy stood next to a fire truck in the middle of a campground that was still closed for the winter, watching smoke and steam rise from Truman's Tahoe. "Someone reported a fire," Lucas had told her during her drive to the campground. "The fire department put it out, spotted the logo on the door, and then called us."

All of Truman's men and Detective Bolton had arrived before her and now stood in a small half circle staring at the vehicle. They'd done a search of the campground and immediate area with the county deputies and found nothing. The Portland FBI office was sending out an evidence team, but they wouldn't arrive for several hours. Truman's missing persons case had escalated. An attack on a police officer was never taken lightly.

No longer would they wonder if Truman had driven off the road. Now they knew someone had taken him and his vehicle.

Why?

Mercy kept staring at the smoking driver's seat, thankful Truman wasn't sitting there, but the torched vehicle didn't bode well for Truman's health. It had been set on fire for a reason. Probably to destroy evidence. Possibly from a deadly crime.

Panic swamped her, and she reined it in.

"They had to know the smoke from the fire would be noticed," she said to Bolton.

"Does that mean they didn't care if the truck was found?" he asked. "Or that they're stupid?"

Mercy didn't have an answer for him.

"Could the firefighters tell how long it'd been burning?" she wondered.

"One of them estimated less than an hour," said Samuel. "It was soaked with gasoline inside. They said it burned fast and hot."

Mercy smelled it. The air was heavy with the pungent scent of gas and burning plastic. She shuddered as the smell triggered memories of her cabin burning two months ago.

Truman hated fire. Twice he'd been burned in bad fires, and he could have lost his life in either.

Fire keeps trying to take him down.

Not yet.

She hated the expressions on the Eagle's Nest cops' faces. They gazed at the truck as if they were mourning their boss.

It wasn't time for mourning. Truman was waiting to be found.

Who started the fire?

"Let's talk to Ryan Moody," she told Bolton. "Has he been notified that his brother's truck was found?"

"No. I wanted to wait until today. Let's go."

The two of them headed toward their vehicles, leaving the smoke behind.

◆　◆　◆

A Ford Explorer was parked in the driveway of Ryan Moody's house. Mercy hoped that indicated he was home.

She rang the doorbell as Bolton stood near the long driveway, watching the side entrance of the house. Impatient, she pushed the doorbell twice and rapped on the door. "Ryan Moody?" she yelled. "I'm with the FBI and want to talk to you about your brother."

Glancing back at Bolton, she noticed the curtains flutter at the home across the street. Truman's report had stated he'd interviewed the woman living there, and that she frequently watched the Moody home. *Looks like we have an audience.*

The handle of the door rattled, and the door opened enough to be caught by its chain. A dark-haired man sized her up. "Did you say FBI?" he asked.

"I did." Mercy held out her ID.

"Is this about Clint? Did you find my brother?" he asked, his voice rising in hope.

"Yes, this is about your brother, but no, we haven't found him."

Ryan's face fell. He closed the door, unhooked the chain, and opened the door wider.

Mercy kept her eyes on his face as soon as she realized Ryan wore only boxers with his T-shirt. He had a bad case of bedhead and a giant crease down a cheek from his pillow. She held out her card, and as he stepped closer to take it, she caught a strong whiff of morning breath. *He looks—and smells—as if he's been asleep for hours.*

Bolton joined her on the porch and handed over his card as well. Ryan opened the door farther and invited them in. He moved some magazines and boxes off the couch so they could sit and gave a jaw-stretching yawn. "Do you mind if I get the coffee going? I can't function without it."

"Go ahead," said Mercy.

He padded to the attached kitchen and stuck a carafe under the faucet.

"I don't think he's been anywhere this morning," she said in a low voice to Bolton. "They roughly estimated that the fire started around six. That's only two and half hours ago. He looks like he's been crashed all night."

Bolton nodded, his gaze on the man in the kitchen.

Ryan shoved the carafe in the brewer and then sat down across from them. He was still bleary eyed. "You said this was about my brother."

"We found your brother's truck last night."

His eyes widened. "Where? How come no one called me? But you didn't find Clint?" He leaned forward, his gaze darting between Bolton and Mercy.

"No one notified you because it was late last night. Do you know the abandoned rock quarry off Bowers Road?" Mercy asked.

"Sure. It was found there?"

"Yes."

"Let me get dressed and I'll go out there with you." Ryan stood, ready to dash to his bedroom.

"Wait." Mercy held up a hand. "It's already been towed away."

"To where? Maybe I can spot something that indicates where Clint went."

"Ryan." She struggled to find the right words. "The truck was up to its windows in a pond. Everything is soaked and muddy."

"You said it was at the rock quarry." He sat back down, confusion and caution on his face.

"There was a pond in the bottom of the quarry from all the rain we've had." She held his gaze.

"Did you search the pond?" His words were slow, as if his brain had just connected with what the location could mean.

"It's happening as we speak," said Bolton.

Indecision flickered in Ryan's gaze. "I don't think I want to watch that."

"You'll be the first to know if we find something," Mercy promised, her heart going out to the sibling. "Have you recalled anything else that might help us find your brother?"

"No. It's all I've been thinking about since that night." He frowned. "Is Chief Daly not on the case anymore? I mean, he's a decent guy and stuff, but I'd much rather have the FBI looking for my brother."

Mercy couldn't speak. For the last five minutes Truman had been off her mind, but Ryan brought her mass of emotions back in a drowning rush.

"No, he's not on the case now," answered Bolton. "Do you know a Joshua Forbes?"

"Is he a suspect?" Ryan's mouth gaped.

"No. But we'd like to talk to him. I take it you know him?"

"Clint hung around with him sometimes. He's okay when he's not pushing that sovereign shit."

Mercy found her voice. "Chief Daly's report said Clint had a fake diplomatic license on him after the bar fight the other day. Did he get it from Joshua?"

"Yeah. He sells them, but he gave Clint one for free. Clint thought it was funny, but I told him to never let a cop see it. Forbes tried to recruit us with all that pay-no-taxes bullshit. They're a messed-up bunch. If we don't pay taxes, who pays for the damn roads and forest management? God?" He shook his head in disgust.

"Have you seen him recently?"

"Nah."

Bolton asked a few more questions, but Mercy knew the interview was done. She reassured Ryan they were doing everything they could to find his brother and thanked him for his time.

Outside, Bolton told her he didn't think Ryan could have torched Truman's SUV. "You were right that he looked like a man who's been sleeping hard for hours," he said. "And there was no scent of gasoline on him or in the house. Usually it sticks to a person no matter if they change their clothes and wash their hands."

"I only smelled morning breath," said Mercy. "How long do you think it will take to drag the pond?"

"Not long. It wasn't very big."

She checked the time as they walked to their vehicles. It was nearly nine. *The same time they last heard from Truman yesterday.*

Tick tick tick.

She bit the inside of her lip to prevent falling apart in front of Bolton, and tasted blood. "I need to get to the office."

He halted, turning to her in shock. "Surely they'll let you have the day off."

"I don't want the day off. I need to keep moving and keep working on Truman's case. I can't sit around and wait. There are plenty of people searching the roads for him, and I can be more helpful directing the FBI's resources along with a computer and a telephone." *I hope that's true.*

Bolton took a hard look at her. "Are you sure you want to work?"

"Positive."

His face said he didn't believe her.

This man doesn't know me at all.

"Let me know when they're done with the pond," she told him. Deschutes County had taken the lead on the Clint Moody case, and Truman's was in the hands of the FBI.

"We're going to find him."

"I'm starting to despise that phrase."

His eyes were full of sympathy.

I'm starting to despise that look too.

TWENTY-EIGHT

His shivering wouldn't stop.

Pale light crept in some of the cracks around the door, and Truman figured it was morning. The concrete floor of the shed felt like a sheet of ice, and even though he knew the temperature was nearly twenty degrees above freezing, he was surprised he hadn't frozen to death. He'd fully expected not to wake up this morning—because of either the cold or his head injury. He'd vomited three times yesterday, and double vision was making him dizzy. No doubt he had a concussion. Maybe something worse.

He'd woken still leaning against the wall, his right arm suspended above him, cuffed to a four-foot-long horizontal pipe along the rear concrete wall of the shed. His hand was long numb. He stood and massaged it, willing feeling back into the icy fingers. Pain finally shot through the nerves in his hand and he welcomed the discomfort. It meant he hadn't destroyed the circulation to his hand. Yet.

The pipe was about three feet off the ground. Just far enough that he couldn't lie down to sleep. Several times during the night he'd stood, gripping the bar for balance and letting the blood run back into his hand. He'd investigated the ends of the pipe. They were firmly embedded in the concrete wall. No hope of getting them loose.

Someone had left him a large jar of water and four empty jars. He'd made use of one empty jar during his vomiting sessions and used another to piss in. He suspected that if he could see better in the poor light, he'd see blood in his urine. His kidneys still hurt from his beating yesterday.

Everything hurt. His hair held several large patches of dried blood. The head injuries had swollen, and touching the spots made him hiss. His lower back felt as if shards of glass were in his kidneys. The worst pain was in his left arm, and he suspected a bone had fractured near the elbow. It hurt like a son of a bitch to move, which doubly sucked because it was his free arm. He licked his dry lips, tasting blood and gingerly touching the rough edges of a large gash on the side of his mouth. His teeth ached on that side but were all present. One positive thing.

Mercy must be going nuts.

It hurt to imagine her frustration and fear at the unanswered phone calls and texts. No doubt she'd gone to his house and wondered what happened.

At least Simon will be fed.

He'd get out of this fucking shed and back to her if it was the last thing he ever did. Pain be damned.

He hadn't seen any people or heard any voices since the attack in his driveway. Apparently the beating had continued after he blacked out. When he woke, he'd found himself in the shed, handcuffed to the pipe, with no idea how he'd gotten there.

Who hates me enough to do this?

Plenty of people got angry when he arrested them, but most eventually understood they'd had it coming. No one had sworn revenge in his presence.

He remembered hearing one of the attackers call him a fucking cop. Hate had infused the word. *Am I here solely because I was the closest available cop to wreak havoc on?*

He'd been in his own driveway.

They must have followed me.

Twenty times over the last year, he'd sworn he would install security cameras at his home. It had never happened. He crossed his fingers that one of his neighbors had cameras and his officers had thought to check them.

Assuming they know where I disappeared from.

His truck would still be in front of his house. He hoped.

Assume nothing.

He had confidence in his men and Mercy. They would push until they tracked him down.

He closed his eyes as another wave of dizziness swamped him.

"Wake up."

A pause.

"Wake up."

Truman jerked and gasped for breath as cold water splashed his face. He tried to lunge forward but was stopped by the handcuff on his wrist. Pain shot up his left arm as he wiped the water from his face, making his vision blur. He sucked in a breath, struggling to stay conscious and look at the man standing before him.

He was tall and lean, with slightly stooped shoulders, wearing a heavy coat and holding a cowboy hat in one hand and Truman's now-empty water jar in the other. Truman couldn't see his eyes with the light streaming in the door behind his captor.

A memory of his field-training officer popped in his head. This man had the same stance and physical build, but Truman didn't recognize him.

My hand. Numbness had set in again, and he slowly slid up the wall to let the blood run to his hand, never taking his gaze from the stranger.

A silent power struggle filled the small shed. Truman knew the stranger was waiting for his captive to ask who'd locked him up or where they were.

Truman kept his mouth shut. He didn't want the stranger to know he knew nothing.

The silence stretched for thirty seconds as Truman stared at where he knew the man's eyes would be.

"Stubborn, eh?" the man finally said.

Truman said nothing.

"Know why you're here?"

Silence.

The man shifted his stance, frustration rolling off him. "Think you're tough, do you? I bet you don't feel so powerful now, chained up like a pig."

In the pit of Truman's belly a small snake of fear started to coil.

"You'll get what's comin' to ya, fucking cop. Fucking pig." The man snorted in laughter. "I was right. You *are* a chained-up pig. Damn, it stinks like pigs in here."

"I'd like some food," Truman stated.

"You won't need food." The man tossed the glass jar in his hand into a corner, where it shattered. "Won't need that either." He shoved his hat on his head and turned toward the door, giving Truman a clear view of a profile with a strong nose and chin. He slammed the door shut behind him, and a bolt scraped across the wood.

Truman slid back down the wall, his heart racing as rampant thirst instantly overtook him. He looked in the direction of the shattered water jar, unable to see the shards. *Fuck me.*

He shoved the image of drinking the only alternative fluid in the shed out of his mind.

What will he do to me?

Mercy's face arose in his mind, and he ached to touch her, feel her warmth beside him. Several nights ago, they'd stretched out on his couch together and watched TV, sharing a bottle of wine and Chinese takeout. Simon had alternated between trying to paw food from their plates and wedging herself between them.

It'd been an intimate, calm evening. And looking back now, he realized it'd been heaven.

He wanted it again.

Hurry up, Mercy.

TWENTY-NINE

Mercy quickly reviewed her current murder cases in her office, getting them ready to set aside. Truman was her priority now.

I promise I won't leave Amy and Alison for too long.

Sporadic updates came from the Eagle's Nest officers and Bolton. No one in Truman's neighborhood had seen anything occur in his driveway. No one had outdoor security cameras. Evidence at the campground did not indicate how Truman's truck had gotten there.

An arson investigator was examining the truck, but Mercy was pessimistic about him finding anything. Yes, it was arson. Yes, it was gasoline. How could there be anything left in the fire to lead them to Truman's abductor?

Struggling to focus, Mercy read the latest reports from the Hartlage investigation.

She was pleased that four of the Hartlages had been positively identified, but the unknown Caucasian male skull she and Dr. Peres had found farther down the slope still bothered her. Only Kenneth Forbes had stated that Corrine Hartlage's brother was living with them. There was nothing else to back up his identity.

She had confidence in Dr. Peres's theory that the Asian skull was a war trophy. Especially after Mercy had done some online research. People collected weird shit.

But that doesn't help me find their killer.

The family's old Suburban hadn't turned up. No one had used their missing credit cards or accessed their bank accounts, so the motive didn't appear to be financial. The post office had closed their mailbox when no one renewed the lease and returned all the mail that hadn't been picked up. The Hartlages got their water from their well and generated their own power. They'd truly been off the grid. So far off the grid that no one had missed them for eight months. A calendar hanging on the back side of a kitchen cupboard door was open to August of the year before. The few pieces of mail that had been found in the home were postmarked last August.

Those weren't confirmations of the time of disappearance, but several of the windows had been left open, and summer clothing was in the laundry. All that was enough to make Mercy pretty darn certain the Hartlages had been gone for eight months, and that had been more than enough time for their remains to skeletonize.

Mercy understood people not being missed for a week or two, but was this family so socially isolated that there was no one to care?

Is that the reason this family was targeted? The killer suspected no one would notice for a long time?

Switching to the Jorgensen file, she wondered if the killer had planned to remove the Jorgensen family from their beds, but been interrupted by the neighbor. That family hadn't lived in isolation like the Hartlage family. Sharla Jorgensen had many social interests, the kids attended school, and the husband had an employer.

The trace evidence from both homes had yet to reveal that a unique presence had visited both homes.

Her gaze fell on Janet Norris's name. The woman had been involved with the Verbeeks and the Jorgensens, and the coincidence still made the hairs rise on the back of her neck. But coincidences did occur. People knew people. The population in the area where the families had lived wasn't huge. It could happen.

Can I connect her to the Hartlages?

Mercy made a note to see if the Hartlages had ever stayed at the DoubleTree hotel where Janet worked.

She switched again to Truman's case.

Joshua Forbes's traffic stop with Truman continued to dart through her thoughts. She and Detective Bolton had yet to track down the sovereign citizen. A county deputy had gone to Joshua's home that morning and reported no one was home.

Did he leave the area?

He could be at a girlfriend's house.

He could be crashed on a friend's couch, venting about his time in jail.

She'd assigned more officers to track down Joshua Forbes. Currently it was the best lead in Truman's case.

The ringing of her cell phone distracted her, and Britta's name and number showed on her screen. Mercy had added the woman to her contacts after she'd called two days before.

"Agent Kilpatrick."

"I've got a problem," Britta stated in a calm voice.

"How can I help?" Mercy leaned back in her chair, determined to win more of the woman's confidence.

"That reporter Chuck Winslow is sitting on my floor. I may have shot him."

"What? Is he dead?" Mercy jumped up as shock shot through her nerves.

"Oh no," Britta assured her. "I was loaded with buckshot and I purposefully shot wide. But he does have some lead in him. He'll live, but he's not happy with me."

"Why did you do that?" she asked in a hushed voice, glancing toward her door, wondering if anyone in the office had heard her shriek.

"He broke into my house."

"Ohhhh." Mercy sat back down, her thoughts racing. "That's not good."

"That was my thought when I spotted him. Fucking asshole." Britta's last two words were said away from her phone, and Mercy suspected they were aimed at Chuck.

"You better call an ambulance."

"He doesn't deserve an ambulance. And a hospital will have to report that he's been shot. That involves the police."

"True." Mercy now understood the reason for Britta's call. She needed an advocate with the police. "Can I talk to him for a second?"

"I'll have to hold the phone."

"Is he hurt that bad?"

"No, but his hands are tied."

Mercy briefly closed her eyes. "That's fine." Chuck had had no idea what he was getting into when he took on Britta Vale. *I bet he knows now.*

"What?"

That distinctive male voice made her chest tighten. "How badly are you hurt, Chuck?"

"She shot me. I've got a dozen holes in my legs and there is damned blood everywhere."

"Any blood spurting or pulsing? Or is the blood flow slow?"

"Does it matter?" he shot back. "I'm going to sue this bitch."

"Yes, it matters. Pulsing could mean you'll bleed out within a few minutes." Mercy felt oddly calm. Talking to the jerk when he was in pain was rather satisfying.

"It's slow. It's mostly stopped," he admitted.

"Are the shots in the front of your thigh?"

"Yes, now call me an ambulance and the police! This woman is psychotic!"

"I'll have her call one as soon as I hang up. I'm coming too." She paused. "Is it true you entered her house?"

"I'm not talking to you."

So yes he did.

"Agent Kilpatrick?" Britta was back on the line.

"Call him an ambulance. I'm on my way. Since he was facing you when you shot, you could have felt threatened. It strengthens the argument that you defended yourself."

"He's no threat. I shot him because he was in *my house.* I also took his gun away from him. He had it in a stupid ankle holster."

He was armed too. Another reason to defend herself.

Britta shouldn't face any consequences for shooting an armed man in her home. Especially since she'd reported a prowler a few nights before.

"Call the ambulance, Britta," Mercy ordered again. "It'll look better if you show you tried to help him, since he's injured."

"All right," she said with great reluctance.

"I'll call for a county deputy to respond, and I'll be there as soon as possible. No more shooting, Britta," she said firmly.

"Of course not." She sounded offended.

Mercy ended the call and sat motionless at her desk for a moment, mentally struggling to leave Truman's investigation.

Deschutes County and his officers are still actively working. I need more leads.

Britta has no one to help her. It won't take more than an hour.

She slowly stood and grabbed her bag, promising to refocus on Truman once she cleaned up Britta's issue.

The ambulance and a county deputy were already at Britta's home when Mercy arrived.

Chuck Winslow sat on the front porch of Britta's home as his wounds were examined and cleaned. Britta stood farther back on the porch, keeping Chuck in her line of sight while speaking with the deputy, who took notes.

Mercy stopped next to Chuck and was greeted with a glare. Chuck was short. Napoleon short. He was in his midthirties, and his clothes always looked as if he'd just rolled out of bed. Today was no exception, but now his clothes sported patches of blood, and the responders had cut away part of his jeans. His legs were whiter than Mercy's—and that was saying something.

She put a fake smile on her face. "What is your problem with Britta, Chuck?" she asked in a saccharine voice, determined not to yell or curse at the man. Two witnesses were working on his leg. They would confirm that she'd been polite if Chuck tried to claim she'd threatened him. "First you publish her new name and her website online, nearly accusing her of hiding something about her family's deaths. Now you're caught in her house?"

Another plastic smile.

Chuck looked away, but the responders glanced at her, obviously listening.

"Do you have any idea how much online harassment she's dealt with since you did that?"

No answer.

"She feared people would come to her home. I guess you were the only one she needed to fear."

Silence.

"I assume you were her night prowler three nights ago. Her dog followed your trail back to the road."

He jerked his head to look at her, eyes flashing. "That wasn't me. I've never been out here before."

The only accusation he denies.

"We'll see." Mercy passed him to join Britta and the deputy. A huge wash of pain took her breath away as she focused on the deputy's uniform, a visual reminder that Truman was still missing. There was one positive aspect to Britta's problem; it'd taken Mercy's mind off Truman for several minutes.

I need to get back to his case.

She forced herself to keep walking and greet the two of them. Britta was tense, like a panther waiting to pounce. She was all black. Boots, jeans, sweater, and her long hair. For the first time, Mercy could read the large, ornate tattoo covering the front of the woman's neck. ASTRID&HELENA.

Her murdered sisters.

Every day she sees that in the mirror.

No wonder she carried survivor's guilt. She wore a constant reminder.

Today she'd skipped the thick black eyeliner, and her pale-blue eyes seemed lost in her face.

"It's pretty clear from the shots still in her wall that the man was in her home," the deputy said to Mercy. "But I'll have a detective and evidence team examine it."

"Good," said Britta. "I didn't do anything."

"Well, I wouldn't say exactly that. He does have a leg full of buck- shot," Mercy pointed out. "He refused to say anything to me except to deny that he was your prowler the other night."

Britta stilled, her breathing silenced. "Then who was it?"

Mercy knew it was a rhetorical question.

"I'm sorry about Truman," the deputy said to Mercy. "We've got every available patrol keeping an eye out."

"Thank you." Emptiness swamped her as the deputy excused himself to talk to Chuck.

"Who's Truman?" asked Britta, her pale gaze locked on Mercy.

"He's my . . . We're a couple." *Boyfriend* sounded juvenile. Kaylie had boyfriends, not Mercy. "He hasn't been heard from since yesterday morning." The words were awkward on her tongue.

"That's horrible. They're already looking for him? I thought they waited forty-eight hours."

"He's the chief of police for Eagle's Nest. They found blood . . ." Her voice trailed off. She couldn't physically say more.

Understanding flashed in Britta's gaze, and Mercy broke eye contact. "I think everything will be fine for you," Mercy said to the woman, forcing Truman out of her immediate thoughts. "Chuck will go to the hospital, and they'll talk to you some more, but even the deputy could see the evidence backs you up. Did Chuck say why he was here?"

"He claimed he wanted an interview."

"People who want interviews call you. They don't break into your home. How did he get in?"

Britta looked at the ceiling. "I left the door unlocked. I'd had my arms full when I got home, and I kicked the door closed behind me."

"He got lucky with his timing."

"He's lucky I was in a good mood."

Mercy held back a smile at the snark in Britta's tone. Her respect for the woman grew each time she encountered her. "I don't think you'll need me anymore. That deputy has your back."

"Thank you." Britta's eyes narrowed. "I hope your man turns up all right."

"Me too," she whispered, and she turned around to leave before she made a fool of herself in front of the tough woman.

Mercy moved down the stairs, passing Chuck. "Good luck with that lawsuit, you stalking creeper."

She didn't wait for his answer.

THIRTY

Truman lost track of the days and nights.

He speculated that two nights had passed, but it had felt like a week. He slept and woke with no discernible pattern. Sometimes he could see light through the cracks around the door; sometimes it was dark. The rain came in showers, pounding on the roof for a long time and then going silent. His dreams were full of Mercy and the tall stranger. He dozed as much as possible. If he couldn't be with Mercy, dreaming of her helped a little.

His longing to see Mercy had settled into a dull pain in every muscle. Or maybe the aches were from his beating. Either way, he knew that if he could hold her, the pain would go away.

When he dreamed of the stranger, the man's face was always barely out of sight, and Truman strained to see him, continuously falling short. If Truman was released now, he would never be able to identify the man.

No food had been brought. The water container remained in shards as the other jars slowly filled. The thought of drinking his urine was still repugnant.

He wondered at what point it would become acceptable.

He alternated between hunching in an almost-ball to stay warm and standing to give his arm relief. It was taking longer and longer each time to regain feeling in his hand.

One more night of sleep might be too much for it.

The tall man had briefly visited again and then left because of the "fucking ripe" smell in the shed. He'd mentioned something about other men and a disagreement, but Truman had ignored him, keeping his eyes closed because it felt as if someone had taken an ax to his skull. Light still flashed behind his closed eyelids, and he watched the show, searching for a distraction from his pain. And thirst.

So much water outside.

The rain taunted and teased him as his lips cracked and his saliva dried up. He'd never hated the rain so much.

Darkness settled in, and Truman wondered if it was from the rain clouds or if night had come.

Doesn't matter.

The door bolt scraped, and Truman pulled his feet closer to his body, turning his face away from the door. He didn't need the stranger swearing at him again. No booted feet sounded on the concrete, and Truman peered toward the door with one eye. A silhouette softly walked toward him, but it wasn't tall and lean, and instinctively Truman knew the person was young. He lifted his head.

"Don't move." The voice was also young.

The new stranger wore a thick coat and heavy-duty hiking boots. His hood was pulled up, and Truman could faintly make out a scarf around his neck and a knit cap under the hood, but his face was dark in the shadows. Truman's gaze shot past the stranger as a dog stepped through the door. Some sort of smallish hound with large floppy ears.

"What are you doing?" Truman's voice sounded as if sand were in his mouth.

"Getting you out." He had the voice of a teenager.

Is this a dream?

"Who are you?" Truman asked as hope sprang to life in his chest.

No answer. The stranger stopped in front of him, and Truman spotted the shape of powerful cutters in one hand. *Yes! I've dreamed of a pair a dozen times.*

The teen felt for the cuffs in the dark, fumbling with the part around Truman's wrist. "Don't know if this will work," the teen mumbled.

"Cut the links between the bracelets." *Is this really happening?*

Cold metal touched Truman's hand, and he hoped his rescuer could see if his fingers were out of the way.

There was a loud metal crunch. Truman's right arm fell to his side, and he wanted to cry in relief.

Using his left hand on the pipe, he pulled himself to standing and nearly blacked out from vertigo and the pain near his left elbow. The teen shoved his shoulder under Truman's armpit and wrapped an arm around his waist, bracing him upright. "Are you sick?" he whispered, worry in his voice.

Will he leave me behind?

"No. Just dizzy from standing up too fast." Excitement and concern over his health battled in his brain.

"We need to go!" Urgency raised his rescuer's voice.

"Where?" breathed Truman, concentrating on keeping his few stomach contents down.

"Out of here. Hurry up." The teen started forward and Truman tried to keep up with his steps. The fresh air filled his nose along with the scent of the rain, and he lifted his face to the heavy drops, opening his mouth.

Nothing had ever felt or tasted so good. *Thank you, God.*

The teen hooked a sharp left, heading behind the shed and toward the forest, the dog right behind them. Truman glanced over his shoulder. A faint light shone in the window of a small house.

"Who lives there?" he asked. *The asshole who visited me?*

"Walk faster!" The boy pushed and pulled him to the woods.

Truman tried to match his pace while his mouth stayed open to the rain, trusting the teen to guide their footsteps.

"Can I use your cell phone?" he asked the teen. He would call Mercy first and then the police.

"Don't have one."

Crap.

"Where are we going?" Truman asked again, overcome by images of a soft bed and hot food. And Mercy. Warmth shot through him at the thought of the dark-haired agent. Soon he would be with her.

"Does it matter?"

"No. Just get me the fuck away from here."

He had a woman to get back to.

THIRTY-ONE

The FBI office was empty except for Mercy.

Jeff had been the last one to leave and had ordered her not to stay too late. It was Sunday, after all.

That had been three hours ago. Another day had passed with no word on Truman. Now he'd been missing for two and a half days. She'd pushed the other agents in the office, not letting anyone sit idle in the search for Truman. They'd had meetings and brainstorming sessions as they used every tool available to them to figure out what had happened. Joshua Forbes was still missing. Deschutes County and Truman's own officers had worked overtime, following up on every possible lead, no matter how ridiculous. A Truman sighting in Portland had turned out to be a local resident. A bloody shirt found in a Bend park garbage can had turned out to be stained with ketchup.

Nothing.

All day the air surrounding Mercy had steadily grown thicker. It was becoming more difficult for her to move, to focus, and to breathe. Everything was heavy, weighing on her shoulders, her mind, and her composure. Pieces of her were splintering off, exposing her nerves and stealing her energy.

She couldn't leave the office. She didn't want to go home and tell Kaylie that there was no news. She was exhausted by the thought of another night of soothing the crying teen while Mercy desperately needed her own comfort. Consoling others as she slowly crumbled inside was too much.

Throughout the long day, the bag in her lower desk drawer had been calling her. An hour after Jeff left, she'd finally given in and pulled out the bottle of wine she and Truman had purchased on their last visit to the Old Mill District. Now the bottle was half gone, and she was no closer to wanting to go home.

She didn't want to see Truman's shirts in her closet or see his toothbrush and deodorant in her bathroom. His scent on the pillow next to her had disturbed her sleep every night. But she refused to remove it from her bed.

It would mean she'd given up. *I'll never give up.*

Touching the screen of her phone, she stared at the background photo. It was a shot Kaylie had snapped this winter of her and Truman outdoors on a snowy day at her cabin. The two of them had been laughing and unaware Kaylie caught them. It was a carefree moment. A scene of two perfectly happy people. Like a magazine ad. But it was from Mercy's real life. One she'd never imagined for herself.

Now her cabin was gone, and Truman was gone.

The pillars of her sanity were being ripped away piece by piece.

Is the universe testing me?

She took another long sip from her coffee cup of wine.

The not knowing was the worst. Not knowing if he was dead. Not knowing if she'd ever see him again. Not knowing *anything.*

When she'd been shot two months earlier, Truman had panicked at the thought that she would die in his arms.

This was worse. She had no one to touch. Nothing to see. Nothing she could attempt to control.

She felt powerless.

A few years ago, at the insistence of a coworker, she'd taken a glider ride outside of Portland. "It's soothing and peaceful," the woman had said. "Just you and the sky."

Peace held a strong appeal.

The plane had towed the glider, the pilot, and Mercy into the sky and then let go. No engine.

The lack of control had terrified her. She'd felt trapped and helpless. Like now.

A text pinged her phone. UNLOCK THE OFFICE DOOR. It was Bolton. She shuffled her way to the front door, surprised at how unsteady she was from the wine. *I haven't eaten since noon.*

Bolton stood outside the glass, a concerned expression on his face. Panic shot through her.

Truman?

Her fingers fumbled with the bolt, but she managed to open the door. "What's happened?" Focusing on his face took more effort than she'd expected.

"Nothing's happened. I was driving home and spotted your vehicle out front. Do you know it's nearly ten?" He moved past her into the office and looked around. "Are you the only one here?"

"Yes."

"You smell like you've been on a wine tour."

"Only a one-bottle tour."

"The whole bottle?"

"Of course not." She was offended.

"How do you plan to drive home?" Tension radiated from him.

She was silent. *I don't want to go.*

"You are going home tonight, right?"

"I would have gotten an Uber."

He relaxed a degree. "What are you doing here so late?"

"Working. Searching for Truman. I can't stop." She turned and walked back to her office. Bolton was right behind her.

"Oh yeah?"

"He has to be out there somewhere." She plopped down in the chair behind her desk and moved a stack of paper, attempting to convince him she had tons to do.

"Anything new?" he asked.

Mercy wouldn't meet his gaze. "Nothing worth mentioning." *Absolutely nothing.*

He sat in a chair and propped an ankle on his other knee, staring silently at her.

Truman sits the same way.

Everything cracked open, and she buried her face in her hands. Sobs emerged from the deepest section of her heart, and hot tears soaked her fingers. Wheezing shallow breaths battled with her sobs. Bolton's hand touched her upper back, and she cried louder.

"It's okay to fall apart. No one can constantly stand tough through what you're dealing with. Not even you."

Snot and tears covered her hands and she yanked a tissue out of the box on her desk, refusing to look at him. *Have I done everything I can?*

Kneeling beside her chair, he placed an arm across her shoulders and gently pulled her against his ribs in an awkward side hug. "I'm so fucking sorry."

She bawled for what seemed like an hour. It wouldn't stop. Every stress and worry and fear she'd bottled up inside broke out. She'd catch her breath and it'd start all over again. Raw and fresh.

"I don't know what to do." Her watery words were pointless, and she blew her nose in the tissue. "I feel so useless."

"You're doing everything possible—we all are," he said against her ear.

"*I hate this.* I don't feel like myself. I don't want to go home because I can't bear to face Kaylie and see his things. That's not like me."

"You're not Wonder Woman. Stop trying to be. Others are here to help you."

"Truman is supposed to help me!" Fresh tears, and she grabbed another tissue.

Bolton didn't answer but tightened his arm on her shoulders. "Let me drive you home. Your niece can bring you back tomorrow."

"I don't want to go home!"

He dug in his jacket pocket for something and shook a pill out of a bottle. He took her coffee cup, sniffed it, shook his head, and then handed her the pill and cup of wine. "Take this."

"What is it?" she asked, holding the tissue to her nose.

"Doesn't matter. It's safe. Trust me, it'll give you some temporary peace until you can gather your strength."

Finally she met his eyes, the eyes that were usually resigned and empty, but now she saw that they reflected her pain.

Temporary peace?

Her brain had been moving at train-wreck speed for days. Peace was appealing.

She took the tablet and stared at it. *Am I really going to take an unknown pill?*

She looked at Bolton again; she trusted him.

After popping it in her mouth, she swallowed some wine and wiped her lips with the back of her hand. "I suspect that wasn't to be taken with alcohol."

"Nope."

A short choke of a laugh bubbled out of her. "I won't die, right?"

"No. You'll thank me tomorrow for a good night's sleep. Let's go."

He helped her stand, grabbed her things, and led her to the front door.

A thought struck her. "You don't drive by my office. You had to go out of your way," she said flatly.

"True."

She turned, halting him with a hand on his chest. "Thank you, Evan." He'd grounded her and kept her from spinning out of control in her self-pity and sorrow.

He met her gaze, and his neck moved as he swallowed. "Anytime."

◆　◆　◆

Truman's visions of a bed and hot food had been crushed.

Once they'd gotten deep into the trees, he'd asked the boy if he had any food. The teen shoved a half-eaten granola bar in his hand. It wasn't hot, but it tasted damn fine.

Beggars can't be choosers.

His rescuer didn't have water but had said they'd come to some soon. *Soon* felt like five hours later, and water meant a meager, muddy creek spilling over a dirt bank. Truman didn't care. He cupped his hands and drank and drank, the single handcuff still around his wrist. He'd asked the boy what time it was, and he'd shrugged and replied, "Nighttime."

Okay.

He and the teen continued to push hard through the forest. A lot of it was uphill, with the boy half carrying him. The rain was persistent, and Truman was thankful for his coat. The captors had emptied all his pockets, taking his badge, gun, and wallet. His head was uncovered and soaking wet. Water dripped under the back of his collar, slowly soaking the lining of his coat and the shirt underneath. He considered putting the coat over his head, but that would mean maneuvering his left arm out of the sleeve. At the moment Truman would prefer to have a tooth extracted.

"What's your name?" Truman asked during one brief break as he sat on a big rock under some pines. The water and granola bar had renewed some of his lost energy, but he still struggled with the pain in his arm and head. The rest he could ignore. Sort of.

The teen, crouching against a tree, looked away. In the poor light, Truman estimated him to be about fifteen. He needed a haircut and he had dirt on one cheek. Body odor hovered around him, but Truman suspected he smelled just as bad.

"Ollie."

"I'm Truman."

Ollie nodded but didn't make eye contact.

"What's your dog's name?"

"Shep."

"He's a good dog." The hound had stuck close to the two of them the entire trek. No leash. No barks. Now Shep sat next to Ollie, eyeing Truman with caution.

At least the dog will look at me.

"He is. He's saved my life two times," Ollie said gruffly.

"That's amazing." Truman wanted to hear more, but Ollie's body language said he was done talking. "I have a cat. I like to think she'd wake me up if an intruder came in the house."

"Cats are stupid."

"I think of them as independent."

Ollie stood. "We need to keep moving."

"Will you tell me where we're headed now?"

"My place."

Truman sagged in relief. A phone. Heat. A bathroom.

"Lead the way."

◆　◆　◆

Truman estimated three hours had passed. Although it could have been ten minutes. "Are we almost to your home?"

He sounded like a little kid on a long car ride. But the pain in his head had tripled in the last few minutes, and his vision was getting narrower and narrower. "I need to stop for a minute," he told Ollie.

In front of him, the teen whirled around. "We just stopped a little while ago." Panic was apparent in his voice and posture.

"I didn't have food or water for a long time," Truman said, coming to a full stop. "That can be hard on a person." Truman didn't dare share all his symptoms or confess that he'd considered flopping under the next tree and telling Ollie to go on without him. The teen had amazing night vision and sense of direction. He'd set his course and never wavered about which way to go.

He didn't want Ollie to leave him behind. Truman was completely lost and suspected his captors could find him without Ollie.

"What happened to your arm?" Ollie nodded at the arm Truman held to his abdomen. It didn't pain him as much if it was bent slightly and held stable.

"They hit it. I think they used a bat. Hit me here and here too." Truman indicated two spots on his head.

"They're assholes."

Truman couldn't disagree. "Who are they?" Ollie had refused to answer any previous questions Truman had asked about the tall man. But judging by the teen's insistence on getting away as quickly as possible, Truman gathered Ollie had a healthy fear of him. Truman didn't want to meet him again either. Ever. Unless the man was behind bars.

He'll get what he deserves for putting me through hell.

"Shhhh! Listen!" Ollie lunged and pulled Truman behind a pine.

Truman clenched his teeth to prevent a shout as Ollie jerked his left arm. When the pain passed, Truman strained to hear over the sound of rushing blood in his ears. *I hear nothing.*

"What is it?" he whispered to Ollie.

"Shhhh." He tugged Truman down to a crouch.

Truman leaned his forehead against the tree, praying his legs wouldn't give out. He didn't know how long Ollie had been leading him through the woods, but he was nearing the end of his strength.

He'd put all his faith in a nearly silent, odd teen. His faith and his neck. *I'm dead if he leaves me behind.*

He closed his eyes, letting his mind drift, imagining he wasn't crouching in the rain in the middle of some fucking forest, running away from an angry man.

"Don't move," Ollie said next to his ear, his words nearly imperceptible. He grabbed Shep's collar and pulled him close, telling the dog the same thing.

Not a problem.

Then Truman heard it. The far-off sound of engines. Either quads or dirt bikes. Voices shouted, too distant for Truman to understand the words. His weak legs started to quiver. Ollie felt it and lowered him into a sitting position. The three of them huddled in the dark.

"It's them," Ollie whispered.

The teen's hearing was as good as his night vision.

Will they hurt Ollie for freeing me? Or worse?

Truman still didn't understand why he'd been beaten and hidden away in a freezing shed in the middle of nowhere. Because of the gradual uphill slope and constant forest, he suspected he was somewhere in the foothills of the Cascades instead of the high desert hills.

Maybe.

He could be in British Columbia or northern Idaho.

At the moment it didn't matter. Ollie was taking him to safety, and then he could call Mercy.

The voices grew more distant, and Ollie gave a small shudder. A million questions ricocheted in Truman's brain, but he didn't have the energy to ask them. He needed all his strength to keep moving. Questions could be answered later.

"Stay here." Ollie vanished into the dark. Shep stayed at Truman's side and didn't move.

At least I know he'll come back for his dog.

He'd just closed his eyes when something touched his arm. *Ollie.*

"You were snoring," he hissed. "I could hear you fifty feet away."

"Sorry," Truman muttered.

"There's a good spot not far from here. We'll stop there for the day."

"The day?"

"Better to move at night."

Truman had no choice but to trust his forest sprite. "Okay. Any food there?"

"No. We'll reach my place tomorrow night."

His stomach protested at the thought of all those hours with no food, and suddenly he smelled pizza. "Do you smell pizza?" he asked.

Ollie sniffed the air. "No."

Great. Now I'm hallucinating food. Or is that a concussion symptom? "Help me up."

Ollie hauled him to his feet. They trudged for another few minutes, and then Ollie pointed at some thick bushes below several close pines. "In there."

Truman followed the teen in and discovered the pine-needle-covered floor was quite dry. He dropped to his knees, lay down, and closed his eyes, cradling his left arm. He felt Shep lie against his back. The needles felt like heaven compared to the concrete floor and the pipe.

He slept.

Truman slept for hours, getting up once to relieve himself outside the ring of bushes. Ollie curled up on his side as he continued to sleep, one hand on Shep's back. Now that it was daylight—although darkened by rain, clouds, and the trees—Truman took a closer look at his rescuer.

The teen's clothing looked as if it had come from the reject bins at Goodwill. Holes and rips dotted his coat and pants, and he wore multiple layers that showed through the holes. He was dressed to keep warm with gloves, scarf, and hat. Much warmer than Truman.

Ollie looked as young as Truman had guessed by his voice. The faintest thin dark hairs had started on his upper lip and chin. They'd never seen a razor. Ollie's hair stuck out from under his hat and hood and needed a wash and cut.

His face was narrow and long, with no extra fat layer under his skin. He was at that age when he could eat all the food in the world, but he'd burn it off. Truman's mother had always claimed he had two hollow legs as a teenager. There was no other explanation for the amount of food he could put away and still stay lean.

This kid probably saved my life.

Shep watched Truman study his master, his black, doggy gaze never leaving Truman's face. "Did he save you too?" he whispered to the dog.

A shiver racked Truman's body, and he brushed something off his forehead. His hand froze on the skin of his face. It was oven hot. He pressed his palm against his temple, checking for heat.

A fever.

Shit. Hopefully Ollie has some Tylenol at his house.

He lay back down in the small thicket, listening to the boy and dog breathe. The homey sounds made tears burn at the corners of his eyes.

Soon, Mercy. I'll be home soon.

THIRTY-TWO

This is not a memorial.

He's only been missing for five days.

Claustrophobia squeezed Mercy's chest as she walked through the crowded church hall. It was as if the entire population of Eagle's Nest and more had come to the rally for Truman. Mercy hadn't wanted the event, but the town leaders had overruled her, stating that people needed to express their sorrow and hope for his return. Truman belonged to the town, not just to her.

David Aguirre had offered to say a few words, but Ina Smythe had claimed the task, saying that if people heard the pastor speak it would feel as if Truman were dead. Ina had known Truman since he was a teenager and had been a surrogate mother when he visited his uncle during the summers. "He's coming back," Ina told Mercy, banging her cane on the floor with each word. The old woman's positive attitude made Mercy feel guilty for every moment she'd doubted Truman would return.

A stream of people shook Mercy's hand and patted her on the back. Women she didn't know hugged her, expressing their faith in Truman's safety. A few men did the same. She wandered the rally in a daze, counting down the minutes until she could leave. *I need to get back to the office and focus on finding him.* She spotted Kaylie in a corner with two of her cousins and immediately looked for their father, her brother Owen.

He was with a small group of men, their heads close, their faces serious during their discussion. Mercy approached and heard "a new chief."

Her heart cracked. They were already speculating on who would take Truman's job. She kept her head up and her eyes dry as she touched Owen on the shoulder. The group broke apart, and the men muttered their sympathies. Owen pulled her aside.

"How are you holding up?" His eyes searched her face.

"By the skin of my teeth," she forcefully joked. He didn't laugh.

"If you need anything . . . I've gone out with the search crews several times." He frowned. "Since there're no leads that point to an area to search, it's been difficult."

"I know. Thank you for helping."

"They'll find him soon."

The platitude was wearing on Mercy, and it made her want to scream. Every time she heard it, her mind questioned whether Truman would be found dead or alive.

"Oh, honey." Her mother suddenly appeared and enveloped Mercy in her arms, reducing her anxiety.

Nothing compares to a mother's hug.

Over her mother's shoulder, Mercy made eye contact with her father and was startled at the compassion on his face. Her mother released her, but Mercy couldn't look away from her father. Ever since she'd returned to Eagle's Nest last fall, he'd looked at her only with annoyance and anger. He'd carried a grudge for fifteen years, and it'd grown stronger when she joined the FBI and when she stood up for Rose's right to be a single mom.

He hadn't looked at her like this since she was a teen, and it meant more to her than all the rally's sympathetic gazes combined.

"He's a good man," her father said in a gruff voice. "Not deserving of this."

"He is good," Mercy echoed, still holding his gaze. "I'm a better person when I'm with him."

Her mother cupped her cheek, turning Mercy's face toward her. "We're all pulling for him."

Mercy gave a wan smile. "Thank you," she said for the thousandth time that evening. She glanced back to her father, but he was in a quiet conversation with Owen.

That didn't last long.

She made an excuse and left her family, heading for the long food table. Every type of cake and cookie covered the surface. *When people grieve, they bring food.* She picked up a snickerdoodle, desperate for distraction. The cookie was tasteless and dry in her mouth.

Like every other bite of food during the last five days.

This morning she'd tightened her belt two holes beyond the usual. Stunned, she'd looked in the mirror, studying herself. Swollen eyes and thinning cheeks. Even her hair looked dull. She had marched out of her bedroom, determined to eat better, starting with a huge homemade ham-and-cheese omelet. She'd managed half of the omelet and then stared at the rest on her plate. She couldn't shake the sensation that she was caught in a slow downward spiral.

Where will it end?

"Hey."

Mike Bevins stopped beside her, a plate with chocolate cake in his hand. He was one of Truman's closest friends.

Mercy swallowed the last of her cookie, searching for a warm greeting. "Hey," she replied.

He picked at the cake with his fork, and she noticed he hadn't eaten a bite. "If anyone can come out of this, it'll be Truman," he said, his gaze on his cake.

"Very true."

"He's tough." He finally met her gaze. "He's not a quitter."

"I know," she whispered.

He set down his cake and pulled her into a long hug. A shudder-ing sigh escaped from her, and she relaxed in his strong arms for a few seconds. Mike pulled back and gave a weak smile. He left without another word.

There are no truly helpful words.

But everyone feels the need to say something.

She knew the words were more for the person speaking than for her. Human nature compelled others to offer comfort, making them feel as if they had helped, done *something*.

Inside she wanted to hit everyone.

She picked up a cup of coffee to occupy her hands and wandered the room.

". . . truck destroyed by fire . . ."

". . . blood in the driveway . . ."

The whispers ricocheted in her skull. Unable to stop herself, she headed for the door, its EXIT sign calling her like a beacon. The door opened just as she approached, and Evan Bolton stepped in. He imme-diately spotted her and frowned.

"Are you leaving?"

"Yes, I can't take this."

He took her arm and moved her to the side of the door. Her mus-cles ached to continue her escape out the door, and she glared at him. He'd ruined her mission.

"You can't leave yet," he said in a low voice. "These people need you."

"No, they don't."

"They're looking to you for emotional support. If they see you can hold your head up, they feel they can too."

"I can't hold my head up anymore tonight," she hissed at him, pull-ing her arm out of his grip.

"Yes, you can," he said firmly. "I'll help you. It's nearly impossible to do on your own."

"How would you know?" she shot back. *No one knows what I'm going through.*

"Trust me, I do." He looked away and studied the crowd. "Looks like something is happening." He placed his hand on the small of her back and guided her to where people were gathering. Fury rocked Mercy; she wanted to be gone.

Ina Smythe had stepped up on the raised dais in front of a microphone. She thumped her cane and it thundered on the wood, catching everyone's attention.

Mercy quailed at the sight of the kind woman. *I can't listen to her talk about Truman.* She started to turn toward the door again.

Evan felt Mercy shift and pressed firmly on her back. "Don't move."

She inhaled, steeling her spine, shutting her eyes, and wishing herself away.

Ina's wavering voice filled the room. She spoke with hope and passion, never once implying that Truman wasn't coming back. Mercy reluctantly opened her eyes and found the old woman looking directly at her as she spoke. Mercy absorbed the strength in the woman's gaze, and her words wove their way into Mercy's heart, patching small rips and tears. She'd always known Ina was tough; the woman had outlasted several husbands, and Truman adored her.

Applause and loud whoops rattled the hall. Ina gave a pleased smile and nod, and then David Aguirre jumped forward to take her arm as she stepped off the dais.

Mercy couldn't remember one word of what the woman had said, but she felt the effects of the speech's power and comfort. The town loved Truman.

I'm not alone.

THIRTY-THREE

Someone was singing.

Truman's eyes stayed closed as a flat voice sang a breathy little tune. He knew the song from somewhere, and it stimulated hazy memories that were content and warm, but he couldn't bring them into focus.

John Henry. Steel. Nine-pound hammer.

His grandparents. His grandmother had sung it while working around the house.

Truman opened his eyes and turned his head to see Ollie sitting next to him on a stool, working on a wood figure with a knife. The boy had taken off his coat, and his sweater had a rip at the collar. Truman abruptly realized he was warm, weighted down by blankets and quilts on a very uncomfortable bed. *Ollie's bedroom.*

When did we get here?

"Ollie?" he croaked. His tongue was so dry it was sticky.

The teen nearly dropped his carving as he twisted to Truman. Wide brown eyes blinked at him. "Are you okay?" Ollie asked.

"I'm thirsty."

Ollie jumped up from his stool and poured water from a small bucket into a mug. Truman tried to sit up and made the mistake of using his left arm to lever up. Explosions of light went off in his vision, and an awkward moan escaped him.

"Let me help you."

The teen put an arm behind Truman's back and easily lifted him to a sitting position, helping him sip the water. Truman was as weak as a baby. He drank what he could, then gestured to be laid back down as the room slowly spun. He clenched his eyes shut against the spin.

"What happened?" he muttered.

"You've been sick. Fever."

"How'd I get here?"

"I helped you walk. You were out of your head."

Visions of a nighttime trek while leaning heavily on Ollie came to the surface. He recalled falling a few times and the boy hauling him to his feet, telling him they were almost home.

"You kept talking about mercy."

Truman's eyelids shot open. *Mercy.* He tried to sit up again and couldn't, flopping back onto the bed. "Bring me a phone," he ordered.

"Don't have one." The teen sat calmly on his stool, watching him.

"Then . . . a computer . . ." *That seems unlikely.* "What do you have?"

Ollie shrugged. "Nothin'. If you want to call someone, we'll have to go to the Lynch place. He has one."

"Okay. Help me up." He held out his right hand.

"I don't think you're strong enough to go anywhere. I practically carried you the last bit to the house."

For the first time, Truman took in his surroundings. The room was tiny, lined with rough boards. The bed he was lying on was framed from similar rough boards, and his covers were a mismatched pile of quilts and blankets. In one corner was a tiny wood stove whose heat Truman could feel on his face. A kettle and a pan sat on the top.

Truman frowned.

He spotted two mismatched wood chairs and a rickety, tiny table holding a few dishes. Shep lay curled up on a blanket under the table, his gaze on Truman.

Comprehension dawned. Truman wasn't in a small bedroom. "Ollie, is this your home?"

"Of course. I said I'd bring you here."

"Thank you." Truman could barely speak. "Do you live by yourself?" he slowly asked. This was the extent of the house. No windows. A rough door. But it was warm, and no rain dripped through the roof.

"Yep." The teen's brown eyes focused on the floor, his shoulders slightly hunched. "I know it's not much."

"It's great," said Truman. "You saw the shithole where they were keeping me. I'm warm and lying in a bed thanks to you."

"It was nothin'."

Lingering pains shot through his left arm, and he clumsily pulled it out from under the blanket. It was wrapped snugly in worn towels and bound with duct tape. A soft splint. His back still ached, and he could feel every lump and bump in the bed. He shifted, moving his legs, and realized he had been sleeping on several layers of blankets on a board. Not a mattress.

I've taken his bed. He tried again to get up and failed.

"I've got some soup," Ollie said, grabbing the pan off the woodstove. He poured its contents into another mug, and Truman salivated at the smell.

Ollie helped him sit up again, and Truman looked in the mug. Chicken and stars.

Another memory of his grandparents came roaring up from the past.

He drank carefully. It was hot. And tasted like heaven.

"How long did I sleep?" he asked between sips, feeling stronger each second.

"Ummm . . ." The boy screwed up his face in thought. "You've been sleeping for two nights, three days."

"What?" Truman sloshed his soup on the blankets. "You're counting the night we slept in the woods, right?"

"No. You've been here for two nights."

He couldn't swallow. "I don't know how many days I've been gone," he said softly.

"They locked you up six days ago."

"H-how do you know that?" *Six days. Six days?*
Mercy must be frantic.

"I saw them drag you in. I had to wait for a good time to get you out." The teen spoke as if it were something he did every day.

"Ollie." Truman remembered how the teen wouldn't answer questions after helping him escape. "Who locked me up?"

"Those crazy guys. My grandfather always said to stay away from them."

"Then why were you there?"

The teen gave the first grin Truman had seen from him. "Because they're easy to raid. They leave food and supplies unlocked all the time."

"You steal from them?"

"Gotta survive."

"Where are your parents?"

"Dead. I lived with my grandfather most of my life. He died two summers ago."

This poor kid.

"I'm very sorry." Truman studied the thin teenager. "How old are you?"

"I turned eighteen last Christmas."

I was way off in estimating his age. Malnutrition, maybe?

"Do you have other family close by?"

"No. Just Shep. We take care of one another."

He has no one.

The dog heard his name and jumped onto the bed, nestling in between Truman's legs. It was uncomfortable, but made Truman happy at the same time.

"Why did you call those guys crazy? Was there more than one? I only saw one person." *But two definitely attacked me.*

The teen's face closed down. "Because they killed my grandfather."

His heart went out to Ollie, and Truman struggled to find words. "Again, I'm so sorry, but why did they kill your grandfather?" He steeled himself for the answer. *What kind of people attacked me?*

"Because he wouldn't work with them anymore. He threatened to go to the police."

"Work doing what?"

"Making the fake stuff. IDs, license plates, the booklets. He wasn't proud of doing it, but he was really good at it and made them a lot of money."

Joshua Forbes. Truman's brain tried to connect the dots in Ollie's story. "Ollie, don't take this the wrong way . . . but was your grandfather a sovereign citizen?"

"Yep." Pride radiated from the young man.

"And when he said he wouldn't do as they wanted, they murdered him? These were the same guys who held me?"

"Yes." The pride vanished. "Ever since they killed him, I've done what I can to make their lives miserable. I've ruined their well, stolen anything they leave out, and taken parts from their cars so they don't run." Determination filled his voice. "When I saw them put you in the same shed they'd put my grandfather, I knew I had to get you out."

Truman realized he had to tread carefully. "Ollie, did you know I'm a cop? I'm the police chief of Eagle's Nest."

"Of course I knew. Well . . . once I got you out. It's right on your coat." He pointed at the insignia on the front of the coat Truman still wore.

Duh. "I can help you, Ollie. I think they put me in there because I arrested one of them a few days ago. He ended up in jail. I can put them all away with your help, but first I need to get to a phone."

Ollie looked skeptical. "No one can touch them. Even the police."

"How about the FBI?"

A measure of respect crossed his face. "You can call the FBI?"

Truman grinned. "Yeah, I can. I know one of their agents real well."

Mercy. A pang struck his heart, but optimism was slowly taking over; he could get back to her with Ollie's help when he was strong enough. "How far away is that man with the phone?"

Ollie considered. "About two days' hike."

He couldn't hide his disappointment. "That's insane."

"The rain washed out the little bridge, otherwise it'd only be a day. We'll have to go the long way."

The long way it was.

"I think tomorrow I can hike out," Truman stated four days later.

At Truman's announcement, Ollie carefully perused him from head to toe, and Truman held up his chin, trying to look strong. His head no longer throbbed, but he still had tender-to-the-touch areas near his ear. His back was the same way. Ollie had told him it was still black and blue, but he could twist and turn with less pain. His arm worried him a bit; all he could do was keep it as immobile as possible. Ollie had duct-taped a couple of sticks to the towels, which kept Truman from moving it. Guilt sparked, since he'd eaten a ton of Ollie's food to gain strength. *I'll buy him whatever he wants when I get home. I bet he's never been to Costco.*

"Think so?" Ollie asked with a heavy dose of skepticism.

"I do. I'm stronger today." Truman had been shocked to discover his pants were extremely baggy the first day he woke from being sick.

He must have burned off ten to fifteen pounds during his captivity and fever. He stank. He'd gone more than a week without a shower or bath. He'd spot bathed here and there, but there was nothing he could do about his hair without asking Ollie for help. He wasn't ready to do that. The smell didn't seem as bad as at first, and he wondered if he was growing used to it.

Ollie had a collection of books. Dozens of yellowed Louis L'Amour Westerns Truman assumed had belonged to his grandfather. And a dozen old Harlequin romance novels with battered covers. "They were my grandmother's," Ollie had told him. "She's been gone for about ten years."

He'd thumbed through an old algebra textbook and a US history textbook that ended with the Vietnam War. According to Ollie, he knew both inside and out. He'd never been to school, but his grandfather had taught him, and these were the only books Ollie had left. He'd abandoned his grandfather's house after he had been killed. Ollie had worried the murderers would come looking for him next—a loose end to tie up. He and his grandfather had built this cabin over the years "just in case," and no one knew it existed.

Truman wished he could thank Ollie's grandfather.

The preparedness reminded him of Mercy.

He desperately wanted to let her know he was alive. *What is going on in her head?*

"Cards?" Ollie asked hopefully. Two faded decks of cards were the only other source of entertainment in the cabin. Ollie knew dozens of games to play on his own, and he'd missed playing against someone. No matter how much his head hurt, Truman tried to play every time he asked, because Ollie hadn't had an opponent in two years.

"Sure. You deal."

The teen creamed him at whatever game they played, but Truman managed to occasionally eke out a win. The contrast of the simple entertainment to the constant phone, computer, and video games the kids played back home made Truman wish technology would slow down. He held long conversations with Ollie; they discussed everything. For someone so isolated, Ollie was a good debater and had a pretty good grasp of what was happening in the world. He confessed to stealing newspapers and magazines on his foraging trips.

Clearly he'd read every word.

"Have you ever run into a problem out here by yourself?" Truman asked as the teen dealt the cards with the skill and speed of a Vegas dealer.

"What kind of problem?"

"Well . . . like hurting yourself or getting sick and not having medication. Or getting lost."

Ollie snorted. "I don't get lost." He gave Truman a reproachful look.

"What about getting sick?"

"Don't really get sick. There was one time that I twisted my ankle during a fall into a ravine."

"What happened?"

He shrugged his thin shoulders, his gaze on the cards. "I wasn't careful and tumbled down a steep hill. At the bottom I realized I couldn't walk, and then my ankle doubled in size."

Truman leaned forward. A simple accident like that with no one around could have killed the teenager. "And?"

"Well, I wasn't going to just give up. I had to figure out a plan and conquer one step at a time. I knew I needed shelter, water, and food. I could crawl—but not good enough to climb out—so I found shade, and there was a bit of water running along the bottom of the ravine." He wrinkled his nose. "Damn, that water tasted nasty. I always have something to eat in a pocket, so I was pretty well set. Just had to wait to accomplish the fourth step."

"Wait until you had the ability to climb out?"

"Yeah, it was really steep. Mostly rock."

"No other way out?"

"Nope. Both ends were blocked. I was lucky that I was in a low area and some water trickled through."

"You could have died."

"Believe me, I thought of that a lot. And I figured no one would even find my body, because the spot was so isolated. I was stupid to go near the edge in the first place."

"How long were you in there?"

"Five days."

"Holy shit!" Truman nearly dropped his cards. *Could I have stuck that out?*

"My ankle got better, but I fell while climbing out and sorta messed it up again and had to wait longer." He ducked his head. "Not smart. It felt as if I stared at those ravine walls forever. I memorized every little indentation and ledge. The next time I tried, I mentally outlined the steps that would get me out and took my time. It worked."

Ollie seemed so nonchalant about it. It had been just another day in his life.

"At least you didn't have to cut your arm off."

Ollie's eyes widened at Truman. "Why would I do that?"

"Never mind. What happened to your parents, Ollie?" Truman asked.

"Car accident."

"I'm sorry."

"I was three. I don't remember." His voice softened. "I didn't grab any pictures when I left my grandfather's house. I don't remember their faces anymore."

Truman silently organized his cards, his single handcuff clunking on the table. He'd learned Ollie hated pity. "Maybe I can try to find something when I get home. If the accident made the papers, there might be photos of them."

"Maybe." Ollie didn't seem to care.

Truman wondered if the apathy was an act or coping mechanism. *Is he too scarred to allow himself hope?*

The two of them continued their game in companionable silence.

The quiet, simple hours soothed Truman's brain. There was nothing he could do about his cases or officers out here; it'd all been forcibly swept off his plate, leaving him relaxed, with a clear mind. He thought and worried about Mercy but soon realized the worry was pointless and making him feel worse. Instead he concentrated on their reunion. It was inevitable, and he couldn't wait.

Soon.

He was able to use the outhouse on his own, he could sit up, and he could read or play cards for hours at a time. He constantly stretched and tested his muscles.

Soon.

Ollie won the hand, and Truman scooped up the cards. "Would you like to go to school, Ollie?" The thought had been on his mind.

"I'm too old."

"No, you're not. No one is ever too old. Anyone can take classes at the community college in Bend. And they have every class imaginable. Geometry, world history, photography, geology. Heck, you could even take dance classes."

Ollie's look of disgust made Truman grin. "Don't have the money."

"Well, there are scholarships and grants." Truman dealt the last cards, knowing he needed to speak carefully. "I'd help you out. Community college doesn't cost too much."

"I won't take charity." Ollie's answer was firm, but a rare spark of hope flashed in his eyes.

"It's not charity. I owe you my life a few times over, and I like to think my life is worth more than a few classes."

Ollie shrugged.

The seed had been planted, and they played in silence for a few moments. "Tomorrow," Truman stated as he took a card.

"Tomorrow," Ollie agreed. "Before sunrise."

THIRTY-FOUR

Mercy stopped counting the days.

She moved in a foggy haze. Head down, working on every minuscule lead in Truman's case. Days blended into one another. Another week had gone by.

Truman's parents and sister had come to town and were involved in the search. Truman's kind mother had hugged her, and Mercy had briefly sunk into her maternal softness. It'd contrasted with the brittle shell Mercy had rebuilt after the night she'd cried in front of Bolton. The sight of Truman's father made Mercy catch her breath; he was Truman in twenty years. His sister was a stunned walking zombie who gazed at her with eyes that looked just like Truman's.

I'm a zombie too.

She left the family in the care of Lucas and the Eagle's Nest Police Department. Being around them hurt her heart. She had her own sorrow to carry, and the weight of his family's pain made her feel as if she were drowning.

Ryan Moody had called her twice, asking for an update on his missing brother's case. She didn't have any new information for him.

The same search groups out looking for Truman had included Clint Moody in their hunt.

Joshua Forbes also hadn't turned up, and Mercy wondered if he should be added to the list with Truman and Clint. Another visit to his home and his father's had been fruitless. She'd asked Kenneth Forbes if he wanted to file a missing persons report, but the man had waved her off, stating his son was known for taking off for a week or two with no communication. He didn't appear worried about Joshua. He was just pissed at the man for leaving without a word after his father had paid his bail.

They had no new leads on the Jorgensen murders. Mercy had exhausted them all. The same was true for the Hartlages.

She felt like a failure. *All those children.*

Britta didn't press charges against Chuck Winslow for trespassing. Mercy had disagreed with her decision, but Britta wanted the incident to go away. Chuck had been silent on the internet—too silent—since he was shot, which made Mercy wonder what rock he would crawl out from underneath next.

"Mercy, Britta is here," came Melissa's voice from the speaker on her desk phone.

"I'll be right out." Time had gotten away from her. Britta had called earlier and asked to meet at three without giving a hint of what she wanted to talk about.

Britta and her black Lab waited for her outside the office. Mercy squatted to greet the dog and received two wet paw prints on her pants.

"Zara!" The Lab wasn't leashed, but she promptly pulled back and sat next to Britta's feet.

"What's up? Chuck hasn't contacted you again, has he?" Mercy asked, crossing her arms against the chill in the wet air. *Is Truman warm?* She shoved the thought away.

"No. But . . ." The tall woman frowned and looked away, her face reflecting an internal struggle. "This is stupid."

Mercy waited.

Britta finally made eye contact again. "Chuck's accusations that I knew something about the murders of my family have reminded me of something."

Every nerve in Mercy's body focused on Britta.

The woman stroked Zara's ears, her lips pressing together. "It's nothing. Like I said, it's stupid."

"Tell me. It's bugged you enough to contact me," Mercy pointed out.

Britta exhaled, her shoulders sinking. "I never saw the man who killed my sisters or hit me. But I often dreamed of that night for years after it happened. I'd forgotten about the dream until Chuck started harassing me."

Disappointment settled over Mercy. "Go on. What did you dream?"

"That I woke and saw my sister Astrid in her bed across the room. She was bloody and silent. I couldn't see Helena because she was in the bunk under me. But *I knew* she looked the same."

"What about yourself?"

Britta's cheeks flexed as she clenched her teeth before continuing. "I saw myself all bloody too. But it was like I was above my bed, looking down. I knew I would die."

"I'm so sorry, Britta. It's completely understandable that you'd have that dream." She wanted to hug and comfort the woman but knew better.

"I saw an angel that night."

I didn't expect that. Britta was too sensible to talk about angels and visions. *This is why she hasn't told anyone before.*

"You nearly died," Mercy said. "I'm not surprised."

"It was all in white and very small. It hovered over Astrid and I knew it was taking her to heaven. Then its face was close to mine. I felt it gently touch my forehead." Britta bent to give Zara a hug, burying her face in the dog's fur for a moment. "I remember floating away and believed I was going to heaven too."

"That doesn't sound like a horrible dream," Mercy said gently. "It sounds almost comforting." *Was that when Steve Harris checked the girls to see if they were alive?*

"I always told the police I didn't remember anything. I was too embarrassed to tell them about the angel. But I'm positive I was awake for a few moments after Grady Baldwin struck us."

"I don't think there's anything in that story that would have helped the police back then."

"I know, but I always felt I was lying to them by holding it back." She stood, a half smile on her lips. "You have no idea how much better I feel now that I told someone."

"I'm pleased you picked me." Her affection for the unusual woman grew. Mercy liked people who pulled themselves up by their bootstraps. Britta had done that times ten.

"I need to leave . . . Come, Zara. Bye, Mercy." Britta abruptly turned and left.

Mercy understood. Sharing a childhood dream had to be an uncomfortable experience for her. She went back to her desk and sat down with a sigh. *I forgot to ask if she plans to move.*

She'd miss the woman—and Zara—if she did.

Her cell phone rang, and her anxiety hit the ceiling at the sight of the Eagle's Nest Police Department number. "Agent Kilpatrick."

"It's Lucas."

"Has something happened?" Tension strained her voice. *Truman?*

"You could say that. Joshua Forbes walked in a few minutes ago and asked for police protection. He's got a story you need to hear." He cleared his throat. "It's about Truman, Mercy," he said softly.

"Is he dead?" she croaked, feeling herself split in two.

"He doesn't know. But he thinks he knows where he was at one point."

She jerked back to reality. *This call could have been worse.* "I'll be there in half an hour."

◆ ◆ ◆

This is Joshua Forbes?

Mercy had spent a lot of time online and in person searching for the man who'd threatened Truman, and for some reason she hadn't expected a quiet young man in a grimy sweatshirt. He had the same eye color as his father, Kenneth—a piercing blue. But he didn't project the ramrod-up-the-spine confidence that his father did. In fact, he looked like a beaten dog.

He's supposed to help us find Truman?

Mercy and Joshua sat in the tiny conference room in the Eagle's Nest Police Department. Officer Samuel Robb stood against the wall, his thumbs tucked in his gun belt, his gaze never leaving Joshua.

"He swears he doesn't know anything about Clint Moody's disappearance, but he told me what he knows about Truman," Samuel said to Mercy. "I want him to go through it again for you." He nudged Joshua's chair with his foot, startling him.

"Where have you been for the past couple of weeks?" Mercy asked. "A lot of people have been searching for you."

"I've been at a friend's. Several friends'. I didn't want to stay in one place too long."

"Why do you need to hide?"

Joshua glanced nervously at Samuel. Mercy didn't blame him; the cop was intimidating.

"I got threats while I was in jail."

"Why?"

"People were pissed that I was arrested. They didn't want me to talk to anyone."

"Talk about what?" She was ready to crawl out of her skin with impatience. Samuel had told her there was no need to rush to the location Joshua believed Truman had been, but he hadn't told her why not.

Joshua gave a heavy sigh. "Our business. I'm part of a business, and they found out that the police knew I was a distributor. They thought I had told the police—but I didn't!"

"Distributor. Are you talking about the IDs, or are you a drug dealer too?"

"No, those stupid IDs and license plates," answered Samuel with scorn. "Apparently someone was making a lot of money and didn't want it to end."

Mercy remembered how Truman had originally pulled Joshua over for the plates.

"You sent Truman a letter saying he owed you three million dollars," she stated. "That had us looking for you when Truman disappeared, even though you got out a few hours after we think he vanished. Then *you* disappeared. That didn't look good."

"I didn't have anything to do with his disappearance," he said earnestly, meeting her gaze. "I didn't even know he was missing. I was just trying to protect my own ass."

"You've got people upset with you?"

His chin dropped. "I don't trust them," he mumbled.

"Why not?"

Joshua didn't answer and stared at the tabletop.

"Where's Truman?" Her heart hammered against her ribs.

"I don't know," he said. "But two days ago I heard a rumor that he'd escaped—but I *swear* I didn't know they had him in the first place."

"The people who head up your forgery business took Truman?" She glanced over at Samuel, who hadn't blinked an eye. *How can he be so calm?* She was ready to dash out the door.

"I *think* they did. All I know is that I overheard a couple of guys talking about the cop who got away."

"When? When did he get away?" She stood up, planted her hands on the table, and leaned toward Joshua, trying to hide her shaking arms.

"It was at least five days ago."

Mercy froze. *Five days?* She slowly sat back down. "Then where is he?"

Joshua looked tormented. "I don't know. I didn't know who they were talking about until I heard something about the missing police chief on the radio. As soon as I realized that the guy who'd arrested me was missing, I knew that's who they were talking about."

"When did you figure this out?"

"Maybe a day or two ago. I didn't know if I should do something or not. I didn't want to get in more trouble with them, but . . ."

"But what?" Mercy wanted to shake him. This story was taking forever to come out.

"I know what they do," he whispered. He slowly lifted his gaze back to hers. "They've killed people who wanted to get out of their organization."

"Were they going to kill Truman?"

"If they were keeping him where I think they were, they were definitely planning to."

"Where is it?"

Joshua told her about a remote property where one of the members of the forgery ring lived. It had an outbuilding where they'd locked up men before.

"What are we waiting for?" she snapped at Samuel, getting to her feet again.

"We're waiting for a warrant and support," Samuel said firmly. "I'm not rushing into a remote situation where armed banjo-playing bumpkins are running their own mini prison. County is pulling together their SWAT team for us." He checked the time. "That takes some time. It's going to be dark out there by then, Mercy. You need to be prepared that SWAT might want to wait and go in during the daylight."

Mercy turned back to Joshua. "Are you sure he escaped? Would they spread that rumor if they'd killed him?" Bile rose in her throat.

"I don't know," he said miserably, looking ready to fall apart. "I don't know anything else. I thought these people were my family."

"Who have they killed in the past?" she asked.

"An old guy. He was a good artist . . . really knew how to make things look professional. He wanted out, and they were afraid he'd talk. They took a vote and put him down."

Like a dog?

"Would they have taken a vote on Truman?" A chill spread over her skin.

He lifted one shoulder. "Probably."

"If this place is as remote as you say, he could be lost in the woods. Is it above the snow line?"

"No."

His answer gave little comfort. The weather had been miserably cold and wet for weeks.

"Samuel, we need to move our searchers to the forest around that place." Her heart fell at the time that'd slipped away. By the time their search parties moved, it'd be too dark.

"County has their search-and-rescue team gearing up too. They'll be ready to head out at first light tomorrow," he told her. "I had the same thought about Truman in the woods."

"I'm sorry I didn't come forward sooner," Joshua admitted. "But . . ."

Damn you for not coming sooner.

We might be too late.

"I know how you've been raised," Mercy told him, thinking of his sovereign citizen upbringing and attempting to keep the anger out of her voice. "It's hard to go against everything that's been ingrained in you since childhood."

I've been there many times.

"But deep inside we all know when the right thing has to be done. If what you've been taught hurts others, there's something very, very wrong."

His posture drooped. "Yeah," he said softly.

Tick tick tick.

THIRTY-FIVE

Mercy stood with Samuel on a remote side road a few miles from the property the SWAT team was about to invade. It was pitch-dark, and the temperature was rapidly falling, but at least it wasn't pouring rain. By the time they'd received the warrant and the SWAT team had organized and made their plan, it was nearly nine at night. A few yards away, the team was reviewing last-minute instructions, their tank-looking armored personnel carrier ready to roll.

"I hope this gets us somewhere," Mercy muttered to Samuel. She was petrified to allow hope into her heart; it'd been shattered too many times recently.

The SWAT team leader had been more than happy to enter the property in the dark.

"Less chance they'll see us coming, but we'll see them just fine." He'd tapped his night vision gear.

The leader was currently conferring over a satellite photo of the area a second time with Joshua Forbes. Joshua had agreed that no structures had changed on the property and stated that up to six men could be in the house. Mercy had already studied the satellite photo, and bile had filled her stomach as she stared at the tiny square Joshua had claimed was the outbuilding most likely to have housed Truman.

She stepped right behind Joshua and spoke in a low voice to the back of his head. "If I find out that you're lying about *anything* regarding this location, I'll personally skin you alive. I'll go all *Game of Thrones* on your ass."

His face blanched as he turned to her. "I'm not lying."

The team leader gave a big grin. He'd heard her threat. "Let's load up!" he told his men.

Frustration filled Mercy as she watched them leave. She had no role to play. Her job was to stand back and wait.

I've been waiting for nearly two weeks.

Fifteen minutes later, she and Samuel got the call to come in. They left Joshua with a county deputy, knowing it was best if the men in his organization didn't connect him with their raid.

The property was less than impressive. A single-wide mobile home with a large barn and a smaller shed to one side. Mercy tore her gaze away from the shed as she strode to the front of the home. *That's the place.* The shed's door was wide open, and the team leader had said it was empty.

Inside the home three men lay on the floor, their hands bound in zip ties behind their backs.

No broken door. No broken windows. No shots. No one injured.

A successful operation.

Two SWAT members stood near the bound men, their weapons ready.

The suspects looked up as she and Samuel entered. Mercy stopped in shock as she recognized one and scanned the room for a certain item. Then she pointedly checked all three men's muddy shoes, went directly to the man in the middle, and squatted next to his head. "Aren't you clever."

Kenneth Forbes turned his face away from her.

"Do you collect disability pay from the government?" Fury shot through her at how easily she'd been conned into believing that he was disabled and reliant on his wheelchair. *Why didn't Joshua say his father was one of the men?*

Then she remembered Joshua's morose statement that he'd thought this was his family.

Did his father put out a contract to kill him?

And Mercy had believed her father was an ass.

It didn't matter. Joshua was upright and breathing. Truman was her concern.

"Where's Truman Daly?" she asked.

No one answered her.

She sighed. "You know his prints will be found in that shithole outside. Don't you want a judge to hear that you cooperated when asked?"

Silence. But one of the men on the floor squirmed. She nodded at Samuel, who was already moving toward the man. He hauled him to his feet and took him outside.

"Do you know what GPR is?" she asked the remaining silent men. "It's ground-penetrating radar. We use it to find buried remains. Rumor has it that there's a grave on these grounds. And in it is a member of your little ring who you wouldn't let walk away from your dirty business."

Kenneth Forbes now faced her but said nothing, his bright blue eyes defiant.

"We were expecting a few more men here," she stated. "Where is everyone?"

After a silent moment, she continued. "Don't tell me you two are the type that can't bear to answer to a woman?" She sighed dramatically. "Poor me, I guess I'll have to wait for Samuel and his testosterone to come back if that makes you more comfortable."

As if on cue, Samuel entered with the third suspect. Mercy was pleased to see the man didn't have a split lip or black eye—Samuel knew better, but she knew his emotions were running high due to his missing boss. Samuel ordered him back on the floor by the other two, and the man didn't make eye contact with his two buddies. "Truman got away several days ago, and three of their men are out searching for him," Samuel announced. "They suspect a kid set him loose."

"A kid?"

"A teenager. Some forest-dwelling hermit who's a pain in their butts. Raids their supplies and damages their equipment."

"I'd like to meet him," admitted Mercy. Some of her worry evaporated. Truman wasn't alone in the woods. "Why do they think this kid did it?"

"The handcuffs were cut with a bolt cutter, and they found dog prints around the shed. The teen always has a dog with him."

"Where do we find this teenager?"

"These guys don't know. I suspect if they did, the kid wouldn't be breathing anymore."

"I want to see the shed. Have county process these guys," she told the SWAT team leader. She followed Samuel outside. He pulled a flashlight from his utility belt and lit the way. "What did you do to the guy you took outside?" Mercy asked Samuel as she stepped around the puddles.

"Nothing."

She smiled in the dark. As they approached the shed, her smile faded. The small wood structure had a metal roof and sat on a concrete slab. It was the creepy place in a horror movie that teenagers should never enter. But they always do.

Her hand covered her nose and mouth against the stink as she stepped inside. A few glass jars were on the floor, the flashlight revealing their contents. Shattered glass covered part of the concrete, and a single handcuff bracelet hung from a pipe along the back wall.

"Oh my God," she whispered. It was too easy to imagine Truman cuffed to the pipe. *How long was he here?*

Samuel shone his flashlight over the floor, and Mercy knew he was looking for blood. There was none. A small relief.

They silently filed back out.

"I'd like a few minutes alone with each one of those guys," Samuel muttered as the two of them stood outside the house, breathing rain-cleansed air.

"He's still alive," Mercy said.

In the poor light, Samuel turned his gaze on her. "That's the first time you've said that. I've heard you say we need to keep looking, but you've never said you believe he's still alive."

"I was too scared to think it. What if I was wrong? It'd tear me apart . . . more than I already am."

"What if you're wrong now?"

"I'm not. I can feel it." She couldn't explain. Two months ago an unusual woman had told Mercy she'd seen an invisible connection that strung between Mercy and Truman. Mercy didn't believe witchy mumbo jumbo, but as she'd lain bleeding out in the snow the day her cabin burned, Mercy had seen . . . something . . . and known it was true.

Is that what I'm feeling? As she'd stepped out of that shed from hell, a confident warmth had filled her chest. It was still there.

Or else I'm finally cracking under the strain.

"That idiot inside gave me the last check-in location of the three guys who are out looking for the teen and Truman," said Samuel. "I'll pass it on to the SAR team. I know they're planning to meet at seven tomorrow morning and start searching as soon as the sun comes up."

"Can you trust what he said?" Mercy asked.

Samuel grinned. "Yeah."

Mercy no longer wanted to know what Samuel had said or done to the man.

"Text the location to me. I'll be there too." She wanted to start searching *now*. "I'm not going to get any sleep tonight."

"That makes two of us."

THIRTY-SIX

"I don't know you, and I don't know what you're capable of. We can't have anyone slowing us down," the search-and-rescue leader stated as he glared at Mercy.

"Trust me, I can probably outlast all of you," she said as she scanned the rest of the SAR crew, ignoring the threatening twinge in her thigh.

She'd been in place that morning before anyone else arrived. Her backpack was stocked for at least three nights in the woods, and she was dressed in waterproof, breathable gear. She wore her most reliable hiking boots and had popped three ibuprofen. She had backups in her pocket. "I know what I'm doing."

The group was composed of various local officers. Three, including the leader, were from the Bend Police Department, one was a Deschutes County deputy, and one was from the Redmond Police Department. They looked experienced and skeptical.

"Aren't you the FBI agent who helped bring down that militia?" asked Anna, one of the officers from Bend.

"Yes."

"She can handle it, Lou," the woman said. "That was some nasty shit she was in the middle of. I heard about it."

Mercy met Anna's gaze and gave a small nod.

"Okay. But if you slow us down, I'm leaving you behind. You armed?"

"Yes." Mercy touched the side of her jacket.

Lou focused on his map. "We're about a half mile from where those perps out searching for the kid and the chief reportedly checked in. They claimed they found footprints at one point, so we're going to operate on the assumption that they're in the right place, because I don't know who else would choose to be out in this crappy weather over the past week."

"If we follow the general direction from the place where Truman was held, it appears the two of them are heading here." Lou circled an area with his finger. "I don't think they would go any further north, because there's a wide section of sheer cliffs that you can't get around. But this is an isolated, sort of protected area. If this mystery kid has a hidden place in the woods, this is where I'd build it. No one goes here."

Mercy couldn't disagree with his logic. *But there's so much forest. What if he's wrong?*

They were truly searching for a needle in a haystack.

As they headed out, Mercy fell into the middle of the line, pleased to be doing *something*.

It finally felt like progress.

I hope my leg doesn't give out.

◆ ◆ ◆

"I think we should have waited one more day," Ollie said, watching Truman catch his breath.

"I just need a moment. I feel pretty strong," Truman lied as he leaned against a tree for the fourth time that morning. There was no way he was going back to the cabin. He could *taste* freedom; he had to keep moving forward. "It doesn't matter if we go a little slow," he argued. "No one is expecting us."

He wanted to ask how much farther but knew he wouldn't like the answer.

Shep touched his nose to Truman's leg and then went back to sit next to Ollie. Truman wondered if he'd passed the dog's inspection. Surely the dog couldn't smell exhaustion, but his eyes looked at Truman in sympathy.

"What will you do when you get rid of me?" Truman asked, stalling for more rest time.

The teen shrugged. "Go back home. Keep preparing for the winter."

The thought of Ollie spending the winter in his little hut made Truman shudder. No doubt Ollie didn't mind . . . or did he?

"What would you like to do with your life, Ollie?"

He tilted his head in confusion. "What do you mean?"

"I guess I'm asking what you want to be when you grow up," Truman said awkwardly.

"Be? I want to be me."

"What kind of job would you like to have? You know, like become a doctor or a lawyer or a fireman." *This is the sort of conversation I'd have with a ten-year-old.*

"Oh." Ollie thought hard. "I wouldn't mind being a teacher. Don't know what I'd teach, though."

"I can totally see that." Truman wasn't surprised. Ollie had used a calm, steadying manner as he'd taught Truman card games. He was patient, kind, and brave as hell. "You should set that as a goal. You're a natural to be a teacher."

"I suppose this is where you talk to me about school again," the teen said.

"I know you want to learn."

"True."

"We'll make it happen. I promise you, once we're out of here, I'll help you explore all your possibilities." He didn't want to see the boy live out his life in the woods with a dog.

"You done stalling?"

"Yes," Truman admitted.

"Let's go."

It was midafternoon when Lou halted and held up his hand, making the line of searchers come to a stop. "Ten-minute break."

Trying not to limp, Mercy took a few steps to lean against a tree trunk. She'd swallowed all her Advil, ignoring the recommended dose. While going down a steep hill, she'd been terrified her leg would buckle under the strain, and Anna had given her a strange look as Mercy wiped heavy sweat from her forehead. No one else was visibly sweating.

At the break, Anna followed Mercy to the tree and removed a bottle of water from her pack. "What's wrong with your leg?" Anna asked quietly between sips, her lips hidden behind her water bottle.

"Nothing."

"Bullshit. I vouched for you to come. Am I going to regret it?"

"No," Mercy said through clenched teeth. "I'm keeping up just fine."

The woman studied Mercy, her green eyes doubtful. "What happened?" she asked again.

Do I tell her? "Gunshot. Two months ago."

A small measure of respect replaced the doubt. "Are you fucking crazy?"

"I have to find him."

Anna looked away, indecision flickering as she took in the men as they rehydrated and rested. "I should tell Lou right now."

"Not until I collapse. Then you can say something."

"What's that sound?" asked one of the men.

Then Mercy heard it. An engine.

The sound wasn't far off and seemed to be coming closer.

"That's a quad," said one of the officers.

"Pair up," Lou ordered.

Mercy and Anna automatically stepped shoulder to shoulder as they drew their weapons, and Lou gestured for them to move ahead. The other pairs of cops were sent in the same direction, sweeping forward but several yards apart.

As they moved, Mercy could hear yelling far ahead. It sounded like cheering. *Did someone else find them?* An eagerness quickened her steps. The forest thinned, and Mercy spotted a small clearing with a group of giant boulders in the center. Three unknown men on quads were circling the boulders, cheering and yelling obscenities at the rocks. Mercy froze and caught her breath.

They must be Kenneth Forbes's men.

Each rider had a rifle.

This isn't good.

She and Anna stopped behind a large pine and looked to Lou. He gestured for them to sit tight. The three pairs of searchers all waited, watching the four-wheelers' tires send mud flying into the air.

A dog darted out from between the boulders, barking at one of the quads. A thin figure burst out and leaped at the dog, caught it around the belly, and then hauled it back to the shelter of the rocks.

Was that the teenager and his dog?

Truman has to be there too.

Mercy tasted blood as she bit her tongue to keep from calling his name.

The four-wheelers came to a stop, each one on a different side of the huge boulder pile to pin down whoever hid in the rocks. The men dismounted. Mercy could see two of them from her angle. Both carried their rifles, casually aiming them toward the rocks.

"Come out, you little shit!" one yelled at the boulders. "If you don't get out here now, I'll shoot your dog first and make you watch as it slowly dies." Laughter from the other two men filled the clearing. "If you do what I say, you can be shot first so you don't have to watch." Peals of laughter again.

"Send out the cop," another one yelled.

Truman.

Joy and terror shot through Mercy, and she fought to keep her focus. Lou gestured for her and Anna to watch the first man who had spoken. One set of cops moved through the trees and around the clearing to cover the man Mercy couldn't see. Lou and his partner had the third.

Lou's suspect aimed his rifle at the rocks and fired twice.

Mercy's heart stopped, and her fingers tightened on her gun. *Did he hit Truman?*

"Police! Put down your weapons and get on the ground!" shouted Lou.

Mercy's man spun around, his rifle pointed at the ground, searching the trees for the location of the shout. She and Anna both had him in their sights, but waited to see if he'd follow orders.

Lou yelled again, his weapon aimed at his suspect. The shooter turned and fired in Lou's direction.

Several gunshots sounded, and Lou's suspect fell to the ground, blood flowing from his chest and neck.

At the same time, Mercy's man threw his rifle to the side and dropped to his stomach in the mud, his hands protecting his head.

Thank God.

No other shots came, and the officers on the other side of the rocks announced that their man was in custody. Mercy and Anna slowly left the trees, their weapons trained on the man covering his head.

As they drew closer, Mercy's suspect whipped out his hand and lurched for his weapon. Three fast steps put Mercy at his head, her gun pointed at his skull. "Just try it," she said in a low voice, as anger raced through her. "Your buddy has several holes in his chest. Do you want some too?"

He slowly returned his hand to the back of his head.

Mercy covered Anna as she cuffed the man. Once he was secure, she exhaled and noticed Lou and his partner checking their suspect. Lou looked her way and shook his head. He was dead. She winced in sorrow for the suspect and for the officers who had fired.

Truman. "Truman?" she shouted at the rocks, her weapon trained on the rocky hiding place. *I don't know who else might be in there.*

"*Mercy?*"

His voice lit up every nerve receptor in her body. *He's alive.* Anticipation made the gun shake in her icy hands. "Are you hurt?" Her voice cracked as she took careful steps closer to the boulders, wanting to dash between them. "The three men out here are in custody. Are there any more in the area?"

"No, just us." A familiar tall figure limped out from the rocks, and she lost her breath at the sight of him. His face was thin and covered with two weeks of beard. His clothing and hair were filthy, but he looked stunningly beautiful to her. She holstered her weapon and ran the rest of the way, flung herself at him, and nearly knocked him down, her thigh forgotten. The only thing that mattered was him.

Finally. I'm not letting go.

His arms went around her and he clung tightly, his beard soft against her cheek. And wet. He started to shake, and she moved him to a rock to sit on and nearly crawled in his lap as she wrapped her arms around his neck. He wept, burying his face against her. A moment later he pulled back and put his right hand on her face, eyeing her hungrily. "I can't believe it," he muttered over and over.

"I thought you were dead," she whispered, moving her hands to hold his face. She couldn't stare at him enough. His face felt foreign yet familiar to her fingertips as they learned the new contours of his sunken cheeks.

"I thought I was too," he admitted. He moved his hand to her shoulder and frantically rubbed it up and down her arm, his gaze still locked on her face. "I didn't think I'd ever touch you again."

His eyes were red and wet, and he continued to quake under her fingers.

"You're not moving your left arm," she noticed.

"I think it's broken."

The pain he must have suffered.

"Is the rest of you okay?" She pulled back and assessed him.

"Everything is okay now."

"No, seriously, Truman. Are you hurt somewhere else?"

"I think I had a concussion, and I know I had a fever for a while . . . I'm a bit banged up, but my arm is the worst of it."

"We'll get you to a hospital." She stood, determined to carry him out if she had to, and nearly bumped into a young man directly behind her. A small hound sat next to his feet and showed Mercy its teeth. Anna stood a few yards behind the young man, her weapon holstered, but her hand ready as she kept a careful watch on the teenager.

"Mercy," said Truman. "This is Ollie. He saved my life." His voice wavered. "I would be dead if he hadn't gotten me out." He straightened his spine and sat up, his eyes widening. "Ollie knows where to find the guys who took me. They are running a—"

"We know." Mercy put a calming hand on his shoulder. "We've already arrested the three men back at the house. Joshua Forbes came in and told us where you might be. His father was one of the ringleaders."

Truman slouched on the rock in relief. "Forbes. It seems so long ago that I pulled him over. One stupid traffic stop triggered this whole thing." He covered his eyes with one hand and shuddered.

He's been through hell.

"Is everyone else okay?" he asked. "My men . . ."

"Everyone is fine. Your parents and sister will be happy to hear you've been found." She glanced at Lou, who had stepped away and was speaking on his radio. The message that Truman was fine should spread quickly.

"I worried what they might think," he admitted, his dark eyes searching her face. "I worried what was going through your head too."

"It was rough," Mercy agreed, unwilling to share her bouts of guilt and doubt and depression. Truman had enough on his plate. She hugged him again, unable to get enough of the feel of his body. *He's safe.*

"Can you drive one of those things?" Lou came back and gestured at one of the quads, raising a brow at Mercy.

"Yes."

"Let's get him loaded up, then, and you can ride out of here in luxury." He glanced over at the dead body. "I'll drive that one out, Anna can drive out the kid, and then everyone else can start walking."

"I'm not a kid." Ollie spoke for the first time. "And I'll head back to my own place. I don't need a ride."

"No," Truman said firmly. "You're coming out. You and Shep will stay with me for a bit."

Ollie looked at the ground. "That's not necessary."

"Yes, it is. We already discussed this." Truman was adamant.

Mercy watched the exchange, wondering what had happened between the two of them in the woods. *Truman has taken him under his wing.* "Ollie, is your family close by?" she asked him. The teenager looked exactly as he'd been described by Forbes's men. A hermit who lived in the woods.

"His family is gone," Truman told her. "He's going to stay with me until he gets his feet underneath him. We've got plans for his future."

Ollie looks less than convinced.

But he needs help.

"I hope Shep doesn't mind cats," she told Ollie. "Simon is the ruling queen of Truman's house."

The teen finally smiled.

THIRTY-SEVEN

Truman was relieved to be out of the woods. *I'll never enjoy camping again.*

After a painful ride on the quad that had continuously jolted Truman's broken arm, Mercy took him straight to the hospital. Ollie refused to let Truman out of his sight and tagged along, which meant Shep was there too. The ER staff banished the dog and Ollie outside while Mercy and Truman spent the next three hours in the emergency room. His parents and sister showed up, and more hugs and tears were exchanged. After an hour he sent his family back to their hotel with promises to see them the next day.

Mercy had sucked in a deep breath at the sight of the colorful bruises on his back and ribs, but there was nothing to be done but allow them to heal. He pissed in a cup and was told his kidneys were doing their job. His head was scanned and his arm was x-rayed. The head looked good, but the arm was broken, as expected. "You're lucky," the busy ER doctor said. "We don't cast this sort of break. Usually a splint is all we do, and it looks like you had a pretty good makeshift one. Keep the arm still and elevate it when you can."

He went home and showered for thirty minutes, letting the horror of the past week go down the drain. Then he ordered Ollie to shower and gave him a spare pair of pajamas. When the teen was sacked out in his guest room with Shep on the bed beside him, Truman finally allowed himself to go to bed.

Mercy snuggled beside him, and they whispered in the dark and touched each other's skin, hair, and face. He couldn't stop touching her to make certain he wasn't dreaming, and she seemed to feel the same. She asked a lot of questions, and he told her the bare minimum. Talking about it brought back too many memories. He pushed aside the flashbacks of extreme thirst and fear of losing circulation in his arm.

"What was it like for you?" he asked her.

"I had a lot of bad days," she admitted. "My emotions were all over the place. The longer you were gone, the deeper I sank. The not knowing . . ." Her voice was raw and earnest. It was a poignant side she rarely exposed.

"This sounds stupid, but I think that you were in a worse mental and emotional situation than I was," Truman told her. "Once Ollie got me out, I knew I'd be okay. You didn't have that luxury."

"You can't say I had it worse. I saw the shed."

"Yes, that was hell." He shuddered. "My mind wants to block most of it. At least I wasn't in there long."

She told him she needed a shower, gave him a long kiss, and disappeared into his bathroom.

It'd been a very, very long day.

Truman would never take his home or mattress or gas heat for granted again. He closed his eyes and appreciated the soft pillow beneath his head, and the vibration of the cat purring on his chest.

Even under the cover of the sound of the shower, he heard Mercy's sobs. Against every desire in his heart, he didn't go to her. She needed to expel the pain and fear in private. She'd come to him when she was ready.

He'd nearly drifted to sleep on a glorious sea of painkillers when he felt her crawl back in bed, smelling of soap and fresh water.

"I love you," she whispered as she formed her body to his.

"I love you more," he answered and then remembered nothing else.

The next morning he woke to the scent of eggs, bacon, and pancakes. And coffee. The heavenly odors reached his starving caffeine receptors and lifted him out of bed. Ollie was coming out of the guest room as Truman stepped into the hall. The teen was following the smells too. Even Shep's nose twitched. Ollie's usually greasy hair was a wild but clean mop on his head. Truman ran a hand over his own facial hair. He hadn't hated the sight of it in the mirror, but he had been shocked at the change in his facial shape caused by his weight loss. He shook his wrist, still not used to his single handcuff bracelet's absence. Mercy had removed it at the hospital.

He and Ollie stepped into the kitchen, where the sight of Mercy cooking while wearing simple yoga pants and a long-sleeved T-shirt brought tears to his eyes. He kissed her long and hard, not caring if Ollie was watching. The teen might as well get used to it. They all sat down at the table and feasted.

"I wasn't sure what to feed Shep, so I cooked some ground beef from the freezer and mixed it with oatmeal," Mercy told Ollie. "I figured that would be fine until we could buy dog food." The way Shep was attacking his bowl of food on the floor indicated he was pleased.

The boy simply nodded, shoveling scrambled eggs into his mouth as fast as he could. Truman watched in amusement. Ollie's eyes had grown huge at the sight of all the food, and he had served himself tiny helpings. Truman had finally loaded the teen's plate for him. Mercy watched Ollie inhale the eggs, raised a brow, got up, and started scrambling more.

Simon wandered into the room and Shep lunged at the cat with a sharp bark. Simon promptly swatted the dog's nose, and Shep howled and dashed to hide under Ollie's chair, where he watched the cat with terrified eyes. Simon sat in the center of the room, ignored him, and groomed her back leg.

"That was settled quickly," commented Truman.

Then the parade of visitors started. Kaylie was first, stopping in on her way to school. She'd insisted on FaceTiming Truman last night in the emergency room and had been horrified by his condition. This morning she launched herself at him, hugged him for a long twenty seconds, and then grabbed a tissue to dry her eyes. She eyed him critically over the tissue. "You look much better than last night."

"Thank you." He didn't know what else to say.

"I don't know about the beard, though." She patted one of his hairy cheeks, her eyebrows coming together in concentration. "Maybe."

She left for school after giving him a short lecture on never disappearing again.

As if I had control over it.

Mercy's sister Pearl was next with a huge plate of pastries from the café and clothes for Ollie. Mercy had called her last night, asking if her son had some clothing that no longer fit. Her son was thin like Ollie but had sprouted several inches in the last year. Pearl had two paper grocery bags full of jeans, shoes, and shirts. "What doesn't fit you can give away. None of it fits him anymore."

Ollie vanished into his room with his bags of riches as Pearl hugged Truman and ran her fingers over his beard.

"What do you think, Mercy? Do you want him to keep it?"

Why does everyone need to touch it?

Mercy tipped her head, pretending to look thoughtful. "I haven't decided yet. The mountain man look has never appealed to me. But it does make him look rugged, doesn't it? Or maybe we could trim it down to a Tony Stark look."

Both women eyed him with fresh speculation. "No Iron Man," stated Truman.

Ollie emerged in jeans, a University of Oregon sweatshirt, and a baseball cap crammed on his mop. He looked pleased.

Truman's men straggled in throughout the day. Ben was first and unashamedly wiped away tears after giving Truman a rib-crushing hug. His bruises shot pain directly into his brain, but Truman didn't care. His senior officer's affection was more important.

"Wondered if we'd ever see you again," Ben muttered. His wife had sent food. Two casseroles and a cake.

Royce's wife sent a complete turkey dinner to feed a dozen people, and Samuel handed him a six-pack of beer. "Thought this might taste good after that long stretch of alcohol-free days," Samuel told Truman. The usually undemonstrative officer gave him a hug with manly back slapping and had a hard time looking him in the eye.

Truman was touched.

Lucas showed up and lifted Truman off the ground in a bear hug. "Damn, it's good to see you." Ollie watched the giant man in awe, his gaze never leaving Lucas's burly arms. Lucas added cigars to all the food offerings, and Mercy wrinkled her nose at the gift.

Truman's family appeared, and his mother and sister took it upon themselves to clean out his refrigerator and restock it. Their energetic presence overtook the house, and Ollie and Shep escaped to the backyard, where they discovered an old tennis ball. His father sat down in Truman's favorite recliner in his study with some of the café's pastries and then fell asleep the moment his wife and daughter left for the grocery store. Truman closed the door against his snores.

In the living room, Mercy had built a fire. She and Truman sat on the love seat across from it, getting as close to one another as possible. She had every part of her body touching him somewhere. *I don't want to get up. Ever.* He didn't use the fireplace often, but as the crackling flames warmed the room, he committed to doing it more. It reminded him a bit of the woodstove at Ollie's place, which had been more efficient at warming a room than his fireplace.

Maybe I should put in a stove in case I lose power.

"I don't think I have the survival skills I need," he mused. "This experience was an eye-opener to me."

"You were held captive and beaten. That's a little different."

"True. But being around Ollie helped me see what's truly vital for survival. He's got it down to a science."

"He had to be lonely."

Truman remembered how Ollie's eyes had lit up during their card games. "Definitely."

"What are your plans for him?"

"Get him in community college. Maybe a job so he can support himself and rent an apartment. I have no doubt he could easily attend school full-time and work full-time. He's focused."

"Is that what he wants?"

"I think so. Part of him would be content to live in the woods for the rest of his life, but I saw how the idea of college and an education appealed to him."

"You're a good man, Truman Daly." Mercy sighed and kissed him, leaning deeper into his arms.

"What have I missed over the last week or so?" His brain struggled to return to work. He'd grown used to letting it relax and focus solely on how to beat Ollie at cards. "Did you identify the adult skulls? Did they belong to the Hartlages?"

"Two of the skulls were the parents," Mercy confirmed. "It feels odd that you don't know this, but I found out the same day you vanished. There's still one unidentified male skull. Dr. Peres sent in DNA samples to see if he's Corrine Hartlage's brother. We should hear back soon."

"What about the other murdered family?" He searched his memory for the name. "The Jorgensens."

"We're stalled until something new comes out of the evidence's lab tests. Right now we've exhausted everything."

"That can't be right," said Truman. "That huge scene? Something left behind has to point to the killer."

"That's what I keep telling myself."

Something prodded him about the Hartlage case. "Wait a minute. You said one male skull wasn't identified. Weren't there two others? What about the Asian one?"

"Oh!" She sat up straight. "Dr. Peres doesn't believe it's a victim . . . well, not a victim from this century, anyway. Someone carved a tiny date and initials inside the skull. She suspects it's a souvenir from the Vietnam War."

"A souvenir?" Disgust created a sour taste in his mouth.

"Right? People collect that sort of thing. It was probably smuggled into the country somehow."

"Then why was it under that road with the victims?"

"That's a question I plan to ask when I catch who put it there."

He had no doubts she'd succeed.

"Clint Moody is still missing," she added. "We'd thought he was taken by the same people as you." She described finding Truman's burned-out Tahoe, her voice shaking as she detailed the damage. Then she told him about Clint's sunken vehicle and her horror at the need to drag the pond. "His brother, Ryan, is going nuts, and I completely understand. Not knowing what happened to a loved one eats away at you," she ended softly.

One-armed, Truman pulled her into him again, ribs and back be damned. She buried her face in his neck but then pulled away, rubbing her nose, an accusatory glint in her eye. "Your beard tickles."

"I'll shave it tomorrow."

The doorbell rang, and she reluctantly pulled away to answer it. He was instantly cold, his body wanting her back.

"I don't think you need any more food dropped off," she muttered as she went toward the door.

He agreed.

It was Rose and Nick Walker. Truman watched Rose greet Mercy, her hand gently touching Mercy's cheek. Rose's pregnancy was highlighted by her formfitting top and the fullness of her face. As usual, Rose brought light and serenity to the room. Her smile and warmth were contagious, and Truman always felt peace in her presence. No wonder Nick was addicted. Truman shook hands with the lumberyard owner and then turned his attention to Rose.

Her resemblance to Mercy was strong, but the coloring was different. And Mercy exuded focus and intensity, not Rose's softness.

That was fine with him.

"Oh, Truman." Rose touched his arm and moved her hand to his face. She froze as her fingertips found unexpected facial hair. Then she grinned. "That's a change."

"It's temporary," he asserted. *What is the fascination with the beard?*

"We were thankful to hear you were okay," Rose said with a wide smile.

Some of Truman's anxiety immediately floated away. It was a skill of hers.

The four of them talked for a short while, and then Rose and Nick left.

"They're crazy about each other," Truman commented. "I see it in both of them."

"I agree. Rose has had a few insecure moments, but she's learning to trust him. We've talked about how she can communicate better with him." Mercy grimaced. "Speaking of communication, do you know what ate away at me while you were gone?"

He knew instantly. "The fact that we argued." It'd ripped up his insides too. "I overreacted about the cabin decisions. You should have the lead on that project."

"You didn't overreact. I need to be more aware of your feelings," she said earnestly.

He kissed her to stop her from talking about it. It was such a small thing in the scope of what had happened.

"I know what's truly important now," he said against her mouth.

He felt her lips curve. "Me too."

THIRTY-EIGHT

Truman went to the police department the next day. He couldn't stay away.

Now that he'd been back in civilization for more than a day, his brain had shifted into fast-forward and he needed to know what he'd missed at work. Mercy had helped him get dressed, and he wore a clean splint and sling for his arm. He had shaved, and now his face looked and felt naked. At breakfast Ollie had looked at Truman as if he didn't recognize him. Truman's father had taken the teen to get a haircut the previous afternoon, and Truman had stared at Ollie in the same manner when he returned, embarrassing him.

Their hair was a symbol of deeper changes. Truman wasn't the same man he'd been weeks earlier, and he planned to transform Ollie's world for the better.

The Eagle's Nest Police Department building felt welcoming and slightly foreign at the same time.

But damn, it was good to be back in his chair.

After catching up on a mountain of paperwork and eating lunch, he saw he had time for an errand before Mercy stopped by. She'd insisted on checking up on him, and he couldn't say no; he had a deep need to see her too. Their separation had left both of them rattled and needing occasional visual reassurance.

Truman walked down the street to pick up more paper for their printer. Lucas had planned to do it, but Truman was ready for a breath of fresh air, rain or not. The outside chill felt good on his bare cheeks. His town was quiet and peaceful, and the stress of his time in the woods was fading.

I'm a lucky, lucky man.

He froze as up ahead a man abruptly lunged out a store door and tripped over his own feet, falling into the street at the curb. A black dog burst out of the store and circled the man, barking madly, and a woman followed. She stopped and stood tall over the man in the street, her hands on her hips, not offering to help. Truman jerked into motion and ran to give a hand.

Not-so-quiet town.

"—following me!" the black-haired woman was shouting at the man.

Truman recognized the nearly bald-headed man on the ground. Steve Harris. The man he'd recently interviewed because he'd found the murdered Verbeek family two decades earlier. Truman halted as the dog planted its feet, made eye contact with him, and growled. The woman grabbed its collar. "Sit." The dog sat, dividing its attention between the man on the ground and Truman.

"Zara won't bite," the tall woman told Truman. "But she isn't fond of men."

"She should be leashed."

"Yes, she should." She released the dog's collar and the animal stayed motionless. The lean woman was dressed from head to toe in black and exuded an alertness and tension that reminded him a bit of Mercy.

"You okay, Steve?" Truman knelt, using his one good hand to help the man up.

"Tripped," he muttered, keeping an eye on the dog.

"He's been following me for days," the woman announced. "Zara picked up on my nervousness in the store and lunged at him. She would never bite," she quickly added.

"Leash her now," Truman ordered. The woman had ignored Truman's first hint to secure her dog. She pulled a leash out of her bag and snapped it on.

"He's been harassing me. I keep seeing him everywhere."

Steve fixed his gaze on the dog. "I didn't touch her or say a word to her," he claimed.

Truman noticed he didn't say he hadn't been following her. "What's your name?" he asked the woman.

"Britta."

He blinked and focused on the tattoo peeking out from under her high collar. He looked questioningly at Steve, who nodded back. "Britta Verbeek—Vale?" he asked her.

Annoyance flashed on her face. "I don't know you," she told Truman. She tightened her grip on the dog's leash.

"I know about you," Truman admitted. "I'm Truman Daly. Chief of Eagle's Nest PD. Mercy Kilpatrick is my girlfriend."

Britta pressed her lips together, agitation present in her expression. *I don't think I just did Mercy any favors.*

Truman looked between the two tense people, wondering where to start. He jerked his head at Steve. "You know he's the one who originally found your family?"

Her face cleared and then went dark again. "Why the fuck are you following me?" she said in a low tone to Steve.

"I saw you for the first time today—a few minutes ago. I heard the clerk call you Britta when he thanked you for your purchase. I came closer to see if it was really you, because I'd heard you were back in town." He looked at his feet. "I've always wondered what happened to you. If you saw me previously, it's only because I'm always in town."

"That's true," said Truman. "I stumble across him almost every time I walk down the street. Did he do anything to you?" he asked Britta.

"He looked at me," she muttered, glaring at Steve. "I could tell he recognized me."

Not against the law.

"I've been on edge lately," she admitted.

"I know," Truman said. "You have good reason." He looked at Steve. "Do you have your confirmation that she's fine now?"

"Yeah." He glanced at Britta.

"Don't ever approach me again." Britta's eyes were pale-blue flames.

Not if Steve wants to keep his head.

"Go home, Steve," Truman ordered. The man was happy to leave, and Truman watched him rapidly make his way down the sidewalk.

He turned back to Britta, who also watched him leave. "Why don't you come chat with me a bit?" Truman asked her. "I'm expecting Mercy any minute. I know she'd like to see you."

Indecision flickered on her face.

He held his hand out to the dog, who leaned forward to sniff it and then enthusiastically licked his fingers.

Truman had eaten a bacon cheeseburger for lunch.

"All right."

◆ ◆ ◆

Mercy was joking with Lucas when Truman walked in the door with Britta and a tail-wagging Zara.

"What happened?" she instantly asked, spotting the restrained fury in Britta's eyes. *She wants to kill someone.*

Truman gave her a rundown of Britta's encounter with Steve Harris.

"You think he's safe?" Mercy asked Truman. "I don't like that he approached her."

"Me neither," added Britta. "I saw him twice earlier this week. Once in the diner and then at the post office. Today made the third time."

"I know it looks bad," Truman admitted, "but I really think he's harmless. When I originally asked him about finding . . . your family, I could see that it had haunted him most of his life. His concern that day for you as the survivor felt very genuine. I've always dealt with him in tense situations because of the fire hydrant in front of his house, so I'd never seen him distressed like that before."

"He's creepy," Britta said. "I need to seriously consider moving. I feel like I'm under a spotlight in this town . . . too many things from the past."

Mercy understood the woman's concern and hated that she was about to make Britta feel even more on center stage. "Britta, do you recall Janet Norris? She was a friend of your mother's." *It feels good to focus on my cases instead of worrying about Truman.*

"I do. They worked together for a little while—the one time Dad allowed her to get a job. Janet talked a lot."

Mercy tried to think of the softest way to deliver her news. "I was going to call you about this later today, but do you remember when I told you a second family had been murdered here recently?"

"Of course," she snapped. "Later I saw it in the news. The Jorgensens. They had two children." Her jaw quivered.

"Janet Norris was their closest neighbor."

The muscles in Britta's jaw clenched as the rest of her went very still. "That's fucked up," she whispered. "How . . ."

"I know. The possibility of her being tied to the two similar murders decades apart boggles my mind."

Fear flickered on Britta's face, and she steered Zara toward the door. "I need to go—"

"Don't leave yet." Mercy stepped after the woman but stopped, knowing she'd bolt if Mercy touched her.

Britta looked over her shoulder. "Today has been too much . . . too many people . . ."

"I'm sorry—"

"It's okay, Mercy. I shouldn't have come back. I was stupid to think it would all be in the past."

The door closed behind her.

Truman exhaled. "I don't know what I think of her."

"She's scared. She's been uneasy all her life," Mercy said, wondering what she could have done differently to stop Britta from running off. "The simple fact that she gets up every morning and functions astounds me."

"I don't know how well she's functioning. I thought she was going to tear Steve Harris to pieces. She's like a loaded cannon."

"Yes, she's tightly wound. Everyone wants a piece of her. Even us," she added. "I feel as if she could help us with the Hartlage and Jorgensen cases."

"Both of them happened after she returned to town," Truman reminded her.

"I haven't forgotten. But we've found nothing to tie her to the deaths."

"Fingerprints, hair samples, footprints. Something has to point at the killer."

"Nothing yet. Even the hammer used at the Hartlages was completely clean and untraceable."

"Start again," Truman suggested. "You've got to find him before he murders again. Go back to the beginning."

Mercy sighed, feeling the weight of Truman's words.

What if he kills another family? Have I done everything I could to find him?

"Do you know how much evidence has been logged?" she asked. "How many interviews there have been?"

"I can imagine."

"It has to break open at some point," she said. "I'll review everything."

I won't rest until I know who killed those children.

THIRTY-NINE

"I know this smell means bad shit," Floyd Cox said solemnly as he led Truman toward the back of his property. His rental business had thirty storage units of different sizes, and they were all full.

Floyd had called the police station, concerned about an odor coming from one of his units. Now the wide sixty-year-old man waddled around the puddles on his grounds. Floyd didn't have any front teeth, but that didn't stop him from constantly grinning or talking. In fact, the short man was one of the most gregarious people Truman knew.

"You didn't call the owners?" Truman asked, thankful it wasn't raining.

"Nope. I wanted the police here when it was opened. If I called the owners, they might clean out something illegal first. I don't put up with that sort of thing on my property. Everyone signs a form saying they won't use the units for anything against the law." He looked over his shoulder at Truman, scrutinizing him and eyeing the splint. "Good to see you back, Chief. Our whole town was mighty worried."

"It's good to be back."

"What happened to the arm?"

"Had a nasty fall," Truman lied.

"You can drive like that?"

"For the most part."

Most of the injuries to his face had healed, but he still had some scabbing. He wasn't about to say he'd had the crap beat out of him—especially to one of the most talkative men in town. The forgers had been charged, and Truman figured he had weeks if not months of trials to deal with. The real story of his injuries would come out in testimony.

"What's the weirdest thing you've ever found in one of your storage units?" Truman asked to divert Floyd's attention. "I imagine people leave stuff behind all the time."

"Haven't found money, that's for sure," Floyd said mournfully. "I keep hoping one of these days someone will leave behind a pile of cash. Hasn't happened yet." He hitched up his pants. "I suppose the weirdest thing was about four years ago. They stopped paying on the unit, and I couldn't hunt them down. When I finally opened it, I found dolls. Hundreds of them in all different shapes and sizes, from Barbie dolls to mannequins." He lowered his voice and waited for Truman to come up beside him. "Every single one of them was naked. Several didn't have heads."

"Were they in boxes?"

"Nope. There were boxes in the unit, but the dolls were sitting on top of the boxes, arranged like an audience. Creeped me the hell out when I went in and found all those eyes staring at me."

I'm creeped out by listening.

"Who does that?" Floyd went on, confusion in his voice. "The image of those dolls still pops into my head at odd times. I didn't understand. Why display them in that way? Probably something *sexual*," he said, whispering the word with disdain.

"People do weird stuff."

"I wish they'd keep it behind their own closed doors, not mine," Floyd asserted. "Here we are." He gestured to a unit that was about six feet wide and eight feet tall with a roll-up door.

Truman smelled it. *Rotting flesh. Not good.* "Maybe an animal got in there . . . or they stored something from hunting."

"I hope you're right." Floyd bent over to unlock the padlock at the bottom of the door. "But you can understand why I wanted a cop here when I opened it."

Truman understood. And wished Samuel had taken the call.

"Holy sheeet," Floyd said as he yanked up the door. He took three giant steps away and dry heaved.

Truman covered his mouth and nose, stepping back from the odiferous wave and clenching his teeth against the bile that rose in the back of his throat.

Something is definitely dead.

Cardboard boxes were stacked high along one wall of the unit, labeled neatly with dates and contents. But Truman had eyes only for the rolled-up carpet on the floor. It was wedged among the legs of several wooden chairs. Fluids seeped from the closest end, and Truman saw hair inside. It was short human hair that appeared to still be on a head.

"What's the name of the renter?" he asked Floyd.

"Moody. Clint Moody," Floyd said between retches.

"Aw, jeez."

◆ ◆ ◆

A half hour later, the Deschutes County Sheriff's Department reported that Ryan Moody wasn't at home and had the day off from his plumbing job.

Truman put out a BOLO on Ryan's truck and wondered if the brother had left town.

"The fucker had me convinced he was worried about Clint," Truman muttered to Mercy as they waited near the storage unit. She'd been his third phone call after the sheriff and the medical examiner.

"You weren't the only one," Mercy said. "I actually felt sorry for him."

"Still not positive he's the one who put his brother in here."

Mercy snorted.

Dr. Natasha Lockhart appeared at the same time as the county forensics team. She greeted Truman and Mercy with her usual perky smile. "I've got good news!" she said to Mercy. "You'll get an email from me later today, but the DNA tests came back on our unknown skull. It is definitely related to Corrine Hartlage. The test indicates a sibling relationship."

"Well, that's one question answered," admitted Mercy. "I assume his last name is Palmer, since that was Corrine's name. We haven't found a paper trail that we can positively link to him. Maybe he simply stayed off the grid most of his life."

"Seeing how the Hartlages lived cut off from everyone, that wouldn't surprise me," commented Truman.

Dr. Lockhart turned her attention to the open unit. "Oh boy. You've got a smelly one here." She opened her bag, shoved cotton rolls up her nose, and put on a face shield. "Looks gooshy too."

Is gooshy *an official medical term?* The visible hair inside the rolled-up rug was eating away at Truman. He'd wanted to yank the carpet out of the shed and confirm it was Clint Moody.

Who else would it be?

The hair color matched what he remembered of Clint.

Dr. Lockhart directed the forensic photographer for a few minutes, showing him the views she wanted, and then asked for help to slide out the rug. Both Truman and Mercy stepped forward, but Mercy waved him back. He'd forgotten he only had one good arm. Mercy, the ME, and two of the techs slid the rug onto a tarp spread out on the concrete. More photos.

The dark-haired medical examiner raised a brow at Mercy and Truman. "Ready?"

No. Truman held his breath as she unrolled the rug. He studied the body for a long moment and then walked away, seeking fresh air.

At the end of the row of units he leaned his good arm against a wall and looked up at the gray sky, breathing deep. A minute later Mercy joined him.

"Clint's wallet was in the back pocket. I think it's him," she said.

"I don't know how you can visually identify him. Someone practically beat in his skull," Truman stated. He'd never get the image out of his head. It'd been seared into his brain. The spots where Truman had been kicked in the skull started to throb.

"That's true, but the height and hair color are accurate according to the license. I bet we'll confirm it's him by tomorrow."

"Or we can get a confession out of Ryan," Truman muttered. When the carpet had been unrolled, his anger toward the man had tripled. "His disappearance is too coincidental. And he would know about and have access to Clint's storage unit."

"The injuries on this body appear to be similar to the Hartlages and Jorgensens. The damaged skulls and the broken teeth. This seems worse because of the amount of decomposition. Clint's been missing for about two weeks, right?"

"Yes." He paused as her words sank in, and he turned toward her. "Are you saying Ryan is also a suspect in those family murders?"

"I don't know. I can't assume anything." Mercy rubbed a hand across her mouth. "As far as I can tell right now, the type of injury Clint has—assuming it's him—is the only thing in common . . . although that could change."

"This body was hidden away like the Hartlages were," Truman pointed out.

"True."

"Someone did a crappy hiding job. They had to know the smell would eventually lead someone to the body."

"Maybe they planned to move him."

"I wonder if they've been back to the storage unit. I wish Floyd had installed cameras. He doesn't have one of those gates where people key in a personal code either."

"Ryan might not be our killer," Mercy stated. "It only needs to be someone who knew Clint had a unit here and had access to his key . . . which was probably on his keychain. I'll get it from evidence. The keys were left in Clint's truck in the pond."

"Didn't they already fingerprint the keys?"

"I don't know. Clint's missing persons case was handled by county once you disappeared. I didn't believe it was related to the Hartlages or Jorgensens."

"I didn't either."

Mercy met his gaze. "But we're both wondering if it's related now. I want a look inside the Moody house."

"Deschutes County was authorized to go into the Moody house to look for Ryan today. A car should still be there in case he shows up."

"Let's go."

FORTY

I never forgot that summer.

My father had burrowed deeper inside himself. Us kids were told to leave him alone and stay out of his way. He stopped going to work, and my mother tightened the household spending. Meals were smaller. Meat was infrequent. We ate a lot of potatoes. She talked about finding a job. My father blew up when she suggested it. "No wife of mine needs a job! I can support this family!"

There was lots of yelling in their room that night, and the next morning her eye was black and blue.

My father started to wander at night. At first he'd pace up and down the hallways, and the boards would creak every time he passed our room. His mumbling continued. The only phrase I could make out was his regular "Stop talking to me," even though he was alone.

Then he started pacing outside, and I'd watch from my bedroom window as he wandered our few acres. Sometimes he dug holes with a shovel. Sometimes he cleaned the pens. Sometimes he'd sit and simply stare at the stars. I would check the holes the next day. There was nothing in them; they were just random holes. Everywhere.

I wondered about the ghosts that tortured him.

Then he started to run. He started wearing shorts at night and running our long driveway out to the main road and back. He'd run for nearly an hour and be dripping with sweat when he stopped. I'd sneak out of the house and hide in the bed of the truck, spying on him from a wide crack in its metal side. I'm not sure why I watched; his actions were boring. But I wanted to know what drove him, why he constantly needed to move. Was something chasing him?

Several weeks after I walked through the Deverell house and saw the blood, I spied on him from my regular spot from the truck, slightly nervous because the moon was full and bright, and I felt exposed. That night he threw down his shovel as he finished a hole. He disappeared into the barn and came out with a large hammer. This was new, and I wondered what repetitive task he'd tackle. Instead he walked directly toward me.

I couldn't move. I froze in place as my heart tried to pound its way up my throat.

He sees me.

He will hit me with the hammer.

I'm about to die.

Instead he got in the cab and the truck started. I lay flat, as close to the cab as possible, and tried to melt into the floor of the truck bed. My relief at not being spotted was brief, and I feared where he was taking me.

A few minutes later he turned off the paved road and onto a gravel one. The ride turned rough, and the moon highlighted the dust clouds rolling behind the truck.

He stopped, and I held my breath, clenching my eyes closed as if that would save me from being seen. His door opened and quietly shut, and I listened to his footsteps crunch on the gravel as he walked away.

Silence.

I opened my eyes. He'd parked under an outdoor security light and it was as if a spotlight shone on me. I scooted on my stomach to the crack in the truck bed and peered through just in time to see him enter a house.

My heart still running a race, I slipped over the side of the truck bed and moved into the shadows of the trees and tried to slow my heartbeat.

I felt secure in the dark, and I crouched behind a thick trunk, keeping an eye on the house. I hadn't been to this home before, but I knew where we were. We'd driven west from our home on the main road and the only turn my father had taken was onto this long driveway.

He's having an affair.

The thought shot through my young brain. I knew what an affair was. He was in love with another woman. Relief for my mother swept through me. Maybe he'd leave her to stay with this other—

The female scream from the house jolted every nerve I had.

In the silence that followed, I felt as if I were drowning, desperate for another sound to help me breathe again.

Instead I only heard the noises of the night. Crickets. Tree frogs. The leaves in a breeze.

A minute later he came out, leaving the front door wide open. He took ten steps and dropped to his knees, covering his face with his hands.

His piercing scream wasn't human.

The hairs on my arms shot upright.

After a moment of silence, he tipped back his head and screamed again, his arms raised to the night sky, the hammer in his right hand.

He's finally cracked.

He lurched to his feet and went to their garden hose on the side of the home, washed his hands, rinsed his hammer, and then aimed the hose at his face and let the water wash over him.

I held my breath.

He finally stopped and shook his head like a dog, water droplets flying everywhere. He threw down the hose and strode toward the truck.

It was too late for me to get back in the truck's bed.

I watched as he drove away and exhaled, briefly closing my eyes. I would walk home. I preferred that to another nail-biting ride.

My legs shook as I stood up, making me put a hand against the tree for balance. I sucked in deep breaths and was relieved at being alone. I started to walk down the driveway to the road.

That scream.

I stopped, horrible visions bouncing through my head.

What did he do?

I remembered the hammer. The determination in his stride as he walked with it gripped in his hand.

I know what he did.

I knew what had happened as surely as I knew the color of my hair, my eyes, my skin.

I turned around and looked at the house. It was silent, and the air around it felt weighted and heavy with pain. Even the normal noises of the night had stopped.

I couldn't think as my feet moved me toward the home. It silently called me, compelling me to go inside. My mind blank, I went up the wooden steps and through the front door. Inside was a dead man on the living room floor. His jaw had been destroyed, and he had several bloody areas on his head. I watched his chest for movements. It was still.

My father did this.

I left and went down the hall. A woman lay on the floor in my way. Her nightgown was up over her hips, showing her underwear. Her hair and head were bloody. I crouched next to her and saw her brain. Blood pooled around her head and streaks of it went up the wall. In the small bedroom beside her, I saw a set of bunk beds and a single bed. Walking silently, I stopped at the bed. A small girl. I could see pieces of bone above her bloody ear. For the third time I saw a bloody, abused mouth and teeth.

The mouths. Was he trying to stop these people from talking to him?

Her hair drained blood onto her pillow, and I recognized a female Smurf on her pillowcase. Her body curled under her covers as if she were still sleeping. I turned around and another girl was in the bottom bunk. She lay in the exact same position, but he'd struck her right eye and her mouth, and her sharp jagged bones poked through her skin.

He couldn't have heard them talk. These two girls never woke.

It's all in his head.

I couldn't see the top bunk. I wanted to.

I stepped on the first rung of the small ladder. Then the second and third. In the bunk was another girl.

Her mouth was bloody, her eyes were open, and she lay in absolute stillness.

A flawless round drop of blood was in the center of her forehead. I reached out and touched it, wanting to spoil its perfection.

She blinked and sucked in a ragged breath, making eye contact.

I gasped and grabbed the railing of the bunk to keep from falling backward. I let go and leaped to the floor. I dashed out of the room and sprang over the body in the hallway.

She saw me.

I tore out of the house and didn't stop running until I reached the road. I stopped, bent over, and rested my hands on my thighs, sucking in deep gulps of air.

She saw me.

She'll be dead by morning.

Repeating this assurance in my head, I walked toward home, reviewing everything I'd seen in that house. I was simultaneously horrified and curious.

Did my father kill the Deverells too?

In my heart I knew he had.

During my long trip home, I considered my options. I could go to the police. I could tell my mother. I could do nothing.

The choices tormented me the whole way home.

I fell into bed, no decision made. The girl's eyes haunted my dreams.

Within a few days, they arrested another man.

I kept my mouth shut.

FORTY-ONE

Mercy saw Truman was right. A county patrol car sat across the gravel street from the Moody home.

She parked on the road behind Truman, and the deputy walked over to talk to them, rain dripping off his hat.

What a miserable job. Waiting in a cold car during a rainstorm.

"No one's shown up," the young man told them. "No one's even driven down the road—it's that quiet here." He gestured at the house directly across from the Moodys'. "Although the lady there did bring me some cookies and hot coffee. She wanted to know what was going on."

"Sally Kantor? Nice lady. Her cookies should be safe," Truman stated.

"Ah . . . I didn't even think of that." Embarrassment flashed on the deputy's face.

Mercy wondered how many cookies he had eaten. "What did you tell Sally?"

"Nothing. Just said I was waiting for Ryan to return home so I could ask him some questions."

"Good." Truman indicated he was ready to head to the house, and she walked up the long drive with him. Far away, thunder sounded, and both of them looked at the darkening sky.

"Have you seen any lightning?" he asked.

"I didn't notice any, but maybe it was too far away. We're supposed to get a good storm tonight."

Mercy focused on the home before them. The house had no flowerpots or happy welcome signs, and large muddy boots sat by the front door. *Men live here.* There was no color anywhere. Everything was brown except the overgrown grass and the tree leaves. She and Truman bootied up and slipped on gloves before they entered. The house had been processed when Clint first went missing, but they had searched only for evidence of who might have hurt or taken the man.

Today she was looking for anything to tie Ryan to the Hartlage or Jorgensen family.

If I only knew what I was looking for.

I could be way off base.

The house appeared to have been built around the middle of the last century. The linoleum and countertops looked original. Again, there was no sign of a female presence in the house. This home was about male needs. Oversize furniture, gigantic TV, game consoles, and food. The cupboards were full of junk food and prepackaged meals. The refrigerator stocked with soda and beer.

At least it was decently clean.

She and Truman quickly searched every nook and cranny, looking for . . . something.

Down the hallway Truman paused in front of a closed door. His throat moved as he swallowed and then opened the door. The mattress had been stripped of bedding, and Mercy knew it had been Clint's room. Black fingerprint powder covered several surfaces. She opened the closet. Clothes hung from hangers and were piled on the floor. She did a quick check inside the pockets, the shoes, and then the boxes on the top shelf.

Truman checked the bathroom and moved to the other bedroom. "Mercy?" he called.

She followed his voice and found him in front of a large gun safe. "It's unlocked," he told her. "Ryan used the combination to open it last time I was here." He seemed hesitant to touch the door, so she reached over and swung it open.

Two rifles were present, and several rectangular containers she identified as handgun lockboxes.

"There were three rifles last time," Truman stated. He picked up one of the lockboxes. "This feels like there's still a weapon in it." He hefted the others until he came to an open one. "I think they all still hold a weapon except this one."

"Did he open the lockboxes for you?"

"Yes. I don't remember how many there were, but they all were full."

"We need to add to the BOLO that he is probably armed." She studied the other contents of Ryan's closet. The gun safe took up a large portion, and his clothes were pushed to one side. She did the same pocket check she'd done in Clint's room and went through the junk on the upper shelf. One shoebox clanked. She removed the lid. "He's got quite a few knives," she commented, counting seven of them. Most of the weapons had old, battered sheaths.

I'd rather find a hammer that could be the murder weapon.

"The garage out back is packed full of junk," Truman told her. "It could take days to go through."

Mercy returned the box to the shelf. She was sliding the closet door shut when she spotted a three-ring binder between the safe and the wall. Sliding her hand into the narrow space, she wiggled it out and flipped it open.

A photo of Britta Vale stared back at her, and Mercy nearly dropped the binder.

"Truman." She couldn't say anything else. Her fingers were ice.

As she turned the page, he watched over her shoulder. Pages and pages of fuzzy long-distance shots of Britta were carefully tucked into protective sleeves. Then came the newspaper articles. They were photocopies of old articles about the Verbeek and Deverell murders. Mercy rapidly flipped through the articles. There was nothing about the Hartlage or Jorgensen murders.

Why Britta?

"Do you think this is Clint's or Ryan's notebook?" Mercy asked.

"It's in Ryan's room."

He's obsessed.

Mercy went back to the photos of Britta. "These are recent. Look . . . this one was taken outside her current house. And this one is at the diner in Eagle's Nest."

"It looks like he's been stalking her, not Steve Harris as she suspected," Truman pointed out. "But why?"

"We need to warn her." Fear for the woman made her throat tighten.

"I think she's already on high alert." Truman reached up and one-handedly grabbed the box of knives Mercy had put back, then set it on top of the safe. "Look at these again." He picked up one by the scabbard and held the wooden handle toward her. "Do you recognize that symbol?"

Mercy leaned closer. "It's an eagle . . . with a swastika below it. Ugh. Are they all like that?" *Were the Moody brothers Nazi fans?*

"No," said Truman. "This other knife has something written in Italian on it. Mercy, these are military collectibles."

She met his gaze as a chunk of her case clicked into place. "Like the Asian skull."

He held out the box. "Between these knives and those articles in the binders, you've got a connection between the old murders and new right here in this house. Ryan Moody." Lines creased his forehead.

"When Ryan was accounting for his handguns the first time I was here, I remember thinking that some of them looked very old."

"War collector old?"

"Possibly."

"You think Ryan could be the one who killed the Hartlages, because we found a war trophy with their remains?" Excitement prickled in her brain. "The victim in Clint Moody's storage shed had his mouth beat in . . . just like the Hartlages and Jorgensens."

"But what's his obsession with Britta?"

"She's the survivor of the original family murders," Mercy suggested. "Ryan is only thirty. He would have been about ten when those murders happened. Wait a minute . . . Did the Moodys grow up around here? I don't remember them."

"I can find out," said Truman, pulling out his phone.

Mercy's nerves vibrated in anticipation as she listened to him make a call. The answer to the murders felt very close, circling in the air just beyond her reach. She worried that if she moved, the tenuous connection between Ryan Moody and the Hartlages would fall apart.

I'm positive it will be confirmed that Clint Moody was the body in the storage unit.

Did his brother kill him?

The boxes in the storage unit.

Mercy struggled to remember what she'd noticed written on the neat row of cardboard boxes stacked along the wall in the unit.

Old dates. Countries. She'd assumed they were possessions of someone's older relatives. Checking the time, she wondered if the evidence team had looked in the boxes yet.

Truman ended the call, a scowl on his face. "Lucas is going to get back to me. He's having computer problems."

"We need to go back to the storage unit."

His nose twitched in memory. "Why?"

"Did you notice the stacks of cardboard boxes?"

"Yes. But I was focused on the carpet."

"I saw dates. Old dates. I remember thinking they were from before I was born and wondered if they held old items. I also saw *Germany* written on one."

"You're right. I did see that but ignored it. I wonder if there are more military collectibles in the boxes."

"Let's take a quick look in the cluttered garage here first," she suggested.

As they went outside, Mercy phoned Britta, but the call went straight to voice mail.

She left a message for the woman to keep her eyes open and immediately call her back. Voice mail didn't seem the appropriate place to explain about the binder she'd found in the Moody home.

A quick search through some very dusty boxes in the Moody garage turned up only old sporting goods and camping equipment, so Mercy and Truman drove back to the storage unit.

The body was gone, but the smell lingered. Dr. Lockhart had left, and two evidence techs remained, taking photos and recording evidence. Rain pounded on the large tent they had set up outside the unit. They hadn't opened any of the boxes yet, and Mercy pointed at the one labeled *Germany* and *1942*, requesting it be opened.

Inside were old military uniforms, magazines, and a metal helmet.

"Okay," said Truman. "One or both of the Moodys were collectors."

"Everything is pointing at Ryan Moody. Where the fuck did he go? Wait a minute." A memory prodded at Mercy, and she strained to bring it into focus. *Where did I see other war memorabilia?* She ran a hand across her forehead. "Truman . . . Britta has swords hanging on her wall and black-and-white photos that could be old war photos." Cold dread unfurled in her stomach. *How many times was it pointed out that the murders happened after Britta moved to town?*

Truman's jaw clenched as he weighed her statement. "She's definitely an unusual woman. I don't know what to think."

"We can't make any assumptions."

"She's been through a lot of trauma in her life," Truman stated. "Who knows how that affected her mentally?"

Mercy checked her phone, hoping to see a missed call from Britta. Nothing.

Please don't have lied to me.

"I need to drive out there," Mercy stated. "At the very least, she needs to be warned about Ryan Moody."

"I need to stop by the station first, and then I'll meet you there." Truman took a hard look at her. "Do *not* go in until I arrive."

Thunder boomed after Truman's words.

Mercy thought of the deadly-looking swords hanging on Britta's wall. "Not a problem."

FORTY-TWO

She was no longer the small blonde girl who had haunted my dreams for decades.

When I first saw her last summer, I struggled to replace my memory of the bloody child with the tall, dark woman who'd returned.

She'd answered her front door, and I instantly recognized her eyes. I repaired the water issue in her new home, a million questions running through my head. I handed her the bill, trying not to stare as my brain screamed, *It's her.* She insisted on writing a check for payment right then. Britta Vale.

Confirmation. *How many women are named Britta?*

After that I followed her everywhere, not that she left her home that often, but I was obsessed with the girl who'd gotten away. The girl who'd survived impossible odds. The girl who'd won against my father.

Her return to Central Oregon released something from the hidden depths of my soul. Evil things I'd long buried now stirred to life. They stretched and yawned and looked around at the world with fresh eyes. They saw my father's work was unfinished.

She walked the streets with confidence, her black clothing and hair like armor, and she never let her guard down. Britta always focused on her surroundings, checking behind her and across the street. It ate away at me that she walked around, living her life as if the world hadn't changed. The night I climbed the bunk ladder and looked into her eyes decades ago, my life had changed.

I learned what my father was capable of. What I was capable of.

I'd noticed after the Verbeek murders that my father was normal for several months. Even throwing a ball with us kids and smiling at my mother. He'd exorcised some demons that night.

My personal demon had pale-blue eyes and now sported black hair. I needed her out of my head.

Her dog was always at her side, a four-legged guard. One time I'd approached her at the hardware store and admired the dog and asked to pet it. She'd refused, stating the dog didn't like people and might bite.

But she never leashed it.

The encounter bolstered my confidence and the need to purge the voices and urges in my brain. I pledged to finish what my father had started. It was the only way I'd find peace. Getting close to her and speaking to her had made it worse. The desire swelled inside me, and I felt unstoppable; I needed to take action, prove my strength.

My father had had strength, but he used it in the wrong ways. Like with his fists on my mother.

When I was eighteen, I took action for the first time. As usual he had passed out in his bed after leaving my mother black and blue. I stared at him from the doorway for a long moment, hating the stink of alcohol and body odor. I strode in and yanked open the drawer next to his bed. He'd shown the weapon to me many times, lovingly stroking it as he speculated about the soldiers who'd fired it half a century earlier.

The gun was always there and was always loaded.

I didn't stop to think. I wrapped his hand around the butt, moved the barrel to his mouth, and pressed his finger against the trigger.

The spray from his skull covered the pillow and headboard. Bits of matter hit me in the face, but I didn't care. I left his hand and gun where they naturally fell on his chest and stepped back, examining my handiwork. A gasp sounded behind me.

I turned and met my mother's gaze.

Relief. Understanding. Accusation. Fear. They all flickered across her face, and I knew she'd dreamed of doing what I had just done.

Probably wished it a thousand times.

My father had been diagnosed with PTSD. He'd visited dozens of doctors and tried every medication. No one would be surprised at his final action.

My brother appeared beside my mother, and the same conflicting emotions shone in his eyes.

"I'll call the police," he said in a monotone. "You'd better wash up and get rid of those clothes."

The police came. The detective came. They looked sideways at my mother, noting her black eye and the two sons who stood firmly beside her.

It was ruled a suicide.

We never spoke of it.

For a long time, his death was enough for me. My burdens evaporated and life was good. But years later, I started to have nightmares. My brother urged me to talk to a shrink, but I refused. There was no statute of limitations on murder, and I feared I'd spill my secret about killing my father. The incident had bubbled up to the surface of my inner thoughts and fought to escape. I yanked it back down, locking it away, but it kept coming back. Bigger and louder each time.

Then my father began to speak to me from the skull.

His favorite keepsake of Vietnam. The one I couldn't bring myself to sell or store away with his other treasures.

I moved the skull to the safe, but I still heard his voice.

Is this what happened to him? Did he hear these voices too?

I remembered how he would drunkenly talk to inanimate objects and the one phrase I could make out: *Stop talking to me.*

Were they talking back to him? Is that what he was trying to escape from all those years?

That is why he battered their mouths. To stop the voices.

For the first time I understood my father's rage and confusion.

How did he combat it?

Then I saw Britta. It was a sign. *Finish my father's work and find my peace again. The voice will stop.*

But I couldn't get close enough to her. I tried and tried. She was always prepared.

Someone else would have to do.

The first time, I came home and confessed to my brother what had happened. I cried and raged as I told him our father had taken over my thoughts and I suspected his soul had entered me after I shot him. *Why else would I feel the need to kill?*

In a panic my brother helped me hide the bodies in the dead of night, telling me everything would be fine, that we'd never talk again about the incident, that it would simply go away. I shattered the teeth of the cursed skull from Vietnam and then added it to the pile of bodies under the road, convinced that would quiet the voice in my head.

It did.

Until it didn't.

FORTY-THREE

I see my breath in the fading day's light as I wait.

I know she is coming soon. I've watched her enough times to know her routine. Every late afternoon, she runs. Rain or shine. She and that dog head west for several miles and then return. On the way back they run by a small rock formation about a hundred yards from her house. It's where I now hide. The rain and wind have picked up, and far away the thunder sounds, but I keep my ears open for the sound of her feet. I am confident in her habits.

She always follows the bank of the dry creek bed during the return part of her run but leaves it behind as she gets closer to her house and passes by my rocks. Today the creek is no longer dry; it is full of rushing water. When I first started watching her, I could see the dirt bottom of the creek bed and how the water had eaten away at its sides over the decades, digging deeper and deeper into the landscape, creating stunning small cliffs. During the winter I saw its dry bottom coated in snow. Only recently did it fill with the first water since last fall. It's narrow and not too deep, but its noise interferes as I listen for her.

The dog is an unknown in the equation, the one factor I'm not confident about, but I've planned the best I can. It needs to be eliminated first. I've worn heavy boots and thick sleeves in preparation. I close my eyes and see myself kick the dog squarely in the face, enough to knock it senseless, and then I swing my hammer at Britta. She'll be too stunned over the attack on her dog to react.

I have my rifle and pistol, but it is the hammer that is important. She needs to be eliminated the same way her family was.

Then my father's voice will be silenced in my head.

I need it to end.

Clint had been about to betray me. After the Jorgensen family died, he refused to help me hide their bodies, and he begged me to turn myself in. I explained that it wasn't my fault; I was driven the same way our father had been. But Clint pushed and pushed, claiming I needed help.

I'd agreed to go to the police in the morning, but I silenced Clint that night. It wasn't my fault. He left me no choice.

I hear her coming.

She breathes hard, her feet making rhythmic sounds on the hard dirt. All our rain hasn't softened that hard-packed ground.

My heart speeds up, and I hold my breath, gripping my hammer. I rise to a loaded crouch, ready to spring.

It's almost over. My peace is at hand.

The dog's black snout comes into view and I leap forward, planting my right foot and swinging my left with all my might. I'm too slow to hit its face and instead catch it in the ribs. Its body hurtles into the air and then slams into the dirt.

Its sharp yelp pleases me.

I spin toward Britta, expecting her to be stopped dead in her tracks at the sight of her immobile dog, but instead a tall black figure tackles me in the gut, knocking me backward to the ground, and I drop my hammer. I wheeze for breath, but my lungs won't function. Britta scrambles to sit on my chest as I suffocate. Stars explode in my eyes as a blow knocks my jaw to the side.

And again.

This is wrong! It's all going wrong!

I taste blood, and a high wail erupts from my throat as my lungs get air. Suddenly her weight is gone from my chest and I roll to my side, still struggling for normal breaths. She kicks me twice in the groin and the blinding pain shoots its way to my head and detonates. I curl into a ball, no breath left to scream. I try to close my jaw, and hot fire shoots from its joints into my brain.

My entire nervous system throbs as I lie in the rain.

I hate her. I hate my father. I hate everyone.

Coughs rack my body, nearly making me vomit, and I feel—and hear—my jaw slip back to the proper place in its joints, creating another explosion of pain that vanishes as quickly as it came.

Blessed sensation of nothing. In my jaw, anyway.

I'm still in a ball, waiting for the pounding in my groin to subside. I manage a blurry, wet look around me. Two feet away, my hammer taunts me from the dirt. At this moment, it might as well be a hundred feet away. Britta and her dog are gone.

I'm not giving up.

Time for plan B.

FORTY-FOUR

Mercy sat in her Tahoe, tapping her fingers on her steering wheel, waiting for Truman.

She had parked out of sight of Britta's home on its long driveway, and the outside lights of the house were on, creating a glow around the bend of the drive. The rain pounded louder on her roof, and she spotted a flash of lightning in the darkening sky. She counted the seconds, waiting for the thunder.

The storm was five miles away.

More lightning flashed, and she saw Britta's unmistakable figure running awkwardly across the flatland for her home. Something bulky was in her arms, and she ran out of Mercy's view. Mercy closed her eyes, seeing Britta's hunched silhouette in her mind. *She's scared.*

Mercy started her vehicle, putting her promise to Truman out of her head.

Something is up.

She parked in front of the house just as Britta dashed through the front door and slammed it behind her. Mercy took the steps two at a time and pounded on the door. "Britta? What happened?"

The door flew open, and Britta grabbed Mercy's arm and jerked her inside the house. She frantically slid the bolts of the door, her chest heaving.

A soaking-wet Zara lay panting on the floor. Britta dropped to her knees beside her dog, gently touching Zara's face.

Zara was the bundle in her arms.

Britta was dressed for running. Mud covered her legs, and her pale eyes were wide in her face.

Mercy knelt beside her, studying the dog. "What happened?" she asked again.

"Attack. He attacked my dog," Britta wheezed.

Alarm shot through Mercy, but she didn't see blood on the dog. Zara's eyes were open, and her tongue hung out as she breathed, but she didn't get up.

How could Britta run with the heavy dog?

Determination.

"Who attacked? A coyote?" Mercy asked.

"No! A man. He was waiting for us by the rocks. He leaped out and kicked Zara in the ribs."

Mercy realized rain wasn't the only moisture on Britta's face.

"I tackled him, but I'm afraid he'll come here next." Determination swept the tall woman's face. "I'll be ready for him."

Ryan Moody? "Britta, did you get a look at the guy?"

"It was getting dark, but he wore a heavy black coat and camo pants. He wasn't old. Dark hair." She sucked in a breath, studying her dog. "He had a rifle over one shoulder."

Mercy stood, tension running through her veins. "We need to get out of here. I'll drive. You grab Zara, and we'll go to a vet."

"She might have broken ribs—"

"Pick her up," Mercy ordered. "You've got a nut outside with a gun."

"I can hold him off. This place is—"

"*Now.* We're leaving now!" Mercy bent over to lift the dog. If Britta wouldn't do it, she would.

"I've got her." Britta scooped up the dog, who whined. "Shhh, girl. We'll get you better." She headed toward the door. "Fucking asshole," she muttered as Mercy held the door open for her.

Mercy knew the curse wasn't aimed at her.

She started to follow Britta across the porch, but the woman shrieked and collapsed as a gunshot thundered, and Mercy dropped to her stomach. Britta writhed as blood spurted from her thigh, and she clutched Zara to her chest, the dog yipping in pain. Mercy shot forward and grabbed the neck of Britta's jacket. On her hands and knees Mercy strained to drag the woman and the dog back into the house. "Push with your foot," Mercy hissed.

Britta planted her left foot, clenched her teeth, and shoved backward with a moan. Her right leg dragged, and blood still gushed. Mercy threw her body weight into a desperate heave and felt something internal tear in her own damaged leg. Not stopping, she hauled the woman over the threshold and then scooted around to shove Britta's legs inside. She slammed the door and threw the locks, her heart hammering in her chest. Her injured leg quivered. *No time to worry about that now.*

"Mercy." Britta's eyes were wide with pain.

"Hang on." Mercy stripped off her belt and wrapped it around the woman's thigh, pulling it as tight as she could. The blood flow slowed. *That's only temporary.*

"What is the most secure room in your house?"

"D-d-downstairs bath. Stocked. Reinforced." Zara was still clasped in Britta's arms, and Mercy figured that was best for both of them.

"Good," Mercy muttered. She couldn't imagine hauling Britta up the stairs. "Are all the windows locked?"

"Yes."

Not that glass will stop anyone.

Leaving Britta in the center of the living room, she drew her weapon and bent over, darting around the first floor, turning off the lights, and closing the shades. The first floor's back door was already locked. She glanced in the bathroom and checked the cabinets. Water, food, first aid, a radio, ammo, flashlight, and a Glock. Reinforced door. Good locks. She grabbed the flashlight.

I knew I liked Britta.

She snatched some pillows and throws off the living room furniture and tossed them into the bathroom. She towed Britta slowly across the floor and settled her on the floor of the bathroom, leaving the door open for the moment. "I'm going to call for help."

"Okay." Britta closed her eyes, and Mercy shone the light on her wound. The seepage seemed minimal, but she'd left a wide blood trail across the floor. Zara settled in the crook of Britta's arm, her gaze on Mercy.

"I'm going to take care of your mother," Mercy promised the dog as she dialed. She gave the 911 operator her location and a rundown on the active shooter.

Then she called Truman.

"Don't come in!" she ordered as his phone picked up. "Stay out on the road!"

"What's going on?" Alarm rattled his voice.

"Britta's been shot, and we're locked inside her house. I think it's Ryan Moody who shot her. He's still outside." Mercy couldn't speak fast enough.

"Is she okay?"

"I've got a tourniquet on her leg, but it's still bleeding. She needs to get to a hospital as soon as possible." *Will we make it?*

"I've pulled over just before turning into her driveway. Did you call it in?"

"Yes," she panted.

Glass shattered as another gunshot roared. Mercy ducked onto the floor next to Britta, but Ryan had shot out a window in the kitchen. Zara barked at the assault on her home, and Britta hushed her.

"Jesus Christ!" Truman exclaimed. "I heard that shot out here. How far away is your backup?"

"I don't know."

"You armed?"

"Of course. And Britta is well stocked." The door to the bathroom was still open, and Mercy crawled out to check the broken window. "He's on the back side of the house. But that window he broke is too high for him to enter through."

Another window shattered. She flung her arms over her head and eyes. Her phone flew toward the fireplace and crashed into the stone hearth.

She shot to the hearth, her fingers scrambling to find her phone. The screen was in pieces. "Truman? *Truman?*"

Silence.

"Shit." Blood pounded in her ears, and her panting filled the room. *I'm armed. If Ryan tries to get in, he's in for a surprise.*

She scooted back to the bathroom, pain shooting through her leg with the awkward movements. "My phone's dead."

"Mine's upstairs." Britta's voice was faint.

"I'm not going up there right now. Help is on the way. We just need to stick it out."

"Okay." In the poor light, Britta stroked Zara's head with shaking fingers. "God damn it. Who would do this?"

"I think it's Ryan Moody. I suspect he killed the Hartlage and Jorgensen families. And his own brother."

"Moody." Britta was quiet for a second. "We had a neighbor named Moody back then. Odd family. The boys didn't go to school. They were taught at home."

"A neighbor of yours?" Mercy breathed as pieces fell into place in her head.

"Well, they lived a few miles away, but in a rural community like ours, we considered them neighbors." Britta's voice trailed off.

"Britta?" *Is she passing out?*

"Tired . . . but Mercy . . ."

"Yes?"

"I hope you shoot that murdering fucker."

There's the Britta I've come to know.

"I'll see what I can do." Mercy felt the pulse at the woman's neck. Slow but strong. She tightened the belt on Britta's thigh. "I'm going to shut the door. I'll be right outside."

"Okay."

Mercy gave the dog a final pat and closed the door. She sat outside, leaning her back against it, and clenched her weapon in her hands as her eyes adjusted to the poor light, studying the remaining windows. *She didn't protest my closing her in.* Britta's acquiescence alarmed her more than the injury. *She's getting weaker.*

I'll be waiting for him right here.

She blew out a long breath, and her nerves settled into preparation mode.

"Just try to come and get her, Ryan," she whispered into the dark.

FORTY-FIVE

"Mercy?" Truman held his breath.

"Mercy?" He looked at his screen. The call had been disconnected.

The shot and shattering glass had made the hair rise on his arms. But Mercy's immediate silence made bile creep up his throat.

He made a quick call. The backup was still fifteen minutes out, and he told the operator to let the responding officers know that he was at the scene.

I can't sit still that long.

Were we right about Ryan Moody?

Images of the Hartlage skulls and Clint Moody's decaying body went through his mind.

"How long can Britta hold out?" he whispered. The worry had been evident in Mercy's voice when she spoke of the woman's wound. She needed medical help soon.

He slammed his good hand on his steering wheel. "Dammit!"

I can't just sit here.

Another shot boomed through the darkness.

Active shooter. I need to move in. Broken arm or not.

"Fuck." He pulled up his location on a map and switched to the satellite imagery. Loading the image took forever. He spotted the long driveway and the rooftop of Britta's house. Mercy had said Ryan was at the back of the house. *But is he still there?* He memorized the surrounding area. Trees on one side of the house. Pastures and a dirt farm road on the other.

Truman turned his engine back on and his headlights off and moved down Britta's driveway, squinting to see through the pounding rain. After a few hundred feet, he pulled to the side of the driveway and parked. *No point in announcing my arrival and becoming a target.*

Crap. Mercy is armed.

He paused, seeking a way to let her know he'd entered the scene but to also stay hidden from the shooter.

There wasn't one.

All I can do is go in.

He slipped out of his truck and darted to the other side of the driveway. Essentially there was no cover except for the orchard on the far side of the house. He jogged along the wood fence lining the driveway, keeping low, his weapon in hand. He felt completely off balance with one arm in a splint. He'd ditched the sling early that day, hating the strap near his neck.

A one-armed cop was better than none.

He hoped.

Delight rolled through me as I saw Britta drop on the porch.

I got her!

She had that damned dog in her arms and was quickly yanked back in the house by a woman.

Who is the other woman?

Through the rain I see the outline of a vehicle near the house; creeping closer I see government plates. *Who?*

The lights shut off in the house, and the blinds and curtains close. I ignore them, focused on the mystery vehicle. The silhouette of Britta's rescuer flashes in my memory. Long, wavy, dark hair. Tall. Lean.

That FBI agent? The one who told me they found Clint's truck?

Chills raise bumps on my skin.

Why is she here?

Did she follow me? Paranoia freezes my muscles. I'd believed I'd convinced the cops that I had nothing to do with Clint's disappearance. *Did they figure it out?*

I snort. *As if that is my greatest sin.*

Lightning flashes and is soon followed by thunder.

I dart to the back of the house, seeking a way in. The back door is locked. I step back and fire at a window with my rifle. The crash of the glass is deeply satisfying, but the window is too high for access. Holding back my laughter, I fire again, imagining the terror that must be filling the women. I move around to the side of the home and choose a third window. At the third shot, a rush of power fills me. I'm making my own thunder and lightning.

I reload, craving more. *Are they armed?*

The house is still silent. No screams. No shots.

You were my brother.

I freeze as the voice fills my head. Clint's voice. *Noooo. Not now.*

You killed me. I was trying to help you.

"Stop talking to me," I whisper to the rain. "I had no choice."

You had a choice.

"No. I had to. You were going to stop me. I needed him out of my head, and the only way was to finish his work." My hands freeze on my rifle, and my knees weaken. I kneel in the mud, terrified I might fall. I wait, scanning the dark sky, but Clint's voice is silent.

Guilt floods me with pain and roars in my head, eviscerating my soul.

"*NOOOOOOO!*" I shriek. The rifle drops as I cover my ears, trying to get rid of the roar. I scream again.

I didn't want to do it!

In my mind's eye, I see my father screaming after he killed the Verbeeks. *Is this roaring in my head what he heard?*

Lightning illuminates the sky, and I see movement to my left by the fence.

A man.

I grab my rifle and drop to my belly, aiming into the darkness. I focus, clearing my head, waiting for another flash of lightning.

It doesn't come.

Where is he?

If I shoot, I show him where I am.

Lightning answers my prayers. The man has traveled fifty feet along the fence, moving past the house. He is hunched over, hiding behind the fence.

I have no doubt he is hunting me.

I smile. I know this property like the back of my hand. I've studied it and walked it. Even in the dark, I can find my way.

Bring it on.

I get up and dart after him.

◆　◆　◆

Did he see me?

Truman jogged along the outside of the fence, cursing the lightning, but also begging for more to light his path. He'd already stumbled three times, the third time catching himself with his left hand. Fire shot up his arm, and he bit his tongue against crying out. That was exactly the type of movement he wasn't supposed to use his healing arm for.

He wanted Ryan to see him; he wanted Ryan to follow.

Anything to get him away from the house so that Mercy could get Britta out and leave.

I'll have to fire at some point so she knows we've moved away from the house.

Apprehension filled him at the thought of shooting. He was shaky, still off balance, and his head had started to throb. *I'm not recovered enough for this.*

He'd probably have one opportunity. After that Ryan would know exactly where he was.

I have to make it count.

The shot had to either take Ryan down or be used as a last resort to signal Mercy.

Rushing water sounded behind him, growing louder and closer as he moved farther from the house. There hadn't been water on the satellite image. But there'd been a dirt farm road.

Not a road. A dry riverbed.

"Who's playing the hero?" came Ryan's voice through the rain.

Truman turned toward the voice, straining to see him and trying to judge the distance. Twenty feet? Thirty?

"I know this land," Ryan called out. "I don't need light to find you."

The large creek was now close on his right. Truman knew Ryan was on the other side of the wooden fence, which gave him a false sense of protection. A few horizontal rails made for lousy cover, but he stayed silent and crouched lower behind them as he stumbled, his legs shaking from the effort.

Now I'm the prey. Weakened prey.

The sensation of being hunted weighed heavily on his shoulders, making his stomach churn. The strength and focus needed to take an accurate shot at Ryan had dwindled unnervingly. It was no longer an option.

Keep leading him away from the house.

He mentally repeated the mantra, ignoring the pain in his arm and head. He needed to get the man as far away as possible. And try to cover his own ass.

Lightning flashed, and Truman dropped awkwardly to the ground, twisting to protect his arm.

He saw me.

The crack of Ryan's gunshot was simultaneous with the thought.

Truman had landed on his right shoulder and now rolled to his back to get his weapon arm free.

His left leg dangled in open air. There was no ground beneath it, and he felt the dirt collapse under the left side of his back.

I'm falling.

Terror gripped him as he flung out his arms to catch himself. There was no foliage to grab.

Gravity pulled him over the edge and into the rushing water.

At the sound of Ryan's primal male scream, Mercy crawled to the closest window and peeked out into the dark.

What happened to him?

Lightning revealed Ryan on his knees about fifty feet from the house, his hands over his ears. Suddenly he turned his head toward the fence that ran along the property.

Mercy caught her breath. She'd seen what had caught Ryan's eye.

Truman was running along the other side of the fence.

She'd know him anywhere. The microscopic split second had been enough to tell her he'd not listened to her order to stay away.

He's running away from the house. And Ryan just followed.

"That damned idiot." Anger flushed her face. "He's leading Ryan away."

He'll get himself killed.

She knew how weak Truman was. She also knew that it would be impossible for her to move Britta. The woman couldn't walk, and Mercy couldn't carry her. Truman's heroic maneuvers would be for nothing.

Unless I get to Ryan first.

Mercy darted back to the bathroom and saw the faint light of the flashlight under the door. "It's me." She pushed the door open, grabbed the Glock she'd seen earlier, and knelt next to Britta. "Take this." She pressed the weapon into Britta's shaking hand. "I'm going outside."

"No." Her voice was almost inaudible.

"Truman's out there. I won't be alone." Mercy ran a hand over Zara's soft ears and then squeezed Britta's shoulder. "You'll be fine. Our backup should be here any moment. Don't shoot any of them," she joked half-heartedly.

"No," Britta said again.

Mercy picked up the flashlight and checked Britta's leg. Still slow seepage. *How long can she last?* "I'll be back in a bit. I'm going to take the flashlight." She leaned closer to Britta, holding her gaze. "I'll get the bastard for you," she said in a harsh voice, her throat swelling with emotion. Britta had been through hell. Multiple times. This was the chance to end it.

Britta blinked moist eyes and nodded.

Mercy turned off the flashlight and shoved it in her pocket. She closed the bathroom door behind her, drew her weapon, and wondered if she'd ever speak to Britta again.

No time for thoughts like that.

She went out the back door and headed in the direction she'd seen Truman go. She silently jogged through the rain, thankful she was dressed in her usual black to blend in with the dark. The ground was uneven, and she moved carefully, favoring her leg and wishing she could use the flashlight. *Why'd I even bring it?*

From her previous visit, she knew the fence kept going beyond the house. But she didn't know how far. Or what else was out there.

She heard the rush of the large creek and wondered if it was near to overflowing from the heavy rain. A new sound reached her ears, and she froze.

Is someone talking?

The voice was male and unfamiliar, but she couldn't make out the words.

Mercy took careful, slow steps, her ears straining to hear more through the rain. The voice was definitely ahead of her, but she didn't know how far. Her gun tight in both hands, she moved forward, rolling heel to toe, keeping her arms taut. She slowed her breathing, concentrating on the dark ahead.

Don't shoot Truman.

She might only have a split second to decide whether to shoot.

Lightning.

The back of a person aiming a rifle appeared twenty feet directly in front of her. He fired as the light disappeared.

Mercy held her fire, knowing Ryan must have shot at Truman. Which meant Truman could be in her line of fire beyond Ryan.

A muffled gasp and then a splash reached her.

The heavens gave her another flash of light, and she saw Ryan peering over the fence rails, his rifle slung over his shoulder on its strap.

She whipped out her flashlight, clasped it against her weapon, and shone the spotlight on the person in front of her. "Federal officer! Raise your hands!"

Ryan's hands slowly went up in the air. He tried to glance over his shoulder and winced at the beam from the flashlight.

"Don't move!" she ordered.

He froze.

Where's Truman?

"I didn't do anything," Ryan called to her.

She wanted to laugh. "We found your brother today."

His immediate shudder pleased something deep inside her.

"We also found a binder devoted to Britta and her family. I assume that belonged to you?"

No answer.

"Grady Baldwin didn't kill those families years ago, did he?" she asked. "Did you help your father with those tasks?"

"No!" he shot back. "I had nothing to do with him."

"Put your left hand on your head." He obeyed, and Mercy mentally ran through the best steps to safely get the rifle away from him. The sounds of faint sirens reached her.

Finally.

"With one finger of your right hand, I want you to slowly lift the strap of the rifle off your shoulder and bring it all the way out to your right."

She took a few steps closer, concentrating on his movements. "Slower!" He finally dangled the rifle with his outstretched hand. "Slowly lower it until it touches the ground, then drop the strap."

Again he obeyed.

"Right hand on your head, lace your fingers. Take four big steps to your left and then two backward toward me."

When he was far enough away from the rifle she exhaled. "You killed the Hartlage and Jorgensen families. Why?"

He muttered something.

"Kneel. Keep your hands on your head. And I didn't hear what you said." She stepped closer, her weapon and flashlight still trained on his back.

"I needed him out of my head!" he exclaimed after he was on his knees. "I needed him to stop talking to me!"

"Who?"

"My father! His work needed to be finished!"

Britta. He means Britta needed to be finished.

"I'm pretty sure the death of those two families had nothing to do with your father. And I bet your brother's murder didn't either."

He lowered his head. "It kept his voice quiet for a while," he said in a softer tone.

"On your stomach," she ordered.

"It's wet."

"Lie down!"

He moved one hand to the dirt for balance and slowly started to lower his body into the mud. The sirens drew closer.

"Where's Truman?" she asked, impatient with Ryan's turtle-speed movements.

"I don't know. I think he went in the water."

The roar of the wide creek intensified in Mercy's ears. *The water?* Horror turned her hands to ice. *Did Ryan's shot hit him?*

I've got to get down there.

Transferring her flashlight and gun to one hand, Mercy slipped cuffs out of her pocket.

At the clank of the metal cuffs, Ryan spun toward her on his knees, whipping a gun from his waistband.

Time slowed.

Ryan's smug gaze met hers as he came around. He grinned, and she saw the muzzle of his weapon.

I didn't search him.

Mercy fired until he toppled over.

FORTY-SIX

Ryan was dead.

Mercy couldn't hear, her ears ringing from her shots. And stress.

She knelt in the mud next to Ryan Moody and shone her flashlight on him as she felt his neck with a trembling hand. No pulse.

Of course not. Look at the holes in his chest.

He would have shot me.

Truman.

She jumped to her feet and lunged at the fence where Ryan had been standing when she first spotted him. Her flashlight showed her an angry rushing creek ten feet below the fence. The water appeared manageable for a strong swimmer, but what about a man with a broken arm? And a possible gunshot wound?

"Truman!" she shouted at the water. She ducked between the rails and stepped carefully to where the ground dropped off down to the water.

The ground gave way under her boot, and she leaped back.

She shouted his name again and started running downstream, projecting her light back and forth over the water.

Close sirens penetrated her hearing, and the rapid flashing of red and blue lights made her path harder to see. Backup had arrived.

I'm not stopping.

"Truman!"

She wouldn't consider that he was gone. She wouldn't. He was somewhere out here in the dark.

She combed the river and its narrow banks with her light. There were no trees or shrubs. Just big rocks that at one time water or ice had deposited in the wash. Her ankle twisted in a hollow, and she went down on one knee. Her bad leg. "Fuck!" She pulled to her feet and pushed on, not trusting her leg. But it didn't matter.

He's not gone. He's not gone.

I forbid it.

He'd just come back to her.

There. She slammed to a halt and squinted at the water. Her flashlight's glow picked up his white face against the black water. He had both arms wrapped around a good-size rock as the water tried to pull him farther downstream. He looked up at the light.

He's almost done.

Ignoring the police shouting for her to stop, Mercy shuffled down the steep bank sideways, her leg threatening to collapse with every step. Reaching the water, she plunged in and quickly found herself up to her waist. The water wasn't deep, but it was fast and strong.

It's so cold.

She pushed through the water to Truman and grabbed his right hand, bracing herself against the rock with her other. She didn't have the strength to get him out, but dammit, she would hang on to him until help arrived.

"Hey." His teeth chattered, and his gaze struggled to hold hers.

"Hey yourself," she managed to choke out. His hand was freezing. "We're going to get you out of here. There's help right behind me. Are you shot?"

"No."

Thank you, God.

"Ryan?" he blurted.

"Dead."

"I heard the shots. I didn't know if he shot . . ." He trailed off.

"He drew on me." She was numb from her twenty seconds in the water; Truman had to feel worse. She rearranged her grip on the rock and clutched him more securely.

He pressed his cheek against the rock and closed his eyes, still clinging with both arms. "I can't hold on much longer."

Hurry up! She squeezed his hand tighter. "It doesn't matter as long as you hold on to me." *I won't lose him this time.*

His eyes barely opened. "Always."

Her heart melted as she met his fatigued gaze. Splashing sounded behind her. The police had entered the water, their shouts unintelligible, but Mercy knew their rescue was minutes away, and she leaned her forehead against Truman in relief.

Never letting go again.

FORTY-SEVEN

For the first time in two days, his home was quiet.

Truman lay back in his easy chair, relishing the silence. He loved his parents and sister but preferred them in small quantities. They'd left for good that morning, and the house had seemed to breathe a sigh of relief. The home was cleaner than it'd ever been, but he'd been unable to relax with them fussing over him. Mercy fussed a little but knew when to step back.

He ran a hand over Simon, who was curled up on his lap. The cat had stuck close since Truman had returned. He'd had to shut the door to his bedroom to keep her from sleeping on his pillow and keeping him awake. She'd meowed her protest and stuck her paw under the door for fifteen minutes before giving up.

Ollie peeked into Truman's study, and Truman waved him in. In the few days he'd been at Truman's house, the teenager had settled into a routine. Kaylie had spent several afternoons with him, catching him up on what a teenager needed to know—cell phones, apps, and clothing. And she had introduced him to the internet, horrified by the thought of him learning from dated textbooks when the world could be at his fingertips. He'd caught on quickly to computers—after several lectures on how to avoid viruses and not to believe everything he read.

Truman wondered if he'd discovered porn yet.

"Mercy asked me to bring you some coffee," Ollie said as he stepped in. At first glance Ollie could blend in with a group of teenagers. The clothes and haircut had done away with the mountain boy. But there was still something that set him apart. A watchfulness in his eyes, an intense studying of his surroundings that was different from the carefree attitudes of most teens. He seemed comfortable under Truman's roof, and Truman wondered how long it would last. Ollie was fiercely independent. Truman liked having the boy around because Ollie made him see the world differently and appreciate everything from dental floss to the flick of a light switch.

Truman took the mug. "Sit down for a minute."

Ollie planted himself on an ottoman, gangly legs akimbo, and Simon abandoned Truman for the new arrival.

Traitor.

"I wanted to tell you what happened the night I went in the water," Truman said. He'd been putting this off until the two of them were alone.

"I've heard." The teen shifted on the ottoman, keeping his gaze and hand on Simon.

"I haven't told anyone about this particular thing."

Ollie looked up, his eyes skeptical. "Even Mercy?"

"Even Mercy." *But I will.* "I was already beat to hell, you know. My arm, my head was still giving me problems, my stamina sucked. I shouldn't have been back on the job."

"You were going crazy doing nothing here. You needed to get back for your sanity."

"True. But physically I wasn't ready." Truman sipped the coffee, appreciating the heat and taste as it hit his tongue. *How many days did I crave coffee while I was in the woods?* "When I fell down the bank and

313

into that creek, the first thing that happened was I banged my head on more rocks. Several times."

Ollie gazed at him in sympathy. Truman knew he looked like shit. The rushing water had tumbled him hard, giving him a bruised cheekbone and scraped chin. And those were only the visible contusions. He had plenty of others hidden by his clothing and hair.

"Water up my nose, down my throat, and my heavy coat acted like an anchor when it soaked through." The terror of that night slammed into him, and the mug rattled as he set it on the adjacent table. "I finally crashed into a bigger rock, one sticking out of the water, and I wrapped my arms around it, ignoring the pain that was shooting up from my broken arm." He gently touched the new splint. The ER doctor had threatened to cast it this time but agreed to let an orthopedist make the decision. Truman had an appointment tomorrow.

"Mercy told me she found you in the middle of the water."

"She did. But what she didn't know was that I'd nearly let go three times. I was long done. The water wouldn't stop dragging on my clothing, trying to yank me from the rock. It continually splashed me in the face, and I think I inhaled or drank a gallon of it. But do you know why I didn't let go?"

Ollie shook his head, his gaze locked on Truman's.

"Because I remembered your story. The one where you'd fallen into the ravine and you didn't give up no matter how bad the odds were against you. You were a teenager, and there was no way I was going to let a teenager out-survive me. If you had the drive to get yourself out of that situation, by damn, I would too. Step one was to hold the fuck on. Remember how you told me you outlined steps to get out and simply focused on reaching the next one?"

The teen nodded.

"I was lucky. I got help at step one. But it was your determination and success that fueled me to hang on. I don't know if I would have made it without the memory of your experience."

Ollie looked away, but Truman saw his jaw tighten, and the teen blinked several times.

"I wanted to thank you, Ollie. You rescued me twice."

The teen snorted and looked back at Truman with a small grin. "So you owe me double now."

"I do," Truman agreed. "You've got a home here as long as you need it. I'll get you set up with college and help you find a job. What else would you like?"

Ollie leaned forward, his eyes eager. "I want to learn to drive."

The pure teenage normalness of the request made Truman's eyes sting. Cars. Driving. The things a normal teen male craved. "You bet."

"Awesome." Ollie's face lit up.

Mercy stood outside the study, blatantly listening to Truman and Ollie's conversation.

I was closer to losing him than I realized.

She sucked in a shuddering breath and wandered back to the kitchen, searching for something to do with her hands and excess energy. She was on leave for two weeks. The doctor said she had created a small tear in her newly healed thigh muscle when she dragged Britta into the house. He said it would heal with time but begged her to follow his advice and restrict herself to light activity. "No pulling bodies around, no jumping into fast creeks, no rushing down steep banks," he'd told her.

"I don't usually do that," Mercy had admitted.

Britta had surgery to repair the artery in her leg, and Mercy had visited her in the hospital after her own doctor visit.

"We have twin injuries," she'd joked with the woman lying in the hospital bed. "Don't overdo it when they let you get out of here. I know from experience that you can't rush the healing."

I need to take my own advice.

"I suspect we have more in common than that," Britta had answered, her pale-blue gaze locked on Mercy's.

Mercy tipped her head as she regarded the woman. They both had violence in their pasts. They both were determined to be self-sufficient. But Mercy still had family. Britta had no one.

"You're right," she answered. "We'll have to keep hanging out together." She eyed the intricate sleeve tattoo on the woman's arm. "I've been thinking about a tattoo. Maybe you can give me some advice since you've had a few . . . unless you're still thinking of leaving town."

Britta sighed. "I've wavered back and forth on a decision. A lot of my reasons to leave are now . . . moot. I've discovered I still love this area. More than anywhere else I've lived. But I don't know if I can live on that property. Sometimes I never want to see it again, but then I think it's a good reminder of what I've survived."

Mercy wanted her to stay. "I can help you look for another place."

A genuine smile lit Britta's face, and Mercy realized with shock that it was the first one she'd seen. "I'll keep that in mind," Britta said. She suddenly straightened up in her bed. "Zara!"

Kaylie had slipped into the room with the dog. She shut the door behind her, breathing heavily and grinning like a crazy person.

"How did you get her into the hospital?" Mercy asked in amazement as the dog darted to Britta's bed and put her paws up on the side, trying to pull herself onto the bed. Britta rubbed the dog's head and ears as happy tears streamed down her cheeks.

"Very carefully," Kaylie admitted. "I know a guy who works in the cafeteria, and he helped me sneak in a back way. The nurses on this hall spotted us but then deliberately looked the other way. I suspect they'll give us a few minutes before they kick us out."

"Has she been good?" Britta asked, her delighted focus on Zara. Kaylie had taken charge of the dog, bringing her to the vet and then back to Mercy's apartment. Zara had some bruised ribs but no broken bones.

"She's been great. Dulce and she are fascinated with each other."

Mercy had stepped back, enjoying Britta's transformation as she tried to pet every part of her dog.

I worried neither would survive that night.

Two of the responding deputies had found Britta in the house and loaded her into an ambulance as more rescued Truman and Mercy from the water. Truman had been so weak, they'd used a stretcher to get him up the bank and into another ambulance.

The FBI and the Deschutes County sheriff were working on connecting Ryan Moody to the Hartlage and Jorgensen murders. Mercy had shared Ryan's confession and directed them to take another look at Grady Baldwin's conviction from twenty years ago. Just as Britta said, the Moodys had lived in the vicinity of the two old mass killings. A brief interview with Ryan Moody's father was even in the Verbeek case files. He'd claimed he knew nothing about what had happened.

Mercy had unearthed the police report of Ryan's father's suicide. The responding officer had made a note of Mrs. Moody's bruised face, but she and both her sons swore the father was unstable and had shot himself. His medical history revealed PTSD and severe chronic depression. Mercy had stared for a long time at the comment about Mrs. Moody's bruises.

Did she or one of her sons kill him?

Mercy would never know.

The investigation of the sovereign citizens' forgery ring had opened a can of worms. Several men, including Kenneth Forbes, were currently sitting in jail, a litany of charges being assembled against them. Mercy was pleased to hear Kenneth Forbes was also being investigated for receiving disability payments from the government. His son, Joshua, would be the prosecution's prime witness. The forgers—including his own father—had threatened to kill Joshua Forbes. The son's anger at his father had loosened his tongue. He'd told the police everything and would get a deal from the prosecutor. Truman wasn't happy about his own role as a witness in the prosecution's case. He'd wanted to forget his time in captivity, stating the men would go to prison for long enough with the other stacks of charges, but Mercy was determined to see the men who'd abused him face the consequences.

Ground-penetrating radar had revealed three bodies buried on the grounds where Truman had been held captive. Tests were under way to see if one was Ollie's grandfather.

The teenager had simply nodded when Mercy told him the news, and her heart had contracted at the flash of pain on his face. She understood he'd already mentally buried his grandfather. Now a painful part of his past was being dug up. *He's tough. He'll get through it.*

Ollie joined her in the kitchen.

"How's Truman doing?" she asked, pretending she hadn't been spying on them minutes ago.

"Good. He says he wants one of Kaylie's snickerdoodles."

"I'll do it." Mercy grabbed a half dozen, taking a bite of one as she went to join Truman. The home was overflowing again with baked goods and casseroles. She stopped in the doorway to his study. He had his eyes closed as he reclined in the big chair. Something inside her burst with happiness at the sight of him safe and in one piece.

My man.

His eyes opened, and he caught her staring at him. "I smelled the cinnamon from the cookies," he told her.

She sat beside him and set the remaining five cookies on the small table.

"I told Ollie *a* cookie," he muttered.

"Like that would satisfy you."

"True." He took a giant bite that left less than half a cookie in his hand.

Thankfulness washed through her at the calm of simply sitting with him and eating cookies. He was her heart. His absence had made that clear to her.

Does he know I feel that way? How many times have I passed up the chance to say so?

An overwhelming urge to tell him opened her mouth. She wasn't going to waste the opportunity. "You know . . ." Her mouth went dry. *Why is this so hard?*

He looked at her expectantly, and she took his hand.

"At one time I steeled myself against feeling the way I do about you. And I did it for the exact reason that just happened to us—I lost you and it ripped my heart to shreds. I was devastated."

"That's understandable, since your family—"

"Let me get this out," she interrupted. "I've wasted too many moments."

He nodded and took another cookie, his gaze never leaving hers.

"I was numb for years after being shunned by my family—cast out by people who were supposed to always have my back. People I loved with all my heart." Her voice cracked as she thought of the time she'd lost with her family. Especially her brother Levi. "I didn't want to ever hurt or feel betrayed like that again, and you know I kept a distance between myself and others. But I've learned from having you and Kaylie in my life . . . it hurts when a loved one is lost. It *hurts like hell*, and I felt as if I'd never recover . . . but the other ninety-nine percent of the time is so worth that chance of pain." She forced out a laugh. "When you were gone, I got angry with myself for insisting on taking our relationship slow," she said quietly. "I thought your disappearance was the universe punishing me. Those days were brutal, but now I have you back . . . I'm never wasting time like that again."

He squeezed her hand. "It wasn't time wasted. You aren't the same person that you were last fall . . . you needed the time to cross over to the dark side." His expression was deadly serious. "You can't rush that sort of thing."

Tears started as she laughed.

He wiped the crumbs from his mouth. "I know this isn't a romantic situation. I'm not on my knees and I don't have a ring, but I want you to marry me."

Her heart stopped. *Is this what I want?*

Truman tightened his grip. "What do you say, Special Agent Kilpatrick? Are you interested in marrying a police chief? Because he wants you with all his heart."

Can I do this?

She studied him. His face was bruised and battered, and he had snickerdoodle crumbs on his shirt. But she loved him with every ounce of her being, and she didn't feel an ounce of fear.

This is right.

He was perfect for her. And so was his proposal.

He gets me.

She lunged into his lap, not caring that he winced or that her leg complained. "I do!"

"That's the answer that comes later. I think right now you're supposed to say yes."

"Yes!" She kissed him slowly, tasting sugar and cinnamon. "But you've got to promise to never disappear on me again."

"The same goes for you," he muttered. "When should we do it?"

"I suspect another wedding will be happening in the next few months," she speculated.

"Rose?"

"Yes. I think she wants to see how Nick is after the baby comes . . . I could be wrong. Maybe it will happen before that, but I don't want to take away any of their limelight."

"Agreed. What about Christmastime? That's about eight months away."

So far off. Her immediate mental complaint made her smile. He was right—she wasn't the same person she had been last fall. "I'd love a Christmas wedding."

"Deal." He kissed her again and pulled her closer. "I told you in the water I'd always hold on to you."

"And I promise the same."

Acknowledgments

This is my thirteenth novel. Unlucky thirteen flowed more smoothly for me than the majority of my books, and I believe it's because I now know Mercy and Truman inside and out. I hear them speak in my head, and I know how they feel when I throw roadblocks in their paths.

My original plan was to write four Mercy books, but my publisher agreed I could write two more. I'm extremely fortunate to write for a house that gives me the freedom to pursue what I want, and I'm thankful every day that Montlake took a chance on me. Anh, Galen, Jessica, Elise, and Colleen are the best in the business. Jessica, you've been the heart and rock-solid core of Montlake—I will miss you terribly!

I appreciate my readers who spend time with the characters I pull out of my head. Your emails and tweets always make my day. Thank you for enjoying Mercy and Truman. I know many of you are waiting for more Mason and Ava—it will happen! I miss them too.

Thank you to Melinda Leigh, who kicks me in the rear when I need it and is just a text away to brainstorm when I'm stuck. The three thousand miles between our homes feel like nothing. It's pure gold to have a friend who shares your love of plotting murders.

Thank you to my family, who are supportive and cheer for me along this unexpected journey. I never planned to write books; I wrote the first to simply see if I could finish one. Then I wrote more to see if I could improve enough to be published. By then I was hooked and had discovered a community of people who loved to read books and write as much as I did.

More Mercy books to come!

WANT TO READ THE ORIGINAL BOOK THAT INTRODUCED FORENSIC SPECIALISTS DR. LACEY HARPER AND DR. VICTORIA PERES? TURN THE PAGE TO READ AN EXCERPT OF THE FIRST BONE SECRETS NOVEL, *HIDDEN*, AVAILABLE NOW.

CHAPTER ONE

Lacey Campbell stared across the hazy field of snow at the big tent pitched against the rundown apartment building. She inhaled a breath of icy air, letting it fill her lungs and strengthen her resolve.

There. That's where the body is.

Her stomach knotted as she trudged toward the site, carefully watching where she placed her feet. She yanked on the sides of her wool hat and tucked her chin into her scarf as she strode through the fluff, blinking away the swirl of snowflakes. Snow was great, unless you had to work in it. And six inches of new snow covered the grounds of her current assignment. This weather was for skiing, sledding, and snowball fights.

Not for investigating old bones in a frosty tent in Boondocks, Oregon.

Two big boots appeared in her downward line of vision. She hit her brakes, slipped, and landed on her rear.

"Do you live here?" The cop's voice was gravelly and terse.

From her ungraceful, sprawling seat on the ground, Lacey blinked at the meaty hand he held out.

He repeated his question and her gaze flew to his scowling face. He looked like a cop who'd stepped straight out of prime-time TV. Solid, tough, and bald.

"Oh!" Her brain switched on and she grabbed his offered hand. "No, I don't live here. I'm just—"

"No one's allowed near the apartment complex unless you're a resident." One-handed, he smoothly hoisted her to her feet as his sharp eyes took a closer look at her leather satchel and scanned her expensive coat.

"You a reporter? 'Cause you can turn right around. There'll be a press conference at the Lakefield police station at three." The cop had decided she was an outsider. Not a difficult conclusion; the neighborhood reeked of food stamps and welfare checks.

Wishing she were taller, Lacey lifted her chin and then grimaced as she brushed at the cold, wet seat of her pants. *How professional.*

She whipped out her ID. "I'm not a reporter. Dr. Peres is waiting for me. I'm a . . ." She coughed. "I work for the ME's office." No one knew what she meant when she said she was a forensic odontologist. *Medical examiner's office* was a term they understood.

The cop glanced at her ID and then bent over to stare under the brim of her hat. His brown eyes probed. "You're Dr. Campbell? Dr. Peres is waiting for a Dr. Campbell."

"Yes, *I am* Dr. Campbell," she stated firmly and tilted up her nose. *Who'd he expect? Quincy?*

"Can I get by now?" She peered around him, spying several figures moving outside the big tent. Dr. Victoria Peres had requested her forensic skills three hours ago, and Lacey itched to see what the doctor had found. Something unusual enough to demand Lacey come directly to the site instead of waiting to study the dental aspect of the remains in a heated, sterile lab.

Or maybe the doctor thought it'd be amusing to drag Lacey out of a warm bed, force her to drive sixty miles in crappy weather, and squat in the freezing snow to stare at a few teeth. A little power trip. Lacey scowled as she scribbled her name on the crime-scene log the cop held out and then shoved past the male boulder in her way.

She plodded through the snow, studying the old single-story apartment building. It looked deflated, concave along the roof, as if it was too exhausted to stand up straight. She'd been told it was home to seniors on small pensions and to low-income families. There was warped siding on the walls, and the composite roof sported bald spots. Irritation swirled under her skin.

Who dared charge rent for this dump?

She counted five little faces with their noses smashed against the windows as she walked by.

She forced a smile and waved a mitten.

The children stayed inside where it was warm.

The seniors were another story.

Small groups of gray-haired men and old women in plastic rain bonnets milled around in the courtyard, ignoring the cold. The rain bonnets looked like clear seashells capping the silver heads, reminding Lacey of her grandmother, who'd worn the cheap hoods to protect her rinse and set. She trudged by the curious lined faces. Without a doubt, today must be their most exciting day in years.

A skeleton in the crawl space under their building.

Lacey shivered as her imagination spun with theories. Had someone stashed a body twenty years ago? Or had someone gotten stuck in the crawl space and was never missed?

A half dozen Lakefield cop cars crowded the parking lot. Probably the small town's entire fleet. Navy-blue uniforms gathered around with hot cups of coffee in their hands, an air of resignation and waiting in their postures. Lacey eyed the steam rising from the paper cups and unconsciously sniffed. The caffeine receptor sites in her nerves pleaded for coffee as she pushed aside the flap door of the tent.

"Dr. Campbell!"

At the sharp voice, Lacey popped out of her coffee musings, froze, and fought the instinct to look for her father—also Dr. Campbell. The bright blue tarp at Lacey's snowy boots framed the partial recovery of a skeleton. Another step and she would've crushed a tibia and sent Dr. Peres's blood pressure spiking through the tent roof. As she ignored the doctor's glare, Lacey's gaze locked on the bones and a sharp rush surged through her veins at the sight of the challenge at her feet.

This was why she accepted assignments in freezing weather. To identify and bring home a lost victim. To use her unique skills to solve the mystery of death. To put an end to a mourning family's questions. To know she made a difference.

The cold faded away.

The skull was present, along with most of the ribs and the longer bones of the extremities. At the far end of the tent, two male techs in down jackets sifted buckets of dirt and rocks through a screen, painstakingly searching for smaller bones. A huge, gaping hole in the concrete wall of the crawl space under the building indicated where the remains had been discovered.

"Don't step on anything," said Dr. Peres.

Nice to see you too.

"Morning." Lacey nodded in Dr. Peres's general direction and tried to slow her racing heart. Her eyes studied the surreal scene. Bones, buckets, and bitch.

Dr. Victoria Peres, a forensic anthropologist, was known as a strict ball breaker in her field, and she didn't take flak from anyone. At six feet tall, she was an Amazon incarnate. A recovery site was her kingdom, and no one dared step within breathing distance of her sites before she gave her assent. And don't dream of touching anything without permission. *Anything.*

When she grew up, Lacey wanted to be Dr. Peres.

Lacey had worked with the demanding doctor on four recoveries before the doctor trusted her work. But that didn't mean Dr. Peres liked Lacey; Dr. Peres didn't like anyone.

Black-framed glasses with itty-bitty lenses balanced on the narrow ridge of the doctor's nose. As usual, her long black hair was in a perfect knot at her neck. No stray hairs had escaped the knot, even though the doctor had been on-site for five hours.

"Nice you could make the party." Dr. Peres glanced at her watch and raised one brow.

"I had to wait 'til my toenails dried."

A sharp snort came from the woman and Lacey's eyes narrowed. *Wow.* She'd actually made Dr. Peres laugh. Well, sort of. Still, it should give Lacey some bragging rights among the ME's staff.

"What'd you find?" Lacey's fingers yearned to start on the puzzle. This was the best part of her job. A mystery to decode.

"White female, age fifteen to twenty-five. We're pulling her, piece by piece, out of the hole that leads into the building's crawl space. Over there's the guy who found her." Dr. Peres pointed through a plastic tent window to a white-haired man speaking with two of the local police. The man clutched a wiener dog with a graying muzzle to his sunken chest. "He was taking his dog out to do its business and noticed several big chunks of concrete had broken out of the cracked wall. The dog crawled into the hole and when grandpa stuck his hand in to haul out the dog, he got a surprise."

Dr. Peres gestured at the gaping hole. "I don't think the body's been here all that long, and it was skeletal when it was placed."

"What do you mean?" Lacey's curiosity rose to code orange. So much for her idea of someone getting stuck under the building.

"I think the hole was recently made and the skeleton shoved in. It was a pile of bones. An undisturbed, decomposing body doesn't end up in a heap like that." Dr. Peres's brows came together in a black slash. "Bones scatter sometimes, depending on the scavengers in the area, but these look like they were dumped out of a sack and pushed into the hole."

"One skeleton?" Lacey's gaze darted back to the skull. What kind of freak dumps a skeleton? What kind of freak *has* a skeleton to dump?

Dr. Peres nodded. "And it looks pretty complete. We're finding everything—phalanges, metatarsals, vertebrae. But what I don't understand is why it wasn't hidden better. They had to know we'd find it. They left the hole wide open and the big concrete chunks on the ground for anyone to trip over."

"Maybe they were interrupted before they could finish. Cause of death?"

"Don't know yet." Dr. Peres's tone was short. "No obvious blows to the skull and I haven't found the hyoid, but both femurs are broken in the same spot. The breaks look similar to what you see in a car accident where someone hits a pedestrian with the front bumper." She frowned. "A high bumper. Not a car. A truck, maybe."

Lacey's thighs ached. "Antemortem breaks?"

"Either postmortem or just prior to time of death. No signs of the slightest start of healing." The doctor was curt, but bent to indicate several wedge-shaped fractures on the femurs.

Lacey's gaze locked on the cracks as she crammed her mittens into her bag and knelt, automatically slipping her hands into a pair of purple vinyl gloves from a box by the skull. The thin gloves were second nature to her hands.

"Someone hit her with a vehicle and hid the body," Lacey muttered, drawing a look of disgust from Dr. Peres. Too late, Lacey remembered the woman hated speculation on the cause of death before an exam was finished. Victoria Peres voiced only facts.

Mentally cringing, Lacey stood and self-consciously brushed at her knees. She'd stepped out of line. *Not my job to figure out the who, what, where, when, why, or how of the death.* She was here to focus on a minute aspect of the skeleton: teeth.

The dirt-sifting technician let out a whoop and added a patella to a growing pile of tiny bones. Dr. Peres picked it up, glanced at it briefly, spun it in her fingers, and assigned it to the left leg on the tarp.

"She seems small." *Too small.* She looked like a child.

"She is small. She'll be around five feet tall or so, but she's a fully mature woman. Her hips and growth plates tell me that." Dr. Peres lifted a black brow at Lacey. "Her teeth indicate that too. But that's your department."

"Hey, I can empathize if she was that short," Lacey stated, unconsciously shifting onto her toes and stretching her spine. Standing next to the tall doctor, Lacey's petite height was making her crane her neck as she spoke. "Can you tell how long she's been dead?"

Dr. Peres shook her head as she turned back to the bones. "There's no clothing to work with. All that's left is bones and blonde hair, and I won't make a guess. I'll know more after I study her in the lab."

"My father said you'd found some interesting dental work."

Dr. Peres's face brightened a degree. "Maybe that could help give us a time line. It was removable, so I bagged it already." She strode six steps to a plastic storage case and started rooting through a pile of evidence bags.

Lacey's shoulders relaxed a notch. Victoria Peres wasn't one of the people who'd mutter "nepotism" about Lacey's job. Maybe the doctor understood the job was tougher when your father was the chief medical examiner of the state. And your boss.

Lacey pressed her lips together. Anyone who'd worked directly with her knew Lacey was damned good at her job.

"That's a rock, not a bone." One of the techs peered at an ivory chunk on his partner's outstretched hand.

"No way. It's gotta be a bone," argued his counterpart.

Lacey glanced at Dr. Peres, expecting her to referee the dispute, but the doctor's attention was still buried in a storage case. Curious, Lacey carefully stepped over the tiny skeleton and held out a hand.

"Can I take a look?"

Two startled faces turned her way. Lacey stood her ground and tried to look like a competent forensic specialist. The men were young. One dark, one blond. Both bundled up as if they were working in the Arctic. Probably college students interning with Dr. Peres.

"Sure." Acting like he was handing over the Hope diamond, the dark-haired tech handed her a narrow piece, shorter than an inch. He cast a quick look at Dr. Peres's back.

Lacey studied the piece in her hand, understanding their confusion. She couldn't tell if it was bone. She lifted the piece to her mouth and gently touched her tongue to it, feeling its smoothness.

"Jesus Christ!"

"What in the hell . . . !" Both men rocked back, identical shock covering their faces.

Lacey handed back the little piece, hiding her smile. "It's rock."

Porous bone would have stuck to her tongue. A trick she'd learned from her father.

"She's right." Dr. Peres's close voice made Lacey jump and turn to face her. The doctor glanced at the men over Lacey's shoulder. "I can never shock those two guys. I guess I need to start gnawing on skeletons more frequently." Her eyes narrowed at Lacey. "Don't repeat that."

Dr. Peres's reputation was hard-assed enough without a rumor circulating that she gnaws on bones.

"I'm still looking for the dental work I removed first thing this morning. Why don't you take a look at the rest of her teeth while I check the other bin?"

Lacey nodded and kneeled by the sparse skeleton, the tarp crinkling loudly. She scanned the lonely remains, feeling quiet sadness ripple through her chest.

What happened to you?

The skull silently stared at nothing.

Lacey's heart ached in sympathy. The dead woman was the ultimate underdog, and Lacey was a sucker for the vulnerable.

Whether a long shot in a football game or an injured animal, she instinctively threw her support to the weakest. It was the same with her job. Every victim sparked Lacey's utmost effort.

But this situation felt different from other recoveries. Was it the freezing weather? The depressing location?

This feels personal.

That was exactly it. The examination felt personal.

Was it because the body was so small? Petite like herself? Young. Female. A victim of a horrible . . .

Stop it. She was projecting herself onto the remains. Lacey mentally pulled back and hammered down her emotions, swallowing hard.

Do the job. Do your best. Report the findings and go home.

But somewhere, someone was missing a daughter. Or sister.

Resolute, she gently lifted the mandible from the tarp and focused. Perfectly aligned teeth with no fillings. But the first molars were missing. Strangely, the second molars behind the missing ones were in perfect placement. She touched one of the empty spots with her little finger. It fit perfectly. Usually when teeth have been extracted, the proximal teeth eventually tip or shift into the empty spaces. Not on this mandible. And the extraction sites weren't new, because the bone had fully regenerated in place of the removed roots.

"Something was keeping the spaces open," she mumbled as she set the mandible down and reached for the skull. She ran questioning fingertips over the smooth, bony surfaces that shaped the head. Definitely female. Male skulls were lumpy and rugged. Even in death, the female form demonstrated a distinctive, smooth grace. She tipped the skull upside down and saw a perfectly aligned arch with all teeth present.

Braces. Or else great genes. The woman's smile had been beautiful.

Large silver fillings covered every surface of the upper first molars.

"She managed to keep the upper set of first molars," she muttered to no one. Lacey squinted as she scanned for any elusive white fillings. "But the bottom set was beyond saving at some point. Something probably weakened her first molars during their formation," she theorized. Lacey eyed the central incisors, looking for any signs of odd development, since those teeth formed during nearly the same time period as the first molars, but her front teeth were white, smooth, and gorgeous.

Lacey touched the bone posterior to the second molars. Bare hints of wisdom teeth poked through the bone. Without X-rays to check the root lengths of the wisdom teeth, she wasn't quite ready to agree that the woman was in her late teens or early twenties, but she hadn't found anything to counter Dr. Peres's premise.

The roar of an approaching vehicle seized her attention.

Her freezing fingers clenched the skull as she watched through a hazy plastic window while a man on an ATV ripped into the snowy parking lot and spun, deliberately covering one group of cops with thick snow.

Lacey jumped to her feet, pushed aside the tent flap, stepped out, and stared, sucking in her breath.

The cops weren't going to appreciate that stupid prank.

The men in blue brushed off the snow, and their disgruntled rumblings reached Lacey's ears. The driver of the ATV gave a shout of laughter as he hopped off and strode toward the incensed group, casually pulling off his gloves.

Was he crazy?

He was tall and walked with confident strides, apparently not concerned with the wrath of the cops. He faced away from her, showing trim black hair below his baseball cap, and she wished she could see his face. To her shock, the circle of cops opened to let him enter, slapping him on the back and shaking hands all around. The knot in Lacey's spine relaxed.

They weren't going to kill him.

Fifty feet away, the rider abruptly turned his head and a laughing, steel-gray gaze slammed into hers. Lacey stepped back at the instant onslaught, her eyes blinking. A solid jaw tensed briefly as he looked her up and down. He gave a deliberate wink and grin, and turned back to his group.

Lust in Lacey's brain jumped up and took notice. *Did he just flirt with me?*

Very nice. Her limbs warmed.

Lacey's fingertip slid into an empty eye socket and she gasped, dropping her gaze to the forgotten skull, terrified she'd crunched a delicate bone. She studied it frantically, searching for fresh cracks. Finding none, she exhaled in a low whistle.

Dr. Peres would have *her* head if she damaged the skull.

About the Author

Photo © 2016 Rebekah Jule Photography

Kendra Elliot has landed on the *Wall Street Journal* bestseller list multiple times and is the award-winning author of the Bone Secrets and Callahan & McLane series, as well as the Mercy Kilpatrick novels: *A Merciful Death*, *A Merciful Truth*, and *A Merciful Secret*. Kendra is a three-time winner of the Daphne du Maurier Award, an International Thriller Writers finalist, and an RT Award finalist. She has always been a voracious reader, cutting her teeth on classic female heroines such as Nancy Drew, Trixie Belden, and Laura Ingalls. She was born, raised, and still lives in the rainy Pacific Northwest with her husband and three daughters, but she looks forward to the day she can live in flip-flops. Visit her at www.kendraelliot.com.